The Dust of Africa

The Dust of Africa

✦

You can't wash the dust of Africa off your feet—African proverb

A Novel

Shel Arensen

iUniverse, Inc.
New York Lincoln Shanghai

The Dust of Africa
You can't wash the dust of Africa off your feet—African proverb

Copyright © 2008 by Shel Arensen

iUniverse books may be ordered through booksellers or by contacting:

iUniverse
2021 Pine Lake Road, Suite 100
Lincoln, NE 68512
www.iuniverse.com
1-800-Authors (1-800-288-4677)

Because of the dynamic nature of the Internet, any Web addresses or links contained in this book may have changed since publication and may no longer be valid.

This is a work of fiction. All of the characters, names, incidents, organizations, and dialogue in this novel are either the products of the author's imagination or are used fictitiously.

ISBN: 978-0-595-49761-4 (pbk)
ISBN: 978-0-595-61237-6 (ebk)

Printed in the United States of America

Dedicated

To the teachers and students of Rift Valley Academy.

And to those who have been privileged

to play rugby on the pitch looking out over Mount Longonot.

May 1983

The small plane jolted onto the paved strip at Nairobi's Wilson Airport. The setting sun glowed like an ember in a dying campfire, outlining the serrated teeth of the Ngong Hills as I stepped onto the still-warm tarmac.

"Your jacket," the pilot reminded me.

I looked up vaguely. He handed me a stained denim jacket. It wasn't mine, but I slung it over my shoulder and walked blankly towards the customs and immigration office.

"Where do you come from?" asked a Kenyan official in a sharply ironed white shirt with silver buttons. My mind pondered as I groped for my passport. Where do I come from? My roots are in Africa. I was born here. I grew up here. I handed the immigration officer my blue U.S. passport with an eagle on the front gripping a wad of arrows.

"I'm not sure," I murmured in answer to his question.

The official frowned. "Your plane? Where have you come from?"

"Oh, you mean right now. Lokichoggio. And this morning from Sudan."

Sudan. I wished I'd never heard the name. The very sound of it hurt my ears and tore at my heart. I put both my elbows on the counter to steady myself against a swirling dizziness. How could Africa—my home and the only place on earth where I felt I belonged—have betrayed me like this?

Book One
Kenya

September 1968

1

"Clay, it's time for your lessons!" Mom called. I scrunched lower behind the silvery leaves of the *leleshwa* bush that grew beside the rusty outhouse. My best friend, Lempapa, crouched next to me. I gripped my dog, Rocky, around the neck and we hid silently. Mom called again, looking past the line of Maasai women who had gathered on the cracked cement veranda of her dispensary.

"Have you seen Clay?" Mom asked, walking over to where my Dad strapped duct tape around a hosepipe on his Land Rover. Dad shrugged and hunched over his work.

"I'll never get Clay through first grade," Mom said in frustration, turning back to her dispensary. A Maasai mother, red beaded earrings dragging on her shoulders, pushed a smeary-nosed baby in front of Mom. When Mom took the baby in her arms and disappeared behind the blue-painted door, I nodded to Lempapa and we slipped into the forest that surrounded our mission station on the Mau escarpment in Kenya.

Lempapa, who had learned to track animals from his Dorobo father, pointed out the bushbuck tracks in the soft forest soil. He eased forward, his knobbed *orinka* held lightly in his right hand. I pulled my club out and carried it just like Lempapa. Rocky pushed against my legs, straining to chase the bushbuck. I gripped his collar and followed Lempapa. Barrel-trunked cedar trees blocked the sun as we worked our way deeper into the forest. Lempapa stopped and pointed at a flash of orange-brown behind some leafy vegetation. He stood up and hurled his *orinka* at the bushbuck. The club whistled as it sped towards its target. But the club caught on a branch near the bushbuck, which started and fled through the forest. I didn't even have a chance to throw my club. I released Rocky and Lempapa laughed as Rocky bayed and crashed through the bushes in pursuit of the bushbuck.

We sat with our backs to a cedar tree. "This may be our last hike together," Lempapa said.

"Why?" I asked.

"I'm joining my agemates for a big circumcision ceremony near Narok. I'm about to become a man."

"Can't I come with you? I want to be a man, too."

Lempapa's eyes sharpened. "You think you could face the knife without flinching? You're still too young. Besides you're not a Dorobo."

"I'm sure my Dad will let me come with you. I was born in Africa. I can do anything you can."

Lempapa shook his head gently and stared up into the branches of the trees above us. "Look!" he whispered.

I squinted and cupped my right hand over my forehead. The large green turaco with a dark blue crest sat quietly on the branch of a Cape chestnut tree. Lempapa stood and aimed his *orinka*. He threw it and knocked the bird to the ground. He ran up and grasped the dead bird, plucking out one of the long red wing feathers. "The feathers will go onto my headdress," Lempapa said. "I have to collect as many feathers as I can. I'll make a hat from bent sticks and cover it with feathers from birds I've killed. The best hunters will have the most beautiful headdresses."

"Are you sure I can't come with you?" I begged.

Lempapa shook his head. "I'm sorry. What the elders teach is for us alone. You can't come."

Rocky crashed through the bushes, white burrs sticking to his shiny black and brown fur, a glossy black chunk of obsidian held in his teeth, drool oozing onto his chin. He settled at my feet, dropped the rock and looked up at me with his watery brown eyes. I stroked my panting dog. I loved hiking in the forest with Lempapa. It sure beat home school with Mom.

Lempapa pulled out some honeycomb from his leather pouch and we sucked on the sweet white honey and chewed the wax like chewing gum before tracking more animals.

Back home after our morning's romp in the forest, Lempapa put his hand on my shoulder as we parted. "*Ole sere*," he said. His good-bye seemed so final.

I arrived at our shambling stone house built on the edge of the Mau Escarpment. My parents sat on the veranda, which looked out over distant Lake Naivasha sparkling like a one-shilling coin on the valley floor. On seeing me, my mother set her teacup down on the stool beside her chair and waved a letter. "Clay," she called. "You've been accepted to start second grade in September at Livingstone Academy."

I stared at the letter fluttering in her hand like a wounded dove, uncertain what to say. I loved our home on the Mau. I didn't want to leave, ever. "Do I have to go away to school?" I pleaded. "Can't I stay here with you guys? I promise I won't run away again. I'll study harder."

Mom looked sad. "We don't want you to leave, either," she said, "but you have to learn and I'm just no good at teaching you. Besides, I never seem to have the time." Her lower lip trembled as she spoke.

Dad put his big, callused hand on my shoulder. Black mud clogged his fingernails. Probably another puncture on the road to Narok. Or he'd had to dig his way out of a mud hole. "I know you don't want to go, Clay. But once you're there, you'll like it. You'll make friends."

I've already got a best friend right here, I thought. *Lempapa—even if he is going to become a man.*

"I went to Livingstone when I was a kid and it's a good school. We pulled some great pranks in the dorm. And now they've got real sports teams that play against other schools. You'll get things at Livingstone that we can't give you. We love you and we always will."

If you love me, I thought, *why are you sending me away?*

Dad blabbed on. "You'll be allowed to come home three times a year for one-month school vacations. And we'll be able to come up a couple times each term to see how you're doing." He stopped talking and I winced with pain as his rough hand clamped my shoulder. "You'll love school," he added lamely.

I didn't share Dad's confidence, but I couldn't do much to change my parents' minds about going away to school. That night as I crawled into my steel-springed Vono bed, Dad stuck his head through the door. "Do you want me to pray with you?" he asked. I nodded. He sat on my bed and closed his eyes. I gazed at his strong chin, covered with one-day stubble, and tried to brand it into my mind. "Dear Lord," Dad prayed, "I thank you for your promise that you'll be with us, even to the ends of the earth. Be with our family now as Clay faces a new challenge of going to boarding school ..." In the soft yellow light of our kerosene lantern, I could see tears glinting in Dad's eyes. He stayed quiet for several minutes. I sat up with my back against my lumpy pillow and my knees pulled up to my chin and soaked in the look of pain on Dad's face. I shoved my right thumb into my mouth and sucked, something I hadn't done for years. It seemed to help. "Comfort and strengthen all of us," Dad finally finished. He cleared his throat and blew out the lantern before leaving the room.

Over the next few weeks I tried to convince myself boarding school wouldn't be too bad.

The day came to pack my idyllic childhood world into a battered old trunk and drive to school. Mom woke me up before dawn. I could hear the gurgling burp of colobus monkeys in the forest. A wave of loneliness swept over me. I wanted to be in the forest with Lempapa eating sweet white honey from the *osu-*

pukiai tree. I took a deep breath and threw off the covers. Dad hoisted my trunk in the back of the Land Rover and I climbed in afterwards.

"*Wootu! Wootu!*" a voice called to my parents asking them to come. Some Maasai men, bright red plaid blankets on their shoulders, stood next to a wheelbarrow. I followed my parents, wondering what the Maasai had brought. One man pointed at a withered old Maasai woman folded into the wheelbarrow and begged my father to take the woman to a hospital. Mom knelt beside the sick woman and felt for her pulse. She stood up, shaking her head. "There's not much I can do for her here. You'd better drive her to Narok."

"Does this mean I don't have to go to school?" I asked, as I helped Dad unload my school trunk.

"I'll be back as soon as I can," Dad answered, stuffing an old mattress in the back. The Maasai gently laid the sick woman on the mattress and then piled into the car and Dad drove off. I wandered back to our porch and sat down next to Rocky.

Dad didn't get back until dusk. Mom met him at the door. "Well?" she asked.

He looked at the floor. "Sorry. It took me most of the day to persuade the doctor at the hospital to admit the woman. And by the time they opened up a bed, she had died."

"At least I didn't have to go away to school today," I said, trying to cheer my parents up.

Dad forced a tired smile. "That's one way to look at it."

"Since we missed the first day of school, do I get to stay here?" I asked hopefully.

He looked at me. "Sorry, Clay. We'll go tomorrow. You'll just be a day late."

We packed the Land Rover early the next morning and I climbed in. Rocky rushed to the car and jumped up, his front paws outstretched up the window. I reached out and rubbed his ears and he whined. Mom, in the front seat, handed me a *mandazi*, a Kenyan-style doughnut, wrapped in newspaper dripping with oil. I broke off a piece and threw it to Rocky.

Dad started the Land Rover and we lurched down our driveway. I looked out the window and saw Rocky chasing after us, a saliva-slick obsidian rock in his mouth. He finally gave up and sat down in the dusty road to await my return.

My parents in the front didn't speak as the Land Rover shuddered, rattled and creaked down the track from the Mau highlands and crawled through thick volcanic dust across the Great Rift Valley. We came to the sharp eastern escarpment that heaved up like a tidal wave from the flat floor of the valley and turned onto a narrow paved road. Dad avoided several battered Bedford lorries that had retired trying to climb up the grade. The drivers had placed a haphazard line of broken-off branches and leaves behind their cars, an African version of warning flares, and left the trucks in the middle of the road. Beside one truck the drivers slept in the grass on the edge of the road.

My father turned off on a dirt road marked by a big stone sign. "This road goes to Baridi where the school is," Dad said. Prickles ran down my back.

I didn't answer. My voice had gotten stuck. An overwhelming sense of fear crept over me. It began to rain. I bounced in the back seat as we slithered in and out of wheel ruts on the five-mile track to Baridi. I could only see the backs of my parents' heads. I shivered from the cold as I sat alone in the back seat.

A low-lying mist hovered over the surrounding forest and ravines as we drove into the school compound. "Here it is," Dad announced. "Livingstone Academy."

"I hear they have good Christian teachers," Mom said, her voice trembling slightly. She turned around to look at me. I had my thumb in my mouth. "Clay, you can't suck your thumb here! That's so babyish! I thought you'd stopped that." I took my thumb out. Tears made Mom's brown eyes look slippery like the shiny mud-slick road.

The long yellow-stone building at the center of the school campus resembled a sleeping monster. Rainwater guttered off the building's roof like tears rolling down its sallow face.

A dried elephant's ear had been nailed to the wall above the door to the school office. "We're the Andrews," Dad said, "and our son Clay is registered for second grade."

The lady in the office looked over her black-rimmed glasses at my parents before rooting around to find some file. "Yes, we're expecting Clay. School opened yesterday. When he didn't show up, we wondered whether you had decided not to send him. We have a lot of children who are waiting for a place to get into this school, you know. We would have appreciated some notice."

"We planned to arrive yesterday," Dad explained, "but an emergency came up at our mission station. When I got home, it was too late to drive Clay here for opening day."

The lady behind the desk sighed. "I guess it was unavoidable. Now," she went on, "you've been home schooling Clay for first grade. I assume he's caught up with his studies?"

"He knows his letters," Mom began eagerly.

"Can he read?" the lady asked.

"It's been difficult finding the time to teach him. There are just so many demands at our mission station. Someone's always coming to the house with some urgent need. And I run a dispensary. Clay's lessons always got shoved aside." She looked down.

"I asked if he could read?" the lady repeated.

Mom shook her head. "He hasn't learned how to read yet."

The lady frowned. "Well, we'll see how he does. The other second graders at Livingstone have already learned how to read."

"Oh, I'm sure he'll catch up," my mother said.

My parents signed some forms and the lady told them how to find the dorm where I'd be staying.

Outside the long, cinder-block dorm, a small gray-bricked shed covered a wood-stoked boiler, which belched out dense silvery smoke. A pile of eucalyptus logs was stacked next to the boiler, the loosened gray bark giving the logs an unshaved appearance. I shivered in the cold highland air. A short lady with brown curly hair came out. "I'm Mrs. Russell, the dorm mother," she introduced herself. "You must be the Andrews." She shook my parents hands, a warm smile on her face. "And is this Clay?" She engulfed me in a big hug. "We wondered what happened when Clay didn't show up yesterday." She led us to the room I would be sharing with three other boys. It had two double bunk beds. Two of the top beds and one of the bottom bunks had been neatly made. The unmade bottom bunk had a blue-covered mattress. "This will be your bed, Clay," Mrs. Russell said. Mom helped me put my sheets and blankets on the bunk before organizing my clothes in the built-in dresser marked number three.

Gray tiles covered the floor. Dirt, caught under a crack in one of the tiles, had created a small hump. Rain dripped off the roof as I looked out the window, barred like a prison.

"We've ordered your school uniforms from a store in Nairobi," Mom said. "They'll be delivered to the school next week."

We had a small family huddle and Dad prayed for me. As they walked to the Land Rover, I panicked. No one had warned me about the terrible, wrenching pain, the jiltedness, the dizziness of feeling your world tugged apart. I clung to my father's leg as if it was the last rock before a waterfall in a muddy African river.

"Please take me home with you," I begged.

My parents looked as sad and bewildered as I did. Mrs. Russell stepped over and said firmly to my parents. "It's best if you leave now. Clay will be all right once you're out of sight, I promise. I've been a dorm mother to lots of little boys. Saying good-bye is hard, I know. It's OK to feel sad because that shows your love for each other is strong. But once you're gone he'll settle in just fine. Be sure to come and visit on field day in three weeks. By then, he'll be so at home here with all the other boys and girls he probably won't even notice you."

Reluctantly Dad tore my arms from his leg and he and Mom climbed into our Land Rover. As they bounced away down the road I stood, stunned and unable to believe they would really leave me. The car vanished around the bend and I began to run after it screaming silently in my heart, "Mommy, Daddy, come back." I leaned against the furrowed gray bark of a wild olive tree and I cried.

2

Mrs. Russell's soft hand touched my shoulder. "Come on, Clay," she said gently, reaching down and wiping the tears off my face. "Let me take you to your class-room."

I looked over my shoulder down the orange-red road that disappeared into the green forest hoping to catch one last glance of my parents' car. But my parents had gone. They'd really gone.

Mrs. Russell walked down with me to the elementary school to meet my teacher. The rain had stopped and the sun began to peak through the bruised clouds. A bell rang and children ran out of the classrooms. Some splashed in puddles wearing black Bata gumboots. Others ran to the swings. All the boys wore khaki pants and shirts. Some had khaki jackets with a red badge on the front left pocket. The girls all wore gray skirts with white blouses and red sweaters. Within a week I, too, would be wearing khaki.

Mrs. Russell led the way to the second grade classroom. "Here's Miss Carlson. She's your teacher."

"Clay! We're so glad you could come to school at Livingstone," Miss Carlson said with a warm smile. "We missed you yesterday. Here's your desk." The forest green desk had been well used and a number of gray spots peeked through where the paint had worn thin. A bossy looking girl with a red headband pushing down her blonde curls marched into the classroom after recess and sat down in the front row. Miss Carlson introduced me. "Class, we have a new student. His name is Clay."

Outside, lightning crackled and the rain began to pelt down so hard on the classroom roof we could hardly hear Miss Carlson. I wanted to cry but I couldn't. Not in front of all the other kids. I tried to swallow the lump that choked my throat like a wedged rock, but it wouldn't go down. Miss Carlson smiled and taught with flair, separating us into work groups and gliding from one to the other encouraging us along. My head seemed to be swimming. I had learned my letters, but today I couldn't focus. I sat lost and alone in a class full of students. The day my parents left.

"Clay," Miss Carlson's voice startled me. "Did you hear my question?"

"No," I mumbled, on the verge of tears.

Miss Carlson's face softened and she leaned over my desk. "I asked you to read the first line on the page." She gently opened a reading book, bent the spine backwards so it would lie flat on my desk, and then pointed out the line she wanted me to read.

I looked at the page, but I didn't know how to read. I wanted to please Miss Carlson and tell her what the words said, but all I could say was, "I don't know how, Miss Carlson."

A snort of laughter erupted from the desk next to me. The girl with the red headband shrilled, "The new boy doesn't even know how to read! Even my sister in kindergarten knows how to read! I taught her!"

Miss Carlson turned quickly to the little girl. "Hush, Susie. Clay has only just arrived. I'll work with him later on his reading. Now, Susie, why don't you read the first line?"

Susie sat up proudly and began to read. I wanted to be home. I wanted to stand up and shout, "Maybe I can't read. But I know how to skin a hyrax. I know how to make arrow poison. I've killed a mousebird with a slingshot. I've chopped off a snake's head with a *simi*." But none of my bush skills seemed to be of much use in this new school. I sat in humiliation as everyone took turns reading. Except me. I couldn't read.

Just before noon Miss Carlson told us to put our books away because it was lunchtime. As everyone else started out the door Miss Carlson asked me to stay.

"I'll bet he's going to be in dutch for sure," Susie piped up to a friend of hers who giggled. "He must really be stupid if he can't read. And he's so tall. He's bigger than all the rest of the class. I'll bet he's old enough that he should be in fourth grade."

My ears burned as I walked up to Miss Carlson's desk. I stood in front of her with my head bowed down. "Now Clay," she began, "if you can't read, you'll have serious problems keeping up with the rest of the class. I'll work with you for half an hour each afternoon after school for the next month. If you haven't caught on to reading by then, I'll have to put you back into first grade. I know that would be hard, but you've got to know how to read if you're going to make it in school."

"I'm sorry, Miss Carlson," I said. "I didn't know I was so stupid."

Miss Carlson stood up and gave me a hug. "You're not stupid, Clay. Many missionary mothers just don't have the time to teach their children, but I'm sure you'll learn to read and you'll fit in fine. Now, run to lunch."

I walked out the door feeling stupid. At least Susie thought so. I kicked a rock on the path that led down the hill. I looked around to see where the other kids had gone, but I couldn't see anyone. I knew it was time for lunch, but I didn't know how to find the dining hall. So I kicked my rock down the path.

As I came around the corner of a kei-apple hedge I gave my rock an extra hard kick. It hit something with a soft plop. A voice roared, "Hey kid! What do you think you're doing kicking that rock at me!"

I looked up in terror as a high school boy, dressed all in khaki, took two giant strides toward me and picked me up by gathering my shirt under my neck.

"Hey, look what I've caught!" the boy shouted. Other big boys in their khaki uniforms sauntered out of the doors in the low barracks-style dorm.

"I think we should have a paddling machine," the boy went on. "This new titchie kicked a rock at me. And he's in our dorm bounds." He glared at me. "Our dorm bounds are off limits for titchies, kid!"

I wriggled and tried to get away. "Resisting arrest, too," taunted my captor. "This kid is in big trouble today. After the paddling machine I think we'll dunk his head in the toilet and give him a swirlie."

"Paddling machine!" the other boys shouted gleefully, dropping books and collecting spanking materials. Some had rubber Bata flip-flops and slapped them on their hands as they waited for the punishment to start. They formed a tunnel by spreading their legs wide. Other boys kept arriving. At least one boy had unstrung his leather belt. I almost wet my pants.

Carrying me to the front of the tunnel, the boy who had caught me set me down and commanded me to crawl through the tunnel. With a sob I plunged into the paddling machine to the hoots and jeers of the big bullies. "Hurry up, titchie, my flip-flop is getting impatient," shouted one of my tormentors. The first blows stung but then, numbed from the slaps, I only thought of getting to the other end of the gauntlet. I glimpsed the boy who'd caught me running back to the end of the line for a second chance. Others followed him. With horror I realized the paddling machine might never end.

3

An angry deep voice interrupted the paddling. "Let the kid up! He's had enough!"

My original captor protested. "Come on Ox, we caught him in dorm bounds and he kicked a rock at me. He's getting what he deserves."

"Shut up you *nusu-nugu*," said the boy who had come to my rescue. He was a tall Kenyan boy with rich brown skin, strong shoulders, and an amused smile, which tugged his lips upward to reveal gleaming white teeth.

"Don't call me a *nusu-nugu*," said my nemesis. "I'm not half baboon. If anyone's a *nusu-nugu* it's you." With that he lunged with a fist at my new hero.

"You are a *nusu-nugu* and you fight like one, too," the Kenyan boy said. He grabbed Nusu-nugu's flailing arm, jerked it tight and then tackled him to the ground and pinned him with his arm painfully pulled backwards.

"Do you give, Nusu-nugu?"

My captor grunted and struggled to get loose but he couldn't. Finally he muttered, "I give."

"Good, now leave this kid alone." Everyone melted away and my protector came over and sat down on the grass beside me.

"Are you all right, kid?" he asked.

I nodded. "I'm new here," I said. "I was just trying to find the dining hall."

"Well, you're too late for lunch now," he said. "But come to my room. I smuggled out some bread and a tin of jam." As we walked he asked, "What's your name, kid?"

"Clay," I answered. "Clay Andrews."

"That's a cool name. I like that. Okay, Clay, my name is Stephen Ndegwa. But my nickname here at school is Ox."

"Does everyone here have a nickname?" I asked.

"No, but a lot of the guys do. There's Sausage, Porky, Peanut, Rat, and, of course, my favorite, Nusu-Nugu. I made it up myself, only Ralph doesn't like it for some reason." Ox laughed to himself.

"Why do they call you Ox?"

"Two reasons. First my name is Ndegwa, which means an ox in Kikuyu. But I also earned the name because I run like an ox when I play rugby," he answered.

13

"What's rugby?" I asked.

"You really are new," said Ox. "Well, it's a game, kind of like a mix between soccer and your American football. Last year we won the Safari Cup and proved we were the best rugby-playing school in Kenya."

"I'd like to play rugby, too," I said, looking up into Ox's face.

"You will if you stay here," Ox said. "They start teaching kids how to play rugby when they're in fourth grade."

"That's two more years," I said sadly. "I want to play now."

"You're tough, kid. You never even cried in the paddling machine. And big, too. I would have guessed you were in fourth grade already. Tell you what. You could be our mascot. Even though rugby doesn't start until third term, a few of us rugby addicts work out every day. You could join us—chase balls that go down the hill and things like that."

"I'll be there," I said.

"Good. Now let me show you around the school so you don't get caught in the senior guys' dorm bounds again. And you also need to know where the dining hall is so you don't miss supper."

Ox showed me around Livingstone Academy starting with the cavernous building made of yellow hand-hewn blocks of limestone where my parents had registered me. "This is the oldest building in the school," Ox said. We passed a small window with bars on it.

"What's in there?" I asked.

Ox shrugged, but he shied away from the window. "I don't really know. It's a window from one of the rooms below ground. Years ago I heard it was the dorm room for titchies like you. Now it's all boarded up. Most titchies say there's a boogey man who lives in there. Others say there's a ghost after one of the titchie boys died of malaria years ago. It's kind of a mystery."

An old cypress hedge skirted the edge of the hill below the old building. The hedge had a few holes with worn patches of smooth dirt in front of them. "The spying hedge," Ox explained. "Titchies love to hide inside the hedge to watch and listen to the high school boys as they stand on the porch and talk to their girl friends."

"What's exciting about that?" I asked.

"You'll find out," Ox said, smiling. "Just don't get caught spying on couples."

We walked around the outdoor concrete basketball court and over to the rugby field which had been cut out of the side of a hill. A sharp drop-off marked the far side of the field. "Now you know why we need someone to chase balls,"

Ox said. I looked down the hill and nodded, gulping at the long tangled grass at the bottom. It looked like snake country to me.

Ox pointed out the dining hall, laundry, chapel and high school classrooms. The courtyard for the senior boys' dorm stood right in the middle of the school.

"Be careful not to trespass on our dorm bounds again unless I personally bring you in," Ox said. "There are other dorms around for junior high boys and for the girls." From the rugby field I tried to identify the buildings as Ox pointed them out at machine-gunfire pace. "I'd avoid the junior high dorm bounds," Ox went on. "Those kids can be pretty mean. Most of them have gotten our paddling machine for one offence or another and since they can't get back at us, they take it out on titchies."

I shuddered. There were so many things to fear at this new school. So many dangers. So much I needed to learn.

"Well," said Ox, "you'd better get up to school." He pointed me up the cedar-lined road that headed up the hill to the grade school building. I walked up alone. I had a new friend, but I still had to face second grade alone. And I still couldn't read.

4

In the playground behind the school a group of first and second graders played a game with a ball tied to the top of a pole. I'd never seen the game before so I stood quietly and watched. A short boy with baggy short khaki pants turned and asked, "Do you want to play?"

I shook my head. Susie sneered, "I'll bet he doesn't even know how to play tetherball."

I turned away, my heart seared from another failure. How could I know how to play a game I'd never seen? I could play *bao* with the old men of the village, dropping seeds that represented cattle into the cupped holes in the board. I could shoot a bow and arrow. I stumbled as I hurried away. A hand touched my arm. The short boy walked alongside me. When he took a step it seemed like his stick-thin legs didn't even touch the sides of his gigantic shorts.

"My name is Tim," he said, "but everyone calls me Titch because I'm so small."

I smiled sadly, happy for the company.

"Don't worry about Susie," Titch said. "She's like that to everyone. Even her friends, and I'm not one of those. Come on. Tetherball's easy. You just have to hit the ball around the pole. Today we're playing teams. After you hit the ball you run to the back of the line and wait for your turn."

We walked back to the tetherball pole. "Clay's on our team," Titch announced in a large voice that seemed curiously out of place for someone so short. His head didn't even reach my shoulder.

I watched the other kids punch the ball back and forth. When I reached the front of our line, I stepped up and took a wild swing. I missed the ball but hit the rope, which tangled around my wrist.

"Ropes!" accused Susie immediately. "You're not allowed to touch the rope," she scolded looking at me. "Don't you know anything?"

I retreated to the back of the line. Titch, right in front of me, hissed, "Just hit the ball, Clay. You're so tall you can get it over everyone. That's the best way to shut Susie up."

I nodded and waited for my turn. This time I gave the ball a solid wallop. Because I hit it from such a high angle, the ball-on-a-rope continued to whirl itself around the pole and no one on the other team could jump high enough to block it.

"We won!" Titch shouted, jumping up and down in excitement. I just smiled.

Susie sniffed. "He's so tall he probably shouldn't even be in second grade. It's just that he's not smart enough to read."

"Let's go," Titch said. "It's almost time for school anyway." As we moved away, Titch confided, "Susie thinks she knows everything. Last year she and I were the only first graders. Both our parents live here at Baridi. She called me stupid all year long."

"But I must be stupid. I really don't know how to read," I said.

"Want to know a secret?" Titch asked. "Neither do I!"

"You don't know how to read either?" I asked.

"Nope! I tried all last year but I keep mixing up the sounds of the letters and stuff. I don't know why. I just can't get it. Miss Carlson works with me every afternoon after school."

"Are you telling the truth?"

"Would I lie to my new friend?"

"I guess not. So we'll both be learning how to read after school."

"Yeah," Titch said. "Miss Carlson's pretty nice."

A sixth grader stepped out of his classroom and began swinging a hand-held school bell. "That's the first bell. We've got five minutes to be in our classroom," Titch informed me. "Let's get a drink at the water fountain first." He stood on his tiptoes to get his drink and then, before I could step forward, he stuck his thumb on the waterspout and squirted me right in the face.

"Gotcha!" he announced, laughing.

It happened so fast I couldn't even get mad. Instead I leaned over and took a gulp of water before hurrying after Titch to the classroom.

The afternoon went better than the morning. Miss Carlson read us a story. Then we did some math, which was easy for me. After that we had P.E. class and played a game of soccer. The soccer ball was a lot easier to kick than the tied-up wad of plastic bags we used for a ball in the village.

When school ended, Titch and I stayed with Miss Carlson. "All right, boys, let's get to work." She laid alphabet cards on the table. "What letter is this?" she asked, pointing.

"T," I answered.

"What sound does it make?"

"T-t-t."

"Right." She set the letter T to one side and fingered another.

"What letter's this, Tim."

"That's E," Titch answered. "It makes the Eh sound."

Miss Carlson smiled. "And this letter, Clay?"

"N."

"Right. Now if I put the three letters together like this, each letter makes a sound and we get a word."

"Ten," I blurted.

"Good! Now, what if I take away the T and replace it with this letter."

"That's a P," Titch said.

"Uh, huh, and what word would we get with a P instead of the T."

Titch frowned. "Pen?" he asked.

"You've got it. Clay, you say you know all your letters. Do you understand how they go together to make words?"

"I think so."

Miss Carlson pulled out a book and we read it together sounding out words. By the time I'd read it once I'd memorized all the words and could read it alone. Miss Carlson nodded. "You're very quick, Clay. You'll be reading in no time." She gave me another book to practice and turned to Titch whose forehead wrinkled as he tried to read the words in his book.

"You keep reading words backwards, Tim," said Miss Carlson. "It's 'on', not 'no'." She sighed.

Titch smiled. "I'm trying my hardest, Miss Carlson, I really am."

"I know you are, Tim. I just wish I knew a better way to help you."

After half an hour Miss Carlson released us. I walked with Titch down the hill towards his home. As we neared the rugby field I heard the thump of a ball being kicked.

"It's Ox and his rugby friends," I said to Titch, starting to run. "I forgot! They asked me to help them practice. Come on!"

5

"Slow down," Titch urged, grabbing my shirt. "How do you know Ox?"

I looked at Titch. "Ox saved me from a paddling machine today. And he invited me to come and help them at their rugby practice."

"How can you help them?" Titch asked.

"Chasing balls that go down the hill, I think. Come help me."

Titch stood with his feet planted and shook his head. "They didn't invite me, and I don't want to get beat up." He headed off on a path that wound down the hill to his home. "See you tomorrow," Titch called as he turned to wave under the shade of an immense blue gum tree.

I sighed deeply. Titch got to go home every night. He could see his parents. A terrible pang of loneliness took a bite out of my heart and my knees started to wobble like Jell-O. I looked down at the rugby field and saw Ox run with a rugby ball and pass it to a friend who kicked it high into the air.

I ran down and stood beside the rugby field. "Hi Ox!" I called, waving my right hand. My left hand was clenched behind my back.

"Hey, kid. Didn't think you'd make it. Get over by the hill. Mike here is practicing his garryowens."

"What's a garryowen?" I asked.

"Kid, what did you say your name was again?" Ox asked.

"Clay," I answered, wondering how my rescuer and hero could have forgotten my name so soon.

Ox bent over and put a hand on my shoulder. Tear drops of beaded sweat trickled down his forehead and off his nose. "I can't teach you everything about rugby. Mostly you'll catch on by watching. But a garryowen is a high up-and-under kick. Your fly-half kicks it as high as he can and your team runs up and under the kick hoping to catch the ball or smear the defender who catches it."

"What's a fly-half? And why do they call that kind of kick a garryowen?" I asked.

"You ask too many questions, Clay," Ox said, his voice rumbling with laughter. "Now go chase balls and I'll think about answering your questions later—after practice."

Mike's next kick sailed extra high and Ox and the others easily ran under it and Ox leaped and caught the ball in the air. After catching it, Ox turned around and started running backwards holding the ball out with both hands. Several of the others ran into Ox, reaching out and grabbing his shirt and wedging in tight and pushing forward. They passed the ball out to Mike again. This time Mike's kick went too flat. The ball hit the ground before Ox and the others reached it and the ball began to roll towards the hill. I ran to get it. The ball took two small hops and then a big bounce. I ran to head it off. But just before it reached me it bounded over my head and down the hill.

"Good try, Clay," Ox called. "Now run get the ball." I stumbled down the hill and soon found the ball in the tawny elephant grass. Picking the ball up, I stroked the soft pebbly leather. There was a two-inch strip in the middle of the oblong ball with yellow lacing. The ball felt soft, almost magical in my hands. Someone had used a black marker to write L.A. 1st XV near the lacing.

As I turned the ball over in my hands a voice snarled at me, "Hurry up with that ball! You're supposed to fetch it, not fondle it!" I looked up quickly to see Nusu-Nugu glaring down from the edge of the field.

Oh no, I'm in trouble again, I thought, scrambling up the steep hill with the ball. I tossed it to Nusu-Nugu who accepted it wordlessly before kicking it over to where Ox and the others waited.

I watched closely as Mike kicked. The ball had felt so good in my hands. Now I wanted a chance to kick it. But Mike kept hitting kite-like garryowens and my job of fetching balls got pretty boring. I sat down and started pulling up straws of grass and sucking on them. Suddenly I heard a shout. "The ball, titchie! Get the ball!"

This time as I watched the rugby ball's bouncing pattern, I timed my run just right and caught the ball after a big hop right before it went down the hill. I turned and kicked the ball like I'd seen Mike do it and the ball sailed right to Ox who caught it and jogged over. "Good kick, Clay. Who taught you how to kick a rugby ball?"

I shrugged, "Just watching you guys, I guess."

"Well, you did a good job. But you'd better head off to supper now. We're going to shower first. I'll see you tomorrow." A couple of the other rugby guys waved, but Nusu-Nugu just scowled before he walked off the field.

I found my way to the dining hall where a feast of beanies and weenies waited for me. Some of the kids complained, but it tasted good to me. I even got a glass of cold milk, bread with Blue Band margarine, some carrot sticks, and two cookies for dessert. When I finished, I wandered alone back up towards my dorm. I passed a brown-red puddle, which had filled up with the morning's rain. Picking up a flat rock, I flung it at the water to see if I could get it to skip. The rock hopped twice and then plopped in the water with a big splash. A man stepped onto the road from a path and the water from my skipping rock splattered all over his blue slacks and white tennis shoes. Turning angrily, the man shouted, "What do you think you're doing throwing rocks about like that, young man?"

6

I stood still, my mouth open but unable to say a word.

"Who's your dorm parent?" the man demanded, coming over and grabbing me by the arm. "I'll see that you get the discipline you deserve!" He bent down and tried to clean off his pants and shoes but only smeared the red mud, which seemed to make him more annoyed with me. I still hadn't answered him. Giving up on his pants, the man straightened up and pierced me with his eyes. "You haven't answered me, young man."

"My dorm Mom's Mrs. Russell."

The man cleared his throat and raised his left eyebrow. "Well, I'm Mr. Russell and I've never see you before. What's your name?"

"I'm Clay Andrews and my parents dropped me off this morning," I said.

"Hmm. I do remember being a boy short yesterday." He was quiet for a moment. "Well, welcome to Livingstone Academy, Clay. Come on, let's go on up to Impala Dorm." He took my hand. "And about splashing mud all over me, I'll be easy on you and only give you twenty logs."

"Thanks," I said, wondering about his weird generosity. "Why are you giving me twenty logs?"

Mr. Russell explained. "The hot water boiler to make hot showers in the dorm is heated with firewood. But the woodpile is about a hundred yards down the hill. So when you guys in the dorm break small rules or forget things like sweeping your rooms or flushing the *choo*, I assign a certain number of logs as discipline. You have to fetch the logs from the woodpile and stack them by the hot water boiler. There's the woodpile now. There's about ten minutes before you have to be in the dorm, so if you hurry you can carry your twenty logs now."

I dropped his hand and ran to the woodpile. Mr. Russell's voice stopped me. "Clay!"

"Yes, sir?"

"You splashed me by mistake. Just do ten logs and come in. I'll introduce you to the rest of the dorm boys."

The eucalyptus logs had been split and I carried three on a trip. As I looked up at Impala Dorm it still looked bleak and gray. I trudged up to the boiler with my first load. As I dropped the logs off, a window opened in the dorm. A head pushed against the bars. "Hey, look!" the boy shouted. "The new kid's got logs already. Wonder what he did to get in trouble on his first day?"

I turned and ran down the hill to fetch more firewood. When I finished I didn't really want to go into the dorm. But the sun set with the suddenness of a dropped window blind. Shadows from the forest covered the dorm and its grounds making the whole place dark and eerie. A blue monkey gave a sharp ee-yonk in the forest reminding me that the dorm was on the edge of untamed Africa. Some lights flicked on in the dorm and the windows glowed with a soft yellow light. Mr. Russell met me on the porch. "Good work, Clay. Now it's time for showers. Then we'll all meet in our living room for devotions."

I walked into my room. Three boys stood there with towels on their shoulders wearing rubber flip-flops. One boy I'd seen in my class that day. The other two were older. The boy from my class said, "Hi, my name is Daniel. I know you're Clay." The other two kind of grunted and moved out of the room.

"Get your towel and soap," said Daniel. "I'll show you how to take a shower."

"I know how," I answered.

"Not in this dorm, you don't. If you don't have somebody to show you, you'll burn yourself. I know. I found out yesterday the hard way." He spoke like a hardened veteran.

"You mean you've only been here one day?" I asked.

Daniel nodded and sighed. "I miss my home," he said.

I found my towel, striped blue and yellow. Mom had bought me a transparent green plastic soap holder and it had a new bar of pink Lux soap in it.

"Who are the other two boys in our room?" I asked.

"Two third graders," Daniel answered. "They're not happy to be stuck in with us two new second graders. They spend most of their time in the other rooms with other third graders. That one there with dark hair is Pete and the blond-haired boy is Mark."

We walked into the shower room, steamy as the hot water mixed with the cold mountain air.

"When you get in," Daniel explained as we waited our turns, "turn the hot one-half turn and then turn the cold on full blast. If you don't, you'll get burned. And if someone yells, 'Flushing,' get out from under the shower right away."

"Why?" I asked.

"If someone flushes the *choo* while you're in the shower, you get burned."

I heard someone yell, "Flushing," and everyone in the showers made a quick scramble out from under the flow.

Two showers opened up and Daniel and I hung our towels on chrome hooks and stepped in. I adjusted the water as Daniel had instructed me. The warm water flowed soothingly over me as I stood under the shower.

Suddenly the water turned scalding hot. I screamed and jumped out. Daniel in the next stall did the same. I heard the gurgling flush of a *choo* and Pete stepped out of the toilet. "Oh, were you two guys still in the shower?" he asked innocently. "Sorry, I should have warned you that I was flushing." The sly smile on his face told me he'd done it on purpose. I heard other boys giggling. I decided to forget it and stepped back into the shower.

Daniel and I finished about the same time only to find our towels had disappeared. "Who took our towels?" Daniel demanded, getting red in the face.

Silence. Daniel walked to the door. "We want our towels or we'll tell Mr. Russell." Our towels were suddenly thrown out of one of the toilet stalls, landing in a thin pool of cold water on the gray cement floor.

Mark calmly stepped out of the toilet stall. "What are you two cry-babies squealing about now?" he asked. "There are your towels in the middle of the floor. Didn't anyone teach you to hang up your towels so they wouldn't get wet?" He walked out the door.

There wasn't much Daniel or I could do but pick up our soaking-wet towels and try to dry off. The towels were cold and I was shivering by the time I'd gotten back to our room and changed into my pajamas.

I donned a brown terry-cloth bathrobe and followed Daniel into the Russell's living room. Mr. Russell had started a fire in the big fireplace and the twelve of us dorm boys huddled close around the crackling fire. The Russells had one little boy of their own about four years old and he sat on his Mom's lap. Mrs. Russell introduced me to the rest of the dorm boys and they all said their names in turn. Mr. Russell read us a Bible story and prayed before sending us all to bed.

Once the lights were off I asked Daniel where he came from. "My parents work in Kampala," he said. "My Dad's a doctor."

"Would you two guys be quiet!" Pete commanded. "We're trying to sleep."

"New kids," muttered Mark. "Whatever you do, don't wet your bed. We don't want our room smelling like a *choo*."

I stopped talking. Soon I heard a quiet sobbing from Daniel's bed. I guess talking about his parents made him homesick. And hearing him cry set off my own pangs of loneliness. I wanted to cry till my insides came out. Instead I slipped my thumb into my mouth and started sucking.

"I hear slurping and crying," Pete said harshly. "Stop it."

I stopped sucking but kept my thumb in my mouth. I thought of my parents and tears began to wet my Donald Duck pillowcase. I didn't want to be at this school. Not even after meeting nice people like Ox and Titch and Daniel. I didn't like being bullied in the dorm. I didn't like getting in trouble for rules I'd never heard of. It seemed like I was blindfolded and surrounded by people beating me with unseen clubs.

I quietly wept myself to sleep with my thumb in my mouth. Mom had figured dorm life would cure me of thumb sucking. She was wrong.

I finally fell asleep. I dreamed of rivers, water, floods, and pouring rain and woke up cold and clammy. I'd wet my bed!

7

I never wet my bed at home. How could it happen now in the dorm? Quietly I got up and struggled to change my pajamas and my sheets in the dark. I piled my wet sheets and p.j.s in the closet and climbed back into bed. But I couldn't get back to sleep. Could I wake up early enough to hide my wet bedclothes before anyone found out?

As the early morning sky turned from black to charcoal to ash gray, I slipped out of bed to stuff my wet clothes into my laundry bag. I hoped I could drop it off at the laundry. As I stealthily stuffed my laundry bag, I heard Pete's voice. "What's the matter, new kid? Wet your bed? Man! I told you not to do that! It smells up the whole room!"

I wished I could disappear. Mr. Russell opened the door to wake us up.

"Mr. Russell," Pete complained. "Clay wet his bed."

Mr. Russell patiently helped me to take my wet things—including the mattress—out to the wash room. As he helped me clean up, he asked me, "Does this happen often?"

"No sir," I replied shaking my head violently. "I can't remember ever wetting my bed. Well, maybe when I used to wear diapers, but ..."

"Sometimes accidents happen," Mr. Russell said kindly, putting his hand on my shoulder. "Especially on the first few nights in a new situation like this. We'll forget it for now, but if it happens again we'll have to call your parents in for a conference."

I thought to myself, *Maybe if I wet my bed again I can go home*!

That thought lasted only until I went back to my room. Pete met me with a smirk. "I hear you wrote a new book, Clay," he said.

"What do you mean?" I asked, falling for his trap.

"Rusty Bed Springs by I.P. Nightly," he said and laughed hard at his own joke. Mark joined him and the two went laughing down to the dining hall, repeating their joke to others on the way.

I knew it wouldn't be long before I was known all over the school as the bed wetter.

Even Daniel seemed to avoid me, rushing down to breakfast by himself. As I walked by the Russells' apartment, Mrs. Russell opened the door. "Clay!" she called.

I stopped, expecting a scolding about wetting my bed. "The school nurse called to say you're supposed to go to the infirmary right after school."

"What for?" I asked.

Mrs. Russell hesitated. "Nothing much," she answered. "Just something about getting a tetanus shot."

A shot! I thought. *Oh no! I hate shots!*

I almost forgot my bedwetting episode in my gloom about having to get a tetanus jab. I walked slowly down to the dining hall wishing I could be home or at least anywhere else in the world but here at Livingstone Academy.

In the dining hall I picked up a metal tray with six various-sized indentations on it. I put a bowl of oat porridge on the tray as well as two pieces of toast. I slapped on some peanut butter and what I thought was jam for my toast. I also picked up a green banana, my favorite kind because it was sweet and tart at the same time.

Picking out my silverware from round stainless steel holders, I carried my tray to an empty table and set it down. I went to pour myself a glass of milk. As I sat down and poured some of the milk around the edges of my gray, pasty-colored porridge, someone sat down next to me.

Expecting Pete or Mark to tease me again about wetting my bed, I looked down at my food and tried to ignore my tormentors.

"You're not in a very good mood this morning, are you?" boomed a deep voice. Startled, I looked up to see Ox sitting next to me.

"What are you doing in the titchie dining room?" I asked.

"Making sure you titchies eat all your food at breakfast," he said. "So start eating before your porridge gets cold and turns to cement. I swear they used leftover porridge last year to fix some potholes in the basketball court."

I started shoveling in the porridge, which despite its color was warm and good. As I ate I caught some oat husks on my tongue and pushed them out onto my spoon and tried to hide them under the bowl.

"We call those toe nails," Ox said. "You don't have to eat them."

I didn't laugh.

"You look pretty glum this morning," Ox said. "What's up?"

I didn't dare tell him about wetting my bed. So I told him about having to get a shot at the infirmary.

"No wonder you look grumpy," Ox said. "I don't like getting jabbed either. They always say it won't hurt, but it does. And then your arm aches like crazy afterwards."

My eyes opened wide. "Sorry," he said. "I'm not making things any easier." He jumped up. "Hang on a second."

I saw him run over to where Pete was leaving the dining hall after dropping off his tray. *He's probably going to ask him if I wet my bed*, I thought.

I turned my attention back to my food. Finishing my oatmeal, I put peanut butter and the orange-looking jam on my bread. Ox came back. "That Pete always tries to get out without finishing his oatmeal. Says it's too full of toenails. But I caught him today. Made him eat it right there, toenails and all."

I smiled thinking of Ox getting Pete in trouble. At least Ox didn't know about my bedwetting.

I took a bite of my toast and grimaced. I wanted to spit it out it tasted so bad.

Ox laughed. "Took marmalade by mistake instead of the jam, eh? They look the same but marmalade is bitter. I'll give you mercy today if you want. I'll eat your marmalade toast and you can go back and get jam. The reddish stuff is plum jam."

"You'll eat if for me?" I asked, not really believing him.

"Sure," Ox said. "I don't like it either, but it'll make me a better rugby player. Whenever you force yourself to do something you don't want to do it builds endurance and toughness."

"Then I'll eat it myself," I said, taking another bite and gagging it down.

"You'll be a tough rugby player, Clay," Ox said. "I was worried when you walked in this morning. You looked lonely and homesick."

"I am homesick, but I've got two new friends," I said. "You and Titch."

"The first few days are the hardest," Ox said. "I remember when I first came to Livingstone in third grade. I could hardly speak any English, and the few words I knew sounded so different from the American twang I heard here. I was the first African student to be admitted to this school. I was so scared and lonely that my first night I cried myself to sleep."

"I kind of did that last night," I admitted.

"I thought maybe you had," Ox said. "But my story gets even worse. That first night I woke up with a terrible urge to take a leak and found that I'd already wet my bed. I was so embarrassed, especially when all the boys in my room teased me about it. Accused me of rusting out the bed springs, stuff like that."

I looked at Ox, not really believing him. "Did that really happen to you?" I asked in a husky voice.

He leaned over to whisper. "Yes, but don't go telling everybody, okay! Our secret. I'm just letting you know so if you have problems, you'll know you're not the only one."

"Yeah," I said with a sigh. "I kind of had the same problem last night. So how did you …"

"After that first night it didn't happen again. I made friends, relaxed and enjoyed school—even though I did miss my parents. I still do."

I had finished my toast and ate the banana to take away the bitter taste in my mouth.

Ox walked over to the exit to check trays. A few titchies had to stop and drink the dregs of their milk. I walked out and handed my tray to a Kenyan man who wore blue overalls and rubber gum boots. "*Habari kijana,*" he greeted me asking how I was. I smiled and answered, "*Salama,*" meaning at peace.

"Thanks Ox," I called, running off to school feeling much better—until I remembered my appointment with a needle.

8

As I walked down the porch of cold gray cement paving blocks to my classroom, Pete and Mark stood leaning against the wall. Pete stuck out his foot to trip me as I passed. I stumbled but didn't fall down. "You're sure clumsy," Pete sneered. "Why can't you watch where you're walking?" Daniel hurried past, head down. I tried to walk on to my classroom. "Come back here, bed wetter!" Pete called.

I turned to face my tormentors. In the village I had learned self-control from my Kenyan friends. But I'd also learned how to fight when necessary. As I stepped towards Pete he curled his hands into fists. But before anything happened Titch stood between us. He firmly put a hand in my stomach and pushed. "Clay, forget it! Let's just get to class."

I followed him down the porch. We could hear Pete and Mark laughing. "Looks like the tall bed wetter needed the smallest kid in the school to rescue him," Mark's voice followed us.

I tried to turn, but Titch kept a firm grip on my elbow. "Don't let those guys bother you," Titch said. "You're big enough to beat them up, but it's better to have friends than enemies."

"I don't think they want to be friends with me," I muttered.

Miss Carlson started the morning with Bible class. She gave each second grader a verse to read from Jesus' sermon on the Mount. Except for Titch and me. When my turn came, Miss Carlson stood by my desk and whispered the verse in my ear. "Blessed are the peacemakers for they shall be called the children of God." I memorized the verse after hearing it once and repeated it loudly for the class to hear. Titch got the next verse. He listened to Miss Carlson but got some phrases mixed up as he said, "Blessed are those which are righteous because of persecution for theirs is the kingdom of heaven."

"That's not right, Miss Carlson," announced Susie. Titch flinched. "It's supposed to read, 'Blessed are they which are persecuted for righteousness' sake for theirs is the kingdom of heaven.' Titch didn't say it right. He couldn't read it for himself and he couldn't even repeat it after you, Miss Carlson."

"That's enough, Susie," Miss Carlson scolded. She smiled at Titch. "You did well, Tim. And I'm sure there are people who are righteous because they've been persecuted."

Miss Carlson asked Titch to pray. He stood up and prayed with a loud voice. At the end he put in a plea for himself. "And dear God, help me to learn to read and not always get things mixed up. Amen." I could see tears bulging from Miss Carlson's eyes after Titch prayed. Even Susie had nothing mean to say.

During that second day of school it seemed like loose pieces of a jigsaw puzzle kept plugging into place in my head. I still didn't know how to read, but I could follow the sounds of syllables as others read. Once I knew what a word looked like, the shape of that word stayed like a picture in my head. When I saw those words in other places, I recognized them without having to sound them out. Even Titch had a good day. After school I left him working with Miss Carlson on his reading while I went to the school infirmary to get my tetanus shot.

I stood outside the double yellow doors with the round glass windows just above my head level. An older student walked through the door and the smell of rubbing alcohol wafted out and choked my nose. I had smelt it often at my mother's small dispensary at home. To me it spoke of needles, pus-filled ulcers, stench, and sometimes death.

A woman in a white dress and white shoes stepped out of the door, a white nurse's cap perched on top of her tightly permed brown hair. Long black bobby pins held the cap in place like the talons of a fish eagle clinging to the top of a yellow fever tree. "And who might you be?" the nurse asked, looking at me over the rims of her glasses.

"Clay," I answered softly. "Clay Andrews."

"Oh yes," the school nurse said, turning back into the infirmary. "You're here for a tetanus booster."

I followed her into the small room cluttered with papers and medical supplies. The nurse took out a long needle and pushed it into a brown bottle and turned the bottle upside down. The syringe filled up with medicine that, seconds later, would be poked into my arm. I gripped the doorframe. As the nurse turned towards me, needle in hand, I turned and ran.

I pushed my way through the double doors and leaped off the infirmary veranda. As I hit the gravel driveway, I tripped and fell, scraping my knee painfully. But I got back up and sprinted away as the nurse came out the door crying, "Come back here, Clay!" I kept running.

Just then Pete and Mark appeared from behind a hedge. "What are you running from?" Mark asked.

I stopped. "Uh, nothing," I answered.

"Clay Andrews, get back here immediately!" the nurse's shrill voice clashed with my statement.

"You were running away from a shot!" said Pete. "What a sissy!"

I walked back to the infirmary to prove I wasn't a sissy. "Sorry," I lied to the nurse, "I needed some fresh air."

She nodded and, after swabbing my arm with a piece of cotton soaked in rubbing alcohol, she made a quick jab that felt like a pinch. "There," she said, "it's over. And don't worry about running away." Her eyes twinkled. "I've got lots of students who panic when they have to get shots. Why, one of the worst is that big rugby player, Ox. He rolls his eyes and starts breathing hard and sweating every time he comes up here. And if I'm not mistaken, he ran away once, too, when he was in fourth grade."

Back at the dorm I met Pete and Mark talking with some of the older boys. When they saw me they stopped talking. They folded their arms and formed a circle around me. Pete was the spokesman. "Here's the guy who ran away from a shot. Clay, your new nickname is going to be Sissy," he stated. "We'd call you I.P. Nightly, but that will probably get us in trouble with Mr. Russell."

"I went back and got the shot," I said, showing them the mark on my arm.

The boys in the circle shook their heads. "Not good enough," said Pete. "You ran away. But don't worry. If you can pass a test, we won't call you Sissy." The other guys laughed when they heard Pete mention a test.

"What test?" I asked after a moment's hesitation. I knew I couldn't go on living in fear of the boys in the dorm. Maybe if I could pass their test they would accept me. Besides, I had gone back to get the shot and it hadn't hurt that much. And the nurse had told me Ox ran away from a shot when he was in fourth grade. And now he was the school's toughest rugby player. So in a surge of bravery I asked about the test.

"He wants to know what the test is," Pete taunted. The others giggled nervously. Pete's eyes narrowed. "Underneath the main school building is a barred window. Behind that window lives the boogey man. No one at this school has ever seen the boogey man. But we've heard him." The others nodded.

Mark added, "Yeah! We've heard him clawing and trying to get out."

I shuddered.

Pete went on, "Tomorrow night after supper you have to go to the boogey man's room, grab onto the bars of the window and stay there for two minutes." He looked at the others. They nodded solemnly. "We'll be watching you and timing you. If you can stay there the full two minutes—no matter what you hear, no matter how bad the boogey man's breath stinks—then we'll know you're not a sissy and we'll stop calling you one."

The group disbanded and left me to think about the dare. I talked about it with Daniel. He wanted nothing to do with it. "Let them call you Sissy," Daniel said. "That's better than going to some dark room to meet a boogey man. Besides, the way I heard the story, that room is haunted with a ghost." Daniel lay down on his bed to read a book he'd checked out of the library.

I sat on my bed thinking. I didn't want to be called a sissy. Ox had showed me the window to the boogey man's room. True, Ox had made a wide pass around the window. But how scary could it be standing by the window and holding onto the bars? I went to Pete. "I'll stand by the boogey man's window tomorrow. I think I can pass the test."

9

Pete put his book down and stared at me. "We'll find out tomorrow if you're a sissy or not."

After supper and devotions I prayed that I wouldn't wet the bed and tucked my black rubber-covered flashlight under my pillow in case I had to run to the bathroom. I tried to sleep. Loneliness suffocated me as I lay alone in a room of four boys. I thought of my parents and my home on the Mau. The buzz of cicadas, the nightly click of tree hyrax, my dog, Rocky. Listening to Dad read the Bible at night to the hiss of a warm pressure lantern. Mom's warm hug and kiss before bedtime. Dad's solemn face, but laughing eyes as he prayed with me. A part of me had died. I forced myself to stop thinking about my parents and home. It made me want to cry. I had to survive. Somehow I had to face up to this boogey man and pass the test and become one of the guys. I thought of what Ox had told me about the boogey man and wondered what really lived in that room under the old school building. I finally drifted off to sleep.

I woke up with a start the next morning. To my relief my bed was dry. I scrambled out of bed and ran to the bathroom. As I came back into the room Mark sat up. "Glad you stopped wetting your bed, Sissy," he said, yawning and scratching his head.

At recess that morning I played with Titch. I told him about the challenge I'd been given to run to the boogey man's window and grab the bars for two minutes. Titch nodded. "I'll go with you after supper," he said quietly

"You will?" I asked. "Aren't you scared?"

"Sure, aren't you?" he replied.

"Yeah, but why would you want to go?"

"You're my friend," Titch stated simply.

Titch and I met below the dining hall after I'd eaten supper. It was almost 6 p.m. and the long dark shadows from the dropping sun cloaked the east wall of the old school building. Pete and his friends came out of the dining hall. "Are you ready, Sissy?" he sneered.

Looking at Titch, Mark added, "Looks like the Sissy got someone to hold his hand."

Titch glared at the growing crowd. "I said I'd go with Clay because he's my friend. He didn't ask me. Did you say Clay had to do this alone?"

Pete shriveled back a bit on hearing Titch's strong words. "I guess we didn't say he had to go alone."

"And have you ever looked into the boogey man's window?" Titch demanded.

"Uh, no," Pete admitted. "But we've heard weird noises whenever we've started to get close."

"You said 'we'," Titch said. "Did you go near the window by yourself or with others?"

Pete didn't answer.

Titch said, "I think you went with others, and no one is calling you a sissy. So if Clay goes and stays by the window, even if he goes with me, that should prove to you he's no sissy."

"Okay," Pete said, grumpily. "Just go down and get it over with. Who's got the watch?"

One of the older boys tapped his wristwatch.

I took a deep breath and closed my eyes in an attempt to squeeze my tears behind my eyeballs. It didn't work. Titch inched towards me, shuffling his dirty brown Bata sneakers. He looked up at me and nodded and we ran across the lawn towards the window. Ahead we could see the small waist-level window about two feet square with two rusty iron bars forming a cross. A torn mosquito screen stretched across the window behind the bars.

Titch knelt next to the window. "Grab the bars," he commanded me. I knelt beside him and gripped the bars. Cupping his hands on the sides of his eyes, Titch peered in.

"What do you see?" I asked. My hands shook.

"Hard to tell," Titch answered. "Looks mostly like dust and cobwebs."

"If the boogey man lives in there, he must not move around much," I observed. A scuttling noise from inside the room startled us into jumping back.

"Let's get out of here!" I said.

"That was only thirty seconds," a voice called. "You let go of the bars. We'll have to start timing again."

"Grab onto the bars," Titch gritted between his teeth. "We're not leaving yet. Unless you face this boogey man the guys in the dorm will keep bullying you. You're my friend and we'll do this together."

I put my hands on the bars and looked at Titch. "We can leave anytime. I'll make up some story. Just because they made this stupid dare doesn't mean I have to do it. Even if they laugh at me and call me a sissy, it's better than being dead at the hands of the boogey man."

"The boogey man can't hurt us," Titch said. "He's behind those bars." I closed my eyes and held on.

"That's thirty seconds," a voice called. "One-and-a-half minutes to go."

Titch edged closer to the window. The scratching, scuttling sound had stopped. "The noise we heard might have been the boogey man's fingernails as he moved against the back wall," Titch whispered. "He's probably more afraid of us than we are of him."

"I don't think so," I breathed, squeezing my eyes shut.

"This wire is so rusty I can't see anything," Titch complained.

Titch hooked his forefinger inside the tear in the wire screen and yanked at it. It broke away leaving a gaping hole in the window. We heard the scuttling sound again! Before either of us could move, a foot-long rat jumped out the window, landed on Titch's back and then tore off across the grass.

In our haste to avoid the rat, Titch and I jumped backwards and landed in a heap in the flame-red geraniums that skirted the building. The bars came loose from the rotten wooden frames and I held them in my hands.

"The boogey man is just a big rat," Titch announced as the other boys rushed closer to see what had happened to us.

"I'm not sure Clay stayed by the window the full two minutes," Pete began.

Titch glared at him. "He held onto the bars like you said. He can't help it if the bars came loose from the window. Clay passed your stupid test. Anyway, the boogey man turned out to be a big rat."

"All right, all right," Pete complained. "You passed the test. I won't call you Sissy anymore. Unless you do something else to show us you really are a sissy." The other boys crowded around and peered into the room and then wandered away.

That night in the dorm room Pete shook his head and commented, "I can't believe the terrible boogey man of Livingstone turned out to be a rat!"

"It sure scared me," I said.

"Yeah," Mark put in. "You're lucky you held onto the bars when the window fell out. Otherwise we'd have had to find some other test for you to prove your bravery."

"Like exploring the back of the Mau Mau cave," Pete said. "Or maybe crawling through the tunnel under the rugby field. But for now you did pretty good. It was funny watching you and Titch fly into the flowers when that rat came out."

He and Mark went into the next room to see the other third graders. They hadn't accepted me yet, but I'd made a step.

10

The next day at breakfast Ox sat next to me. "You don't have to come to rugby practice this afternoon."

"Why not?" I asked.

Ox smiled. "It's too long a story for a kid like you. Most of the guys on the rugby team are on restriction for a week. We have to stay in the dorm compound when we're not in class or at meals."

"What did you guys do?" I asked, worried. "I don't know all the rules in this strange place yet. Maybe I could get put on restriction, too. After all, Titch and I broke a window yesterday."

"I can't tell you," Ox answered.

"But I want to know so I won't get in trouble for doing the same thing," I pleaded.

"All right," Ox agreed. He took his bowl of oatmeal and put it to his lips, drinking down the remaining porridge and brown sugar. He burped politely and told me what had happened.

"We went for a nature run yesterday down to second ravine before doing a steep hill climb up to the railway tracks. We jogged back along the tracks. On the way we heard a train coming. One of the guys climbed up the overhang above the tracks and thought he'd try to toss some mud clods at the train." Ox hesitated. "One of the clods must have had a rock in it. Anyway, his last throw went right through an open window in the caboose and it hit the conductor in the face. The engineer stopped the train and we sprinted out of there. But officials from the railway called the school and we all got summoned into the principal's office."

"But why'd you all get in trouble? Why didn't the principal just punish the guy who threw the mud clod?"

"We never let on who actually threw the mud clod so we're all taking the punishment," Ox answered. "As the captain, I should have told Nusu-Nugu—I mean the guy who was throwing the mud clods—to stop. I never imagined he'd actually hit an open window. But when the conductor stuck his head out the window with blood running down his cheek, I trembled. He yelled, '*Ninyi watoto wa Wazungu ni wakora*,' meaning, 'You white kids are thugs.' I felt terrible because I'm not white. I'm a Kenyan." Ox's face looked sad, almost embarrassed.

"Anyway, kid, that's what happened, so we won't be practicing rugby for a week."

I must have looked disappointed because Ox said, "If you want, I'll give you a rugby ball and you can practice with it this week."

"Do you mean it?" I asked.

"Sure," he said. "Come by the window to my dorm room this afternoon after school. Speaking of windows, what did you mean when you said you and Titch broke a window yesterday?"

I told him about how Titch and I had gone to the boogey man's window on a dare and how we'd discovered the boogey man was a rat. "You're a spunky kid, Clay," he said. "With your toughness you'll make a good rugby player some day."

As I walked up to school from the dining hall I heard a turaco calling in the forest. The chirring sound sent a chill of homesickness to the center of my heart. I thought of Lempapa and how he'd taught me how to hunt turaco with a club in the cedar-filled forest behind our their tiny mission station. I thought of Mom and her one-room dispensary. I could see Dad struggling with tire irons to fix yet another punctured tire. I could hardly breathe. A blanket of grief smothered my lungs. I wanted to go home. My eyes blurred with tears as I neared the school building.

A hand struck me on my back. I jumped and raised my arm to hit back. I turned and saw Titch putting his forearm over his head to protect himself. "Hey, I'm sorry," he said. "I didn't mean to scare you."

I smiled. "Hey, Titch! I'm all right. I was just thinking about home and you surprised me."

We walked into our classroom together. Miss Carlson's bright smile and welcome brought some relief for my sadness. She encouraged us through the tasks of learning. Reading seemed less cumbersome and the words I had learned slotted into formation in my mind like tiny soldiers, each in its proper place. As we worked on addition and subtraction my mind lined up the numbers like tottering piles of dominoes, meandering from zero up to one hundred. Titch scratched his head furiously during our reading sessions and made wild guesses at what the words were. Miss Carlson didn't become angry, but once, after going over the word "where" with him four times in a row, she did take a big breath and clenched her fist a couple of times. Finally she said, "We'll work on this some more after school."

At lunch there was mail call and Mark, who had collected all the mail for Impala dorm, waved a letter at me. "Hey, new kid, there's a letter from your

Dad." I ran to get it, but Mark hid it behind his back. "Don't be grabby, new kid. You'd think you'd never had a letter before. How do you ask?"

I just had to get that letter. "Please …" I began and tried to reach around behind his back. Pete started to laugh. A big black hand engulfed the back of Mark's neck. A deep voice boomed, "Give him his letter, kid." It was Ox. Mark's eyes clouded with fear and he handed me the letter. Ox glared at Mark and Pete. "Teasing and bullying is one thing," he said. "But don't ever hold back a letter from anybody. That's from his parents. Now don't be playing any tricks like that again on Clay or anybody else or we'll use you two guys for tackling practice."

"Yes, Ox," Mark agreed, nodding his head furiously.

"Yeah, sorry Ox," Pete added.

I ripped open the envelope and stared at the letter. It was written on a white sheet of paper with a black-and-white ink drawing of Mt. Kenya across the bottom. I could make out the words Love, Dad at the bottom. But the rest was written in letters that looped and joined together. I'd learned to read a little, but I couldn't even recognize letters with Dad's joined up writing. I wanted Dad to talk to me through the letter, but I couldn't read what he'd written. My jaw quivered as I tried to hold back tears of frustration.

"Bad news?" asked Ox, putting his huge hand gently on my shoulder.

"I don't know," I whispered.

Ox led me to a nearby bench in the brilliant noontime sun. "Can't read it, huh," he said gently. "Here, let me tell you what it says." He took the letter and began to read:

Dear Clay,

Your Mom and I miss you very much. Saying good-bye to you when we left you at school was the hardest thing I've ever done. I've cried myself to sleep for the last two nights. We went to Nairobi after we left Baridi to buy some supplies. We head home tomorrow. I'm writing this so I can drop it off at the post office. Home won't be the same without you. Mom misses you, too. We're praying for you. I read the story of Hannah today and how she left her son Samuel at the temple and only saw him once a year. And he was her firstborn. So I can sort of understand her feelings. She only saw Samuel once a year. We'll be up in two weeks for titchie field day. We have bookings at the missionary motel at Baridi. Mom's already planning what cookies and other treats she's going to bake to bring up to you.

Love, Dad

I blinked back my own tears as I heard how Dad cried because he missed me. Ox folded the letter and gave it to me. "Keep this, man," Ox said. "You've got a good father who loves you very much. Hang in there, little buddy."

I put the letter in my pocket.

"Hey," Ox said, "why don't you come get that rugby ball now instead of after school."

I walked with him up to his dorm and stood outside the dorm bounds while Ox walked in and opened the scarred brown door to his room. Two senior guys had put mattresses in the courtyard and were lying out in the sunshine during lunch break.

One of them sat up and scowled at me. "Hey titchie, what are you staring at? You're awfully close to getting the paddling machine."

I stepped back a few steps. Ox appeared carrying a leather Gilbert Match rugby ball. "Leave the kid alone," Ox growled. He tossed the ball to me. "Here you are, Clay. Practice passing it and kicking it." He showed me how to hold the ball in an upright position between both hands as I ran. He demonstrated how to pass the ball backwards by sweeping it across my middle, again using both hands and sending the ball straight and smooth.

"Try to pass the ball so it stays in an up-down position like an egg in an egg-cup. That way the person catching the ball doesn't have to deal with a twirling ball. He can just catch it and it's ready for him to service the next player with another pass. The ball should flow down your back line like it's sliding down railway lines from one player to the next." I nodded and we passed the ball back and forth a few times.

"You're getting the hang of it," Ox said. "Well, enjoy yourself. I'll tell you when we get off restriction and you can help us at our practice sessions again."

I waved good-bye and raced up to school carrying the rugby ball in both hands like Ox had taught me.

I hid the ball in the coat closet in the back of the classroom and told Titch we could practice rugby after school. His face fell. "By the time my reading session with Miss Carlson is over," he pointed out, "we may not have much time to play."

Miss Carlson gave me my assignment from a workbook after school and I began to whip through it. Titch's lesson took a bit longer.

They went over the same few words again and again and Titch still mixed the words up when they appeared in a sentence.

"You know your letters and the sounds they make," Miss Carlson said, sighing. "I just can't understand why you read them backwards so often."

Titch shrugged. "It's like I'm standing on the outside and I can see the whole page as a big circle. I can walk around it and I seem to see the words from all sides. So I never know where to start reading. The words keep dancing up and down on the page and I can't get them to stand still long enough to read them."

Miss Carlson frowned. "I wish I knew something I could do to help you master this," she said. She shook her head. "Let's try writing some words down on flashcards."

Somehow seeing the shape a word made on a single card helped Titch.

They went over four or five words on cards. Titch stared at the words as if burning them into his mind. Finally he said, "I think I've got those words now, Miss Carlson. This way really helps." He beamed.

Miss Carlson placed four word cards on the table in a line. "Read them in order, Tim."

Titch scratched his nose and read, "The cat is fat!"

"Right!"

"I can read!" Titch exulted.

"We'll see if you remember the words tomorrow," Miss Carlson answered, not sounding as confident as Titch. "Remember this. You are a very smart young man. Learning to read may take you a bit longer, but you will get it. Your mind seems to work in a different way from other kids. But it doesn't mean you're not clever."

I collected the rugby ball from the closet and said to Titch, "Let's go practice some rugby." We ran up to the field and began passing the ball back and forth.

Mark and Pete walked by. "Hey!" Pete called. "Where'd you get that rugby ball?"

"Ox loaned it to me," I said, passing it to Titch.

"Let me see it," Pete asked. When Titch passed it to him, Pete examined it. "This ball looks too good for second grade kids. I think we'll just keep this ball for a while. What do you think, Mark?"

He passed the ball to Mark and the two of them began to run away with the ball.

11

As Pete and Mark ran away with the rugby ball my heart filled with frustration and rage and I tore after them.

"Here comes the new kid," Pete taunted, flipping the ball to Mark.

"Yeah, what was your name again kid? Something like dirt? Or was it mud?"

I lunged at Mark, slamming into his midsection with my shoulder. Mark fell backwards and landed on the ground with me on top. A hiss leaked out of his lips like a bike tire that's hit an acacia thorn. The ball bounced slowly towards Pete who picked it up and started to run. I jumped to my feet and chased him. He ran down the hill yelling, "Leave me alone, Clay!" My long legs flew over the grass. Pete looked back over his shoulder and I saw fear in his eyes. I launched myself and rammed him square in the backside with my shoulder. My arms snaked around his waist and we both went down in a heap. Pete dropped the rugby ball and it careened down the hill like a drunkard. I jumped up and ran after the ball. When I corralled the ball, I walked back up the hill. Pete sat hunched over, picking grass and dirt out of his scraped knees.

My anger had passed. I stopped next to him. "I'm sorry you cut your knees," I said.

Pete looked up and nodded. I stretched out one hand and helped him stand up. He winced as he started walking. "You tackle hard, Clay," he said. I looked down and saw my own knees had strawberry-colored scrape marks.

We walked towards Mark. He'd gotten his breath back and stood next to Titch who'd come to check if Mark was hurt. Both Mark and Pete looked down. Finally Pete spoke. "I'm sorry, Clay. We shouldn't have taken your ball."

"And we were mean to tease you in the dorm," Mark added. Their faces pleaded with me to forgive them. Maybe they were scared I would tackle them again. Or maybe they feared I would tell Ox. But I needed friends more than I needed tormentors, so I said, "No big deal. I forgive you. Come on, let's go practice rugby."

"Not tackle practice, I hope," Mark said rubbing his ribs gently. We called some other boys over and passed the ball around. "Here's how Ox taught me to pass a rugby ball," I said, demonstrating with a crisp pass to Titch. The others paid no attention and heaved the ball around any way they felt like.

"Let's run up the field in a line passing the ball like the first team does," suggested Mark. When the ball came to me I greeted it with both hands. I hugged the soft leather gently to my chest for a split second before passing it to Titch who had lined up next to me. He ran hard, pumping his short legs up and down like pistons before passing the ball the Pete who dropped it.

"This is too much like work," Pete complained, kicking the ball away. "Let's play something else." Some wandered off to swing on the rope that hung from the giant pepper tree. Others climbed the monkey bars.

I looked at Titch. "Let's do some pushups to get strong." We managed a few trembly-armed pushups before I had a better idea. "Let's go down to the big rugby field and kick the ball around," I said.

Titch's eyes appeared to fill half his face. "Not me, man," he said. "Who knows what the big kids will do to us if they find us playing on their rugby field."

"Don't worry," I said. "The whole rugby team is on restriction for throwing dirt clods at the train. No one will bother us. Come on. We can really boot the ball and see how far it will go."

Titch reluctantly agreed and we ran down the hill to the big rugby field. As we came through the trees, the field spread before us like a green carpet. Two sets of rugby poles—tall uprights with a crossbar—were planted, one at each end of the field, towering, straight and gleaming with fresh white paint. White lime lines faintly marked the touch lines and the halfway line. Titch and I ran onto the pitch and started kicking the ball back and forth. I held the ball in both hands at a slight angle, just like I'd seen Mike doing at rugby practice. I dropped the ball and hit it on the outside part of my foot and the ball spun off in a wobbly spiral. "I'll have to keep working on that one," I called to Titch as he scampered after the ball. Titch booted it back. He didn't care about form. He just walloped the ball with every ounce of energy he had. I caught the ball on the run and kicked the ball without stopping. The rugby ball flew over Titch's head, bounced past the touch line out of bounds and disappeared in some long grass.

Titch stopped running and covered his mouth while shaking his head. "Come on, Titch," I yelled. "Why aren't you chasing the ball?"

As I came up to him he whispered, "You kicked the ball down the tunnel."

"What do you mean? What tunnel?"

Titch carefully led the way to the grassy bit where the ball had disappeared. He stopped on the edge of a gaping black hole. I stopped behind him and peered over his shoulder. The black hole had swallowed the ball.

"What am I gonna do?" I asked, feeling like I had rocks rolling around in my stomach. "Ox gave me that rugby ball and now I've lost it down a hole. What kind of hole is this anyway?"

"It's a drain for rainwater," Titch said, pointing to a nearby ditch on the hillside "My Dad built the tunnel a few years ago after a big rainstorm almost ruined the rugby field. I watched them lay big round concrete pipes under the field. This ditch sends all the water here and it goes underneath and comes out the other side."

"Well, maybe the ball rolled out the other side," I said and we ran across the field and down the hill to where a big concrete pipe stuck out of the hill like a cigar hanging out of an old man's lips. The ball had not rolled out of the tunnel. We clambered down and peered into the tunnel. Blackness, dark and moist, stared back at us.

"I'm going in to find the ball," I said.

12

"Don't go in, Clay," Titch pleaded. "The ball must be really stuck in there. We could just wait for another rain to flush the ball out." He looked up at the sky, which churned with ash-gray clouds. "See, it looks like it could rain tonight. We could find the ball tomorrow, dry it off and give it back to Ox and the rugby guys."

"What if someone else found it first?" I pointed out. I crouched and looked into the tunnel. My arms shook with fear. But I feared losing Ox's friendship more than I feared the hole. I gulped and pushed my head in. "I'm getting the ball, Titch," I said and squirmed into the tunnel. I sprawled flat out, pulling myself along with my elbows, which squished into three inches of red mud left over from the recent rain. I tried to look over my shoulder but could only catch a glimpse of light and the shadow of Titch's head. I kept heaving my body forward. My elbows began to sting, raw from rubbing the gritty cement pipes. I started pushing with my toes as well.

The darkness enveloped me. I couldn't turn around. I closed my eyes and pulled myself forward. My hands hit a rock, the size of a soccer ball. I couldn't crawl over it so I pushed it ahead of me. After several agonizing minutes snailing forward, the rock plopped into a mud puddle deep enough to swallow the rock. I paddled my hand in the puddle and wondered what to do next.

A shout echoed from behind. "Are okay?"

I could barely turn my head, but I shouted back to Titch, "I'm okay!" I decided to go through the puddle. It didn't feel too deep and I thought I could brace myself against the sides of the concrete culverts with my feet.

I eased into the puddle, feeling like the crocodile I'd seen slithering into the Mara River on a recent camping trip with my parents. The water wasn't too deep but the force of the rain had eroded the concrete bottom of the tunnel leaving jagged edges, which bit into my elbows and knees. I passed the puddle but soon ran into a bigger rock blocking the tunnel. I reached behind it and my hand oozed into a mound of slippery mud that had piled up behind the rock. I couldn't get past the rock. The narrow tunnel prevented me from turning around and when I tried to go backwards, I got snagged by the broken bits of concrete in the bottom of the tunnel. I began to panic.

"Help!" I shouted. "Titch! Help! I'm stuck!"

My voice echoed in the darkness. I strained to hear Titch's voice. I heard nothing. The black tunnel stood silent save for the thumping of my heart and the steady drip of water somewhere in the distance. I shouted for help again but the echoes faded away unanswered.

I began to pray and I struggled but couldn't back out of the tunnel. The drip of water changed to the sound of a faucet running. *What if it rains hard?* I thought. *What if this tunnel fills with water?* I wished I was home with my parents. If only I hadn't come to this stupid school none of this would have happened.

I prayed again but the darkness seemed to swallow my prayer. Water began trickling over the rock that blocked the tunnel. I wriggled and tried again to push myself backwards, but this time my foot stuck under a piece of eroded concrete. As I pushed forward to release my foot, my hand brushed the big rock. It had moved towards me. The rainwater was pushing the rock and mud down the tunnel! I would be squished by the rock. I twisted and managed to turn onto my back. I pushed my feet into the floor of the tunnel and laid my back and shoulders against the rock, trying to stop the rock from tumbling on top of me and burying me in mud and water.

Water spouted over the top of the rock and I had to move my face to the side to keep from drowning. I thought I saw lights, like stars in the blackness. Then nothing. I woke to feel someone fumbling around my waist. I tried to sit up and cracked my head.

"I am here to help you, *kijana*," a soft voice said. "Stay still while I tie this rope." I recognized the lilt of a Kenyan accent.

"*Nisaidie*," I murmured. "Help me!" The man cinched the rope and I could hear scratching sounds as he moved away from me. The rope drew taut and he began to tug. I bit my lips to keep from screaming as my knees and elbows scraped along the tunnel. I heard a gurgling sound behind me and a steady stream of water iced my back. But the wetness seemed to make it easier for the man to pull me through the tunnel. A circle of light loomed ahead. A slender African man slid out of the tunnel ahead of me and reeled me in. It was Kinyanjui, one of the school's cooks. He hugged me to his chest as a cheer rang out. I was vaguely aware of a crowd of students standing in the driving rain. Mr. Russell stepped up and I collapsed into his arms. He carried me to the school infirmary.

The same nurse who had punctured my arm earlier put me to bed. I woke up later. Titch stood beside my bed, his hands behind his back. Mr. Russell towered over Titch. "Are you okay?" Titch asked quietly. I stretched and yawned. A sharp pain stabbed me between my shoulders and as I bent my elbows, newly-formed scabs split open.

"Ouch, that hurts," I answered, touching my sores. "How did Kinyanjui know I was stuck in the tunnel?"

"As soon as you went in I got scared you'd be stuck so I ran to get help. I found Mr. Russell who called some of the men from the kitchen."

Mr. Russell took over the narrative. "Kinyanjui volunteered to go in with a rope and pull you out. By then it had started to pour and everyone was afraid you'd drown in there. Kids from the school heard someone was stuck in the tunnel and they came and stood around the entrance. I asked everyone to pray."

"I heard everyone cheering when Kinyanjui pulled me out," I said.

"After Mr. Russell carried you to the infirmary, a big rock came rolling out of the tunnel, shoved along by mud and water," Titch said. "And guess what came out with it?"

"I don't know," I answered groggily.

Titch took his hands out from behind his back. They held the rugby ball. He shoved it onto my bed. "The ball," he said.

I caressed the ball and held it against my chest. I smiled. The nurse came in. "Visiting hours are over." Titch gripped my hand before running home. I went back to sleep.

In the morning I had more visitors. Ox came by first. "I heard you almost killed yourself to get my rugby ball," he said gruffly. A smile crept onto his face. "Man, you're one tough kid. You'll make a great rugby player."

Later Miss Carlson brought the whole second grade class, and finally my dorm parents came with all the boys in Impala Dorm. Mrs. Russell touched my forehead. "We were so worried about you. We all prayed for you and are so thankful you're safe." I smiled at all the attention. I felt like I was part of a family. Livingstone Academy, my new school in the misty highlands of Kenya, had become my home.

13

My parents picked me up at the end of first term and took me home for the month-long December vacation. A dip into a pothole crunched yet another a shock absorber and we lurched up our driveway. I jumped out of the Land Rover and called for my dog, Rocky. Dad got out of the car and looked warily at Mom and then at me. "Where's Rocky?" I cried.

"I'm sorry, Clay," Dad said, wrapping an arm around my shoulder. "I should have told you. Rocky died of tick fever about a week ago. I meant to tell you right away, but I didn't have the heart." Tears ran down my cheeks. Rocky had died? How could he? I had waited all term for Rocky to slobber on me. I wanted to rub my head in Rocky's sturdy chest. Dad showed me the small heap of earth that marked Rocky's grave. My stomach churned as I looked at the mound. I stood there weeping as Dad unloaded the car.

That night I hardly tasted the roast warthog with mashed potatoes and gravy that Mom had cooked especially for my homecoming. I cried myself to sleep that night. The next morning I planted a cross and then lined the edge of the grave with chunks of shiny black obsidian, the rocks Rocky loved to chew. I sat and cried some more.

The next day I went to look for Lempapa. In the village I met Lempapa's father. "Lempapa has gone away hunting with the other warriors from his circumcision group."

"Can't I go with them?" I asked.

Lempapa's father shook his head sadly. "Lempapa is now a man. You're still a school boy." He spit on the ground before walking away.

My vacation dragged on. I mourned the loss of my dog. Even more, I mourned the loss of my best friend. Our worlds, once knitted as one, had been torn apart when I went away to school. Lempapa had been circumcised and after a period as a warrior, he'd marry and become an elder in his tribe. As a man, Lempapa would have adult status, but I would just be a white schoolboy. Lempapa would get to do all the things we'd learned together—hunting, collecting honey, making arrow poison. I would go back to school.

I moped for several days, confused at the changes. I loved being home with my parents, but nothing seemed the same. At Christmas my Dad gave me a leather rugby ball from Nairobi Sports House. I rubbed dubbin into the leather to water-proof it. I carried the ball with me everywhere. I even slept with it. When vacation ended, I eagerly jumped into the Land Rover. I wanted to be back at school with my friends. I had a new home and a new calling. Lempapa had become a man and now lived with his agemates as a warrior. I had to become a warrior in my own way. I had to absorb everything I could so I could be a rugby player.

When rugby season started I saw my first rugby game. Ox had made me captain of a group of ball chasers. We sprinted down the hill as soon as school ended. We watched Ox and Mike and Nusu-Nugu and the other first fifteen players warming up for the game. Ox ambled up the hill from his dorm. He carried his rugby boots in his right hand, thumb between the back of the heels and index finger and middle finger inside each boot. The leather boots glinted with polish. Metal studs jutted from the bottom of the boots like rake fingers. Ox's thighs bulged at the edge of his short black rugby shorts. He wore comfortable mud-stained tennis shoes with red-and-white hooped socks, which sagged around his ankles. Ox's rugby jersey draped over his left arm. We titchies whispered in awe. "Look at his chest muscles!" "Ox is the toughest." "I wonder how many push-ups he had to do so his muscles would ripple like that?"

Ox's jaw worked up and down as he chewed on some gum. He sat down in the grass and took off his tennis shoes and began lacing up his boots. He stood up and pulled his socks up to his knees, folding over the top two inches. Plunging his arms inside the jersey, he stretched the shirt to fit his swelling chest. He pulled the shirt on, white with a wide red hoop across the chest. The colors, I'd been told, represented Jesus Christ. Red for his blood and white for the cleansing power of that blood to all who believe.

Other players arrived and dressed for the match. Ox rubbed Vaseline onto his legs and behind his ears. Ox arranged the team in a circle and they began stretching out. The coach, a South African, stood in the middle of the circle and gave last minute advice.

A brisk wind whipped the red-and-white flags planted around the edges of the pitch. The hill above the field had earthen seats cut out of the bank. Students and staff assembled. One teacher rang a cowbell. Two students in red t-shirts blew blasts on a horn as they encouraged the others to cheer.

The only thing missing was the other team. The Livingstone players spread out on the field and began some unopposed warm-ups. The forwards lined up for a lineout. The ball was thrown in and caught, then passed out to the backs who ran it up the field with crisp lateral passes. The winger would stop as if tackled and the forwards would quickly surround him, win the ball for second phase possession and then swing the ball out to the backs again. After about half an hour of this, the players came off the field. Maybe the other team wasn't coming. Maybe their bus had broken down.

A junior high boy sprinted to the field and shouted, "We just spotted their bus turning off the main road. They should be here in about fifteen minutes." The junior high dorm had a view all the way back to the main road and one boy was always assigned to sit with binoculars and announce when the opposition bus arrived.

Ox took his team into hiding up on our titchie soccer field to get them psyched up for the game.

A gray and white bus girdled by a maroon stripe groaned wearily to a stop above the rugby field. Duke of York School had arrived from Nairobi. The players in their maroon and white striped rugby shirts jumped off the bus and ran into the forest first to relieve themselves. Then they quickly prepared for the game. The referee came over and checked their boots and fingernail length before telling them the game would start in five minutes.

The crowd on the hill began to cheer. The Livingstone first fifteen came thundering down the hill and sprinted in a line before stopping in front of the crowd. They sang the school song and then ran onto the field. I could hardly contain my excitement. I wanted to play. But for now I would be the best ball-retriever in the world.

The ref whistled for the captains. Ox and a player from Duke of York went to the center of the field for the coin toss. Ox won and elected to kick off. "We always want to get the first hit on them," Ox said in explanation later when I asked him. "That way we can intimidate and set the tone from the beginning."

Ox led his team in a brief huddled prayer before spreading out across the field. Ox took the forwards to the left in a bunch. Mike, the fly-half, carried the ball to the center. He twirled the ball in his hands several times. He kicked a small wedge in the grass with his heel and balanced the ball upright. He took two measured strides back from the ball. The referee's whistle shrilled. Mike lifted his left hand while looking left at his forwards who were crouched and ready to run. Mike dropped his hand, stepped forward and lofted a high kick. A Duke of York player caught the ball. As he did, Ox thundered into him, lowering his shoulder at the Duke of York player's waist. The two players slammed to the ground and the ball skidded away. Nusu-Nugu dove on the loose ball and the rest of the Livingstone forwards formed a ruck over the ball, gripping each other with a strong bind and then pushing over and around the ball. The Livingstone scrum-half picked the ball up and hurled it out to the backs who began to attack the Duke of York defense.

A Duke of York player made a desperate tackle and the boll rolled free. Another Duke of York player fly-hacked the ball with his boot and it sailed down the hill. "Hey, titchie, get the ball!" barked the linesman, a red-haired British student at Livingstone.

"Right," I said, ripping my eyes off the field. I scampered down the hill and gathered up the ball.

Ox scored a try early in the game, banging through three players before barreling over the line to put the ball down in the in-goal area. Despite hard running and breath-crushing tackles, no one else managed to score. Late in the second half, Ox hung back from a loose scrum. As the Livingstone scrum-half picked up the ball, Ox thundered down the blind side, inches from the touch line. The scrum-half faked a long pass to the backs, then pulled the ball back and popped a short pass to Ox who churned up grass as his glossy legs drove him forward. A big-eared white player from Duke of York slammed into Ox and the two of them rolled down the hill. As they stood up, the white player shoved Ox away from him and said in a plummy accent, "You bloody wog!" The words slammed into Ox like a Maasai club.

Ox reeled back a step. I saw fire dancing in Ox's eyes and he clenched and unclenched his fist. Then, taking a deep breath, he smiled and ran up the hill and handed the ball to the linesman. The white player plodded back onto the field. He looked sour. A few minutes later the final whistle blew. Livingstone had won.

After watching that first game, I couldn't wait until I was old enough to play in a real rugby game. I wanted to run and tackle like Ox. I went up to him and told him so. He put his hand on my shoulder. I could see some red gouges on the back of his hand. "What are those?" I asked, concerned.

"Stud marks from someone's boot," Ox said. "Rugby's not a game for fairies. I get stepped on and kicked a lot."

I didn't like the sound of that. "Why?"

"Because of who I am," he answered.

I paused. "What's a wog?"

Anger stamped its curious blend of smoke and fire into Ox's eyes again. His voice cut like a knife. "A wog is …"

The big-eared white player from Duke of York who had used that term to describe Ox moved closer, several of his friends flanking him. "Yes, do tell us what you think a wog is."

Ox looked around. Most of the Livingstone players had moved away. Several had taken off their streaked and sweaty rugby jerseys and given them to their girl friends, who had promised to wash them.

Ox ignored the white players and looked down at me. "Clay, wog is a rude word used by brainless whites to describe an African."

The Duke of York players stepped closer, hemming Ox in.

I thought for a moment before saying, "Well, if you're a wog, I guess that makes me a wog, too. I was born here. Africa's my home."

The Duke of York players exploded with laughter. "The little kid thinks he's a wog."

I didn't get the joke. Ox grabbed my arm. "Let's go," he commanded.

14

I didn't find out until some years later how rude it was to call an African a wog. But I truly meant what I said when I told Ox that if he was a wog, then I was a wog, too. More than anything, I wanted to be like Ox. Ox graduated the next year and went off to university in the US. But I continued to admire the school's rugby players. More than anything I wanted to be a rugby player. The thought of playing electrified me. I finally got my chance in fourth grade. The announcement came at chapel.

"There will be try-outs at 4 p.m. today for a Titchie Colts rugby team to play against St. Mary's in three weeks." A shiver crept down my back.

After chapel I grabbed Titch and said, "Let's try out for the rugby team." Titch didn't look as excited as I was. As we tossed the ball back and forth during recess, I asked Titch why he wasn't excited. "We've been waiting for this since second grade!" I pointed out. "What's gotten into you?"

"Look at me," Titch said. "I'm the shortest kid in fourth grade, girls included. How am I supposed to make the rugby team? You're big, Clay. You'll have a chance against those fifth and sixth graders. I think I'm too small. I may get smashed."

"Come on, Titch," I encouraged. "Size isn't everything. You're tough and you can pass and kick better than a lot of the sixth graders. Every rugby team needs a few smaller guys for positions like scrum-half and hooker. I think you'd make a great scrum-half. Why don't you practice a few diving passes?"

Titch took a deep breath and nodded. He put the ball on the ground, motioned to me to move back and stepped towards the ball. He picked it up with both hands as he dove headlong and threw me a perfect pass.

"Good pass!" I shouted back to him after I'd run forward to catch the ball. "You'll be a great scrum-half."

We walked back into class, Titch trying in vain to wipe off the green grass stains from the knees of his khaki school uniform trousers. I could hardly concentrate the rest of the day. About thirty kids showed up at the try-outs that afternoon. The first team coach, Mr. Prinsloo, with helpers from the first fifteen, welcomed us. "Rugby is a great game," he began. "And the best way to learn it is when you're young. You are the future of Livingstone rugby. I'll be with you today to explain the basics of the game. After that Mr. Stone here will be your titchie colt coach. Work hard. Learn everything you can. Practice, practice and then practice some more and in a few years you'll be playing for me on the first fifteen. Now let's form a scrum." Coach Prinsloo grabbed my shoulder. "You'll be a great lock forward," he said. He pulled Bean, a skinny sixth grader over. "And you'll be the other lock." He draped my arm across Bean's back. "Grasp his shorts," Coach Prinsloo commanded. "Your arm goes across Clay's back here," Coach instructed Bean. "Your two arms should form an X."

Coach Prinsloo sized us up and said tersely, "Tighter. Bind tighter." He nodded. "Now kneel down together." We did and Coach stuck our heads between the hips of the front row forwards. The friction of pushing my head into the tiny slot between the bony hips of the hooker and the prop rubbed my baboon-like ears raw.

After some passing drills, Coach Prinsloo finally taught us how to tackle. "Get on your knees, Bean," Coach ordered. "And the rest of you, watch closely." Bean knelt and Coach Prinsloo knelt opposite him to demonstrate. As Bean shuffled along on his knees, Coach tackled him by driving his shoulders into Bean's thigh. He tucked his head behind Bean's hip and reached around with both arms and clamped Bean's legs together. Bean toppled over with Coach on top. "That's the proper way to tackle, lads. If you do it like that, it won't hurt. And the other player will go down with a bang, no matter how big he is. No one can keep running when his legs are tangled together."

We practiced tackling on our knees. "Looks like you're getting the hang of it," Coach commended us. "Now let's do it on our feet. Get in two lines. First man in this line, run straight at the first man in the tackling line. Tacklers come out and take your man down." On my first chance, I crouched and started to tackle a big sixth grader. But he pushed me down with his hand and I ate dirt while he galloped past. I struggled up and went to the back of the running line. Titch tackled next and he ducked under the runner's hand-off and latched onto his legs and knocked him onto the coarse Kikuyu grass with a thud.

"Good job, Titch," I yelled. Everyone else kept quiet, faces red from exertion, sweat leaking down cheeks, as we learned to tackle. I did better on my next chance, lunging forward with my shoulder and pinning the runner's legs together. His own weight brought him crashing to the ground and I landed on top of the back of his legs.

"Enough tackling," Coach Prinsloo shouted. "Let's have a fifteen-minute scrimmage." He and his helpers organized us into two teams. On the first kick-off one of the guys on our team dropped the ball so that it fell in front of him. The whistle shrilled. "Knock-on!" called the coach. "We'll have a scrumdown right here." He ground his heel in the grass at the spot and, standing facing sideways, he pointed his arm towards the other team, showing that it was their put-in at the scrum.

We bound together as we'd been taught, but as their scrum-half put the ball in, one of our props collapsed with a groan. The whole scrum tumbled in together. My face smashed into the ground under the weight of the whole pack. "Up you get lads. Let's see if there are any injuries," Coach Prinsloo called out, his whistle dangling next to his bristly chin.

"The skin above my eye stings," I said.

Coach Prinsloo came close and put a hand on top of my head as he examined my eye. "Just a scrape. Nothing to worry about."

He turned to the props. "You have to hold the scrum up lads. I've chosen you to be props because of your strength. But you also have to be in the right position. Crouch before binding and don't let your shoulders dip lower than your waist. It's illegal and dangerous for your necks and for the rest of the players." We formed another scrum. This time we stayed standing, though I don't think we pushed too hard. I made one open field tackle, but the rest of that first practice was kind of a blur of bodies.

Coach Prinsloo called us into a huddle. "Not bad for a first practice, lads. Not bad at all. From here on you'll be under Coach Stone. I have to work with the first fifteen. Work hard. You're the future of Livingstone rugby."

After practice, we headed down to supper. By then the scrape above my right eye had become a bright-red strawberry. "Wow! Doesn't that hurt?" asked Linda, a new fourth-grade girl from Zambia.

I touched the wound gently. Then I wrinkled my nose and stated proudly, "Naw! Rugby players always have strawberries from hitting the ground."

By the next day the strawberry had started to darken and scab over. I thought it made me look like a pirate with his eye patch pushed up on his forehead. I was disappointed when the scab fell off a week later, but at least it left a white scar that lasted for quite awhile before various sunburns darkened the skin to match the rest of my face.

After two weeks of practice Coach Stone announced, "After supper I'll post the team list of twenty players who will travel to St. Mary's next Wednesday." After supper we raced to the school bulletin board to read the list. I arrived at the board late. I'd stayed to eat another helping of pizza to gain strength, and because I always seemed to be hungry. I couldn't see the list as a pack of other kids crowded around the locked, glass-covered bulletin board. But as the others finally moved aside, I edged closer. My heart began to drop as I ran down the list. I reached number fifteen and still hadn't found my name. I bit my lower lip and tried to stifle the sob that wanted to burst out. Then I saw it. My name! Clay Andrews. Second from the bottom. And Titch's name was number twenty. We were both subs, but we'd made the team! I turned and saw Titch running towards the bulletin board on the worn wooden porch of the old school building.

"I had to run all the way up from home," he said. "My Mom made me eat supper with the family." He saw me smiling. "Well," he demanded. "Did we make it or not?" I stood in front of the board. He squirmed his way around me and started reading down the list. Even with his reading problems, Titch recognized his own name at the bottom of the list. He looked at me with a huge grin on his face. "Yes!" he exulted.

We examined the list again. We were the only two fourth graders on the team. And as subs, we wouldn't have much chance to play unless someone got hurt. But we'd get to ride in the bus with the team to Nairobi. We couldn't wait.

At the bottom of the team list Coach Stone had added the following instructions: Wear a white t-shirt and black shorts. Be at the bus at 3:15 p.m. Don't be late or you'll be left.

On the Wednesday of the game, I finished lunch and ran back to the dorm. I changed out of my khaki school uniform and into my rugby uniform. I had bugged Dad for a pair of rugby boots, but he'd told me money was tight. So I had to wear my worn Bata tackies. It didn't quite have the effect of a pair of rugby boots clicking on the cement floor of the classroom. But my black and white uniform drew stares and whispers from the other kids.

Titch and I got to leave class twenty minutes early and we ran down to the bus with the other players on Titchie Colts. The first fifteen and the second fifteen were also playing that day so we crowded onto the bus together. The smell of newly-polished rugby boots and liniment filled the bus as we set off for my first rugby game.

Titch and I joined in the singing that got everybody ready for the game. "Everywhere we go-o, People always ask us, Who we are, And where do we come from, And we always tell them, we are the buffaloes, we come from the forest, and if they don't hear us, we shout a little louder, We are the buffaloes we come from the forest …!"

At St. Mary's Titch and I shied back as the older players filed off the bus. The big field with the stone pavilion dominated the sports area. That's where the first fifteen played. They sent us to a smaller field. Our game started almost right away so we would get a chance to watch the final minutes of first team game.

The St. Mary's players looked a lot bigger and older than our team. And it showed. On the kick-off, they had a big prop who caught the ball and barreled through our whole scrum. Finally our fullback did tackle the big guy, but as he went down he passed the ball to a fast, tall Kenyan player who ran it across the line and scored between the posts.

The game got worse from there. Our forwards got pushed back on every scrum so St. Mary's won almost all possession of the ball. Our backs tackled bravely, but when they had to tackle on every play, they eventually got overwhelmed. At half time, Coach Stone tried to instill some morale. But our team was whipped. The score was already 36-0.

Bean, who played lock, had a bloody nose. Coach Stone looked at it and then motioned to me. "Clay, you'll go in the second half and replace Bean, here." He looked around at the dejected faces. "Anyone else hurt?"

Every hand went up as players cited injuries ranging from bruises to cuts. "Well, I can't replace all of you," Coach Stone said, "but I'll send in all the subs. It will be good for all of you to have a chance to play."

He went over to the St. Mary's coach who agreed to let us do a mass substitution of all five subs. I looked over at Titch. "You okay?" I asked. He nodded bravely. He looked about half the size of the guys on the Saints team.

They kicked off to us to start the second half. It was a high kick and the ball came right to me. Taking a deep breath, I called for the ball and actually caught it. Two big Saints players smeared me, but as I hit the ground I played the ball back like the coach had taught me. Our forwards managed to form a ruck over the ball and Titch dug the ball out and passed it to our backs who had a chance to run for the first time in the game. Our second center slipped through a tackle, but as he passed the ball out to our winger with room to run, the St. Mary's winger stepped in and picked off the pass and ran it in for a score.

We never did score that day. We lost 66-0. But Titch and I both got lots of chances to tackle and after the game we boasted about how we'd played. We'd survived. Coach Stone shook our hands after the game and said, "Well boys, you've been properly blooded."

We compared strawberries and bruises as we walked over to watch the end of the first fifteen game. Thankfully, they beat Saints that year, 15-12, so the bus trip home was festive, filled with singing and cheering. I had entered into a brotherhood. My body ached and my t-shirt oozed from my own sweat. Grass stained the filthy shirt, as did dirt and blood, but just as Lempapa had passed through the test of circumcision to become a man, I had passed my own test. I was a rugby player.

Book Two
Yakima, Washington

August 1973

15

"We're going back to the States in July for a one-year furlough," Dad announced during April vacation during my sixth grade year.

I sensed a crisis looming. "Why?" I asked. I didn't want to leave Africa or Livingstone.

"We need to see our families and churches that send us financial support," Dad explained. "We're supposed to go back after four years. It's been six years since we visited the States, but our ministry has been so urgent we didn't feel we could leave."

"Not having the money for airplane tickets is another reason we've stayed so long," my mother put in, a sour look on her face.

Dad sighed and rolled his shoulders and looked at Mom. "I know finances have been tight these last few years, but we have the tickets now and we're going."

"Tight!" Mom muttered. "That's an understatement."

"I don't want to go to America," I stated. "Can't you leave me at Livingstone for the year?"

"Don't be ridiculous, Clay," Mom snapped. "Your grandparents haven't seen you for six years. Of course you're coming to America with us."

I had no choice. I had to spend seventh grade in my parents' home country instead of at Livingstone. I had expected to make the Senior Colt rugby team in seventh grade, since I now weighed 140 pounds and stood five feet eleven inches tall.

I packed up my old trunk, scratched and bent from all the luggage-destroying trips between our home and Livingstone, and went home at the end of the school year. Mom sorted through my stuff and threw most of it away. Clothes I'd outgrown, ratty old pairs of underwear with nametags curling loose from the elastic, socks reddened with the orange mud from the playing fields at Baridi. I insisted on keeping a scarred old leather ball that no longer held air. I wiped off the dust that clung to the ball. It was a gift from Ox, the rugby ball I'd set out to rescue in the tunnel.

We flew into Chicago on a chartered Air France plane crowded with other missionaries. As we hiked through the humid, heavy air in the airport, sweat leaked from my armpits. I missed the cool highland breezes of Kenya. I didn't like the weather in this new country my parents called home.

In Chicago we stayed with my aunt and uncle and I met some cousins I never knew I possessed. As the adults talked, I followed my cousins to the rec room. "Did you ever see Tarzan?" they asked. I felt like a lion in a zoo.

"No," I answered. I picked up a Flintstone comic book and started to read. My cousins quietly discussed this surprising mystery that I could read. I'm not sure what they expected. When we left, my uncle insisted that I keep the comic book. "Dad, that's our comic book," my cousins cried.

He glared at them and hissed, "I'll buy you another." My cousins didn't say good-bye. My parents bought a big white station wagon. Dad stuffed the back of the station wagon with our suitcases, scratched and ripped in places. He'd also brought several large cardboard packages tied up with hairy sisal twine and filled with some of his hunting trophies. He had zebra skins, a buffalo skull, impala horns, and even a warthog skull. He had an idea about decorating the place where we would live to remind him of Africa. Mom wasn't too impressed.

Once we'd loaded the luggage into the station wagon, we waved good-bye to my uncle's family and drove west. Along the way we visited other relatives in Minnesota, and still others in North Dakota. I didn't know I had cousins all over the place. But they all seemed to think I was some oddball for growing up in Africa.

Round about Montana, I found out we didn't have any relatives left to visit. So we had our first chance to stay at a motel. I'd never stayed in one of these and hoped it would have a TV. We pulled into the city of Butte late one hot summer evening. We stopped at a motel with a bright colored sign announcing the place had TVs. I could see a swimming pool inside a black wrought-iron fence next to the parking lot. Mom walked in to make arrangements. In less than a minute she hurried out of the office. "Drive on!" she ordered Dad as her door slammed shut. "We're not staying here. Not at the price that man is asking."

"But Mom!" I pleaded from the backseat. "They had TV and a swimming pool."

But she was firm. "No motel could be worth what that man is charging. TV or not, we'll look for something else." Finally on the far side of the little town, we found a motel that suited Mom's purse. A neon sign spelling the word VACANCY glowed a dull orange. The NO in front of VACANCY wasn't lit. The motel consisted of ten small rooms, all lined up neatly, but with faded pale green paint starting to peel in places. There was no swimming pool and when we opened the door to the room, I could see it had no TV. Mom was happy it had a bathtub.

My parents decided to get up really early the next day and drive all the way to my grandparents' house in Yakima, Washington. Mom called Grandma collect and told her to expect us the next evening. The motel without a TV had almost broken the bank, and with no more relatives to land on in between, we had to suck it up and get home. Or to Mom's home. I didn't feel at home at all. And I could see it wasn't all that easy for my parents, either. They argued about money. Or lack of it. And where it had all gone. You'd think we'd gotten robbed or something. Dad looked puzzled. "How could we have spent so much so quickly?"

"It's not my fault," Mom answered defensively. "Everything costs so much more than I'd expected." Dad hunched his back a bit as he adjusted his position on the blue vinyl of the driver's seat. His jaw worked as he gripped the steering wheel and pointed the car down the highway. He kept his window partly open to keep the car cool. His thinning hair flew in the air like elephant grass blowing in the breeze. Even if it took all day and some of the night, he was determined to sleep at Grandma's house that night.

I sat, eyes fixed on the passing sage brush and yellow prairie grass of eastern Washington, fascinated by the translucent heat waves that rose from the baked earth. "This looks like the plains in Kenya," I commented to my parents.

Dad rolled his shoulders to stretch the tired muscles and nodded. "Yup, this part of Washington sure does look like the grasslands near Narok, doesn't it?"

Mom groaned and reached her hand behind her neck as she sat up from her sleep. "Oh, my neck has a crick in it." She shook her head gently from side to side and plunged her fingers into her stiff neck and began massaging. "Where are we?"

"Somewhere between Spokane and Ellensburg," Dad said. "I need to rest and the car needs fuel. Maybe we can stop for a burger and fries."

"And a chocolate milkshake," I chipped in. I'd found a few things in America I liked and chocolate shakes headed the list.

Mom examined the state of our finances and said we could afford lunch and gas for the car as well. We pulled off at a small town and found a roadside restaurant with a big red EAT sign on top of the roof. A board sign shaped like a milkshake glass, complete with a straw angled out the top, advertised fresh berry shakes in season. "You should try a fresh strawberry shake, Clay," Dad said as he got out of the car. A dark sweat stain shaped kind of like the continent of Africa spread out over the back of his lime green shirt. He put his hands on his hips and swiveled his back in a circular motion. I could hear soft crackling noises emanating from underneath the African continent. "Aah!" Dad said. "That's a bit better.

I tell you, my back is in bad shape after bouncing our Land Rover over those crazy Kenyan roads."

"What we drive on in Kenya can't really be called roads," Mom said, pulling open the glass door. A brass bell attached to the inside handle jangled. "The thing that's impressed me most about coming back to America is the smooth roads."

We sat at a booth and ordered burgers and fries. I decided to try a fresh strawberry milkshake. Dad wanted one as well, but Mom warned him it would make him fat. "It's your Mom's cooking that will make me fat," he said, a satisfied smile spreading across his face. "I can't believe I'll be eating your Mom's home cooking tonight!" Mom's face clouded over at that comment, but Dad didn't order a shake. Instead he snuck some sucks out of mine. As I sucked hungrily at my milkshake, a strawberry chunk clogged the straw. I lifted the straw out of the shake and ate the partially-inhaled strawberry off the bottom, before sucking in some more. I found I liked strawberry shakes better than chocolate ones. Even as I devoured my hamburger and finished off Mom's french fries—chips as we called them in Kenya—I could tell something had come between my parents. Mom stopped talking and Dad avoided looking at her.

As we got back in the car, Mom broke her silence. "Why are you looking forward to eating my Mom's home cooking? Do you like her cooking more than mine?"

"I didn't mean that," Dad answered. "But you know how your Mom is. Whenever we come she pulls out all the stops. Fresh corn on the cob. Mashed potatoes, fried chicken. And I mean chicken that melts in your mouth, not the bouncy chicken meat we get in Kenya. Then there's the desserts. Cherry pie, apple pie, all kinds of ice cream. And sticky buns for breakfast. You know your Mom."

Dad pulled into a gas station. I could see tears in Mom's eyes. And they didn't seem to be tears of joy. When Dad got back into the car and drove off towards Yakima, Mom spoke again. "You do like my mother's cooking more than mine. It's not my fault that Kenyan chickens are tough because they run around the *boma* for years before they're butchered and that we can't get apples or cherries or that we don't have a freezer for ice cream. I do my best." Tears started flowing in earnest.

Dad had the sense to pull the car off to the side of the road. "Oh, honey," he said, pulling her close to him. "I'm sorry. I didn't mean to hurt you by describing your Mom's cooking. I love you and I love the way you work so hard in Kenya to produce good meals. We eat well in Kenya. And the bouncy chicken meat is good exercise for my jaws and teeth."

"Then why did you get that far-away 'I'm in heaven' look in your eyes when you talked about my Mom's cooking?" Mom demanded.

Dad shrugged. "When I met you in college, I was a half-starved missionary kid from Africa, miles from my parents. And my Mom had struggled with rocks in the rice and weevils in the flour for all our growing up years. And the food at Livingstone in those days when I went to school was unimaginable. So when we came to meet your parents, and your Mom fed me one of those meals, I thought I'd died and gone to heaven."

The look on Mom's face told me Dad hadn't gotten out of trouble yet. He reached over and kissed her. I couldn't believe it! Right there by the side of the road. "I love you," he said, "and I love your cooking. It's more the vision of having all this food available that we haven't had a chance to eat in six years. I certainly wasn't trying to say I didn't like the way you cook. I love you and everything about you. But your Mom's from the generation that believes people aren't happy unless they're stuffed. She stacks the table until it creaks and then won't even sit down to eat. Instead she hovers around the table making sure everyone has more than enough."

"I'll never be able to match up to my own mother," Mom said, wiping tears.

"I don't expect you to. I didn't marry you to be my mother. I married you because I love you. But it is special when your Mom welcomes us home with a big meal. At the same time, I couldn't go back to living under her roof. Your Mom wants to control my every move."

"And mine, too," Mom said. "Living with them on our first furlough almost drove me crazy. I'm glad the church found us a place to live for this year."

They hugged each other, and I said gruffly from the back seat, "I'm glad you guys are friends again. Now, let's get going. I can't wait to eat Grandma's feast."

16

We drove up the gravel driveway to my grandparents' two-story white wooden house in the apple orchard late in the evening. Grandma came running down the steps from the front porch and attacked Mom and then hugged Dad and me as well. Grandpa, wearing faded but pressed overalls, stood and waited for us on the porch. Even as we marched up the steps and hugged Grandpa I could smell the food. Dad had been right. It was fried chicken and mashed potatoes. And I saw at least four pies on the kitchen counter.

"I'm sure you're all hungry after your trip," Grandma said, and in short order had us all washed up and seated at the table. Grandpa smiled, but it didn't seem like he knew who we were. Dad told him about our trip and Grandpa responded by saying, "Yup," or "Yah, sure, you betcha," after every sentence. I ate and ate. And then I ate some more. Suddenly I loved America with its soft chicken meat and smooth mashed potatoes. In the village I'd often eaten *enkum*, a heavy meal of mashed potatoes and beans, but I'd never had butter-smothered mouth-melting mashed potatoes like Grandma made.

Grandma never sat down, she just kept piling the food on as fast as I could eat. I heard the throaty gurgle of a coffee percolator and the sweet aroma of coffee wafted in from the kitchen as grandma rattled around, preparing the dessert. She offered us the choice of cherry or apple pie. I couldn't decide and received two large pieces of each, both covered with a huge slab of ice cream. I ate so much I thought I looked like a pregnant Kenyan goat.

After supper, we moved onto the front porch of the old farmhouse where my parents sat on a swinging couch and my grandparents rocked back and forth on their rocking chairs. "Tell me how your work is going among those natives in Africa," Grandma asked.

Dad grimaced. "Africans don't like being called natives."

Grandma smiled, oblivious to his comment, and asked again, "So are the natives becoming good civilized Christians?"

Dad cringed at her words, but he decided to ignore it and began to answer her question. "On a recent trip preaching trip to a Dorobo village, ten people decided to become Christians …" A sharp snore interrupted him. Grandpa had fallen asleep.

"Don't mind him," Grandma said, "tell me more. Do the natives wear clothes now? I so admire what both of you do there in Africa. I'm always telling everyone in church about your noble work among the savages there."

"Mom," Dad said, "they're not savages. They're people like you and me."

Grandma looked blank. Then she smiled and nudged Grandpa, "Wake up Carl! You should hear the stories about the savages in Africa."

Dad sighed and looked away. Mom looked unhappy. "We're a bit tired," she said, yawning to stress her point. "Maybe we should get to bed."

Grandma stood up and led us upstairs. She opened the door to a small bedroom with one bed in the corner and a dark old dresser against the wall. "This will be your bedroom for the year, Clay," she said.

Mom, coming in behind, raised her eyebrow and asked, "What do you mean it will be Clay's bedroom for the year? I thought we would be in the missionary house the church renovated recently."

"Oh, that house," Grandma said, waving her hand. "It's on a busy street right near the church. I told them you wouldn't be needing it because you would much prefer to stay here on the apple ranch with us. Just like your last furlough. This was your room then, Clay. Though you're a lot bigger now."

"Wait a minute, Mom," I heard my Mom say to Grandma. "We appreciate your sacrificing to make space for us. But we want to have our own house near the church. We'd see you just as often and ..."

"Nonsense," Grandma said. "You're my family and this is where you'll spend the year. Besides, when I told the church you wouldn't need the mission house, they gave it to the new youth pastor. You'll adore them. They're such a cute young couple. They've even got twin girls, almost two. You know, I can't wait to show you all off at church tomorrow." Grandma pointed Mom and Dad towards a larger bedroom, then disappeared down the stairs.

I heard Dad mutter, "I love her cooking, but I told you she likes to organize everything for us and this is a bit much."

"I agree," Mom answered. She noticed me listening. "Just get to bed, Clay. We'll talk with the church missions committee tomorrow about our living arrangements. But don't worry, we won't spend another year cramped into this attic."

As I sat down on the bed, which creaked under my weight, I heard Mom talking in low tones with Dad. "I can't believe my Mom would go and do something like that."

Dad's deep-voiced reply rumbled like a lion, but I couldn't hear what he said. I lay on my back and stared at the all-white ceiling which was so different from the view from my top bunk bed in the dorm with brown rain stains creating modern-art-looking patterns on the ceiling boards. I sighed and stood up to undress. Pulling back the covers, I lay down on top the sheets in the sweltering Yakima heat. Sweat beaded up on my forehead. *And people think Africa's hot,* I thought to myself. I threw open the window hoping for a breeze, but the pungent smell of a skunk wafted into the bedroom. I resigned myself to a sweaty night and closed the window.

I didn't have any bad dreams on that first night in my grandparents' house, but the next day at church was a nightmare. I hated being paraded in front of other people like some kind of freak because I grew up in Africa.

As we stepped out of our station wagon at the church, an older man came up and shook my parents' hands. "I see you're driving a missionary station wagon," commented the man, whose bald spot glowed shiny and red. "All missionaries seem to drive station wagons." His eyes twinkled, but I could tell Dad felt a bit embarrassed.

"Well, yes, it's good for carrying luggage on all the trips we have to make," Dad explained.

The old man lost interest. Looking at me he leaned and put his hand on my head. I thought maybe he'd learned this greeting from the Maasai. "And this must be Clay," he said. "My how you've grown." I think I heard that phrase a hundred times that morning. Of course I'd grown! Did they still expect me to be the size of a kindergarten kid? We'd been away for six years!

Grandma came over and dragged us to the church entrance. "Stand here," she commanded, then beamed as she introduced us to every church member. "And this is my grandson, Clay," she said. "Hasn't he grown?"

Everyone would murmur agreement. "Must be all that monkey meat you feed him over there," joked a heavy lady whose black eye shadow had smeared as she'd given Mom a hug and a kiss. I wanted to shake her and tell her we didn't eat monkey meat. But instead I stood, sweated, and smiled.

When we finally stepped into the church, my parents herded me to the junior high Sunday school class. "Clay has just come from Africa," Mom explained to the teacher who smiled at me. The hubbub from three boys in the back row abated and their eyes pierced me. I wanted to disappear. But the teacher called the class to order and announced, "We have a visitor in class today. This is Clay and his parents are missionaries in Africa. I'm sure Clay would love to tell us stories about the wonderful things God is doing in Africa."

"I really don't have any missionary stories," I mumbled. The teacher looked a bit surprised, but then recovered. "Well, I'm sure you can say some funny sounding words for us from the African language over there." My ears glowed and I wished I could sink out of view forever. I didn't want to be singled out as different. Finally I said gruffly, "*Jambo* means hello in Swahili."

"*Jambo*! That sounds so African," the teacher gushed. "It must be wonderful living over there and helping all those people." I shuddered inwardly. But she left me alone and began teaching her lesson. I slouched alone in the front row and retreated into a daydream, watching myself plough through a scrumful of players to score a try. The teacher's words interrupted my daydream. "I'm sure you know the answer to that question, don't you Clay?" I wasn't sure what question she meant. "You've probably memorized that whole chapter from the Bible, haven't you?" she went on.

"What verse are you talking about?" I asked. Some of the students behind me laughed. I wanted to go outside and find a tree to climb. I needed to get away, but I couldn't escape.

After Sunday school the other students whispered and stared at me as I marched out of the room and found my parents. Dad looked about as awkward as I did. I'm sure he would have preferred a small wooden church in the forest with a rough-hewn pulpit. The necktie he'd put on that morning had been pulled loose, and now hung askew on his suitcase-wrinkled shirt. Mom seemed to enjoy all the attention. This was the church where she'd grown up and she seemed to know everyone. During the main church service, the pastor had our family stand up in the front so he could pray for us. My best trousers had grown a little short after my most recent growth spurt and my brown-stained white socks, which had no elastic left, sagged around my ankles, visible for all to see as we stood on the platform.

17

Thankfully American church services are timed to finish in one hour so my embarrassment eventually came to an end. A kind-looking woman with oval black-rimmed glasses pulled my mother aside after church. "Come downstairs and choose some clothes from the missionary barrel," the woman said. She grabbed my arm. "You too, Clay." She led us to a small closet in the church basement. A slew of cast-off clothing had been jammed into a big box. "You can choose anything you want," the woman said, beaming. I didn't see anything I wanted to choose. My mother pulled out a few items and thanked the woman profusely.

Afterwards the mission committee chairman took our family out to an all-you-can-eat buffet called the Chuckwagon. "You can eat all you want," Mom informed me.

"You're kidding!"

"No, I'm not. 'All-you-can-eat' means you can keep going back for more."

I piled on heaps of mashed potatoes and baked ham and roast beef. I blotted out my horrible morning by gobbling up the food. "You can drink as much soda as you want as well," Dad said.

"Where's the waiter so I can order?" I asked.

Dad laughed and pointed to a machine. "Get a glass and fill your own from there." I picked up a glass and stood in front of the machine, not sure which button to push. I saw the familiar red-and-white Coca-Cola symbol. I put my hand out and pushed on the Coke logo. Nothing happened. A Y-shaped metal lever jutted out from underneath the Coke sign. I reached down and pushed the lever. Frothy Coke dribbled all over my hand. Now that I could see where the liquid flowed out, I put my glass in the right place and filled it. I came back to the fountain again and again. They even had a soft ice-cream machine and I polished off three bowls covered with thick chocolate sauce and peanuts.

As I sat down at the table with yet another bowl of ice-cream, I heard my father ask the mission chairman if we could live in the mission house. The man pulled out a wrinkled white handkerchief and mopped his forehead before answering. "I'm sorry, but we've put the new youth pastor there and we don't have any more funds for another place. We had it all ready for you after you'd written and said you wanted to live there this year. But then your mother-in-law insisted you didn't want to stay there. I thought maybe you'd been too polite in your letter to say no. And since your mother-in-law is so forceful, well, I'm sorry, but apart from renting your own place, there's not much we as a committee can do."

I could see Mom biting her lip. On the drive home Mom said, "I'll look into what it will cost to rent a house. I think I can survive a week or two with my Mom, but for our sanity, we'd better find a place of our own."

Mom hefted the Sunday newspaper from the porch and flipped through it until she found the classified ads. Dad grabbed the sports page. I soon heard sniffling from Mom and she threw down her section of the newspaper. "We can't afford to rent a house even in the poor section of town!" she said in answer to Dad's raised eyebrows.

"I'm sure the Lord will provide," Dad began.

"I'm tired of hearing that!" Mom fussed. "Here we've sacrificed all these years in Africa and we can't even have a house of our own. Sometimes I wish you'd gotten a regular job after college. At least we'd have a place of our own."

Dad's jaw tightened.

"I love my parents," Mom said, "but I feel like a failure, a kid who never grew up. If we have to live with them again this year, Mom will treat me like a little girl."

Dad grabbed the classified ads and ran his finger down the homes for rent section. "Here's one in our price range," he said.

Mom looked over his shoulder. "That's in a real sleazy area," Mom said. "We couldn't live there."

"Well, maybe I can get a job," Dad said. "Most of our church meetings are on weekends and during the evenings. It might squeeze my time and I may have to cancel some of the longer trips, but we could use the extra money to rent a house."

"It's no use," Mom said. "Your preaching schedule is so full you couldn't find a job to fit around our travels. And I'm not going out to any churches on my own. Besides, you have no work experience here in the States. Who would hire you? I mean, I'm proud of you for being able to preach in Maasai and all that, but how will that help you get a job here?"

"So we stay with your parents and make the best of it?" Dad asked. "Or what would you suggest?"

"Oh, I don't know," Mom wailed. She ran out of the room. I looked at Dad and he shrugged.

"We'll work it out, Clay, don't worry."

Just then Grandma came into the room adjusting the waist of her blue flowered dress. "Did I hear some arguing going on in here?" she asked.

"Oh, no, Mom," Dad lied. "Everything's fine. Hey, since it looks like we'll be staying here for the year, I wondered if I could put up some trophies from Africa. I've got a zebra skin, a mounted buffalo head and even a warthog skull. I'd planned on using them to decorate our house."

Grandma glared at Dad, "My house is decorated just as I want it. If you want any of those animal things around, go put them up in the barn. But don't mess my house up with those old stinky bones and horns from Africa."

Dad had the sense not to argue, but I could see the hurt in his blue eyes. "Come Clay," he said. "Let's go put that buffalo head inside the barn. And there's an old basketball hoop over there, too. Maybe we can shoot some baskets."

As we hammered some nails and mounted Dad's trophies on the inside of the barn, I asked, "Is Mom really mad at you?"

He smiled. "Seems like it. Actually, we're both really off balance. I know we say we're coming home to the States, but truth is America doesn't always seem like home. We have a hard time fitting in. Mom sees people she grew up with living in big houses with swimming pools and we have to squeeze in the attic here. She doesn't think it's fair. And being preachy about trusting God isn't the message she wants to hear right now. But we still love each other."

I handed Dad an impala head with its wide-sweeping horns. He hung it from a nail. "Don't worry. Your Mom and I will learn to adjust, even if we do spend the year in the attic. And I'm sure you'll learn to like it here, too. Did you enjoy your first Sunday at church?"

"No," I answered bluntly. "Everyone thinks I should have a tail since I grew up in Africa. I can't stand the way everyone stares at me. And I don't know anyone."

Dad put his arm around my shoulder. "I've been there," he said. "It's not easy, but this place will become home as you make friends."

"It'll never be home, Dad. Besides, I look so different. Did you see how short my trousers were today in church? I need new ones and new socks. I heard one of the girls say I looked cute wearing floods and saggy socks. But I think she was making fun of me. Then some lady took Mom and I to choose clothes out of the missionary barrel, but everything looked wrinkled and ugly."

Dad laughed. "We'll get you some clothes before school starts," he said. "Don't worry."

18

Mom took me over to Rattlesnake Valley Junior High School a few days before school started. She signed me up as a new student. "Oh, look, they have a boys' glee club," she said and registered me in the glee club as one of my elective classes.

"What's a glee club?" I asked, worried.

"It's like a boys' choir. You'll love it. You have such a good voice, Clay."

Singing in a boys' choir gave me no thrills. But even when I protested, I couldn't change Mom's mind. I figured it was something I'd have to do to adjust to America. We didn't have glee clubs in Africa.

On the first day of school I put on the best clothes I owned. I wore a button-down white shirt with gray trousers, which were a bit snug around my waist but at least reached the edges of my Bata Safari boots, the boots that said I knew Africa. Mom pushed me out to the edge of the road where she assured me a yellow school bus would soon appear. The bus trundled into view and stopped. The front door flipped open with a hiss. I stepped into the bus and a whole new world. I strode quickly to an empty seat and wedged myself against the window. I heard laughing and chatting but I focused my eyes out the window. At another stop five boys bustled into the bus. One sat next to me. I didn't look up but I could feel his eyes boring into me. I turned. He seemed amused. He nodded his head slowly and said, "You're sure different." His tight blue Levi jeans, white t-shirt, and scuffed cowboy boots contrasted with my attire. "What kind of shoes are those?" he asked.

"Safari boots," I answered.

"Safari boots? Sounds like some fancy African word. Where you from, anyway?"

"Kenya," I said, "and I got these shoes there."

"Kenya!" the boy said loudly. The chattering and giggling on the bus stopped as everyone looked toward our seat. "You must be joshin' me. You can't be from Kenya. You ain't even black!"

Everyone started to laugh at me. "He says he's from Africa," my seatmate went on, "but he don't even know Africans are black. Even I know that." He turned from addressing the bus to me. "So, where you from, really?"

"Chicago," I said softly, naming our port of entry into this alien country. He gave me a final questioning look before losing interest and leaning across the aisle to visit with a friend.

The bus pulled up to the square red-bricked school buildings. A flagpole jutted into the air with an American flag flapping in the breeze. As we filed off the bus, I noticed that even though this school didn't have a school uniform like we did at Livingstone, all the guys seemed to wear blue denim jeans and a white t-shirt. My button down shirt labeled me as being very out of step. I followed the herd to the gymnasium for the school-opening assembly. As the principal stood up on the platform he asked us to say the pledge of allegiance. I'd never heard of such a thing. I glanced around at the others, not sure what to do. Everyone put a hand on their chest and started reciting something beginning with, "I pledge allegiance to the flag ..." I put my left hand on my chest and pretended to mumble along. A pretty girl to my right looked at me with shock registering on her face. "You're supposed to use your right hand!" she hissed. I dropped my left hand as if it had been stung by an African bee. But before I got my right hand up, the murmuring recitation ended.

I listened as the principal droned on. I gathered I was supposed to head for a home room and get a locker assignment. I had a home room number, but I didn't know where it was. I was too afraid to ask anyone so I went looking. How hard could it be to find room 120? It took me a long time. By the time I arrived, the teacher had already given instructions and frowned at my late arrival. Everyone turned and stared as I stumbled and sat in a chair. The legs of the chair squealed as I pushed them back so I could fit in under the shiny wooden desk.

The teacher came over and handed me a sheet of paper with some numbers on it. "This is your locker number and locker combination," he informed me. "Don't lose it. You have fifteen minutes to find your new locker and put your things in it before going to your first class."

Chairs scraped as everyone pushed towards the door. I hung back and looked at my paper. Locker number 154. Then three numbers: 24-6-24. I had no idea what they meant, but I followed the crowd and saw all the others twirling black dials on the side of the locker doors. I found locker number 154. I tried twirling the black dial to the required numbers. It didn't work. I could hear lockers opening and slamming. Mine stayed firmly shut. I rattled on the handle. It still didn't open. I wanted to go home to Livingstone.

A voice behind my ear asked, "Having trouble?"

I turned to see a boy with straw-colored hair that fell over his blue eyes and curled on his white t-shirt collar. Blue jeans hid his tree-trunk legs and his gut hung out under his shirt and partially covered the cowboy belt with the silver buckle. *He'd make a great prop on a rugby team*, I thought. He smiled and went on, "I'm Bobby. Bobby Fuller. What's your locker number?"

I showed him the slip of paper. He reached his meaty hand over to the combination lock and dialed deftly and the door opened.

"How come it worked for you?" I asked.

"Did you go left-right-left and pass over the number in the middle the first time?" he asked.

Dumbly I shook my head. I hadn't even understood what he said. "I've never used a combination lock before," I confessed.

"Where'd you go to school before this?" Bobby asked.

"Livingstone Academy," I answered.

Bobby looked blank.

"It's in Africa," I said quietly.

"You're from Africa? Really?" he asked.

"Yes," I replied waiting for him to mock me.

"That's great!" Bobby said. "I'd love to visit a place like Africa. You'll have to tell me all about it. Now, where's your first class?"

I had the registration paper Mom had given me. "Uh, boys' glee club," I said doubtfully.

"You're not serious!" Bobby said. "I didn't think there would be any cool guys in boys' glee club. I hate to sing, but my Mom insisted and signed me up."

I smiled. "My Mom signed me up, too."

"Well," Bobby said, "let's get over there. Lucky for you I know the way. I flunked seventh grade last year and I'm doing it over again. So I know where everything is." We walked off down the hall. "You look pretty tall," Bobby said. "Do you play football? I'm on the football team. Least I was last year and I guess I'll make it again. I play guard on offense. You ought to join the team."

"I've never played football," I answered, "but I play rugby for my school in Kenya."

"Rugby? I hear that game's insane. No pads, nothin'. And you hit and tackle just like in football. If you play rugby, I'm sure you can play football."

We arrived at the music room and walked in as the choir director began handing out sheet music for a sea shanty. I glanced around at the rest of the boys in our class. I'd never been in an all boys' choir before. The director ran us through a few voice exercises and then had us singing, "A-rovin', a-rovin', since rovin's been my ruinin', I'll go no more a-rovin' with you fair maid."

Bobby rumbled away in a false bass to irritate the teacher. Most of the rest of us had squeaky in-between voices that slid up and down the scale at random. Roving. Always wandering. The song sure described my life. No roots. Always moving around. And even when I stayed in one place, others around me slipped away and disappeared—sometimes forever.

I survived boys' glee that first day, but I had a problem in gym class. Bobby's schedule had diverged from mine after our singing class and I ended up in the locker room trying to change my clothes for P.E. We'd been told to bring shorts and a white t-shirt along with our tennis shoes. Our P.E. teacher handed us each a heavy combination padlock and told us to choose a locker where we could keep our P.E. clothes. He sternly warned us to have our clothes washed regularly. "Especially your socks," he snapped. "I don't want this locker room smelling like sweaty old socks."

I stripped down to my underwear and then played with my combination lock, trying to remember Bobby's instructions. I finally got it to open up. But as I stood up to finish getting dressed and lock my clothes away, cold metal pressed against my buttocks. I looked over my shoulder and saw some joker's hand gathering the rear of my underwear between the elastic band and the leg hole. Before I could pull away, he used his other hand to snap a padlock shut around my underwear. The boy, who had curly brown hair, smirked and slipped behind the next row of lockers. "Stop!" I pleaded, pushing panic back. "Take your lock off!"

19

The curly-headed boy popped his head around the locker and shouted, "It's not my lock. I don't know the combination. You'll have to ask around until you find the owner." With a giggle, he disappeared again.

Humiliated, I walked to each one left in the locker room and showed them the lock and asked if it was theirs. Everyone laughed and I got redder. But I finally heard a boy shouting, "Who stole my lock?"

"Is this yours?" I asked, hurrying over to him.

He looked down. "Why are you wearing my lock on your underwear?" he demanded. "That's gross!"

"Just please get it off!" I begged. "Someone locked it on me when I wasn't looking."

The boy grunted in disgust, but he undid the lock. Released, I ran back to my locker, put on my gym clothes and locked my school clothes in the locker before rushing out to the gym.

Curly Head, who I found out was named Adam when the teacher called roll a few minutes later, winked at me and laughed. I tried to ignore him. After a short warm-up the teacher told us we'd be learning wrestling the first two weeks of school. He showed us a few basic moves and then paired us up. Adam became my partner. As I knelt down in the starting position, he knelt beside me with one hand on my elbow and another over my back. The coach blew his whistle and Adam jerked my arm and twisted. Within seconds I found myself pinned to the blue mat.

"For a big guy you're not too good at wrestling," Adam taunted. "Still thinking about that lock on your undies?" I ignored him and watched as the teacher explained some basic moves. I realized how Adam had whipped me so easily. The teacher also showed how to defend against certain moves. In our next match I managed to hold my own. And on the third try, I flipped Adam and my superior height and weight helped me to pin him down. In frustration, I held him firm against the mat until I heard the teacher say, "Clay, that's enough. Let him up. I didn't ask you to strangle him."

Adam sat up and shook his head. Drops of his sweat splattered on my face. I stood up and wiped the sweat off. Adam looked at me with doubt in his eyes. "Be careful with my neck," he said. "This is just P.E. class, you know."

I put my hand out. "I'll lay off if you stop playing pranks on me," I said.

Adam avoided my hand and walked away.

I caught up with Bobby at lunchtime. He had a huge sack lunch with four baloney sandwiches, several apples, a pint of milk, and more. He spread his lunch out on a table on the porch outside the main cafeteria. "I always bring my own lunch," Bobby said waving his hand over his food. "I could never afford to buy enough food from the cafeteria."

I, too, had my lunch in a brown paper bag. I had feared I'd be the only one with a sack lunch. Most of the other students went through the line and sat down at the inside tables with their hot meals on orange trays.

I opened my lunch. Bobby leaned over. "What do you have?" he asked.

Mom had fixed me two tuna fish sandwiches, something I'd never gotten in Kenya. I also had a small fruit pie and a banana.

"Trade you an apple for that banana," Bobby said.

I agreed. "These bananas here in America are tasteless," I said. "My favorite bananas in Africa are green."

"Green?" Bobby mumbled around the banana he'd stuffed into his mouth. "Aren't green bananas unripe?"

"Some are, but some African bananas are ripe when they're green. We have short finger bananas that are really sweet. We even have red cooking bananas. They taste like potatoes."

"Red bananas? You're putting me on," Bobby said, smiling as he crunched into a red apple. "Red to me means an apple. And the bananas taste like potatoes? Africa sounds like a great place. Tell me more."

"What I really miss is *chai*," I said, draining the last of my can of Coke.

"What's *chai*?" he asked.

"Kenyan tea. Mostly milk and very sweet. And if it's boiled in a big *sufuria* on a wood fire, it has a smoky taste."

"I'd love to try some *chai*," Bobby said, patting his generous stomach. "I'm fascinated by all kinds of food and drink."

"My Mom could make us some *chai*," I said. "Why don't you come by my place after school?"

"I'd love to, but I can't today. I have football practice. Aren't you going to try out?"

"I'm only a seventh grader. Do you think I have a chance?" I asked.

"You're big enough," Bobby said. "I'll tell the coach you want to try out. He'll hold a place until tomorrow, I think. Just get your Mom to sign the permission slip. Better yet, we could go now and I'll sign it for you." He raised his eyebrows. "I've learned to be a great forger. I sign my Mom's name for everything."

"What about your Dad?" I asked.

Bobby looked up at the sky and said nothing. Then he stared at me and shook his head sadly. "See you around," he said. "Maybe I can try some *chai* this weekend. Do you think it would be okay to visit your home and meet your Mom and Dad?"

"I'm sure it would," I said. "My Dad would love to show off his animal skins and horns and skulls and tell stories about his hunting trips." Bobby waddled off, crumbs spilling from his t-shirt.

I concentrated on finishing the day without making a fool of myself. I remembered one of my Dad's favorite proverbs. "Even a fool is thought to be wise if he keeps silent." So I didn't say much in any of my classes. The teachers didn't seem too frightening and it looked like I might survive in this foreign place. As I trudged to the bus, I was glad I had at least one friend. I remembered how Bobby wanted me to play football, so I changed direction and went by the office to pick up a permission form. I hurried to the bus parking area with the paper fluttering in my hand. The line of yellow buses looked like a train of hairy caterpillars from the African forest. I tried to remember the number of the bus I'd come on, and realized with a sinking feeling in my gut that I had no idea. Getting picked up in the morning had been no problem. Only one bus came by my house. But how would I find my bus home? Kids laughed and boarded the buses as the drivers waited patiently. I ran along the side of the buses peering into the windows to see if I recognized anyone. All the buses looked the same, loaded with kids I didn't know. As I passed one bus, a girl stuck her head out the window. "Hey, Africa Boy. Are you looking for your bus?"

She looked friendly so I said, "Yes. Is this the right one?" I strained to remember whether she'd been on the morning bus or whether she'd been in one of my classes during the day.

"Don't you remember the number of your bus?" she asked.

"Uh, I guess not," I answered.

The bus made a hissing sound as the driver released the brakes.

"Our bus is number 19," the girl said. "You'd better get in or you'll be left behind." I scampered onto the bus. The driver telescoped the door shut and I had to look for a seat. The girl who'd called out to me had an empty space next to her. Heart beating from my scare of almost missing the bus, I sat down next to her.

"Thanks," I said.

"I've never known someone to forget their bus number," she answered. "Are you stupid or something?"

I shriveled inside, but answered bravely. "You can't forget something you don't know. Today's the first day I've ever traveled on a school bus."

"How'd you get to school in Africa if you didn't ride on a bus?"

"My Dad loads my old trunk on our Land Rover and we drive for three hours," I explained.

"You drive three hours to school every day?"

Now I wondered who was stupid, but I didn't dare say it.

"Actually, I only travel to school once every three months. My parents say good-bye and I live in a dormitory with other boys my age."

The girl's mouth sagged open. She'd never heard of such an arrangement.

"It's a fun school," I went on. "On Saturdays we hike to the waterfalls or to the hot springs. I play rugby after school and …"

"Your school sounds weird to me," the girl said. Then she put her chin on her fist and stared determinedly out the window. I had to look sharp to make sure I got off at the right stop. Thankfully I recognized the cherry trees that lined the front of the driveway to my grandparents' house.

I clumped off the bus and ran home. Grandma welcomed me home with a plate of chocolate chip cookies and a big glass of milk. "How was your first day at school?" Mom asked.

"Fine," I mumbled. I didn't mention my locker disaster or the padlock on my undies. I pulled out the football consent form and asked her to sign it.

"Are you sure you want to play football?" she asked. "It means staying after school every afternoon and I've heard some of these football coaches are mean. I'm not sure I want you playing football." She looked over the form, running her finger down every line. "And here it says if you get hurt we as parents won't hold the school responsible."

"Mom, please. You don't understand. In a whole day at school I've only met one guy who even talked to me as if I was a normal person. He's called Bobby. I don't think he has a Dad, but can he come over this weekend? I told him you'd fix him some *chai*. Bobby's on the football team and really wants me to try out. I could make friends. I may even learn something to help me be a better rugby player when I go back to Livingstone."

Mom chewed the end of her pen. "I'll have to ask your Dad," she said.

I smiled. I knew I'd won the battle.

20

Dad dragged in at supper, dark sweat stains under his armpits. He smiled at me. Then he handed Mom fifty dollars. "I've been picking pears," he said. "And you can use some of that money to buy school clothes for Clay."

"You look like a migrant worker from Mexico," my Grandma complained, a frown wrinkling her face. "Are you sure that mission of yours can't give you a better salary?"

Mom's eyes sparked, but Dad touched her lips.

"Sometimes you have to go out and get dirty," Dad said. "Reminds me of summers trying to earn money for college. I'm off to take a shower."

Mom disappeared into the kitchen with Grandma. I heard a low murmuring. Then Mom burst out crying and ran upstairs, tears trickling down her cheeks. I didn't want to think of Mom crying so I stepped outside and sat on the porch next to Grandpa. He looked at me and nodded. "Yah, sure, you betcha!"

Grandpa's old cocker spaniel, Joe, uncoiled from next to Grandpa's rocking chair and came over and sat next to me. I clutched Joe's silky coppery hair and received a lick on the chin for my attention. I remembered Rocky and I hugged Joe with both arms and choked back a sob. Grandpa's eyes brightened. "Old Joe likes you," he stated. He went back to rocking and puffing air out of his mouth like an old steam engine. "It's hot," Grandpa blurted. "Don't you get tired of the heat?"

I nodded and buried my face in Joe's fur. Something about the earthy dog smell comforted me. I felt a hand on my shoulder. Dad sat next to me on the edge of the porch and dangled his bare feet over the edge. "Do you miss Kenya?" he asked. Without waiting for me to answer he went on, "I sure do." He got a far off look in his eyes.

Grandma called us to supper. Dad stood up. "That first wad of cash is for you and Mom to spend on clothes."

"Thanks, Dad," I answered. "All I really need is a pair of jeans and some white t-shirts. That's what all the kids are wearing."

Dad smiled. "Fashions don't change much around here."

After supper, Mom announced, "I'm taking Clay over to Montgomery Ward to buy some school clothes." We climbed into the station wagon while Dad and

Grandpa sank into two recliners facing a hazy image on the old black and white TV and watched the news. "Wait," I said to Mom. "I need Dad to sign my football permission form. And there's some things on the paper I need to buy at the store."

I ran into the house and asked Dad to sign the form. He examined it, then looked at me. "Is this something you really want to do?" he asked. "Football can be a bit brutal."

I nodded. "My new friend Bobby Fuller really wants me to try out."

"All right," Dad said, pulling out a pen and signing the form. "It says here you need to buy a jock and a cup. Can you buy those with Mom or do you want me to come with you?"

"What's a jock?" I asked.

Dad stood up. "I'll come with you," he replied, choking back a chuckle.

At the store, Mom marched to the young men's section and started examining khaki slacks. "These look good, Clay," she said. "They're permaprest so we won't have to worry about ironing them in Kenya. And you could even use them for school uniform pants at Livingstone."

I shook my head. "I only need some jeans, Mom. No one here wears khaki pants. This is my first year at a school where I don't have to wear a school uniform, so I sure don't want to wear khaki."

I pulled out some Levi's 501 blue jeans. I found a pair that fit along with several white t-shirts. "Let's buy these," I said.

Mom carried my jeans and t-shirts to a cashier as Dad walked with me over to the sports section.

To my horror, he walked up to a counter and pulled out a small cardboard box with a picture of some funny looking underwear on the front, and the word Bike emblazoned on the box. He pulled out the underwear. "Dad," I hissed. "What are you doing? Those underwear don't have any rear end, just two straps!"

He smiled and shook out the odd-looking contraption. The straps jiggled in the air and the label BIKE jutted out of the front waistband. "This, Clay, is a jock, also called a jock strap. It's what guys wear for sports to protect their more—uh, how should I put it—more sensitive areas. Now what size waist did you say you wore in those jeans?"

"Are you sure this is what I have to buy?" I asked, looking over my shoulder to be sure no one saw us.

"You're not embarrassed, are you?" he said. "Now, what size waist are you?"

"Thirty-two inches," I said. "Do I have to try this thing on?"

"No you don't have to try it on. Here we go, size thirty-two waist. Now for a cup."

I saw a pyramid of coffee mugs with logos from various football teams. I expected him to buy me one of them. I wasn't sure why I needed a cup for joining the football team. Maybe we'd have an after game tea like we did after a rugby game and Americans required everyone to bring their own cup. But Dad ignored the coffee mugs and rummaged around near the jock straps and pulled out something flesh-colored and vaguely heart-shaped. It looked like some sort of gas mask.

"I think this will do," Dad said.

"What's that?" I asked. "I think the cups are over here." I pointed at the stack of mugs.

Dad laughed out loud. "This is a cup." He leaned toward me and whispered. "You slip it into a pouch inside your jock strap. It's extra protection for some vital body parts."

A blush exploded on my face. "Is that what a cup is?"

Dad nodded. "I'll show you how it all goes together when we get home. Now, do you want to buy these?"

I shook my head. "You can buy them," and I hurried away to distance myself from the man buying a jock and a cup.

21

I headed to school the next morning feeling more confident in my blue jeans and white t-shirt, though I'd had to do ten squats to loosen up the tight-fitting jeans. At least I could blend in with the herd. I met Bobby Fuller at our homeroom. "Did you get your permission slip to play football?" he asked.

When I said yes, Bobby's rounded cheeks wrinkled as he broke into a huge smile. It felt good to be wanted.

After school I went into the locker room for practice. I handed the coach my paper. He leaned back against the wall and squinted at the permission form. "Okay, Clay," he said, "I'm Coach Burke and I'm in charge here. We run a tough football program. If you can survive my practices, I'll make sure you play on my team." He paused and smiled before leaning closer to me. "But if you can't handle the heat, get out of the fire. I can tell after one practice if you'll make it on my team. Now go get your equipment from the manager. You can keep your stuff in your PE locker." He jerked a thumb at a room surrounded by a metal cage. An eighth grader with black-rimmed glasses and a pencil behind his ear sat on a tall round metal stool.

"What do you want?" the eighth grader asked.

"Uh, Coach Burke told me to ask you for my football equipment."

"What all do you have?" the manager asked.

"Well, I have a cup and a jockstrap," I began.

"Ha! Where did you come from? Everyone has his own cup and jockstrap. I don't hand those out. I'm asking if you brought your own helmet, your own pads, or anything like that."

"No, I don't have any of my own equipment," I mumbled.

Sighing, the manager slid off his stool and began rummaging through some cupboards. He threw me a battered helmet that had scarred blue paint on it. "Last one, I'm afraid," the manager said. "Hope it fits."

He piled a heap of other equipment on the counter and asked me to sign for it. "There's your football pants, two knee pads, two thigh pads, your girdle, and your shoulder pads. I already gave you your helmet. And here's a practice football jersey. You also have to wear a mouth guard, but I ain't got none of those, so you'll have to buy your own."

I nodded and signed. When I got back to my locker, most of the other guys had dressed and run out to the field. I dropped my football paraphernalia on the floor, not sure where to start. The helmet rattled a yard away, then rocked back and forth upside down. I looked at the shoulder pads. *They must go on my shoulders,* I thought. I slipped them over my head, but they got stuck around my ears. I yanked them off and looked again. Seeing laces on the front, I undid them, loosened the pads and slid them over my head. When I had them comfortably balanced on my shoulders, I tightened the laces. I turned the football pants over and noticed pockets on the inside. I took the thigh pads and knee pads and inserted them. Then, putting on my jock and cup first, I pulled the skintight white football pants up. I struggled to pull my football jersey over the pads, but finally I managed that and put my helmet on. It was too large and wobbled uncertainly on my head. I laced up my tennis shoes. Then I noticed a belt-looking contraption under the wooden bench. *Why did the manager call this thing a girdle?* I wondered. *I hope it's not important.*

Adam rushed into the locker room and started dialing his padlock. "Forgot my mouth guard," he grunted to me. "You better hurry up. Coach is in a foul mood today. I think his girl friend canceled his date for tonight."

"I'm trying," I said. "But I'm not sure how to put this thing on." I held up the girdle.

Adam looked at me like a cat realizing he's cornered a mouse. "You really don't know how to put on your girdle?" he asked.

"Nope," I answered. "I've never played football before, and I've never even seen a girdle."

Adam smiled cunningly. "Here, I'll show you," he said. Holding the girdle up by one end he explained, "These two pads here are to protect your kidneys. And this flat curved piece that looks like a shoe horn is to protect you if someone tries to lift a knee in your groin."

"I thought I already had a cup for that," I pointed out, not sure of his directions.

"This provides double protection," he assured me. "Now, slide down your pants, and I'll help you buckle this up from behind." The all-important curved protection piece gouged its way between my legs. I had to walk bow-legged.

"Are you sure this is right?"

"Absolutely," Adam answered. "Now cinch up your pants and get out to practice. I'll see you there."

I followed his instructions and began to waddle out to the field, the oddly fitted girdle chafing between the front of my thighs. The other players minced their way through a series of old car tires as the Coach Burke bawled out instructions. Seeing me, he called out, "Get over here Andrews and step through these tires. Show me you've got what it takes."

I lifted my knees and started to run through the tires. The coach's voice thundered, "Stop!"

I stopped.

"Andrews, bring your ass here," he called.

I obeyed.

"Do you always run with your legs spread like you're sitting on the can?"

"No," I replied.

"You will address me as sir. When I ask a question you will answer, 'Yes, sir,' or No, sir,' do you understand me?" He shoved his stubble-covered chin within an inch of my nose.

"Yes, sir," I answered.

"Now, why are you waddling like a goose?"

"I'm not used to football gear, sir. In rugby we only wear a pair of shorts."

He peered at my football pants. "What is that bulge in the front of your pants, Andrews?" he demanded.

"My girdle, sir, and it hurts."

"I'm sure it hurts. You've got the thing on inside out and backwards. What in the world persuaded you to put it on back to front? It's a tailbone protector."

I heard a giggle from behind a faceless helmet as the other players had huddled around.

I wanted to blame Adam, but answered, "I'd never seen a girdle before and I just guessed on how to put it on." I glared at Adam. "I guessed wrong."

"You certainly did," Coach Burke fumed. "Now go back to the locker room and do it right. You'll do extra tire ladders after practice. If you try any more stupid stunts like this, you're off my team."

As I duck-walked away to reverse my girdle, Bobby stepped next to me. "Sorry, man," he whispered. "I should have helped you put on your football gear."

In the locker room I considered throwing all the equipment back at the manager. I knew what David felt like when Saul dumped all his armor on top of the little shepherd boy. All I really needed was a pair of rugby shorts. But I'd come this far, and I didn't want to be called a quitter. So I unhooked the girdle, and reversed its direction. The shoehorn piece felt much more comfortable flat against my tailbone. I could move normally. I sprinted out the to field to show the coach I really wasn't inside out and backwards.

I found all the players kneeling on one knee as they huddled around the coach and listened to him berate them about being lazy. He glared at me. "Glad you figured out how to put on a football uniform, Andrews," Coach Burke drawled. "Now, since you say you're a rugby player, why don't you go hit Adam over there."

I didn't know what he meant. Hit a man who was kneeling and listening to the coach talk?

"Are you deaf?" Coach Burke howled. "I said hit him! Go on! Show me how hard you can hit, rugby boy."

I hesitated. Did he want me to tackle Adam? Or punch him? I stood there uncertainly.

Disgusted, Coach Burke spit on the ground. "Adam, it doesn't seem like Andrews wants to hit you. So you hit him instead."

Adam sprang to his feet and rushed at me. Before I could move out of the way, he lunged at me with his helmet, ramming into my chest and hurling me to the ground. I groaned as I struggled to regain my breath.

I looked up at Coach Burke's face as he knelt over me. "Andrews, learn one thing and learn it quick. I'm the coach. I'm the law here. Do what I say when I say it." A gold filling glinted in one of his molars.

I nodded and sat up, gripping my ribs and wondering if Adam had broken one of them. I was mad. Mad at Adam for hitting me. Mad at Coach Burke for his army-style commands. Mad at my parents for taking me away from Africa. Mad at everyone, even Bobby Fuller for talking me into going out for the stupid football team.

"Stand up, Andrews," Coach Burke ordered. "Now, I want you to hit Adam." Coach Burke's eyes narrowed. In blind anger my feet dug into the grass and I churned several steps and nailed Adam so hard he flew backwards and crashed into Bobby Fuller. All three of us landed in a heap with me on top.

I stood up. Coach's eyes were wide with surprise. "Thank you, Andrews. You really do know how to hit pretty hard. From now on, when I ask you to hit, do it. All season long. Get used to it. Football is a game of hitting. Knocking our opponents back on their cans. You used your shoulder, though. I want you to lead with your head when you tackle. Use your helmet as a weapon. Now, all of you, back to the tires. This time, show some effort. Andrews, lead the way."

Bobby Fuller huffed like a puff adder on the scalding floor of Kenya's Rift Valley. His barrel-like legs moved in slow motion. I lapped him twice. But Bobby always slapped me on the rear and said, "Be tough, Clay." Coach Burke didn't reprimand Bobby for his plodding speed. When Coach shrilled his whistle to end the tire ladders, he went over to Bobby. "You're not fast, Fuller, but you sure are fat. I can teach guys how to tackle, block, and pass, but I can't coach anyone to be as big as a blimp. You're wide enough to block pass rushers without even moving. Let's go over to the blocking sleds."

Bobby grinned and nodded. "I'm a cinch to make the team," he said to me.

Coach Burke demonstrated blocking techniques and then set us loose to attack the sleds. I got in line behind Bobby. When he hit the sled, it shuddered and moved backwards. When I tried it, I thought I'd run into a tree. I felt a vertebra in my neck crack. I massaged my neck as I got back in line. "Get lower," Bobby hissed at me. "And pretend the blocking dummy is Coach Burp, I mean Coach Burke." He chuckled at his joke and thundered into the sled again.

On my next turn I came in at a lower angle and the blocking sled jerked backwards a few inches. My tennis shoes slipped and I went down on one knee. I felt a hand grasp the back of my collar and lift me up. "Andrews, you need to buy a pair of football cleats. Do you understand me?"

"Yes, sir," I answered.

"I think he likes you," Bobby whispered.

22

The rest of the practice blurred into one long line of torturous drills and hitting practice. When Coach Burke blew his whistle after the last wind sprint and told us to hit the showers, my knees buckled. I sat in the grass, sucking in oxygen. A boy near me cried softly. He jerked off his helmet and spit. "I'm quitting," he said.

I considered following his example until Bobby Fuller waddled up. "Good practice, Clay. Wasn't that great!"

Bobby had skipped the last fifteen minutes of wind sprints by barfing behind the stands.

"Are you feeling better?" I asked as he reached a hand down and pulled me up.

Bobby looked both ways and then winked. "I'm fine. I just hate to run. So I stick my finger down my throat and puke. Coach is worried I might have a heart attack or die of heat stroke or something. So he tells me to skip the running parts. What I really like is blocking and hitting."

"You faked your own puking?" I asked as we limped toward the locker room.

"No, I really do puke when I poke my finger down my throat. I couldn't fake coach out by just gagging. But now I'm hungry. I'll have my Mom buy me a burger and fries on the way home. And a chocolate milkshake."

"Chocolate milkshakes are my favorite part about America," I said. "I could down one right now."

"Maybe I could have my Mom drive both of us home and we could have that milkshake together on the way," Bobby suggested. "Just call your parents and tell them you're coming home with me."

"I don't know how," I answered.

"What do you mean," Bobby asked, his forehead furrowing into a puzzled frown. We'd just walked into the locker room. "There's a payphone right there. Just go and call your parents. Don't you want a milkshake?"

"I do want a milkshake, Bobby, but I don't know how to use a phone. We don't have too many in Kenya and, well, I've never used one."

"For goodness' sake," Bobby said. He clumped over to the payphone and popped in a dime. He asked, "What's your phone number?"

I shrugged. Bobby clanked the phone back on the hook. "You don't even know your own phone number? Clay, you really need me to be your friend. I don't know nobody who don't know how to call their own parents on the phone. We'll just wait until both your parents and my Mom come and we'll ask them then. Here, help me pull off this football jersey." Bobby leaned forward. "Take the bottom of the shirt and peel it over the shoulder pads," he instructed.

I managed to pull his shirt off with a great deal of grunting and groaning. "Now, I'll help you," Bobby stated. All over the locker room the other players helped each other struggle out of the tight sweaty football gear. Bobby gathered up our pants and shirts and took them to the manager to be washed before the next practice. Bobby showed me how to stack the rest of the equipment in the locker before grabbing white towels and hitting the showers. Steam billowed out and I couldn't see any free shower heads. Bobby shoved someone aside and called to me, "Here's a shower for you, Clay."

The hot water cascaded over my head and stung my back. I groaned as the warmth seeped into my aching muscles. After showering, I tied my towel around my waist and went back to my locker.

Bobby stood up on a bench and clapped his hands. "Attention, everyone. We want this to be the best football team Rattlesnake Junior High has ever seen. I know some of you want to quit. But don't. I've made friends with a new kid named Clay." I looked around nervously as Bobby mentioned my name. "Clay has every reason to quit. He comes from Africa and he doesn't even know how to play football. He didn't know how to put on his football gear, but he went out today and worked his tail off, even if he did have his tailbone protector on back-wards." The locker room echoed with nervous laughs. "Clay's not quitting. Let's all stick with it. If we work with Coach Burke, we'll have a great team this year."

I heard the steady cadence of someone clapping at the other end of the locker room. Coach Burke stood there nodding and clapping. "Good speech, Bobby. But be sure you apply it to yourself the next time you feel like gagging yourself on my football field. That trick has worked for the last time."

Bobby's jaw sagged open. He jumped off the bench. His belly quivered when his feet hit the floor. "Yes, sir, I'll work hard this year. You'll see."

"Right now you're a tree, Fuller. But trees are rooted. They don't move. And neither do you. I want you to be more like a hippopotamus. Big, fast and deadly. Hippos kill more people than any other animal in Africa, isn't that right, Clay."

"It's true, sir," I answered. "How did you know?"

"I went on safari to Africa once," he said. He turned and closed the door to his office.

Coach's comment had made it cool for me to be from Africa. "Have you really seen hippos?" asked the boy who had threatened to quit.

"Once a hippo surfaced next to our fishing boat in Lake Naivasha and we always hear them spluttering and wheeze-honking."

He listened with open eyes. "My name is Eric and I've decided not to quit football after all."

Bobby came over, a bit stunned that coach knew his trick of gagging himself. "I may have to run tomorrow," Bobby said, his voice trembling at the prospect.

"You'll be okay," I reassured him. "Besides, if you learn to run, I could teach you to play rugby. You'd make a great prop."

"I know as little about rugby as you do about football," Bobby said. "I still can't believe you put your girdle on backwards."

"Someone on the team told me to put it on that way. He even helped me cinch the belt from the back."

"Someone played a trick on you! Now that demands a court hearing." Bobby heaved himself back onto a bench and called out, "Kangaroo court! Kangaroo court!"

The others, in various stages of getting dressed, gathered around Bobby. His ample gut flapped over the towel he had wrapped around his waist. Bobby had black chest hair growing in a cross shape across his chest and down the middle of his stomach "We have a case to try. It seems that today, my friend Clay began putting on his football equipment. And one member of this team, realizing Clay didn't know how to put on his gear, told him to put his girdle on backwards. He even helped Clay put it on. Do we get a confession, or do we have to go to testimonies." A few people laughed nervously. No one admitted to the crime.

"Clay, can you identify the joker?"

"I can," I replied.

"Last chance, then," Bobby intoned. "For an open confession, the punishment will be a cold shower. For a forced confession after a positive ID by Clay, the punishment will be a swirlie. Head down the john and the toilet flushed. What will it be? This is the last chance for a confession."

Adam stepped forward. His head hung a bit. "I did it," he confessed.

"Adam!" Bobby said in a dramatic voice. He stepped off the bench. "How could you be so cruel? A new kid from Africa. To the shower with him!"

Several players ran ahead gleefully and turned the water on. My mind swirled with the memories of being bullied during my first days at Livingstone. I thought of the paddling machine and vicious towel snaps in the shower. I called out. "Stop!"

Everyone halted and looked at me. "I don't want to spoil your fun, but I'd like it if you let Adam go."

Bobby walked over to me and glared. "We have a guilty verdict. We need to punish him."

"Sorry, Bobby," I said, standing up to him. "I'm sure Adam won't do it again. I'd rather we be friends." I held out my hand to Adam. This time he shook it. "Friends?" I asked.

"Friends," Adam said. "I'm sorry. And I'm sorry for putting the lock on your undies. Thanks for not getting me in trouble with coach out there. You're okay, Clay."

Bobby shook his head. "Out of court settlement," he declared. "Kangaroo court's over. Everyone get dressed and go home."

He hauled on his blue jeans, sprayed a whiff of Right Guard under his armpits that had spidery black hairs crawling out the edges, then pulled on his shirt. "Let's go get a milkshake, Clay."

I followed him outside. I saw Dad standing next to our station wagon in the parking lot. He waved.

"There's my Mom," Bobby said. A woman wearing a white outfit sat behind the wheel of a rusted out Chevrolet Impala. A pair of black oval glasses bracketed her worn-looking face. She chewed on the filter stub of a cigarette. "Hurry up over here, Bobby," she called. "I have to work the evening shift at the hospital."

"But Ma," Bobby pleaded, "I wanted you to take me and my new friend here to the drive-in for burgers and shakes on the way home."

"No time today, Bobby." She jerked a thumb at the door.

Dad stepped over. "Maybe I can take the boys home and stop by the drive-in," he offered.

Bobby's Ma glared at him for a second. Then she softened. "That would be mighty nice of you. I'm late to work already. Bobby, the house is open. And there's food in the fridge if you're still hungry. I'll be home too late to say good night. And if I'm not awake in the morning, have a good day at school tomorrow."

Bobby jumped into our station wagon. "Thanks Mr. Andrews. I'm starving after practice. Clay tells me you're from Africa. Do you know where the Sno-freeze Drive-in is? They have the best burgers and shakes in town. And I promised to buy Clay a milkshake." He wiped the sweat from his forehead. "We about melted out there today, didn't we Clay?"

I told Dad about practice as we drove to the drive-in. "Grandma's got food for us at home," Dad said, "so just the milkshake for now, Clay."

Bobby ordered a triple-burger, large fries, and two large milkshakes. When the order came, wrapped in a white paper bag, he handed me my shake. Between slurps and burps, Bobby guided us to his home. Mangy grass fringed the house. A rusted pick-up adorned the rest of the yard. The screen door sagged.

As Bobby eased out of the car, I turned to Dad. "I need to buy a pair of football boots."

"Football boots!" Bobby interrupted. "Who calls football cleats boots? Boots are what cowboys wear."

"In rugby we call our shoes rugby boots," I tried to explain.

Dad's face showed sadness as he shook his head. "I'm sorry, Clay, but I don't think we can afford a pair of football boots or cleats or whatever they're supposed to be called. I used up the last of our money buying those clothes last night. And I couldn't work today. I didn't feel too good this morning. Maybe I worked too hard yesterday or sweated too much or something."

Bobby, who'd been tractoring his way to his house, turned around. "I can help Clay buy some football cleats. He needs them or Coach Burke might really get mad. I earned some money this summer and I'd be glad to buy Clay a pair of cleats."

At first Dad refused, but Bobby kept insisting. So Dad invited Bobby to have supper with us and then he'd drive us to the store to buy the cleats. I wondered how Bobby could eat anything else, but he sat down at Grandma's and tucked into the roast beef, mashed potatoes and gravy as if his triple burger had been a dainty appetizer.

"Can you make some *chai*?" I asked Mom. "I promised Bobby he could try some. I know he'll like it."

Mom smiled. "I'd love to fix some *chai*. I even brought some Brooke Bond Green Label tea from Kenya."

She went into the kitchen. Soon Dad, Bobby and I were drinking *chai*, sweet milky tea the way Kenyans made it except without the smoky flavor. Grandma and Grandpa didn't want to try any. They'd had it once before and it was too sweet to their liking. They drank black coffee instead.

"It's polite to burp after a meal in Africa," I informed Bobby. I belched quietly.

Grandma's eyebrows lifted and Grandpa looked down at his dog Joe and said, "Shame on you!"

Bobby grinned and fired off the biggest burp I'd ever heard. Mom wasn't pleased. Grandma huffed, "Well, I never! What is Africa doing to my grandson?" She stalked into the kitchen and rattled dishes around.

Dad stifled a smile and told Mom he'd bring me back after we'd gotten the football cleats. In the car Dad told me to be careful where I burped. "I'll be careful, too," Bobby said. He burped again. All of us giggled.

I chose a pair of Adidas football cleats with rubber studs. "That way I can use them to play rugby when I get back to Kenya." I paused. "They'll magically change into rugby boots instead of football cleats."

Bobby smiled as he pulled out a wad of sweaty, wrinkled one-dollar bills and paid the clerk. He put his arm around my shoulder. "We'll turn you into a football player, yet."

As we dropped Bobby off, Dad asked, "So where's your Dad, Bobby."

Bobby shrugged. "Took off when I was in third grade. I've been the man of the family ever since. Mom works hard as a nurse, but I grew big and sometimes eat more than she can provide. So she's learned to glean on some of the nearby apple ranches. We get by."

"Does your Dad ever call?" my Dad asked.

Bobby's eyes misted. "Nope!" He straightened his back. "Well, gotta go. I'll see you in school tomorrow, Clay. You'll punish the blocking sled now that you have football cleats."

23

"All right, take a break," roared Coach Burke. I heaved huge gulps of air, and knelt on one knee with the others in a circle around the coach. His snakeskin cowboy boots glistened orange in the fading sunshine.

"Tomorrow's our first game of the season," Coach Burke informed us. "Jefferson Junior High have whipped us for the past three years. Tomorrow will be different. Right?"

"Right," we all echoed.

"Say it louder," Coach Burke ordered, his nostrils quivering.

"Right!" we shouted.

Coach Burke glared at his clipboard and announced who would be starting in tomorrow's game. "Clay," he looked over his clipboard at me.

"Yes sir!" I answered.

"You'll start at defensive end. I want to see you knock those Jefferson runners on their tails."

"Yes sir!" I answered.

The hint of a smile tugged at his lips. "You know, for a guy who came here inside out and backward, you're learning pretty fast. Even if you don't tackle head first."

After practice, Bobby clapped me on the back. "You made it Clay. I knew you would. I think we should have milkshakes to celebrate."

"Sounds okay with me," I smiled.

My parents had gone on a one-month trip to visit some churches and tell them about the missionary work in Africa. I was supposed to stay with my grandparents, but Bobby had begged me to stay with him. His Mom worked evenings at the hospital, so I struggled to do my homework while Bobby watched TV and ate potato chips and downed gallons of soda.

"Don't you ever study?" I asked.

"Naw!" Bobby answered. "I don't get good grades, but I get by. I've only flunked once. At this point, I'm so big, the teachers keep pushing me through, whether I've learned anything or not."

I frowned. "Don't you like to read?" I asked.

"It's too much work. I'd rather watch TV."

Bobby and I wore our new ocean-blue football jerseys to school the next day. My number, 88, painted in white and edged in red, seemed to glow. As Bobby and I walked down the hallway, I noticed some of the girls nudging each other and pointing.

"Pay no attention, Clay," Bobby said. "All the girls think football jocks are hot."

They let us football players out of class for the last period so we could get ready for the game. The Jefferson school bus rolled up as Bobby and I headed for the gym. It wheezed to a stop and the Jefferson football team swaggered off the bus. A pimple-faced boy with greasy black hair struggled to offload the football equipment.

"Hey, most of the guys on their team are black," I pointed out.

"Yeah," Bobby answered. "Jefferson's in town. Our school out here in the orchards is almost all white."

"This will be just like playing rugby in Africa," I said, grinning.

"You're crazy, Clay. Just watch yourself. Some of these guys are big and mean."

Coach Burke stalked around the locker room growling at everyone. Bobby helped me pull my football jersey over the molded plastic shoulder pads and we went to stretch out.

Jefferson's pumpkin-orange uniforms gleamed in the autumn sun. Students piled into the bleachers. The stripe-shirted officials started the game with a shrill whistle and we kicked off. We ran downfield to tackle the ball carrier. I ran into a giant wall of Jefferson blockers. I could see the runner behind them and pushed and shoved in vain. I couldn't get past the huge Jefferson blockers. Neither could any of the rest of our players. Their runner sprinted down the corridor and scored a touchdown.

"Watch out, white boy," a hulking Jefferson player warned. "This is our game."

Coach Burke threw his clipboard on the ground and kicked it. "What do you guys think you're doing!" he shouted. "This is a football game! Now go out and hit someone!"

We spent all game being hit. Jefferson outsized us, outblocked us, outran us, outscored us, and hammered us into submission. I wasn't sure I liked football after all. Coach Burke's face had turned purple and his voice finally disappeared in the third quarter from ranting up and down the sidelines. He walked up and down and slapped players on their rear ends and sent them in to the slaughter.

I'd been blocked out of almost every play all day. But as we entered the fourth quarter, I realized that the big offensive tackle against me was tiring. On the next play, as he pushed off his three-point stance to drive me away from the quarterback, I stepped sideways, and slipped around him. In two steps I reached the quarterback. I launched myself and hit him around the thighs. The ball tumbled out of his hand as my tackle dropped him to the ground. I leaped on the loose ball and picked it up. I started sprinting towards their goal line. My sack of the quarterback had surprised the Jefferson players and no one was in a position to catch up with me. I ran across the goal line and touched the ball down on the ground with two hands, just like I would have scored a try in rugby.

Bobby bounced in from the sidelines and pounded my back. "Great job, Clay. You've scored the first touchdown of the season!"

We lost to Jefferson 49-7, but I was the hero for scoring our only touchdown.

Coach Burke glared at all of us in the locker room. "Pathetic, boys, just pathetic," he rasped. "Wait until tomorrow's practice and you'll never want to lose a game for me again." He stopped next to me and murmured, "That was a good hit on the quarterback, Clay. But you should have hit him in the ribs. Or broken his collarbone or something. When will you learn not to tackle around the thighs? And why did you set the ball down like that between the goal posts?" He wheeled and disappeared into his office.

Bobby grinned at me. "Don't worry, Clay. You're my hero. A touchdown in your first game. I've played for years and I still haven't scored a touchdown."

Our season didn't improve. Despite Coach Burke's threats, we lost game after game. But I learned to slip past the big blockers and caught a lot of quarterbacks.

The last game of the season arrived. My parents had come back from their missionary ramblings. "Can you come and watch, Dad?" I asked.

Mom smiled. "We'll both come, Clay. We're sorry we've missed your other games, but we've been so busy sharing what the Lord is doing in Kenya. We need these churches to keep supporting us if we want to go back to Africa. But I've really missed seeing your games. Did you know I was once a cheerleader when I was in junior high?"

"You?" I questioned. "A cheerleader?"

"Yes," she answered, putting her chin up slightly. "Two, four, six, eight, who do we appreciate—Clay!"

I raised my eyebrows. "Just promise you won't cheer like that at this game, okay Mom?"

In the locker room before the game, Coach Burke glowered at us. "Burke the jerk isn't happy with us," whispered Bobby, winking.

"We've lost a lot a games this season," Coach began. "In fact, if we lose today, we'll set the school record for the worst losing season ever." He paused. "But my manager pointed something out to me this morning. We can also set another record this year."

We perked up. I looked at Bobby. He shrugged.

"We have a player who has made fourteen quarterback sacks this season. The school record is fifteen sacks in a season. So," he turned to look directly at me and went on, "if Clay can get one more sack today against Wilson Junior High, he'll tie the record. And if he makes two sacks, he'll hold the record."

Bobby smashed my back with his fat hand. "Go get 'em Clay."

"Let's all go get 'em," I said. "Let's win at least one game this season."

I saw my parents in the stands. Mom waved. I gave a tentative nod. My heart warmed to see them there, but it seem a bit weird to wave at your parents in front of the other guys.

Bobby nudged me. "I'm glad your parents got to see you play a game. Someday …" His voice dropped off.

"Someday what?" I asked.

"I dunno. Mom comes sometimes to watch me and I like that. But I dream of the day my Dad will show up after a game and say, 'Well done, son.' Aw, I'm just dreaming. Come on, let's go win this game."

24

Our offense stunk. Our quarterback couldn't pass straight and our backs ran like crabs trying to find gaps in their defense. But our defense really came together. Early in the game, I brushed off a block and crashed into the quarterback. *There's one*, I thought.

On the sidelines, Bobby crushed me with a bear hug. "Fifteen QB sacks!" he said.

We held the other team to almost no gain on every possession and the game stood at 0-0 late in the fourth quarter. Wilson had possession with one last chance to win the game. We stopped them on the first two downs. But on third down they blasted a hole in our defensive line and their fullback plunged through, rambling for thirty yards before our cornerback pulled him down. As the play ended, I saw Adam, who played defensive tackle beside me, on his back groaning and clutching his right knee.

Coach Burke called a time out. They stretchered Adam off. Coach looked at us. "We may not win, but if we hold them, we won't lose. Bobby, I know you're tired from playing all game in the offensive line, but now you'll have to play defensive tackle, too. I need a big body in there. Please, guys, stop them."

Their center snapped the ball to their quarterback. Bobby strained and grunted, drawing the attention of two offensive linemen. His hulking presence opened the hole I needed. I squeezed through and hurled myself at the quarterback. I hit him just as he turned to hand the ball to the fullback. He crashed to the ground with me on top and the ball squirted free. I jumped to my feet and snatched the ball. Maybe I could run it in and score the winning touchdown. I sprinted for the line. But their fullback chased me down. On my side I saw Bobby hurtling down field to join me. I slowed and slanted my run to the left to allow the fullback to catch me. As he leaped to tackle me, I turned my hip towards him to take the brunt of his tackle and flicked a lateral rugby pass to Bobby. He swallowed it into his bulging belly and stormed across the line.

The referee lifted both hands above his head to signal a touchdown.

Bobby flung the ball into the air after scoring. He jumped up and down like a toddler having a temper tantrum. He grabbed me and lifted me up in a gorilla hug. Winning had never felt sweeter.

We still finished with the worst record in our league, but we had won a game. We mobbed Coach Burke and poured a cooler of ice water on his head. As he shook the ice off like a black Labrador after a bath, Bobby and I grabbed coach Burke and hoisted him to our shoulders and carried him in front of the stands. The cheering and foot-stomping on the metal bleachers blasted our ears. My parents waved and I waved back. I didn't care who saw.

The noise finally eased off. We set Coach Burke down. He looked at me and said, "For a kid who started the season inside out and backward, you did pretty well this year Clay. I wish you'd be here next year. You could become a great football player."

The public address system crackled. "Final score, Rattlesnake 7, Wilson 0. We also want to announce that a school record was set today. With his last-second sack of the quarterback, Clay Andrews has sixteen quarterback sacks, the most ever by a Rattlesnake player in one season."

The crowd cheered again and my cheeks flushed hot. Bobby gripped my arm and waved it for me. "Way to go, Clay," he said.

My parents came up. Dad gripped my shoulder and Mom hugged me. "I'm glad we got to see you play. I didn't know you were setting records," Dad said.

"It didn't seem important, I guess," I started. "Besides, you weren't here for most of the football season."

I looked over and saw Bobby, eyes scouring the stands. His eyes suddenly looked hollow.

"What's wrong, Bobby?" I asked.

"Nothin' I guess," Bobby answered. "I just thought maybe ..."

His voice stuck.

"Are you looking for your Dad?"

Bobby nodded, eyes now glistening. He sniffed. "Seeing you with both your parents made me feel jealous."

"Funny," I replied. "That's how I felt about Titch being able to live with his parents at Livingstone while I had to live in the dorm so far from my parents."

My parents took us out to a pizza parlor to celebrate. Bobby ate large two pepperoni pizzas all by himself.

Soon after football season ended, the skies turned steel-gray and the temperature dropped. I shivered as I stepped onto the front porch and headed for the school bus. "Looks like it might snow today," Dad said. He handed me a maroon-plaid jacket. "It's wool," Dad said. "If it snows, you'll need it."

I saw a flash of yellow and ran for the bus, the coat on my arm. I shrugged the coat over my shoulders as I pushed my way up the steps of the bus. I noticed the other kids were bundled into warm coats as well. But theirs were different. They had brightly colored nylon parkas, stuffed with down. I sighed. Would I ever wear the right clothes? How did anyone learn what the right clothes were?

At school I met Bobby in the hall. He eyed me and asked, "Is that your grandpa's coat?"

"Is it that bad?" I asked.

Bobby pondered. "I guess not. Not really. It's different. But lots of people think different is cool. Just wear your coat with pride."

"At least it's warm," I muttered.

It started snowing in the morning. At lunch, Bobby invited me to join him in a snowball fight in the school courtyard. He showed me how to pack the snow in my hands and hurl it at unsuspecting students. I made my first snowball. "That's cold!" I commented.

Bobby frowned. "Where are your gloves?"

"I don't have any," I answered, throwing my snowball at a nearby birch tree. It burst into powder as it pounded the trunk.

Some of the other football players had joined us and soon we had a war going with the basketball team. After ten furious minutes, I couldn't feel my hands. A teacher came out and told us to stop. In the hallway, I blew on my red, chapped hands.

"I can't believe you don't have gloves," Bobby said. "You need to warm your hands up. Let's go to the bathroom and run cold water over them."

"Cold water? I want to get my hands warm!" I complained.

Bobby laughed. "Cold water will feel warm on your freezing hands. Hot water would hurt. I know. I tried it once when I rode my bike in the snow one day without any gloves."

I thanked Bobby for his help and gradually I got the feeling back into my hands.

I learned to enjoy the snowy Yakima winter. I went tubing down the slopes of the Cascade mountains with our church youth group. This time I brought winter gloves that Mom had fished out of the church missionary barrel. But inwardly I longed for the hot African sun.

One morning at the breakfast table, Dad pointed out the window. "Look at the apple and cherry blossoms on the trees," he said. "The season's changing. Spring's coming. Those blossoms are a sign of the fruit to come in autumn. By then we'll be back in Africa. We've had a season of time here in America. But now it's time to head back."

"That reminds me," Mom said, as she added coffee to Dad's mug. "We have our physicals scheduled for this week."

Dad groaned. "I hate seeing doctors. They always think I've got TB because I had a shot against it when I was a kid. Then I have to get chest X-rays and they're always negative."

Mom smiled. "Don't be such a whiner. You know the mission won't let us purchase tickets to go back until we have medical clearance."

Dad sighed. "All right, what day?"

She looked up at the big calendar on the wall and ran her finger across the squared off dates. "Thursday at 10 in the morning," she said.

"Do I get to miss school?" I asked.

Mom nodded.

As Dad had predicted his TB inoculation caused a false positive test result and he had to have an X-rays.

About two weeks after the physicals, I came home and saw Dad looking unhappy on the couch. Mom came in from the kitchen. "Clay, we have some possible bad news," she began.

"What's going on?" Grandma asked, coming in wiping her hands on a dish-towel.

"Mother, please, we want to have a small family conference. I'll explain to you later," Mom said.

Grandma drew back. "Well!" she accused as she left.

This sounded ominous. "Is something wrong?" I asked, sitting down.

25

"Clay, the doctors discovered something when they did my physical," Dad began.

"What kind of something?" I asked.

"A growth of some kind on my kidney. Now they don't know whether it's a bad growth or not, but they can only find out by doing an operation."

"How bad can it be?" I wanted to know.

Dad shook his head.

Mom spoke up. "It could be just a cyst. But it could also be cancer. If it's cancer, that could be very bad."

"Is Dad going to die?"

"Not from the surgery," Mom said. "He'll go into the hospital and the doctors will cut out the growth to see what it is. After that …" She paused. "Who knows."

"I'm sure it will be okay," Dad said. "I'm in God's hands."

"We wanted you to know so we can be praying as a family. And even if Dad is okay, this will delay our return to Africa," Mom went on. "It will take time to schedule the surgery. Then it takes time for the lab to determine whether the growth is something to worry about. And after that, Dad has to recover enough to travel back."

"*So when do we go back to Africa?*" I wondered.

"We don't know for sure, Clay. Even after the surgery, we don't know if they'll approve Dad's health to go back."

"You mean—we might have to stay here in America?" My own words jolted me. Staying in America? Would I ever get home to Africa?

Mom didn't answer right away. Then she said slowly, "I'm sure we'll go back to Africa, Clay."

I didn't know if I could believe her words.

It took almost a month before Dad went into the hospital. I rode in the backseat as we drove to the old red-brick hospital. Once inside they put Dad onto a wheelchair. We huddled around him and prayed for Dad and the doctors. My personal prayer was more selfish. "Oh God," I groaned, "don't take Africa away from me." When we finished, my jaw ached. I realized I'd been grinding my teeth.

I sat with Mom in the waiting room, leafing through old copies of Sports Illustrated. They had lots of American football stories and articles about basketball, but nothing about rugby.

After a few hours a doctor came and summoned my mother. I sat alone in the waiting room. "God, please!" I pleaded. "Help Dad get better. I want to go home to Africa."

Mom came back. "Dad's surgery is over," she stated. "He came through it fine. He's in the recovery room now. Later they'll move him to a private room. We can visit him when he wakes up."

"He's okay? What about his kidney?" I asked.

"They removed a small growth. They won't say whether it's dangerous or not until they've sent it to the lab to be examined. So let's go home for lunch."

"Can we buy a burger and milkshake on the way?" I asked.

Mom smiled. "I think we can handle that."

At the burger place Mom asked, "How would you feel if we didn't go back to Africa?"

I dropped my hamburger on the plate. "I'd hate it," I stated bluntly. "I don't belong here. We have to go back! I'm sure Dad will be okay."

"I hope he will," Mom said. "But there's more to it than just Dad. At this point we don't have enough money to buy tickets to fly back to Kenya. And at least two churches have chopped their support. They say they believe in what we're doing, but their members are older and some have died off. So the churches say they have to cut back."

"So you think we should stay? Just because we don't have enough money? You guys are the ones always talking about faith."

"Sometimes God leads through circumstances. We're already delayed because of your Dad's kidney. Maybe he'll be all right. Maybe he won't. And now our support money is short, too. Maybe God is trying to guide us to stay here."

"Don't you want to go back?" I asked, shocked at the idea of losing Africa.

"Of course I do," Mom said. "The needs are so great. My mind floods with the patients who might have died of pneumonia if I hadn't been there to give them penicillin. And your Dad's the only one starting churches with the Dorobo and the Maasai in that area. I wonder how things could possibly go on without us? But I also realize it's God who will build his church. We want to be part of what God is doing, but if he chooses to keep us here and use someone else to work in Kenya, then I'll trust God."

"I'm not sure I could live in America," I answered. I munched on my hamburger, but now it tasted like sawdust.

Mom put her hand gently on my shoulder. "We'll keep praying and see how God leads," she said.

That evening we went to see Dad. His words slurred a bit and he kept falling asleep as we talked. I wanted to ask him to promise me to take us back to Africa. Instead I told him to get better.

The next day, Dad smiled and reached out to hug Mom. "Oww!" he yelped. "That hurts." He rolled back into bed. "I guess I can't stretch my muscles quite yet."

Dad showed me his stitches. I winced at the sight. "Don't worry, Clay, it will heal. The doctors say they'll have a report on the growth within a few weeks."

"I want to know now, Dad," I demanded.

"Sometimes we have to wait," he said. "You're anxious to get back to Africa, aren't you?"

I nodded.

"So am I, Clay, so am I." His eyes glistened.

Two days later as we visited Dad, a doctor whisked into the room. He looked over his glasses at Dad. "How are you feeling today?" he asked.

"Still sore," Dad said, "but ready to be out of this bed."

The doctor nodded. "It shouldn't be too long before we release you."

Dad came home a day later.

"We got the results of Dad's biopsy," Mom said one evening after supper a few weeks later.

"What did they find out?" I turned towards Dad.

"The growth on my kidney is something called a cyst. And the cyst is benign."

"What's that mean?" I whispered to Mom.

She smiled. "It means it's harmless. It's not cancer. Your Dad is going to be fine. However, the doctor said no air travel for at least another month."

"But that will make us late for the start of school at Livingstone!" I blurted.

"Yes," Dad said, "but I'm glad we get to go back to Kenya."

As Dad healed at home, Mom kept busy at the desk in their bedroom writing letters and making phone calls. "It's no use," she said, flopping onto the living room couch one torrid evening in late summer. Grandpa was out on the porch in his rocking chair.

"What's the matter, honey?" Grandma asked.

"We haven't told you yet, but our support is too low to return to Africa. We need at least another $600 a month. And we need several thousand dollars right now for tickets. Everywhere I turn I get the door slammed in my face and I'm tired of it."

"Maybe you should stay with us," Grandma commented.

Mom looked at her, then rushed out of the room, sobbing. Dad followed her. I went out to the porch to sit with Grandpa. He had a far away look in his eyes. "Sure is warm," he said. "Yeah, sure, you betcha." He put his leathery hand on my shoulder and kept it there. It felt strong and soft at the same time.

Dad came out and sat next to me and put his hand on my other shoulder.

"What are we going to do?" I asked.

"Have you ever thought of setting more football records for Rattlesnake Junior High?" he asked.

I jerked my shoulder away from his hand.

"I'm just kidding," he said. "We'll do what we've always done. We'll pray and leave the rest up to God. He hasn't failed us yet."

"But what if he tells us to stay in America?" I asked. "I think I'd die."

Dad chuckled. "I think I would, too, but who am I to say no to what God wants to do in our lives. One thing's for sure, if God opens this door, we'll certain he wants us back in Kenya." He stopped.

After a few minutes, Dad said, "Hey, Grandpa, why don't you pray for us? We need God to provide a hefty chunk of money if we're going to make it back to Kenya."

I wasn't sure Grandpa understood. He sat and rocked, his jaw working. After several minutes, he began to pour his heart out. I was stunned. I thought Grandpa had forgotten who we even were, but as he prayed I shivered. It seemed like he was talking with his best friend. He pleaded for God to show the way, to break down the barriers, to provide since he was Jehovah Jireh, the provider. He went on for almost ten minutes. Then he touched both of us and said, "God is faithful." He stood up and tottered back into the house. The dog followed him, nails clicking on the wooden porch deck with the peeling gray paint.

A week later, a pickup truck pulled up to the old farmhouse. An apple rancher stepped out and, carrying his battered tan cowboy hat in both hands, strolled to the porch. "Is your Dad here?" he asked me.

"Dad!" I called. "Someone's here to see you." I wondered if he'd come to offer Dad a job picking fruit.

The rancher and Dad walked to the pickup and drove away. Dad came back after lunch with a pleased look on his face. Dad slapped an envelope on the kitchen table and announced, "We've got our tickets to fly back to Kenya. We leave in two weeks."

Mom looked puzzled. "What's going on?"

"Bart Hillman came by this morning. He said God had been speaking to him," Dad explained.

"Bart? Doesn't he attend our church sometimes?" Mom asked. "I've never thought of him as someone to be talking alone with God. He never says anything at church, just nods and tips his hat."

"Well, he said God had nudged him to buy our plane tickets. And he said God told him to give $600 a month to our regular support. So we're set. Isn't God amazing? Bart took me downtown and we purchased the tickets from a travel agent."

Mom opened the envelope, stunned. "I guess God does want us back in Kenya," she said, a look of relief erasing the worried wrinkles around her eyes.

"Yes!" I exulted. "I'm going home! And I'll only be a few weeks late to school." I ran out to the porch. "God answered your prayer Grandpa. We're going back to Africa!"

Grandpa looked blank and grunted, "Shucks, yah!"

The only one who didn't seem happy was Grandma. She threw her nervous energy into cooking and baking. As she dished out a massive serving of mashed potatoes and gravy on my plate that evening she grumbled, "Never know when you'll have a chance to eat my cooking again, young man."

I showed my appreciation by consuming her food in large quantities. I devoured her fried chicken. I thought of the food at Livingstone and realized I would miss America after all. I'd gotten used to Grandma's cooking. I'd fallen in love with milkshakes and burgers. Could I go back to gray oatmeal full of toenails and stew made from mystery meat?

I pushed the thought away. I wanted to go home to Kenya.

Two weeks later, our suitcases stuffed with clothes for the next four years, we drove to the small airport in Yakima. It seemed the whole church had come out to say goodbye. I spotted Bobby Fuller in the crowd. His Mom stubbed out a cigarette and stood at the fringes of the church group. Bobby rushed over and gave me a hug.

"I'll miss you," he said. He carried a big brown paper bag.

I went over to Bobby's Mom to say goodbye. "You've been a big help to my Bobby," she said, gruffly. "He's changed since attending your church youth group." She reached out and hugged me.

"Maybe I'll see you again in four or five years," Bobby said bravely, handing me the bag. "Just a few snacks for the trip." I peeked in and saw potato chips and chocolate bars.

"All right! Thanks!"

Bobby smiled. I broke open a chocolate bar and we shared it as my parents checked the luggage in.

Mom came over with a worried expression on her face. "We're overweight, Clay. Can you put these clothes on?" She handed me a couple of shirts and a jacket with books stuffed in the pockets. I pulled on the extra clothes, including the jacket. The early evening heat stifled me and I started to sweat.

Bobby looked me over carefully. "Looks like you'll need this bottle of pop," he said, pulling it out of the bag he'd given me. He laughed. "You remind me of the day you had your football girdle on backwards."

I tried to laugh with him, but the extra clothes made my skin prickle. They announced the boarding of our plane. I shook hands with Bobby, waved to the rest of the people, picked up my hand luggage, where Dad had stashed all his new camera equipment. It weighed almost as much as our suitcases. I noticed Dad also had on extra layers of clothing. Sweat trickled down his temple as he waved and we trundled out to the airplane.

An hour later, we transferred to a larger plane in Seattle and flew into the dark night air, heading home to Africa.

Book Three
Kenya

October 1974

26

As we drove up the winding dirt road to Baridi, my stomach flipped. I couldn't wait to be back at Livingstone. My parents dropped me off at the broken-down junior high boys dorm. After a brusque kiss goodbye to Mom and a hug from Dad, I dumped my battered suitcase in the dorm lounge and ran out to find Titch.

I spotted him on the soccer field. "Titch!" I shouted. "I'm back."

Titch turned and waved. A whistle blew. "Titch!" the coach called. "Pay attention. We're having a practice here."

"But my best friend Clay is back from America!" Titch answered, running off the field.

Titch ran into my arms. I gripped his forearms in my hands, pushed him back and looked at him. His black curly hair had rounded out into an afro. Even with the extra hair, he only stretched as high as my shoulder. "Titch! It sure is good to be back," I said.

The soccer coach, a new teacher, sidled over. "Hey, Clay! I'll bet you don't remember me. I'm Mike Layton. I played fly-half here at Livingstone back when Ox was our team captain."

"Mike! Yeah, I used to chase rugby balls for you and Ox and Nusu-Nugu when I was in second grade."

Mike smiled. "Well, I finished college and got married. Now I'm back teaching at Livingstone. And I'm your dorm parent as well. So I guess you'll have to call me Mr. Layton. That still sounds strange to me. I expect everyone to call me Mike and I feel more like a student than a staff member. Anyway, Titch says you're an excellent athlete. We could use your help."

"My best game is rugby," I said. "I only play soccer to keep in shape until rugby season."

"Let's see what you can do," Mr. Layton said. "Go out and play center half."

Wearing jeans and a t-shirt, I really wasn't kitted out to play soccer. But I was so thrilled to be back on the green playing fields of Livingstone that I hustled onto the field. Titch encouraged me. "You'll be great, Clay. Just like old times in grade school." I booted the ball a few times and nobody managed to dribble around me. After a few minutes, I had to slow down to catch my breath. I wasn't used to the mile-and-a half altitude of Baridi. My lungs felt like I was rubbing sandpaper on the inside, but I kept playing.

After practice, Titch and I lined up at the drinking fountain. "It's great to be back," I said. "Everything looks the same."

Titch nodded. "It's been a long year without you. A lot of new guys have come into Livingstone in junior high. We used to have only fifteen guys in our class. Now we have almost forty." I didn't recognize most of the guys who were collecting their gear and heading to the dining hall.

"Come on, I'll walk with you," Titch said. We caught up with two guys. "This is Kevin and this is Derek," said Titch.

Kevin nodded. "Hi, welcome to Livingstone. We've had an empty bed in our dorm room. I guess you'll be our roommate." He pointed to Derek. "Derek is in our room too, as well as Steve. Steve doesn't play soccer."

Derek kind of grunted. I had a sinking feeling. I didn't know any of the guys in my dorm room. And they greeted me like I was the new kid. I guess I was.

"I started at Livingstone in second grade," I said.

"Where did you live in the States?" Kevin asked.

"Washington. The state not the capital city."

That didn't seem to impress Kevin who said, "Derek, Steve and I all come from Texas. The biggest and best state in America. Did you know Texas used to be an independent nation?"

We neared the dining hall. "Hey," Derek pointed out, "see the chicks over there? Let's get in line and sit with them." Derek and Kevin hurried away.

I looked at Titch who shrugged. "I told you there's a lot of new guys. You'll have to make some new friends in the dorm, but I'll always be your best friend." Titch grinned, punched my shoulder and took off for home. I stood in the supper line by myself. Derek and Kevin flirted with the girls. They pointed at me. I reddened.

When I reached the front of the line, I took my tray and filled it with pasty white macaroni and cheese and a pile of bread and peanut butter and jam. Sitting down at a table by myself, I suddenly missed my parents. I'd gotten used to being with them every day and I felt again the wrench of loneliness. The macaroni and cheese stuck in my throat. I imagined a sweet straw full of chocolate milkshake and looked down at the pale noodles and lost my appetite. I wanted to dump my tray out and run to the dorm. A staff member stood against the wall checking outgoing trays for wasted food.

"I'm back at Livingstone," I told myself. I forced myself to eat the macaroni and cheese. I filled my glass with milk to wash down my peanut butter sandwiches. I heard giggling and saw two girls coming over to my table.

"Can we sit here?" they asked.

"If you want," I said doubtfully. "I was just getting ready to leave."

"Please stay until we've eaten," said the one with blonde curls. "You're Clay aren't you?"

I nodded, tongue tied with fear and peanut butter.

"We were in sixth grade together. Don't you remember? I'm Jenny."

I remembered vaguely. "Oh yeah. Good to see you again, Jenny."

Her friend smiled and introduced herself. "I'm Karen. I came to Livingstone last year."

Not having anything to say, I sat quietly while the girls chatted and ate. "Eighth grade is much tougher than seventh," Jenny babbled on. "We have a new English teacher this year. Miss Marker is making us diagram sentences! And we have writing assignments every week. Remember Mr. Bateman in sixth grade? We hardly had to learn anything."

I laughed. "I do remember Mr. Bateman," I said. "All we had to do was ask him to tell us a hunting story and he'd go on for hours. We did learn a lot about hunting."

"But not much about English," Jenny said. "Mr. Bateman has left Livingstone. Had you heard?"

I hadn't.

"And there are lots of other new teachers. Why, you wouldn't think Livingstone was the same school anymore."

"Is Mr. Prinsloo the rugby coach still here?"

Jenny jolted me by saying, "No, he went back to South Africa last year because his father was sick."

"So who coaches rugby?" I asked.

Jenny looked blank. "I'm not sure. The rugby team wasn't very good last year."

My mind clouded. I didn't hear much of the conversation after that. I walked out and handed my tray to a tall Kenyan man wearing blue overalls and black Bata gumboots. "Clay, *umerudi*, you've returned!"

I focused on the man's smile and brown fluoride-stained teeth. "Kariuki! You're still here! Yes, I'm back!"

"Welcome young brother," Kariuki said.

"Hey, quit holding up the line," a voice behind me complained.

Derek and Kevin and another guy with a scowl on his face crowded forward.

"Sorry," I mumbled, hurrying to get out of the way.

Karen and Jenny said goodbye and I trudged towards the dorm. I looked up at the thick forest that surrounded Baridi. I could hear the chuckle of black-and-white colobus monkeys in the trees. Some things didn't change. I walked up by the school chapel and looked down on the rugby field. The tall poles pierced the sky and framed the orange-flamed sun as it dipped behind a huge volcanic crater sitting in the valley below. The rugby field hadn't changed, but so much else had. Mr. Prinsloo our South African rugby coach had left. I didn't know any of the guys in my room. We had new teachers. Had I really come home?

Back at the dorm, I carried my suitcase to my room. I found Kevin, Derek and the guy who scowled. "This is Steve," Kevin said. Steve just glared at me. Kevin pointed at a closet with chipped brown paint. "You can stick your stuff in there," he said. "We've used the rest of the space. There's not much room for four guys in here."

He was right. We had two bunk beds on each side of the room with cracked gray floor tiles covering the floor between the bunks. If all four of us stood on the floor together, no one could turn around without hitting someone else. A glass beer mug sat on the one scarred desk in front of the room's one window. The mug was filled with water and an electric heating coil hissed gently in the water.

"This is my coil for making *chai*," Steve spoke for the first time. "Don't ever use it."

One of the window bars had been pried sideways. Derek saw me looking at the window. He smirked. "That's Steve's escape route."

Steve stepped over to me and pointed a finger into my chest. "You don't be a stool pigeon when I'm out on my evening business, you hear?"

I wasn't sure I wanted to be back at Livingstone. After stashing my stuff, I wandered around the dorm. I met a few guys who had been at Livingstone before. But even they seemed to have grown and changed. I found Daniel, my second grade roommate. We talked for a while before he excused himself to do his homework.

A pang of loneliness gripped me. I grabbed my towel and shampoo and took a shower. When I came back to my room, I only saw Derek and Kevin. "Where's Steve?" I asked. His empty glass *chai* mug with lumps of powdered milk stuck to the side sat on the desk.

Derek shook his head slightly. "Don't ask," he whispered.

My joy at returning to Livingstone turned to a stone in my gut. I didn't really belong here after all. Two days of traveling by plane caught up with me and I crawled into my bed. "I'm tired. I need to sleep," I said.

Derek and Kevin ignored me. They seemed tense. I fell asleep as soon as I pulled the covers over my head. Maybe it was jet lag, but I woke up a few hours later. The room was dark. I heard a rustling sound at the window. I propped myself on my elbow and saw Steve pythoning himself through the window. He dropped quietly to the floor and a strong scent of acrid smoke filled the room. Steve opened the door and disappeared down the hallway.

I lay on my back and wondered what to do. Steve had snuck out to smoke. But if I reported him to our dorm parents, I'd be called a squealer and I'd lose any chance of making friends in this new dorm.

Steve eased back into the room. I closed my eyes and pretended to be asleep. My stomach churned with more than hunger.

The next day I got hammered with homework and books. I had to catch up on almost three weeks of work. I complained during *chai* break to Titch, who laughed. "Don't worry, Clay. I've been here all three weeks, and I'm three weeks behind, too."

"Reading's still a struggle?" I asked.

"Yeah," Titch replied. "I keep thinking it will get easier. But every year they give us stuff to read with bigger and harder words. So I always feel like I'm back at the start of the race. And this year there's so many bright new kids. Especially the girls. The teachers are so excited that they can pile on the homework and expect the kids to do it. And that leaves me walking in the dust as usual."

"We can work together during study hall," I said. Even though Titch couldn't read fast enough to keep up, he could remember almost everything he heard. So in study hall I'd read assignments to Titch. But because his spelling was so atrocious, Titch still got horrible grades for all his writing assignments.

One day at the end of English class Miss Marker gave our book reports back. Mine had a big A+ on the top. Titch flipped his paper upside down, but not before I saw the D-and a red ink scrawl screaming, "Learn to Spell, Tim!" Titch crumpled the paper into the back of his English textbook.

"Are you okay?" I asked Titch as we walked out of class.

"No big deal," he answered. His sad basset hound eyes betrayed him. "She just doesn't appreciate my creative spelling." He tried to smile. After that I proofread Titch's papers and he'd rewrite them with the right spelling. But Miss Marker often gave short in-class essays and I couldn't help Titch with those. Titch's essays came back bleeding red with corrections and Miss Marker's sharp comments about his inability to write.

27

A week after midterm Derek, Kevin and Steve kept whispering all study hall. I watched, puzzled, as they pulled stuffing out of the old mattresses from their beds. I saw Steve cram a box of matches in his pocket as well as some newspaper. Kevin shook some tea leaves into a plastic bag. Steve looked directly at me, his rust-colored eyes cold. "Clay, you're free to join us if you want." He looked at the others. "That way if he's part of us, he won't turn us in." He turned back to me. "If you choose not to join us, that's fine, too. You're the one missing out on all the fun. Just don't squeal on us."

After lights out, all three moved to the window. "Are you coming, Clay?" whispered Kevin. I felt torn up inside. I didn't want to join them in smoking their homemade cigarettes, but I wanted so much to be part of the in-group that I almost said yes.

As I hesitated, Steve said curtly, "Leave him behind." They slipped out the window.

I tossed and turned in my bed and tried unsuccessfully to sleep.

Suddenly the light in our room switched on and Mr. Layton, our dorm Dad, stood there. "I'm just doing a room check," he said. "Where are the others?"

"I really don't know," I answered truthfully.

He raised his eyebrows and turned off the light. I heard the door open and close. I turned over and shivered. What if I had gone with the others?

I heard a soft sound. My heart pounded and I squinted into the darkness. Had Steve and the others returned? Should I warn them that Mr. Layton was looking for them? But no one came through the window. I heard the sound again, and realized it was the sound of breathing. Mr. Layton had stayed in the room. I lay on my back stiffly waiting for the confrontation.

Finally I heard a scratching sound and whisper. I saw the curtain flicker open and Derek crawled in, followed by Steve and Kevin.

"Which did you like better?" Steve whispered. "The girls' lips? Or my home made cigarettes?"

"Snogging is better than smoking," Kevin answered. "Your cigarettes are vile, Steve." He giggled.

"You're right, tea leaves and mattress stuffing don't make the best smoke," Steve said.

The light clicked on. The bright light blinded me for a few seconds. I blinked to clear my eyes. Mr. Layton stood there, arms crossed. Steve and the others looked like rabbits in the python's cage at the Nairobi snake park. "Would you three care to come to my office and explain what you were doing outside?" Mr. Layton said evenly.

He stepped outside and my roommates followed. As he went out, Steve elbowed me violently. "If I find out you turned us in, Clay, you'll pay for being a squealer," he hissed.

I started to defend myself, but Steve had already slammed the door. Misery settled over me like a blanket.

Eventually Steve, Kevin, and Derek returned. Steve shook my shoulders and glared. "So, did you squeal on us, holy Joe?" He reached down and grabbed my wrist.

"No, I didn't," I answered. "Mr. Layton came in and did a dorm check on all the rooms." Steve's grip on my wrist tightened.

"We can find out if you're telling the truth," Steve said. He motioned to Kevin with his head. "Go find out if old man Layton did a room check."

Kevin slipped out. He came back quickly. "Clay's telling the truth. Layton checked all the rooms. And we weren't the only ones caught. Layton found two guys in room three climbing out their window and they're in trouble, too. Layton told them he used to live in this dorm when he attended Livingstone and he knows all the tricks of sneaking out of the dorm."

Steve released my wrist. "Okay, Clay, I'll believe you this time. But be warned. Don't ever turn me in. I make my own rules."

Kevin laughed. "Whatever punishment they give me, it was worth it to kiss Jenny."

"Jenny?" I questioned.

"Look, Clay, just because she started chasing you, doesn't mean she'll wait forever for you to kiss her," Kevin said. "She said you took too long to catch on to her hints for a kiss."

Hints? I thought. I hadn't noticed any hints that Jenny wanted me to kiss her. "Will the girls get in trouble, too?" I asked.

"Not from our lips," Derek said. "They had a key to the fire escape of their dorm and we made sure they got back in safely. I'm sure Layton will kick up a fuss, but if they don't talk, neither will we and they'll be safe."

Steve chuckled, "You know, I've already got two demerits this term for being disrespectful. They just might suspend me tomorrow after we talk to the principal. Then I'll get to go home."

"Do you want to go home?" I asked.

Steve shrugged. "Home's boring. My Dad makes me help out at the hospital. But it's sure easier to get real cigarettes in the town. My favorite brand is Sportsman. You should try them, Clay, since you seem to be such an athlete."

I didn't know how to respond. The others undressed and talked in whispers and murmurs. I finally turned over and pulled my pillow over my head.

Steve did get suspended the next day for excessive demerits. We found him packing up at lunchtime. He seemed happy. "Even if my Dad gets mad at me, at least I'll be home until the end of term," Steve commented.

Kevin and Derek got two demerits each and were restricted for two weeks to the dorm area when they weren't in class.

That night Kevin looked up and asked, "Do you want to sneak out with us tonight, Clay?"

"Are you crazy?" I responded. "You got two demerits for being out last night. Besides, I really don't want to try smoking. I want to be the best rugby player Livingstone has ever seen."

Kevin raised his eyebrow. "That's quite a goal, Clay. Have you seen those varsity rugby players working out every day in the weight room?"

"I've been watching them since I was in second grade," I said. "Ox, the rugby captain that year, taught me how to kick a rugby ball and ever since I've wanted to be a rugby player. Even better than Ox."

Kevin shook his head. "Okay, Clay. Maybe we should call you scrumboy or something like that."

"I like that," Derek said. "Good nickname, Kevin. Clay, we dub you Scrumboy."

I smiled. "That's fine with me."

Kevin pushed back the curtain. We all saw it at the same time—a blackened scar on the metal window frame. "They've welded shut our escape route!" Kevin wailed.

"I guess you won't smoke tonight," I said.

"I don't care about smoking. We only took a few puffs to make Steve happy. But I made a date to meet Jenny again outside the boiler room. What will I tell her tomorrow? She'll think I chickened out. And she promised to bring a few friends in case I brought some other guys along for kissing lessons."

"You guys are crazy," I said. I picked up my literature book and tried to read the short story we'd been assigned for homework.

Kevin and Derek sat down by the desk. "Dang!" Derek said. "We're locked in. Oh well, might as well make some *chai*."

He went out to get some water in a battered aluminum kettle.

Kevin looked up. "I played rugby last year, but it's a tough game. Being short, they stuck me in as hooker. I thought my neck would get twisted off after the first scrum. I'm not sure I want to play again this year."

"Your neck wouldn't hurt if you got in properly," I said. "Here, I'll show you." I leaped off the top bunk and showed Kevin how to bind properly in the front row. I interlocked my head under his shoulder and stuffed his head under my shoulder.

Derek walked in. When he saw us, he jumped backwards, splashing the water on the floor. "What are you two guys doing?" he asked. "Kevin, you got some kissing last night. You don't need to start hugging Clay."

Kevin pulled away and glared at Derek. "Clay was showing me some rugby binding techniques," he said.

"Sure," Derek said, laughing. He put the immersion coil into the kettle. As the water began to boil and bubble, he asked, "You want to make some *chai* with us, Clay?"

I accepted the African offer of friendship. We gathered around the desk and made *chai* together. I pulled out my huge green mug and put two spoons of powdered milk and three spoons of sugar in the bottom. Derek scooped some tea leaves into a big strainer, then poured the boiling water through the tea leaves into my mug. As I stirred my tea, some lumps of powdered milk refused to dissolve and floated on the top of the *chai*.

"Looks like you've got monkey turds in your *chai*," Kevin pointed out. He twisted his spoon crazily in the bottom of his mug to soften his powdered milk before Derek poured the hot water into his mug.

I sucked some of the milk lumps into my mouth and chewed on them. "They're my favorite part," I said.

Kevin wrinkled his nose. "I can tell you've been at Livingstone for a while. I still can't stand monkey turds." He used his spoon to fish out the few milk lumps that swam in his *chai*. He flicked them against the wall.

I raised my eyebrows. "Won't that make dorm cleanup harder at the end of term when we have to wash the walls?"

Kevin laughed. "Last year we got some titchies to wash our walls in exchange for a look at one of Steve's dirty magazines."

"Steve's gone," I pointed out.

Kevin shrugged. I walked over and wiped the milk lumps off the room with a wad of pink made-in-Kenya toilet paper flecked with bits of aluminum foil.

I looked at Derek. "Did you play junior colt rugby last year?"

"For part of the season," Derek said. "Then I broke my arm when a scrum collapsed on me, so I missed the rest of the games. I don't think I'll try out this year."

"Let me show you something." I opened my trunk and pulled out a flat oval piece of leather.

"What's that? A dead rat?" Derek joked.

"This is a rugby ball that Ox gave me." I told them how I'd climbed into the tunnel underneath the rugby field to retrieve the ball. I stroked the ball and stretched it a bit. Flecks of dirt stuck to the seam. The old bladder inside had been patched so many times it was useless to try again. "When Ox gave it to me, he said it was my job to keep the rugby spirit alive at Livingstone. He said he was passing on his love of rugby to me so there would be another generation of rugby players at Livingstone to keep winning games. That's what I plan to do, but I can't do it alone. All of us in eighth grade have to work together to create the best team Livingstone has ever seen. I've seen how fast both of you are at soccer. I know you'd be great backs. We'll all be on the Livingstone First XV in 1979 when we're seniors."

"You're rugby mad, Scrumboy," Kevin said, but he had a grin on his face.

"Just touch the ball," I begged. "This ball has the spirit of Livingstone rugby in it."

"Kind of like a good luck charm?" he asked.

"More than that! It has the history of Livingstone's best players. Ox and his team of 1969. Did you know that's the last time Livingstone beat Duke of York School?"

"Duke of York? I've never heard of them," Derek said.

"They changed the name of the school to Lenana after some old Maasai leader," I said. "But they still wear maroon shirts and Livingstone hasn't beat them since Ox's team." I squeezed the ball under my arm. "We have the ball Ox's team used. And we have to regain Livingstone's old rugby glory. But we have to do it together."

"Well, you've almost convinced us," Kevin said.

"Yeah, maybe I'll give rugby another chance," Derek agreed. "But we're a long way from rugby season."

"It's never too early to start," I said. "Ox and his team practiced rugby year-round." I put Ox's ball away and pulled out another ball, which had air in it. "Catch!" I tossed the ball to Derek. He jerked back and spilled his *chai*.

"Look what you've done, Clay. We can't play catch with *chai* mugs in one hand."

"Why not?" I asked, cheekily. "It will teach you to catch with one hand. You might need that when we play Lenana and someone's grabbing your hand as the ball comes at you."

Derek set his mug down and picked up the ball and passed it to me.

"Not like that," I said, showing him how to hold the ball with two hands.

A few guys from the next room knocked on the door. "What's going on in there?" they demanded.

I opened the door. "We're preparing for a winning rugby season in 1979. Want to join us?" They squeezed into the room.

"Let's go to the dorm lounge where we have more room," suggested Kevin.

28

I found my niche as the rugby expert. We'd often go to the rugby field after supper and kick and pass the ball around. Titch joined us. He'd improved his scrum-half dive pass and leaped fearlessly to sent the ball streaking to the fly-half. "You're great, Titch. I'll bet you'll make the second fifteen this year."

"As an eighth grader?" Titch shook his head. "You've always been a dreamer."

"Ever since second grade I've dreamed of playing on Livingstone's top teams," I answered. "There's nothing to stop us trying out at the end of second term. We'll get some good experience, even if we get cut. But I'm serious, Titch. You're good."

During second term, we kept practicing. We created a new school rule: no tackling without staff supervision. It happened when we played a game of ten-on-ten and I'm afraid I had a big part in creating the new rule. We'd finally persuaded Daniel to abandon his books and join us one evening. Daniel was thin, but quite fast, so we'd put him on the wing. He was playing on the other team and after one scrum, they passed the ball swiftly to Daniel who flew down the sideline. I had been sprinting towards the corner flag like Ox had taught me. I caught up with Daniel and hit him hard from the side. When he hit the ground, I heard a thump and a loud crack. Daniel writhed around as I stood up. "Are you okay, man?" I asked.

Daniel pulled his right arm against his chest and held it gently with his left hand. I could see that I'd broken Daniel's arm. "Let's get him to the infirmary," I said. We surrounded Daniel and carried him to the school nurse.

She looked at Daniel uncertainly. "Maybe he should soak it and check with me in the morning," she said.

"His arm's broken," I pointed out. "You can see where it's broken. It looks like an old Dorobo man's arm who came into my Mom's clinic after falling out of a tree while collecting honey."

The nurse furrowed her eyebrows and looked closer. "I guess we'd better take you to see the doctor and get an X-ray."

Daniel's arm had a clean break. But the next morning in chapel, the principal announced the new rule. So we stopped playing tackle, but we didn't stop practicing rugby.

Except for Kevin. It seemed that Jenny, who could no longer slip out of the dorm for evening makeout sessions, had told Kevin he had to choose rugby or her. For now, he'd chosen Jenny and they met behind the boiler room when the rest of us practiced rugby.

Titch and I led the sessions. We ran hill climbs up to the old quarry. At the quarry we passed heavy rugby-ball sized building rocks to strengthen our arms, before heading back to school. Others got bored of our enthusiasm. But even when only Titch and I showed up, we ran, spurring each other on.

A few weeks before the end of second term, Mr. Layton stood up in chapel and made the announcement I'd been living for. "Rugby try-outs will start this afternoon at 4 p.m. This is for all guys from seventh to twelfth grade. Come on out. Livingstone rugby needs you."

At the practice we stretched out as Mr. Layton laid out his plan. "Some of you may know I used to play rugby at Livingstone when I was a student here. Well, this year I'll be coaching, and I want to win back the Safari Cup. I understand we haven't had the cup here since Ox led our team back in 1969. In order to have a great first fifteen, we need to have good teams at the lower levels. That's why we're putting emphasis back on our younger teams." Mr. Layton—I still thought of him as Mike—introduced a few other teachers who would be coaching the younger teams.

Introductions over, Coach Layton emptied a dark green duffel bag full of rugby balls onto the grass. "Get in groups of six, one ball per group," he instructed. "Everyone take a few moments to hold the ball. Feel it with your fingers. Then form a small circle." Some of the guys wandered around trying to get partners.

"Come on," Coach Layton barked. "It can't be too hard to count up to six and pick up a ball." Titch and I hustled into a group.

"Now in your circles, start passing the ball around the circle. But before you do ..." He went on to show how to hold the ball in both hands and pass it in front of our teammates who had their hands outstretched in front of their waists to receive the pass.

"Catch the ball and then release it right away. One movement. One motion," he said, taking the ball from one of the seniors and pointing out how much wasted motion he had when he passed the ball.

"If that's how you passed the ball last year, it's no wonder you didn't win any trophies," Coach Layton almost snorted. I liked him already. He could see the flaws and point them out. But he wasn't nasty like my football coach. Cheeky, maybe, but not mean. We went from passing to mauling and rucking drills.

"Go in hard and low," Coach Layton instructed. "Get used to hitting people." Another of the senior players went into a rucking drill almost upright. "Lower your angle," Coach instructed. "If you go in standing up like that, you'll get your ribs cracked. Even if you don't, you sure won't drive anyone off the ball." He used his forearm and hand to form a flat line about waist height and parallel with the ground. "That's how low you should be when you hit a ruck or a maul."

Tackling came next. I loved this part the best. Titch and I lined up next to each other. "Hard and low," Titch whispered to me. Then he smiled. "Low isn't hard for me, I'm so short already!"

"I'm ready," I answered. "I haven't tackled since I broke Daniel's arm first term." The first person to run at me in the tackling drill was a big senior prop named Bill. He rumbled along and I crouched and then exploded my shoulder into his thigh and wrapped his legs. His weight helped me to take him down like a felled tree.

"Good tackle, Clay," Coach Layton complimented me. He rubbed his chin briefly with his left index finger. "Keep it up."

I noticed Kevin and Jenny and a few other eighth graders on the bank watching practice. Kevin looked annoyed. We ended up doing some wind sprints. Many of the older kids were sucking air after only one or two. Titch and I just flew. Our hill climbs and after school sessions had paid off.

The supper bell rang and Coach Layton called an end to the practice. "Not bad for a first day," he complimented us. "Some of you obviously have a long way to go on fitness, but I'll take care of that. If you play for me, you will be fit. Be sure to bring your boots tomorrow. We'll build a couple of scrums and then have our first scrimmage."

As we scattered after practice, Coach Layton called me and Titch over. "What's with you guys?" he asked. "Where'd you get so fit? And your tackling is excellent—both of you."

"We've been running and practicing after school since the end of first term," I said.

Mr. Layton raised his eyebrows. "Sounds like you learned something from watching Ox and the rest of us all those years ago."

"I sure did," I answered. "But when we run the tracks, we don't throw mud clods at the caboose."

"Ouch, a bad memory," Coach said. "I'd hoped everyone had forgotten that."

At the scrimmage the next day, Titch and I teamed up. I slotted in at eighth man and Titch played scrum-half. We'd practiced so much together that we meshed like the hands on a clock, each doing its essential part without getting in the way of the other. Coach Layton had mixed up the players so there wasn't just one big team of senior guys. We got the ball out easily to our backs and when we had chances to tackle we both hit hard and solid.

After a week of practice, the coaching crew announced the squads. Titch's name was first on a list for the second fifteen. My name followed soon after. Titch made a fist and shook it in front of my face. "We made it!" he exulted. We were the only eighth graders to make the second fifteen. The rest were on senior colts or junior colts.

I sat on a bench near the dining hall and pulled off my rugby boots. "Well, Titch, we made it!" I slipped on a pair of battered tennis shoes and stood up.

"We sure did," Titch answered, his smile as wide as a hippo's mouth on Lake Naivasha.

Coach Layton walked by. "Congratulations," he said. "I don't think many players have made the second fifteen in eighth grade. Not since Ox back in the sixties."

Titch headed for home and I walked into the dining hall. I sat down with my tray piled with food. I paused briefly to bow my head and pray for the meal. When I looked up, there was Jenny. "Congratulations, Clay! Or should I call you Scrumboy," she gushed. "I hear you made the second fifteen. I'm so proud of you."

I raised one eyebrow. "Uh, where's Kevin?" I asked.

"Kevin? Oh, Kevin and I broke up today. Can I sit here? Have I ever told you how much I like watching rugby?"

29

By ninth grade, Titch and I were already veteran second fifteen rugby players. Kevin made the team that year, now that he didn't have Jenny to distract him. He was still short, but had filled out so Coach Layton trained him to be our hooker. Daniel played on the wing, and Derek had made it as our fullback.

"When we get to be seniors, we're going to be the best team Livingstone has ever seen," I promised the other freshmen on the second fifteen.

Coach Layton had turned the first fifteen into a tough, fighting squad. They'd lost in the quarter-finals of the Safari Cup the year before. They had a good chance this year.

He talked to our second team early in the season. "The only way we'll make it is if you on the second fifteen push the varsity players. Every practice, every tackle. The tougher you make it for them when we scrimmage, the better they'll be."

The guys elected me captain of the second team. "Way to go, Scrumboy," Kevin cheered after the vote, a grin on his face.

The first team reached the semi-final of the Safari Cup that year. Then the epidemic hit. It seemed that over half the school came down with the trots, our euphemism for amoebic dysentery. At first they blamed the cafeteria, but then found that some sewage had leaked into the school's drinking water system.

Somehow, our dorm was spared. The day of the semi-final the first fifteen only had ten available players, and most of those were weak and pale.

Coach Layton called us over after chapel. "Clay, you'll have to play eighth man for the first fifteen today. Titch, you'll have to start as well, along with Kevin and Daniel. I've got guys desperate to play, but they can't stay away from the john for more than ten minutes, and I doubt the ref will stop the game every ten minutes to let them run for it." He smiled grimly before tossing us our first team jerseys. "You guys are young, but you've got the spirit."

I looked in unbelief at my white shirt with the red stripe around the middle. "Titch! Our first varsity game!" We all sat stunned.

The bus belched out black smoke as we clambered on and sat on the clammy brown-plastic-covered bus seats. I jammed my knees into the narrow space and looked down. My rugby boots had been polished and I had the laces tucked into my socks. Titch squeezed in next to me, his face tense.

"Can you believe we're playing Lenana in the semi-finals?" he asked.

"Maybe we'll make our dream come true before we're seniors," I replied.

"I could start a butterfly farm with the butterflies fluttering in my stomach," Titch said. "I think I'm going to be sick."

"You don't have the runs?" I asked in shock.

Titch's face paled. He shook his head. "No, just nervous."

Coach Layton walked down the bus aisle counting heads. "Okay, we're all here," he said. "At least the able-bodied players. Let's pray for the trip."

I tried to cheer Titch up, but after a few miles, I shut up. His nerves were contagious. We were only ninth graders. We weren't ready to play at this level. At least not yet.

Coach Layton sat down in the seat in front of us and twisted his body to look at us. "You two guys don't look too excited."

Titch didn't answer.

"I'm excited," I said. "But we're both really scared."

"I'll tell you a secret," Coach Layton said. "When I played at Livingstone, I'd be so scared I could hardly spit before a game."

"So what did you do?" Titch asked. "I remember watching you when I was in second grade. You were so icy calm."

"Once I make my first tackle on the field, everything's okay. That's why I always have the captain elect to kick off if we win the coin toss." Coach Layton laughed. "You two will do fine. You've got a great combination at the base of the scrum." The expression on his face grew serious. "Clay, you'll have to watch their burly eighth man closely. He loves to pick up the ball from the base of the scrum and attack the gain line. You're a good tackler. Hit him low and he'll go down."

Coach moved off to encourage some of the other second team recruits. I closed my eyes and dreamed I was driving the Lenana eighth man backwards every time he ran at me.

We arrived at Lenana School and saw a mass of students in maroon school sweaters surrounding the rugby pitch. No one was allowed on the field except for the first team players. Titch whispered, "My butterflies have returned."

I grabbed a ball and stuffed it in Titch's gut. "Get the feel of the ball. The spectators can't play. There will only be fifteen of their guys on the field."

We stretched and Coach Layton gave us last minute instructions. A rumbling roar interrupted him as the spectators began shouting, "A mean maroon, a mean maroon!" over and over. The Lenana first fifteen burst out from behind a nearby building. Their shoulders looked as wide as trucks in their white-and-maroon hooped shirts. Their Vaseline-slick legs shone in the late afternoon sun.

"Come on, boys," Coach Layton urged. "Concentrate on what you'll do on the field. Don't worry about looking at them. Doesn't matter how much Vaseline they have on their legs. If you tackle them hard, they'll go to the ground. We can win this game."

I closed my eyes and took a deep breath. My first game for the Livingstone first fifteen was about to begin.

Our captain won the coin toss and chose to kick off. Our fly-half kicked the ball high. As it fluttered end-over-end in the air, I chased under it. The Lenana eighth man caught the ball and lowered his shoulder into me just as I reached him. I managed to duck under his charge and entangle his legs. He crashed to the ground. I struggled to get to my feet as a ruck formed over us. Lenana had pushed over the ruck and their scrum-half ferreted the ball out. I moved behind the back foot of our last player in the ruck to stay onside and sidled to the open side where the Lenana backs had lined up to receive the pass.

As their scrum-half flung the pass wide, I sprinted forward. Their fly-half caught the ball and shoveled it along before I could tackle him. I kept moving down the line, finally catching up to the ball as it landed in the hands of their winger. He tried to jink inside, but I managed to grasp his shirt just as our winger also moved in for the tackle. Together we bustled him out of bounds. They hadn't even reached the gain line and we would have the throw-in at the lineout.

Titch positioned himself alongside the line of forwards who were getting ready to leap for the inbounds throw. I smiled and asked him. "Still got butterflies?"

He grinned back. "Gone completely. Great start Clay."

The game see-sawed back and forth. We managed to stop all their attacks, but without our regular players, our own offense ran like a balky Leyland truck filled with sand. We trundled ahead, but couldn't get anywhere. The score at half time stuck at 0-0.

Coach Layton walked around our circle of bruised and battered players. "Great start, boys," he said. "Keep tackling and they won't score. But we have to make a few changes in our offense. Our backline just isn't breaking through. We're going to have to create our attack from the base of the scrum." He turned to me. "Clay, that means you'll have to pick up the ball and run with it. Take on one or two of their players, then slip the ball to Titch. Titch, if the opportunity is there to cut through their defense, go for it. Otherwise, get the ball to the backs. That way our backs will get the ball moving forward."

On our first scrum after the break, I picked up the ball from the base of the scrum and drove forward. I met their flanker and their hefty eighth man who slammed me to ground. I didn't even have a chance to get the ball to Titch. They won the ball from the ruck that followed and spun the ball wide. Daniel couldn't hold his man and Lenana scored in the corner. Our captain pulled us into a huddle behind the try line. Daniel's face oozed sadness like the face of an old wildebeest. "Sorry, guys," he mumbled.

"Don't worry," our captain said. "You did your best. That's only one score. We can get it back. Don't give up on me now."

We all nodded and clapped. I rushed the Lenana kicker's conversion attempt. I doubt if I unsettled him, but his kick went wide. Lenana led 4-0. I continued to pick the ball up from the base of the scrums, but couldn't make much headway against the Lenana backrow. But I did get the ball to Titch after taking on the tacklers. We made some gains but couldn't score.

Late in the game, our fly-half decided to hoist a garryowen to test their fullback. Under heavy pressure, their fullback misjudged the kick and knocked the ball on. The ref called a scrum for Livingstone and looked anxiously at his watch. I knew we didn't have much time left. As we formed for the scrum, I pulled Titch aside. "This time, loop deep behind the scrum. I'll pull the ball out and pop it to you as you go forward. That will force their backrow to move wide to tackle you. Then look for me on the inside."

We won the strike and our hooker guided the ball back to me. I shifted it to my right foot and pulled my head out to see where Titch was. He'd made a deep loop and started charging towards the gain line. I released my bind and picked up the ball and passed it to Titch in one motion. The Lenana backrow broke off and sprinted wide to tackle Titch. My legs ached with fatigue, but I drove myself forward. Just as the Lenana players looked set to squash Titch like a flying ant on a windscreen, he popped a pass inside. I gathered it up and was through the defense. I only had another ten meters to the goal line. Their fullback moved up to tackle me. I slanted my run to the right and just before he tackled me, I launched myself forward like a missile. I landed inside the goal line with the ball under my shoulder.

The ref lifted his hand to signal a try as he blasted on the whistle. Our fly-half stepped up to convert the try by kicking the ball through the posts like a point-after in American football.

He gazed at the posts, then down at the ball. Back in our own half, I knelt on one knee breathing a prayer. He strode forward and stroked the ball through the posts. Two more points! The ref looked at his watch again and then blew his whistle to signal the end of the game. We had beaten Lenana 6-4 on their own field! Our whole team danced and hugged in the center of the field.

30

As we walked to our school bus, Titch limped. "Are you hurt?" I asked.

"No," Titch answered, grimacing.

I gazed into his eyes. "You're lying," I said. I ducked down and slipped my shoulder under his armpit.

"I'm okay, Clay. Stop making a scene."

"Lean on me," I ordered.

Coach Layton caught up with us at the bus. "Where are you hurt?" he asked.

"I'm fine," Titch insisted. The pain in his eyes disagreed with his words.

Coach Layton knelt down and ran his hand down Titch's left leg. When Coach touched Titch's ankle, Titch winced and squeezed his eyes shut. "I'm going to send you back to the school in somebody's car," Coach said. He hurried away.

A few minutes later, one of the teachers who had driven to the game in his Land Rover, pulled next to the bus. I helped lift Titch into the car. They laid him down on some blankets in the back.

"Can I go with him, Coach?" I asked.

He nodded. "Take him right to the mission hospital and get some x-rays of that ankle," Coach Layton told the teacher. I hopped into the Land Rover and crammed myself next to Titch. "Keep his rugby boot on for now," Coach said, sticking his head in through the back door. "At the very least he has a badly sprained ankle. We don't have any ice here, but the boot will keep the swelling down until you get to the hospital."

"I'll take care of him," I promised. Coach patted Titch on the shoulder before shutting the door.

"You'll be okay," I encouraged Titch. He swallowed a sob.

I tried to steady his ankle as the Land Rover bounced over the potholes in the tarmac road. The last five miles of dirt road tortured Titch and his injured leg. All I could do was hold onto him.

At the hospital the missionary doctor tenderly probed Titch's ballooning ankle. He pulled off the boot and sock. I held them, the orange mud of Lenana's rugby field staining my palms. Titch's ankle looked an angry red. The doctor took Titch in for some x-rays. When Titch came out, I sat with him on a white-painted bench holding a plastic bag of ice against his ankle. The melting ice dripped cold against my hands leaving a muddy puddle on the concrete floor.

Coach Layton came in with Titch's parents. "How's my favorite scrum-half?" Coach asked.

Titch gave a tired smile. "Winning the game sure makes the pain worth it."

His Mom knelt in front of the bench. "Oh, Tim, you'll have to stop playing that dangerous game. I pray every time you go out on the field."

"I'll be okay, Mom," Titch answered.

The doctor came out, squinting at some grayish looking x-rays. "Some good news," he said, looking at Titch's parents. "There's no break, so we won't need to cast it. But it's a nasty sprain." He knelt beside Titch. "The ligaments took quite a hit, from the feel of your ankle. Sometimes sprains take longer to heal than a clean break. Anyway, we'll wrap it up and give you some crutches. You won't be able to put much weight on that foot for a few days. Your foot will swell and turn very blue. Then you'll have to rebuild the strength back into your foot. You definitely won't be playing rugby for two or three weeks, maybe longer."

Titch's sickly smile reversed. "That means I'm out for the rest of the season."

Coach Layton said, "Sorry, Titch. You played great today. You got us into the finals. Now you'll just need to heal up for next year."

"Get better soon," I said lamely. We left Titch with his parents getting the crutches and some painkillers. Coach Layton drove me up to the dorm.

The next week the first fifteen players had recovered from the runs. By Saturday's Safari Cup final against St. Mary's School, Coach Layton had his whole team back. But he invited me to travel with the team as a reserve. "You got us into the finals, Clay. You deserve to be there."

The final game started poorly for Livingstone. Our forwards won the first lineout and our backs passed the ball quickly. Our inside center made a beautiful break only ten meters from the try line. But as the defense closed up, he passed the ball wide without looking. A speedy St. Mary's winger poached the pass and sprinted the length of the field to score between the posts. Livingstone fought bravely, but could never overcome that first six points, losing 21-15.

"Our best finish in years," Coach Layton encouraged the players at the end of the game. I circled up with the others to sing the Doxology. "Praise God from whom all blessings flow," we chorused as I vowed in my heart to hoist the Safari Cup before I left Livingstone.

All of our freshman players who won that semi-final game against Lenana made the first fifteen the next year as sophomores. We lost that year in the semi-finals, but we gained a lot of experience. In our junior year, everything came together. We hammered the opposition by controlling possession in the scrums and lineouts. I had grown to six-feet-four inches and dominated the lineouts and ruled the base of the scrum. At the end of every game it became the custom of all our players to pat me on the head as they ran through our victory tunnel and say, "Way to go, Scrumboy."

We met Nairobi School in the final that year and we beat them 39-0. It was the most lopsided final in the history of the Safari Cup.

Back at Livingstone, we carried the cup into the school assembly hall where the drama department was putting on a play called the Mousetrap. We marched in during the middle of the production, cheering and waving the cup. The whole crowd broke into cheers. The drama teacher glared at us for interrupting the play. He shooed us out of the hall. On Monday the principal gave us demerits for disruptive, disrespectful behavior.

"I don't really care," I said to Titch during *chai* break as he worried how to tell his parents. "We won the Safari Cup. We've been dreaming of this for years, Titch. We had a right to celebrate. This school has no sense of humor and the rules are squeezing the life out of me."

"That doesn't sound like you, Clay," Titch said.

I shrugged. "A year from now we'll be out of here, Titch. Why can't we celebrate winning the Safari Cup?"

"We don't have to break rules and be rude to celebrate," Titch answered.

I grunted.

I still roomed with Kevin and Derek and during the week Derek suggested celebrating our victory in style. "Next Friday we can sneak off campus after classes. We can hitchhike into Nairobi, have a meal at the Hong Kong, visit a disco and then catch a bus back to school."

I surprised myself by agreeing. Somehow I felt I deserved a victory celebration. The three of us caught a ride on a sagging lorry. Diesel smoke and charcoal grit from the gunny sacks we sat on covered us when we arrived in Nairobi. We went to the Hong Kong restaurant. I ordered sweet and sour chicken and a Coke.

"I'm having a beer with my meal," Kevin stated.

"Me, too," said Derek.

Suddenly I felt very uncomfortable. I might get some demerits for being off campus, but if we got caught drinking, we could get kicked out of school.

"I don't think that's a good idea," I put in.

"Lighten up, Scrumboy," Kevin said. "You're too straight. All the Bible says is don't get drunk. We won't get drunk on one Tusker each. And we won't get caught unless someone at this table tells."

I strong hand gripped my shoulder. I looked up into the eyes of Coach Layton. His wife in a delicate red dress stood beside him. "Celebrating your victory, boys?" he asked.

"Uh, sure," I began.

"Funny, I don't remember signing any off-campus permits for you three. But tell you what. If you need a ride home, I'll give you one. Now excuse me for a while. I'm on a date with my wife. When you're done eating, wait for us outside."

Kevin took his napkin and wiped the beads of sweat that had gathered on his forehead. "That was close, Scrumboy," he whispered. "Thanks for making us slow down before ordering our Tuskers. What do you think Coach would have done if we'd had beers at our table?"

Derek couldn't enjoy his meal. "Coach knows we're in town without permission. I'm sure he'll turn us in when we get back to school. Whose idea was it to come to this restaurant anyway?"

"Yours," pointed out Kevin, smirking. "Just relax. If he's letting us eat our meal, we won't be in too much trouble. Maybe a demerit or two. Nothing to get sent home for."

"Unless you've already collected a ton of demerits," Derek grumbled.

"Oh, that's right," Kevin remembered. "You and Brenda got busted for sneaking out of the movie last week and sitting under the stars by the edge of the rugby field."

"I'm ready to be out of this school," Derek said. "I want to make my own decisions about when I can sit with a girl, what I can drink, when I have to be in the dorm."

"We've just got one more year," I said. "Our senior year at Livingstone will be our last. Then freedom." As I said the words, a pang of fear clutched at my heart. Livingstone had been home for so long, I wasn't sure I could survive somewhere else.

We finished and wandered outside. "I want some ice cream," I said, walking down the street to the Sno-Cream and ordering a chocolate dip. The others followed me. We sat on the ledge of the show window for the Mercedes Benz dealer beside the Hong Kong. Between licks, Kevin pointed at the silver Benz behind the window. "When I get a good job in the States, I'm going to drive one of those babies."

I laughed. "I'll probably end up back here in Africa bouncing around in an old Land Rover."

Coach Layton and his wife came out of the Hong Kong. "My car's over here," Coach said. "Let's go."

We followed like scolded children. Once in the car, Coach Layton drove towards the big traffic circle. Avoiding careening *matatus* stuffed with passengers, he spoke to us in the back. "You guys didn't have permission to be in town, did you?"

We looked at each other but didn't answer. Coach Layton laughed. "I didn't think so. Did I ever tell you about the time Ox and I hitchhiked to Nairobi? We had a meal at the steak house. Afterwards we caught a ride as far as Limuru. So we started thumbing for another lift. Imagine our surprise when a gray Volkswagen came by. It was the Principal of Livingstone. We tried to duck. But the Principal just rolled down his window. With a crafty smile on his face, he waved and said, 'Have a nice walk boys.' When we finally did catch a ride, we were sure we'd be busted back at Livingstone. But the Principal never brought it up. I guess he figured we'd had punishment enough just worrying about what might happen.

"Anyway, I'm going to take you back to Livingstone, and that will be the end of it as far as I'm concerned. But hang in there guys. I know Livingstone sometimes seems like a prison. Believe me, most of the rules are for your good. At this point you may not see that. For now, stay out of trouble. I want you here next year so we can be repeat winners of the Safari Cup."

31

At the beginning of our senior year I started dating my first serious girlfriend. Leah and I were assigned to work on some page layout together for the school yearbook. Her shoulder-length dark hair framed her pretty face, and I found myself staring at her, not the layout. "Come on, Clay," she prodded with a laugh. "We have to get this assignment done."

"Right," I said. The mole on her right cheek looked like a chocolate chip. "Leah, do you have a date to Saturday night's movie?"

"What?" she asked. "Clay, we're working on the yearbook."

"I know, but will you answer my question?"

Leah sighed. "No, I don't have a date for Saturday."

"Would you go out with me?" I asked.

Leah pondered. "Will this get you back on track with our assignment here?"

"Yes," I lied.

"Okay," she agreed, a heart-warming smile crossing her lips.

"Titch," I said that afternoon at soccer practice. "I have a date for Saturday night!"

"Does this mean you won't be sitting with me?" Titch said in mock astonishment.

"You can join us if you want," I said.

"I'm just kidding," he said. "I'm glad you have a date. A lot of girls have been chasing you the last few years."

"Leah's different. I'm chasing her," I pointed out.

First term at Livingstone we played soccer. It didn't give me the same thrill as rugby, but it kept me in shape. At soccer practice our coach waved a letter as we circled up to stretch. "Rockpoint, a Christian college in California, has written to me asking me to recommend some players for soccer scholarships. I think most of you could find a place on a college soccer team. So if any of you are interested in a good education and a chance to play soccer, see me after practice and I'll give you more information as well as a recommendation letter."

As we ran during practice, my mind turned to the coach's offer. I hadn't given much thought to college yet. I just knew it was the next step after Livingstone. California beckoned with Beach Boy music, surfing and the beach. Sounded like a better spot to go to college than some cold wintry place. I'd rather have gotten a rugby scholarship, but I didn't know any places that even played rugby in the States. At the end of practice I asked the coach for information on Rockpoint College.

I showed the papers to Titch. "Why don't you try to go to Rockpoint, too?" I asked. "I'm sure you're a good enough soccer player. We could stay together."

Titch shook his head. "You'll do great in college, but I'm not cut out for it. I've talked with my Dad and there's a technical school where I can learn the mechanical side of drilling boreholes. I won't have to worry about all that reading and writing stuff. I'll work for a few years as an apprentice on a well-digging team. Then I hope I can come back here to Africa to drill wells."

"You've got it all figured out," I said surprised. "Why didn't you tell me before?"

"My Dad and I only talked it out a few days ago," Titch answered.

At student center that night after study hall, I saw Leah with some friends. I walked over. "Can I buy you a Coke?" I asked. Leah's smile answered for her. As we sat down on one of the couches, a song by the Mamas and Papas blared on the turntable and caught my attention.

"Do you hear that song?" I asked.

"Sure, it's California Dreamin'," Leah answered. "It's one of my favorites."

"Funny, just today I started thinking about attending Rockpoint College in Santa Barbara, California, and now that song comes on." I told her about the possibility of a soccer scholarship.

"It's sure worth a try," Leah said. "I've applied to Wheaton. If my SAT scores are high enough, I might get an academic scholarship."

"Wheaton's cold," I pointed out.

"My parents come from Chicago," Leah said, "and that's where we always stay in the States. You get used to it."

I shivered. "I don't think I could ever adjust to cold winter weather. One year in junior high was enough."

Back in my room that night, I filled out the application form and mailed it off the next day.

I had a lot of fun on my date with Leah the next Saturday evening. Usually I got all tongue-tied on dates. I'd say things like, "So, what's the name of the movie we're watching," or something equally inane. But with Leah I relaxed. She talked easily about topics as varied as Beowulf, which we were reading in English class, to a hornbill she'd seen in the cedar tree next to her dorm "It had a huge casque on top of its bill and had a clattering kind of call."

"You're a bird watcher?" I asked.

She laughed gently. "With my Dad, it's hard not to notice the birds around us."

"My Dad's a bird nut, too," I admitted. "I know a lot of bird species, but I usually don't tell others. They think it's kind of nerdy."

"What's wrong with enjoying God's creation?" Leah said. "The Bible says God cares about sparrows."

At the intermission they sold cold sodas and candy in the back of the assembly hall. Standing up, I asked Leah, "Want something to drink?"

Leah smiled appreciatively. "Sure. I'll come with you." I found myself staring into her copper-brown eyes. We bought Cokes and went back to our seats. The last half of the movie started. When Leah had finished her Coke, she whispered, "My hand's cold from holding that soda. Can you warm it up for me?"

I gladly took her hand in mine for the rest of the movie. We held hands in the dark as we walked back to the dorm. At the door we leaned against the wall for a few minutes to talk. A window opened above us. It was Leah's dorm Mom. "Get inside girls," she commanded. "You boys get back to your dorm now."

"I really enjoyed this evening," I said to Leah. "Could we do this again?"

"I'd love to," Leah replied, eyes sparkling. She squeezed my hand and slipped into the dorm, turning in the doorway to wave good-bye.

Within a week, Leah and I were going steady. When I wasn't on the playing field, I was with Leah. We ate meals together, visited during student center hours and had dates to all the movies.

During December vacation Leah went home to Tanzania. I'd never felt so lonely. Even seeing my parents drive up to take me home couldn't dispel the feeling of loss.

When we came back to school in January, I couldn't wait to see Leah again. Would she still like me? Was it really true love? I began to worry.

At the dorm I said good-bye to my parents, never an easy moment, but so different from the first drop-off back in second grade. I carried my bags of cookies into my dorm room. My dorm Mom said I had some mail that had arrived during vacation.

I picked the letters up and took them to my room. I sat down on my bed and riffled through the envelopes reading the return addresses. One letter came from Rockpoint College. I ripped it open. It was an invitation to attend their school on a full tuition scholarship if I played on their soccer team.

As I held the letter, I suddenly realized that in seven short months, my life at Livingstone would be over. It hit me that I didn't want to leave Africa. I didn't want to leave home and go away to college. I dropped the letter on the bed. My hand trembled as I picked it up and read it again. It was there, coldly typed onto the stiff stationery. An invitation to a foreign world. Another threshold to cross. College.

32

When I saw Leah later that afternoon, she asked if I was all right. I nodded and smiled wanly. "I missed you and I'm really glad you're back."

Leah's friendly smile perked me up. We wandered over to the rolling edge of the hillside and looked at the sun bleeding away behind the jagged rim of Mt. Longonot on the floor of the Rift Valley.

"I received sobering news when I got back to school today," Leah said.

"What?"

"I got accepted at Wheaton," Leah said. She sighed. "I guess that's great. But as I read the letter, I began to cry. Going to college means leaving Africa. And Africa's my home." Tears slipped from her big copper-colored eyes, made even shinier by the fierce blood-red sunset.

I held her hand and squeezed it gently. After a minute or so, she sniffed back her tears and said, "I'm sorry. You must think I'm such an emotional mess."

"Actually, I think I understand. I got accepted to Rockpoint College in California. Full ride tuition scholarship to play soccer. I thought I'd be happy to get free schooling for playing sports. Instead, all I could think of was that I didn't want to leave Africa."

"Oh, Clay, leaving will be scary. I'm not sure I want to go."

I reached an arm around Leah to comfort her. We sat there, holding each other as the sunset faded to rose pink.

"That looks a little too close to me!" an icy voice interrupted us from behind. I turned to see our math teacher, her little dog on a leash, looking at us grimly. "I'm afraid I'm going to have to turn you two in to the school disciplinarian."

Leah pleaded, "But ..."

"No excuses, now. Just get on back to your dorms. I'm sure you'll find out what your punishment is tomorrow."

We stood up unsteadily. I started to walk with Leah towards her dorm. "Not together," the math teacher commanded.

"Sorry, Leah," I mumbled. "I'll see you later."

Leah ran to her dorm. I heard her stifle a sob.

"Maybe leaving this school won't be so bad after all. What stupid rules!" I murmured.

"What did you say?" the math teacher asked.

"Nothing," I answered, and slipped down the hill to my dorm.

Leah and I received a one-week couple's restriction, which meant we couldn't talk to each other or spend time together for the next week. We got around the no-talking bit by passing notes. Titch became my envoy. Funny, that week of enforced restriction actually opened up our communication. I learned I could say a lot more from my heart by writing a note. We carried on our conversation about our fears of leaving Africa for life after Livingstone. I stared at Leah during class until I caught her eye. She'd blush and I'd smile.

After a week, our punishment was over. We decided there wasn't much we could do about leaving, so we'd better enjoy our last months in Africa. Several weeks before the end of second term, we started rugby practice again. This would be my last season at Livingstone. I knew we would have the best team Livingstone had ever seen. We would lift the Safari Cup two years in a row.

"We'll start with fitness," Coach Layton announced as we circled around him and stretched out. "We're going to run the nature trail, down the first ravine, then straight up the cliff to the railroad tracks before circling around and coming back to the rugby field."

"No throwing mud clods at the train," I called out. I winked at Coach.

"We don't want to talk about that bad memory," he said, running his hand through his thinning hair.

Halfway up to the railroad tracks, I had to lean forward and scramble up the path, grasping at grass on the side to keep my momentum. I heard the gushing groan of someone puking behind me. Sweat poured off my forehead by the time I reached the top. I stood and turned to encourage the others. Titch arrived second. I reached down and pulled him over the crest. "Turn right at the railroad tracks," I called, pushing the others along. When the last player arrived at the top, I started running again, sprinting along the tracks and catching up with Titch before the trail dropped back down to Baridi. We arrived back at the rugby field together.

We worked hard, carrying each other piggy-back, running wind sprints, followed by tackling practice, rucking and mauling drills. By the end of the first practice I had skinned knees and my lungs burned. "I love it!" I commented to Titch, who grinned. Some of the others looked sick.

"We have a friendly game with the Harlequins Second Fifteen in Nairobi next week," Coach Layton announced. "So thank you for your hard work today. I know it hurts, but it will pay off when we start playing games."

Our traditional season-opener against the Harlequins turned out to be a tight contest. Quins had big forwards and fast backs. We had a hard time winning the scrums as our front row crumpled under the weight of the stronger club players. We had to tackle like crazy to keep them from scoring. I was able to outleap their jumpers in the lineouts and we got some good possession when the ball went out of bounds. By the second half our superior fitness began to wear out the older Quins players and we scored a couple of tries in the dying minutes to win the game.

"Great game!" Coach Layton enthused. "If we can take on club players, we'll certainly be able to run over other schools. Now, don't lose your fitness during your month-long vacation. Find a hill somewhere near your house and run. When we come back for third term, we can work more on skills instead of having to start over again with fitness."

During school vacation I wrote a letter to Leah every day, but I only got them mailed once a week when I went with Dad to Narok, the closest post office. I kept fit by running up and down a bushbuck trail in the ravine below our house. I wore heavy hiking boots to build up my calf muscles and carried a backpack for upper body strength.

Back at Livingstone to start our final term of high school, I realized I would lose Leah when school ended. I thought if I didn't see so much of her, maybe the parting wouldn't hurt so much. The first evening back at school I ignored her at student center and sat with the other rugby players daring each other to chug Cokes in one glug. Leah's eyes showed her confusion and pain. I deliberately walked back to the guys' dorm alone.

The next day after lunch, which I ate with my rugby buddies, I looked up and saw Leah staring down at me. "We have to talk," she said firmly.

"All right," I answered.

"Ooh! Sounds serious, Scrumboy!" Kevin teased. I dropped off my tray before following Leah outside.

"What's going on?" Leah demanded when we reached the shade of the old green tree in the school parking lot. "You write great love letters during vacation. Then you won't sit with me at student center. Now you won't sit with me at lunch. If that's the way you're going to treat me, we might as well break up."

"I'm not sure how to say this," I began.

"What? Is there someone else?" Leah asked.

"My first love has come back to me," I joked. "Rugby!"

Leah opened her mouth in shock. "You love rugby more than me! That's it! We really are through!" She stomped away.

For the next week I focused on rugby only. I ran early in the morning. I used my blue Bic pen to design tattoos on my hand saying, "Beat Nairobi School." I refused to talk to any girls. I sat and talked rugby at student center. But every time I saw Leah, my heart hurt. Finally one evening I went to where she sat drinking a Coke by herself. "Can I sit down?" I asked.

"I don't care," Leah said, refusing to look me in the eye.

"Listen, I've come to say I'm sorry. Rugby isn't the real reason I was ignoring you."

"It sure seemed like it."

"I'm not good at explaining my feelings, but when I realized that at the end of this term we'll be splitting up and going to different colleges, it hurt worse than sliding across a dry rugby field and gouging a six inch strawberry on your hip."

Leah looked at me, puzzled.

"I thought maybe if we weren't quite so close it wouldn't hurt so much when we had to say good-bye," I went on. "But it didn't work. I'm miserable without you by my side."

"Oh, Clay, I'm sorry for misjudging you." Leah's lips trembled.

"Does that mean you forgive me?" I asked.

Leah nodded. "I sure do."

"And we're back together again?"

"Yes. I don't even want to think about leaving you at the end of the year. Let's enjoy the time we have left. Together." I took her hand and gave it a firm squeeze.

33

We mowed down the other schools in the Safari Cup schedule, qualifying for the playoffs. After a bruising semi-final victory over Saint Mary's School, we were set to play against Lenana in the final. The game would be played at the rugby football union field in Nairobi. As we drove into the game, our ninth grade manager crawled up and down the aisle of the bus polishing our rugby boots.

The game started well. Titch scored the first try after I picked up the ball and drove through two of Lenana's backrow forwards. As they grappled at me desperately, I popped the ball out to Titch at a full sprint. He squirted between their defenders and scored between the posts. Soon we scored two more tries and Derek slotted the conversions. We led 18-0.

But Lenana wouldn't give up. They started pecking away at our lead. A drop goal for three points. Then two penalties. At halftime we led 18-9. We couldn't get untracked after the break and clung desperately to our lead. One of their centers penetrated our defense and after breaking the gain line, he shoveled the ball to his winger who scored in the corner. Their kicker missed the conversion, and our lead stood at 18-13.

A knee planted in my face resulted in a bloody nose. After treatment—a bucket of cold water and a sponge—I rejoined the fray. But Lenana kept threatening. Time crept by as we tackled furiously stopping them time and time again on our goal line. Our fly-half unleashed some powerful kicks to relieve the pressure, but Lenana kept coming back. In injury time Lenana won a lineout and their backs swept forward. Our defense spread wide. Their center made an inside break and slipped. As he did, our defense squeezed in. *We've stopped them!* I thought. But somehow before the Lenana center hit the ground, he flung the ball as wide as he could. Their winger clung to the pass and flew past our defense. He scored his try in the corner. Our lead had been cut to 18-17.

As their kicker set up the ball for the conversion, I prayed. "No, Lord, don't let him make this kick." We rushed at the kicker, but he thumped the ball before we could charge down the kick. I turned and watched in dismay as the kick curled right between the posts. The linesmen's flags went up. Lenana had a 19-18 lead. The ref looked at his watch and blew three shrills on his whistle to end the game. We had lost. The Lenana players jumped on top of each other in elation. I sat down in the middle of the field alone and started to cry. I tried to choke back the tears when Titch came and knelt beside me, a hand on my shoulder. Tears dripped off a one-inch cut under his left eye. I couldn't move.

As the initial disappointment passed, I stood up and Titch and I walked over to the Lenana players and shook their hands. Coach Layton had gathered our players in a small circle. He motioned for us to join them.

"I'm proud of you boys," Coach Layton began. "You have nothing to hang your heads about. You fought hard to the last second. Let's thank the Lord for the game, even if we didn't win today."

I didn't close my eyes as he prayed. I looked into the gray, darkening sky. How could we have lost the Safari Cup?

As we headed to the bus, I shook Coach Layton's hand. "Sorry Coach, for letting you down."

To my surprise, Coach Layton smiled. "You didn't let me down. You played a great game. You have a great future in rugby if you can join a club in the States."

"I guess I let myself down," I said. "I wanted Livingstone to be the best rugby team in Kenya during my senior year. I've dreamed of it ever since I saw you and Ox play back when I was in second grade."

"Life is more than a game. We won the Safari Cup last year. This year it was Lenana's turn. For me the victory came when I saw you take the knee in your face and you didn't retaliate. You showed real character. And after the game you went over and congratulated the Lenana players. For some strange reason, we always laud good sportsmanship, but really don't have a chance to show it until we lose. I'm proud of you, Clay."

"So this is Clay," a deep voice rumbled. I looked up to see a rhino of a man with an outstretched hand. "I haven't seen you since you were a skinny little kid."

I gazed into the dark beefy face. "Ox?" I asked.

"You don't recognize me, your rugby hero?" Ox asked. He laughed. "I filled out a lot while I studied at university in the States. Too many fatty burgers and milkshakes."

"When did you come back to Kenya?" I asked.

"I've only been back about a month. I heard that Mike was coaching rugby at Livingstone so I decided to come see a game. Sorry you lost, but my goodness, you play a tough game of rugby, Clay. You should join my club in Nairobi after you graduate."

"Do you play for Harlequins?" I asked.

Ox shook his head. "A group of us has founded a new club. We call ourselves Udongo RFC."

"You call your club dirt?" I asked.

"Soil would be a better translation," Ox said, raising his head. "All of the clubs in Nairobi were started back in colonial days and we wanted a new start. A rugby club run by real sons of the soil."

"A blacks-only club in response to the whites-only clubs of days gone by?" Coach Layton asked.

"Race is not the issue," Ox said. "Being a son of the soil is. Clay here was born and raised in Africa. He's welcome. So are you, Mike, since you grew up in Africa. Anyway, it's just a statement. We wanted to make it clear that we Kenyans can run a good rugby club."

He turned to me. "You sure grew up, Clay. And you played a great game today."

"We won the Safari Cup last year," I said, desperate to defend myself. "I guess that's not too bad. We had it for a year."

"That reminds me, I have to turn the cup over to Lenana," Coach Layton said. He hurried away and came back with the cup. "Here Clay, you're the captain." He gave it to me and we carried it to the Lenana team. Before I handed it back, I looked at the metal shield attached to the base of the cup. Livingstone—1978 was engraved on it.

Maybe we didn't win it again this year, but at least we put our mark on the cup, I thought to myself. I presented the trophy to the Lenana captain. A shout went up as he hoisted the cup.

I turned and walked to the bus, a hollow feeling in my gut. I'd spent a lifetime at Livingstone in pursuit of that trophy. I'd won it briefly, but now it had been snatched away.

Leah had saved me a seat on the bus. I didn't feel like talking and sat glumly during the hour-long trip back to school. Leah tried to cuddle her head against my shoulder. I sat stiffly and brooded.

Our last week at school tasted like dust. I didn't do any assignments. Titch tried to get me to help him. "Why bother?" I told him. "We're graduating in a week. They can't do anything to prevent that. Why do school work?"

Titch frowned. "The world isn't coming to an end, Clay."

I shrugged. "Kind of feels like it is." I spit in the dirt as we walked to my dorm room for a mug of *chai*. "The world as we know it is about to explode," I commented.

It exploded the next Saturday at graduation. As I sat in the front seats of the school's auditorium listening to the speaker drone on and on about the end really being a beginning, I thought only of the end. The end of Livingstone. The end of years of close friendships. The choir sang a South African song called Ma-yi-bu-ye about Africa calling us back home. I didn't want to be called back to Africa. I wanted to stay.

Our senior class speaker read a poem she'd composed called uprooted and rootless. The words drilled into my heart. Planted in African soil. Watered and grown in the dust of Africa. Now being uprooted and cycloned around the world to a new land where we had to grow in a new place with no roots. I looked over at Leah. She dabbed at the corners of her eyes and her mascara streaked and black tears dripped down her cheeks. It tore a chunk out of my heart to see her crying. I choked back the sobs bubbling in my chest.

Soon we stood and filed forward to receive our high school diplomas. Shouts went up as I received mine. "Scrumboy! Scrumboy!" shouted some of the rugby guys. I smiled and waved my diploma before hurrying off the platform.

We marched out of the assembly hall where we'd sat through years of required chapels. I slapped the lintel as I walked out. I was free from the laws according to Livingstone. I always thought I'd be elated. Instead sadness settled like a cloak on my shoulders.

I found Leah and gave her a hug and a kiss. No one could give me couple's restriction now. Titch found us and our parents took pictures. We sniffed back the tears and smiled. The cafeteria had prepared our final meal, but I had no appetite. Soon parents and graduates were carrying dilapidated suitcases to waiting cars. A lifetime of Africa had been stuffed into suitcases not allowed to weigh more than forty-four pounds. Dust swirled as cars drove towards Nairobi. I kissed Leah goodbye and she climbed into the backseat of her car. She wound the window and waved slowly as the car disappeared around green tree where we'd climbed as titchies and caught chameleons. "See you at the airport tonight!" she called. I waved back.

"Are you going to bring your suitcase and trunk, Clay?" Dad asked.

I nodded and walked away, numbed by the blast swirling our class around the world. I met Titch sitting by the jacaranda tree in front of our dorm. He stood and reached for my hand and we walked to my dorm room, arm in arm.

"I've got your address," Titch said bravely.

I cleared my throat. "Yeah, I'm sure we'll see you in America. California isn't too far from Oklahoma."

"America is the land of cars," Titch said. "My first goal is to get a job and buy my own wheels. Then I'll come see you in California." He blinked his eyes fiercely. In a trembling voice, he whispered, "I'll miss you, Clay."

"I'll miss you too, Titch."

He helped me carry my suitcase and trunk to our Land Rover. "You'll have to keep my trunk here in Kenya, Dad," I said. "I can only take the suitcase on the airplane."

"Good-bye, Clay," Titch said with a final handshake.

We drove off down the same road that had brought me to Livingstone ten years before. I tried to memorize the deep green of the forest that surrounded the school. I caught a glimpse of something black and white moving through the trees. I wondered how long it would be before I saw colobus monkeys again.

I was booked to fly out by myself on KLM that evening. Dad had arranged for me to get a month of work at my uncle's apple orchard to earn spending money for my first semester in college. Leah was flying out at almost the same time with her parents on Air France. Other classmates would fly out that evening. Titch had opted for a week or two in Africa before heading for America.

My parents took me out to an Indian restaurant to celebrate my graduation. After feasting on spicy tandoori chicken, Mom took out a small box and handed it to me. "This is our graduation present to you," she said.

I opened it up and found a Swiss watch inside. I thanked them, inwardly wondering how often I'd use a fancy watch. Dad cleared his throat and said, "Clay, we're proud of you. You're now moving into a new stage of life. We'll be praying for you as you work your way through college. We'll come back to the States next year for the summer."

Funny, I didn't think I'd miss my parents as much as I'd miss my classmates from Livingstone. My parents had been a steady part of my life, but they seemed firmly rooted in the hazy background. I knew they loved me. We had great times during school vacations. But my friends at boarding school had been like brothers and sisters. When I'd been sick in the school infirmary, it had been my friends who visited. When I got lonely, it was my classmates who had stood shoulder to shoulder and shared chocolate chip cookies and Kool-Aid with me.

Leaving my parents to attend college didn't seem too much different than being away at boarding school. But the bonds of friendship after years of living together at Livingstone were strong. And my heart was bursting with sorrow because of the slashing of those bonds.

I thanked my parents for the watch and told them I'd be fine at college. We drove to the airport. A huddle of Livingstone students dominated the veranda in front of the check-in desks. I saw Leah. I went over to her and hugged her and gave her a kiss. Her father glared at me and started to say something. Leah's Mom touched his arm and pulled him away. "Let them say good-bye."

"We're all checked-in," Leah said. "It seems to unreal. So final. When will we ever see each other again?"

My throat tightened. "I don't know. You've got my address, Leah. Please write."

"I will," Leah promised. Her Dad tapped his foot and looked at his watch. His bald patch gleamed blue under the fluorescent light. Moths fluttered around the lamp and his head.

I kissed Leah again, not caring who saw. My Mom looked embarrassed.

"Let's go, Leah," her Dad called.

Leah held my hand and looked into my eyes. "Good-bye Clay."

"Yeah, I'll see you," I answered.

Her hand slipped off mine. Then she was gone. Others in our class waved and called, "Good-bye Leah!" There were hugs and tears. I got in line to check in my luggage and get my boarding pass. My parents stood back.

I reached the counter and handed my ticket to the agent. I looked back at the scrum of Livingstone students. I squinted and let my eyes fall on each one. I tried to drink in the smiles and tears on their cheeks. I memorized the emotions plastered on their faces. Who knew when we'd ever meet again? Titch wasn't there. I'd hoped he would come to the airport for the last good-bye.

I got my boarding pass and walked back to the group of students. "Well, I'm off to seek my fortune," I said, trying to keep it lighthearted.

"Just like Jack in the Beanstalk," laughed Kevin. His eyelids were red from crying. I shook his hand.

"Hang in there, bro," I said. "You've been a good roommate."

"Texas isn't too far from California," Kevin answered. "We'll get together."

It sounded so hollow. I nodded. I hugged a few more and then waved good-bye. I stopped by my parents who gave me their parting words of advice. "Uncle Mel will meet you at Sea-Tac Airport," Dad said.

"Be sure to write to us once a week," Mom added.

"I will, Mom," I promised. I hugged both of them. I walked away into the departure lounge. A tinny voice on the loudspeaker announced the boarding of Leah's Air France flight. I found a seat next to my gate and sat down and stretched my feet out in front of me. My canvas tennis shoes, stained red by the dirt and mud of Africa, suddenly looked cracked and old. I took a deep breath and tried to hold in the sob that threatened to break out. I squeezed my eyes shut to keep the tears from leaking. My world had been shattered. Could I ever put the shards back together again?

Book Four
California

July 1979

34

My uncle Mel, Mom's older brother, met me at the airport. "Welcome home to America, Clay," he said, hand outstretched. He hoisted my worn-out suitcase and hustled towards the parking lot. My stomach churned with hunger and fear. I had never felt at home in America. He dropped my suitcase in the back of his Chevy pickup. I stood by the left front door to get in. Uncle Mel looked at me strangely. "Planning on driving?" he asked.

"No," I answered, puzzled.

"Then get in on the other side of the car," he said, laughing. "In America we drive on the right side of the road and the steering wheel's on the left."

"Sorry," I mumbled as I hurried to the other side of the car and climbed in.

"We'll head straight to Yakima," Uncle Mel said, glancing at his silver watch, which seemed almost hidden under the thick hair of his forearms. "We can get a burger and milkshake at a drive-in at North Bend before heading over Snoqualmie Pass."

"Sounds good to me," I answered.

At North Bend I stretched and used the bathroom while we waited for the food. I saw myself in the shiny bathroom mirror. My wrinkled white t-shirt glared back at me. *I'll have to get some new clothes*, I thought, wondering what clothes were even in style.

I gulped down my burger and sucked on my straw to pull the thick chocolate shake down my throat. It tasted wonderful. I thought of Leah and my stomach lurched. Would I ever see her again?

"Are you okay?" Uncle Mel asked.

"Sure," I answered, trying to swallow my sorrow under more milkshake.

We finished and the pickup pulled back onto the highway. I must have nodded off to sleep, because the next thing I knew we were pulling up at Grandma's house. Grandpa had died the year before and Uncle Mel had taken over the ranch. Grandpa's dog Joe bounded off the porch. He greeted me by wagging his tail and licking my hand.

"Seems like he remembers me," I said.

"He does that to everyone," Grandma said gruffly, opening the screen door and coming out on the veranda. "How's my long-lost grandson?" She hugged me warmly. "Want some fried chicken?" she asked. Without waiting for an answer, she shuffled into the kitchen and within minutes had a meal on the table.

After supper I went to bed and crashed. I woke up in the middle of the night feeling strangely hungry. I snuck into the kitchen and found some leftover chicken. As I tore off chunks of meat with my teeth like a Dorobo hunter, I heard a swishing noise. I turned to see Grandma in her white nightgown.

She looked bewildered. "Are you okay?" she asked.

"Sorry, Grandma, I can't sleep. My days and nights are still kind of mixed up. My stomach thought it was time to eat."

She smiled. "I can't sleep either. It's been getting worse since Grandpa passed on." She sighed. "But I don't feel like eating. I have a hole in my life that no amount of eating will fill. I miss my husband and I wish my daughter was here."

She reached out and hugged me. I didn't know what to say, so I hugged her back. I could feel tears wetting my shoulder from her soft wrinkled cheeks. Finally she let me breathe again and stepped back and looked me up and down. "Eat as much as you like," she said in a soft, rattly kind of voice. Then she was gone.

I washed the chicken down with a glass of milk, then raided the freezer and found some chocolate chip ice cream. I wandered back to my bed, my stomach bloated. I kicked off the covers and lay on my back and thought of Kenya. And Leah. And Titch. And Livingstone. And my parents. I missed Africa badly. Tears trickled unbidden onto my pillow. I scolded myself for being so sentimental and turned over, but I still couldn't sleep. Our last-second loss to Lenana in the Safari Cup came back to me. I replayed each painful moment in my mind. I wanted the chance to go back and do it over again. I don't know when sleep came, but I woke up to find Uncle Mel jostling my shoulder. "Come on, Clay. I've got work for you in the orchard."

After two weeks I had earned almost two hundred dollars from propping apple branches and my uncle dropped me off at a shopping center to buy some clothes for college. The rows of shirts and racks of jeans and shorts bewildered me. I wandered up and down several aisles. The more I saw, the more confused I became. What did I need? What kind of clothes did people wear, anyway? Why did I need crisp new white underwear when I already owned several comfortable pairs, even if they were frayed and mud stained. I finally bought two pairs of tube socks and left the store, sweat beading up on my forehead despite the air conditioning.

When my uncle picked me up later in front of the store, he saw my small bag. "Is that all you bought?"

"I couldn't make up my mind," I mumbled. "Maybe I'll try again tomorrow."

He nodded and drove me to Grandma's. In my room I pulled on my new white tube socks. They almost glowed. I put my shoes on and noticed how dingy brown and stained they were compared to the new socks. I shook my head. "At least I'll buy a new pair of tennis shoes tomorrow," I vowed before heading out for an evening training run through the apple orchard.

A week later, Uncle Mel called me over after work. "There are a couple of students driving down to a college in Los Angeles. They've agreed to drop you off in Santa Barbara on the way. They leave tomorrow morning early." He gave me the rest of my wages—almost $100.

I packed what I owned into my old suitcase, stuffing my high school yearbook next to the dirty old rugby ball I'd rescued from the tunnel. As I placed the yearbook in the bottom of the suitcase, I flipped it open and read the page where Leah had said her good-byes in her gentle, lilting cursive. Her memories of times spent with me warmed my heart. I laughed when she mentioned being arrested for PDA (public display of affection) by our math teacher. Livingstone seemed so far away. I prayed I'd find a letter from Leah when I arrived at college.

The next morning my stomach tightened at the thought of heading into the unknown. Grandma gave me a tin of dried apricots and a hug. Uncle Mel shook my hand. My ride arrived, a brown AMC Rambler with two college-age guys with hair curling down to their shoulders. "Let's go!" they called. I threw my suitcase in the trunk and climbed into the backseat. I waved as we tore out of the gravel driveway.

We headed down the highway for Oregon. I touched my pocket to assure myself I had my money.

"I'm Aaron," the driver said. "This here's Mac. Short for MacKenzie." Mac smiled and nodded his head.

"I hear you're from Africa," Mac said. "What's it like over there?"

I hesitated. How could I explain a lifetime of Africa in a few sentences?

"Do you have snakes in Africa?" Aaron asked.

"Yeah, we have snakes. At our boarding school we killed a python, once. It had eaten some missionary's dog and was so stuffed it couldn't escape. We dissected it for biology class before taking the meat home and eating python steaks."

Mac's face turned baby powder white. "Python steaks?" he asked, his voice gurgling.

"Yeah, and then we boiled down the fat into a yellow oil. We used it for over two months to make popcorn in the dorm."

"You cooked popcorn in python fat? That's too wild," said Aaron. He clenched his jaw and hunched over the steering wheel.

I retreated into my thoughts. Longing for Africa pinched my heart. I closed my eyes and leaned into the backseat.

Soon I heard Mac whisper to Aaron, "Do you think he really cooked popcorn in python fat?"

"No way," Aaron answered. They drifted into a conversation about the latest movies and if some girl name Barbara still loved Mac.

I vowed not to embarrass myself by telling anyone too much about Africa. How could I expect them to understand?

35

We arrived in Santa Barbara late the next afternoon. We saw the sign for Rock-point set into a brick wall. We found the gym and I pulled my suitcase out of the trunk and went to look for someplace to check in. I found the school's basketball coach coming out of his office next to the gym.

"I'm Clay Andrews," I said, reaching out to shake his hand. "I'm here for soccer camp."

"Soccer doesn't start until tomorrow," the coach said. "Didn't the soccer coach send you a letter?"

"He did," I answered. "But this was the only day I could catch a ride from Washington."

The coach made a growling noise. "Well, we'll see if we can find a bed for you until the others come in tomorrow. You'll have to find your own food though. The cafeteria's not open yet."

He made some phone calls, then came out and motioned with his thumb for me to follow him. I ended up in a dorm room with two beds. "You can stay here until the soccer coach opens up someplace else tomorrow. The other players should be coming in after lunch."

"Thanks," I said as he clomped off.

The beds had no sheets or blankets. I knew Grandma had packed some sheets, but I felt too tired to make a bed. I pulled out my red-and-black checkered Maasai blanket and spread it on the bed, kicked off my shoes and lay down. I soon fell asleep, only to wake up several hours later in the dark. My stomach growled in hunger. I turned on a light and checked the watch my parents had given me as a graduation present. It was 9 p.m. Too late to hike the three miles back to the closest grocery store I'd seen. I remembered a vending machine in the lobby of the gym. I hiked over, rattling a few coins in my pocket, hoping I had enough to buy a snack.

The doors to the gym were locked and I could only drool at the candy bars in the vending machine behind the glass. I sighed and walked slowly back to the dorm room. I remembered the dried apricots Grandma had sent. I sat on the bed and ate dried apricots before lying down again.

I couldn't sleep. I felt lonelier than my first night at Livingstone. At least there I could hear the familiar sounds of cicadas buzzing in the trees and tree hyrax rasping their peculiar throaty rattle. I thought of Africa, rugby, Titch, and Leah. I thought of Mom and Dad in their rambling stone house on the Mau. My throat constricted and I had to choke back a sob. I needed to talk to someone.

I had a phone number for Leah's grandparents. Maybe she would be there. I stumbled to the payphone in the hallway and stared at it. Bobby Fuller had tried to teach me how to use one in junior high, but I was a bit rusty. I knew I had to pick up the receiver. I did and listened to a rattling buzz. *Not too different from a cicada,* I thought. I pulled out a dime and dropped it in the slot. I tried to dial the numbers from the small square-folded sheet of paper but I couldn't get the phone to ring through.

Maybe I need the operator to help me since it's long distance, I thought. I checked the phone for a crank handle to spin like we had on the dorm phone at Livingstone. Our dorm Dad would spin the handle and shout into the phone. "Hello, Naivasha! Hello, Naivasaha! Is this the operator in Naivasha?" If the operator answered, which wasn't often, he would put the call through. I held the phone in my hand, not sure how to contact the operator. I jammed the phone back into its slot.

"Forget it," I muttered and crawled back into bed.

I woke up in the morning with a gnawing hunger spreading across my stomach. I put a few dollars in my pocket and jogged the three miles down the hill to a supermarket where I bought a loaf of bread and some peanut butter. Back in my dorm room I opened the bread and took out several slices. I twisted off the peanut butter jar top before I realized I didn't have a knife. Shrugging, I dipped my finger into the jar and spread the peanut butter on the bread before licking my finger. I ate several peanut butter sandwiches before walking slowly around the new campus. I stood above the soccer field, where a man in white shorts and a t-shirt waved at me.

"Help me put these nets up," he called.

"Are you setting up for soccer camp?" I asked.

"Yeah, I'm Coach Davis."

"I'm Clay Andrews from Kenya," I said, reaching out to shake Coach Davis's hand. He dropped the net and shook my hand.

"When did you arrive?" he asked. "We didn't expect anyone until this afternoon."

He apologized profusely when he heard about my early arrival. "Once we get these nets up, I'll take you out for an early lunch," he said.

After lunch Coach Davis opened up the wing of another dorm where all the soccer players would be staying. I transferred my stuff and then went down to the gym to meet the other players who were starting to arrive.

Luis Gomez, a soccer wizard with Mexican roots who lived in Santa Barbara, came first. He started juggling a ball off his thighs and feet before flicking it to me. I failed to trap the ball and had to chase after it. Luis smirked. "Rookie," he mocked and wandered off to kick his ball against a large green wall.

Later Coach Davis introduced me to my roommate for soccer camp, a tall player with a dark brown afro. "I'm Ron," he said. "Ron Hartwig. Coach Davis says you're a missionary kid from Africa."

"That's right," I answered, ready to retreat from the subject.

"Well, I'm an MK, too," Ron said. "I grew up in the Philippines and went to a missionary boarding school in Manila. Sometimes I don't think I'm much of an American. Know what I mean?"

The smile that filled my face started deep in my heart. "I do know what you mean. I'm not sure I belong here. I keep wishing I was back in Kenya."

"That's how I felt all last year about the Philippines," Ron said. "Playing soccer was my salvation. You'll learn to adjust. What position do you play?"

I almost said eighth man, my position in rugby, but I caught myself. "Fullback," I answered.

"Well, I'm a halfback, so we'll be working together. Let's go drop my stuff off at the room then go to the welcome barbecue."

The next morning we began grueling two-a-day workouts. We ran sprints, did passing and shooting drills, ran more sprints, listened to chalk talks, ran hill climbs, then ran some more. By lunchtime my body screamed for a rest. In the dining hall my first tray had eight glasses of ice water and juice. I downed most of them before getting any food.

Ron smiled. "I lose up to eight pounds a day during these hot summer workouts," he said. "So keep drinking liquids."

During our lunch break, Ron took me to the campus post office. I received my post box number and the combination code. I peered into the small window of my post box and saw several letters. In my haste I messed up the combination twice before I got the door to slide open. I found three letters with Leah's name on the return address. I drew the letters to my nose and smelled a faint flowery scent.

Ron snuck up behind me. I jerked the letters away from my face. He laughed. "Letters from your girlfriend?" he asked.

I nodded.

"My high school girl friend ended up across the States in Virginia. We wrote letters and made long distance calls for about two months. Then she wrote and quoted a song. "If you can't be with the one you love, love the one you're with." It was her way of telling me she'd found someone closer. Long distance relationships are hard. So, what's your girl's name?"

"Leah, and she's in Wheaton," I answered. "We kind of broke up when we left Africa. Gave each other permission to see others. But since I've been back, I've missed her more than I thought possible."

"Go read your letters," Ron said. "I'll see you back at the soccer field."

I found a tree and sat down on the grass in the shade. I arranged the letters by postmarks and started reading them in order. Leah filled her letters with details of her trip through Europe and visiting relatives in the Midwest. She signed the first letter, "I still love you and miss you lots." The second letter ended with, "I really miss you." The third letter chided me for not writing to her. "Where are you?" she wrote. "I'm not sure I can live without you."

I reread the letters, and remembered our last few months in Kenya. Why had we decided to study at different schools? Was it too late to transfer? I took a deep breath and stood up. Gripping the letters in my hand I hurried down to the soccer field.

I had the beginning of a blister on my left heel. I asked the trainer if he had any talcum powder.

"Why?" he asked.

"For a blister. I need to slit it open and fill up the blister pouch with talcum powder for lubrication."

The trainer shook his head and pulled out a big plastic jar. "Never heard of using talcum powder. We treat blisters with bag balm," he said. The jar had a drawing of a cow's teat. "This stuff is for cow udders, but it's great on blisters." He scooped out a dollop of the yellowish ointment about as thick as Vaseline. "Put your foot up here." He rubbed the bag balm over my heel. "That should take care of it," he said with a smile.

"Don't waste your time on rookies," a voice growled. I pulled my foot off the bench and jumped back. A bearded player scowled at me. "Seniors go first," he said in a menacing tone. "Don't forget that, rookie."

Back at the locker, Ron nudged me. "Don't let Killer bother you. He's like that with everyone. But coach keeps him around because he plays a rugged defense. He's probably worried that a talented rookie like you might knock him out of the starting lineup."

"His name is really Killer?" I asked.

"It's Kelly, but everyone calls him Killer because of his style of play. Just try not be get partnered against him in the one-on-one dribbling drills or he'll kick your shins into pulp."

I stayed out of Killer's way for the afternoon practice. By the time Coach Davis whistled a halt at about 5 p.m. my legs quivered with fatigue. No one else had fared much better. We staggered to the locker room for a shower. I sat on the bench in front of my locker, a white towel around my neck, trying to get the sweat to stop dripping.

Suddenly I felt a fiery sting on my left shoulder. I turned to see Killer, a crooked smile on his face and a wet towel in his hand. Before I could respond he whipped the towel at me again, this time leaving a red mark on my left rib cage.

"Leave him alone, Killer," Ron said leaping to my defense.

"Does the rookie need protection?" Killer said. He pointed a finger at me. "Listen to me, rookie. You want a place on this team? Then learn to be tough. But don't expect to replace me." He turned and stalked into the shower stalls.

"Why's he so upset with me?" I asked Ron.

Ron shrugged before leaning over and whispering. "We'll talk about it later. Just stay out of his way."

"I thought I did," I answered.

After showering, I asked Ron. "Can you help me make a phone call this evening?"

"Sure," he answered. "Do you need someone to hold your hand when you call your girl?"

"Actually, I couldn't figure out how to use a payphone my first night here."

Ron laughed before confiding, "I couldn't get up the courage to use a phone for the first two months I was in the States. I'll help you make your call. Make sure you have lots of coins."

At the cafeteria I changed almost ten dollars into quarters. Back at the dorm Ron picked up the phone and dropped a ton of coins into the slot and then dialed the numbers. "It's ringing," he said, handing me the phone.

"Hello?" a man's voice questioned.

"Uh, yes, hello to you, too," I stammered.

"Can I help you?" the voice went on, puzzled.

"Sorry, I meant to call Leah. Maybe I have the wrong number." I started to hang up.

"Leah's here. Just wait a second," the man's voice said.

Soon I heard Leah's voice. "Who's this?"

"Leah!" I said with relief. "This is Clay."

"Clay! How are you? You haven't answered any of my letters," Leah began.

"I just got to college and found your letters today." I paused. "I miss you, Leah."

Leah chatted effortlessly telling me about their trip through Europe. I tried to hold every word in my head. The telephone interrupted saying I had to put in more money. I squeezed a few more quarters into the slot.

"I'm sorry, I'm using up all your money," Leah apologized. "Writing letters is a lot cheaper."

"It's okay," I replied. "Keep talking until the money runs out. I just need to hear your voice. You sound so far away."

Leah laughed, melting my heart. But she talked on until the phone clunked off. I stood holding the phone to my ear, trying to absorb my latest contact with Leah.

"Hang up, rookie!" a voice commanded. "I need to make a call."

36

I looked up to see Killer in the hallway. "It's all yours," I said quickly, putting the phone back on the hook. He glared at me as I hurried back to our room.

"You don't look good," Ron said, concerned. "Trouble with your girlfriend?"

"Leah's fine," I answered. "It was sweet to hear her voice." I paused. "It's that Killer guy. He chased me off the phone. What's his problem? I can't think what I've done to bother him so much."

"Everything bothers Killer," Ron said. "We went to the same school in the Philippines."

"Killer's an MK?"

Ron nodded. "He didn't have a good experience in the dorm and he's angry at his parents, at God, at just about everybody. He feels his parents abandoned him and says he doesn't like being used as a pawn in God's big game of bringing salvation to the lost. Anyway, when he sees other MKs who are well adjusted, it makes him boil. So I think he tries to twist us and make us just as sour as he is. Last year I was the main object of his wrath." Ron smiled. "I'm glad you're here this year. Now Killer has someone new to pick on."

I looked at him with a frown.

"Just kidding," Ron said. "Anyway, that's what's up with Killer."

I shook my head. "I never would have guessed Killer was a missionary kid."

"Not everyone appreciates growing up in a different culture," Ron answered. "Especially when it means long times away from home. I sometimes resented it when my parents dropped me off at school. But I enjoyed my friends. I loved sports at school. I loved vacations when my parents would rent a cottage on the beach and I'd go snorkeling and look for shells."

"Do you collect shells?" I asked. "I've got a collection from the coast of Kenya."

"I'd love to see them," Ron said. "I love sea shells."

I rummaged through my suitcase and pulled out a small box. "I left most of my big shells in Africa with my parents. But I brought some of my special shells to remind me of home."

I opened the box and spread the shells on the desk. I picked up a mole cowrie with its dark chocolate base and caramel and brown stripes. "I found this during senior safari in a gap between two reefs," I said.

"I've got mole cowries from the Philippines," Ron said. "Mine aren't quite as big as yours. What's senior safari?"

I looked out the window where I could see a full moon rising. "Our school, Livingstone Academy, had a tradition. The senior class raised money selling food like hamburgers and hot dogs at sports events. Then for five days near the end of our senior year, we booked a hotel on the coast. It took a day to travel there by bus. But for five glorious days we forgot about school, we played in the sun, we surfed, we snorkeled ..." I paused before going on softly. "I went on long moon-lit walks on the beach with Leah. It was heaven. After senior safari, school seemed dull and lifeless. Most of us couldn't wait for the final month of school to finish so we could leave. But here I am, and all I can think of is wanting to be back at Livingstone."

"I know I'm not Leah, but let's go for a walk on the beach," Ron suggested. He grabbed the keys to his Mustang and we drove down to east beach and walked in the moonlight with the sand rasping against our feet.

"Maybe it's because I'm a beach bum from the Philippines," said Ron, "but whenever I feel homesick, I come down here and walk in the sand and smell the salty air. Somehow it makes me feel better."

After an hour of roaming the beach, we headed back to the car.

"Thanks," I said.

The next day at soccer practice, coach sent all the defensive players to one side to work on ball-stealing techniques. He showed us how to keep the offensive players away from the goal by our body position. He warned us not to dive in. He scoffed at slide tackles, which he said only served to take us out of the play. "Stay goal side and cover him like a wet towel." I thought of Killer and his towel snaps in the gym. "When he makes his move, then step in and steal the ball," Coach Davis droned on.

"Now here's the drill." We went into a one-on-one drill, one player with the ball trying to advance around the other. I was in the dribbling line first and the defensive player who came out to challenge me was Killer. I faked left and tried to slip around Killer to the right. Killer booted me hard and stole the ball. I felt a crushing pain in my shin and I crumpled to one knee. Killer didn't show any pity. "Get tough, rookie," he growled. I limped to the back of the line. I could see a red welt growing above my socks, which had sagged down to my ankles.

Numbers worked out that I faced Killer again. I crouched in a good defensive position, eye fixed on the ball. Killer didn't fake at all. He charged right into me, driving his shoulder into my chest. I fell on my can. "Not much chance of you taking my place," Killer taunted.

I ground my teeth together and tried to control my anger. When I faced Killer again, I tried a wide loop around him. It almost worked until Killer grabbed my shirt and reeled me in. Another sharp kick to the same shin brought tears to my eyes. But I refused to show Killer how much it hurt and I ran to the end of the line.

By the end of the drill, my legs were battered and aching.

After practice, I limped outside with Ron, heading for the dining hall. "Your shins look nasty," Ron commented.

"Killer hammered me," I said.

A loud sputtering noise erupted in the parking lot. I turned to see Killer astride an old motorcycle. His forearms flexed as he revved the bike and tore off down the road. "That's funny. Killer doesn't have any rearview mirrors on his bike," I noted.

"Sounds like Killer," Ron replied. "He doesn't want to waste any time looking back."

I survived soccer camp and coach kept me on the team. I seemed buried in the reserves, but I still felt a thrill at our first game, putting on our all-white uniforms, crisp and new. I don't think I'd ever had a new uniform at Livingstone. Everything was mud-stained and used season after season. Even though I only got to play the last five minutes of that first game after we had a 4-0 lead, I made the most of the time. I stole the ball twice, blocked a close range shot and on the subsequent corner kick I leaped high and headed the ball away. Not much, but not bad for a rookie.

After the game, several freshman girls stood giggling and talking by the sidelines. As Ron and I walked towards the locker room, a girl with long blonde hair, who I'd noticed in my Intro to Philosophy class, leaned forward and said, "Good game, Clay."

"Thanks," I answered. "But I really didn't play very much. You should congratulate Ron, here. He played all game."

"Or a real player like me," Killer said coming up behind me. He gave a big smile to the girls. "Don't waste your time on a rookie." He stopped for a moment. "There's a party tonight at Alfredo's. Do you girls want to come? It's for the soccer players and their invited guests. Consider this an official invitation."

"We'd love to come," the blonde girl consented for all of them. "We'll see you there."

Killer walked off, a knowing smile on his face.

37

"Are you going to be there, Clay?" the blonde girl asked.

"Maybe," I answered. "Actually, it's the first I heard of the party. Does coach always have a party when we win?"

Ron glanced away. He whispered. "Coach doesn't know about this party. But if you want to go, I'll make sure you get there."

I guess I was a bit innocent. Parties at Livingstone involved watching a movie and having Cokes and candy.

Alfredo's parents had a huge house and I could smell meat cooking on the barbecue in the backyard. Killer, in a mellow mood, waved his silver Coors can at us. "Welcome to the party boys," then turned to flirt with some girls.

I grabbed Ron's shoulder. "What about coach's training rules that we don't drink beer during soccer season."

Ron looked away. "You're the one who wanted to attend this soccer party," he said. "I usually avoid them. Yes, coach has his rules, but a lot of the guys like to booze after a game, especially if we win." He sidled away, looking uneasy.

Someone turned on a sound system and the bass thumped loudly in my ears. Some couples started to dance on the paved veranda. A hand tapped my arm. I turned to see the blonde-haired girl. She wore a short white skirt and sandals and a blue sleeveless blouse. Her California-tan arms and legs looked almost orange in the artificial lights. "I see you made it," she began.

I nodded.

"My name's Sierra," she went on. "My parents named me for the Sierra Nevada Mountains here in California. They love to backpack in the mountains every summer."

"Well, I'm Clay," I introduced myself.

"I know who you are, Clay," Sierra said with a sly smile.

My heart thudded. Did this mean she'd been watching me? Reading my name on my paper over my shoulder in our philosophy class?

"I also hear you're from Africa," Sierra went on. "That sounds so exotic to me. What's it like to live in Africa?"

Did she really want to know? So many people didn't even care. I decided to risk it and began telling her about our old stone house in the Mau, the car-swallowing mud holes, life at Livingstone, snorkeling on the Kenya coast, rugby. "Sorry for rambling on," I said.

Sierra looked serious. "You seemed to be in a different world."

I smiled. "I guess I was back in Africa. Want some meat?" I plucked a chicken breast off the barbecue.

Sierra raised her eyebrows. "No thanks," she said. "I'm a vegetarian. Something I inherited from my parents, I guess."

"I've never met a vegetarian before," I said. "You really don't eat any meat?"

"I never have," Sierra replied. "Having grown up without meat, I have no desire to try it."

"Boy, wouldn't the Dorobo be surprised to hear there are people in the world who have never eaten meat. Meat is the main food in the Dorobo diet. Meat and honey."

"I love honey," Sierra said. "Honey is the perfect food. Anyway, enough about food. Do you want to dance?"

I choked down the piece of meat in my mouth. "I don't think so," I answered. "I've never danced before."

"Now it's my turn to be surprised. Don't Africans dance? I've heard about the drumming and the rhythm in African dances. And you don't know how to dance?"

I laughed. "I'm a white African and the school I attended frowned on dancing. So I've never learned. I watched a disco one time when I stayed in a hotel on the Kenya coast. Some kids in our class went out and tried dancing. They looked hilarious. And then they got busted by some staff members for breaking the school rules."

Sierra looked incredulous. "Kids in your school got in trouble for dancing? What did you do for parties?"

I shrugged. Sierra tugged at my arm. "Come on, I'll teach you. It's not too hard. These days, you just go out and move to the music."

I wolfed down the rest of my chicken breast and allowed Sierra to drag me to the dance floor. *This is foolish*, I thought, trying to move my arms and shake my body the way Sierra did.

She kept smiling at me and gyrated, as if in a trance, to the beat of the music. "Play that funky music, white boy," the song blasted. I'd never heard the tune before.

The song ended and Sierra held my hand. "You did great for the first time."

I tried to move away from the dance floor. Once was enough. Then a slow song started. "Come, Clay," Sierra pleaded. "Let me show you how to slow dance."

She pulled her body close to mine and clasped her hands around my back. She felt soft and nice. "Put your hands on my hips," Sierra whispered. "I'll guide you." We glided slowly in time with the music. I wondered what Leah would think of me dancing with a California girl.

When the dance was over, I said, "That's all the dancing I can take for one evening."

Sierra started to protest, but walked off to the side, holding my arm. We sat on some chairs away from the blast waves of the music. Ron came by and joined us. Other groups of soccer players stood around laughing and drinking. Part of me thrilled at my freedom to be at a drinking party. Another part of me felt guilty seeing so many guys breaking coach's training rules.

"Do you want a drink?" Sierra asked.

I noticed Ron only had a Coke. "Just a can of soda," I answered.

As she walked away, Ron said, "I'm going to leave soon if you want a ride. I don't really like these parties."

"I'll come with you," I said. "I don't like the drinking. Probably a hangover from so many years at a strict Christian school that kicked you out if you even sniffed alcohol."

Ron laughed. "The beer is the least of it. Do you smell the smoke coming from over there?"

I sniffed and detected a sweetish aroma. "What about it?" I asked.

"It's marijuana," Ron said. "The soccer players aren't smoking it, but I sure don't want to be around when people start smoking pot."

"You mean we could all get arrested?" I stood up, alarmed.

"I doubt anyone will bust this party. But I'd rather not stay much longer."

Sierra arrived with two cans of Coke. I popped the tab and told Sierra that Ron and I would be leaving soon.

"But the party's just started," she pleaded. "Don't you want to dance some more?"

"Maybe another night," I said.

Sierra pouted, then went off to find someone to dance with her.

"Let's go," Ron said.

We picked our way through the crowd that seemed to be getting bigger and louder.

Ron had the top down on his Mustang and as we drove away, the wind seemed to blow away the foul smoke of the party.

"Well, now you've been to a party," Ron pointed out.

"Funny," I answered. "My last years at Livingstone we dreamed of getting away from the rules so we could go to parties like that. In fact, we did sneak out once. But now it all seems a bit pointless."

On Monday at soccer practice, Coach Davis pulled me aside. "You're going to have to work hard Clay. You'll be starting at left fullback in Wednesday's game against Cal State Fullerton and you've still got a lot to learn."

I wrinkled my brow in a puzzled frown. "But Killer plays left fullback ..." I began.

"Not anymore," Coach Davis said grimly.

I began to sweat, wondering if Killer had been suspended from the team for drinking. What if Coach Davis knew I'd been at the party, too!

"Killer broke his leg over the weekend," Coach Davis explained.

"How?" I began. He'd been fine at the dance party. A bit drunk perhaps, but ...

"He pulled in front of some car with that crazy motorcycle of his," Coach Davis went on. "He said he never knew the car was behind him. Anyway, the car hit him and flipped his bike and he has a compound fracture of his left tibia. He'll heal, but not before the end of the season. So get to work, Clay. You've got some good raw talent, but you've got to learn how to remain in a good diagonal position with the rest of the defense."

38

Ron and I visited Killer in the hospital. He acted gruff. "Guess you got your way, Rookie, taking my place on the team," he began.

"You're better and tougher than I'll ever be, Killer," I said. "I didn't take your place. You just broke your leg and can't play for awhile."

Killer grunted and we stood silently. Finally Killer spoke again. "I'm surprised you two visited me here," Killer said. "I've got lots of friends, but none of them have bothered to come see me. And you're the two guys I've kicked all over the soccer field."

"No one likes having their shins kicked to a pulp, Killer, but that doesn't mean we wouldn't come and see how you're doing," Ron answered. "We're from the same school, remember."

"I'm trying to forget, Ron. I don't want to think about the Philippines anymore," Killer said. "I'm done with that. I'm an American now." He paused. "I think every missionary kid should feel like I do. What I can't figure out is how you two are so happy?"

"I loved the Philippines," Ron said, "and I'd love to go back. But I've learned to get along here as well."

"And I'm actually miserable here in the States," I told Killer. "I just cover up well. Inside all I want to do is go back to Africa. I miss all my friends, and I don't know how to fit into this place. Sometimes I think I'm riding a motorcycle backwards."

"Maybe I wouldn't have had my accident if I had ridden my bike backwards," Killer muttered. He looked up. "Anyway, thanks you guys for the visit." He looked out the window and seemed to be brooding. Ron motioned to me with his head to leave and I followed him out of the room.

At my Intro to Philosophy class the next day our teacher, a graying professor with frown lines furrowed in his forehead, asked, "How many of you have heard of Unamuno?"

No one ventured an answer. The professor took off his glasses and leaned back against his desk. "Not one of you has heard of Miguel de Unamuno, one of the most influential Spanish thinkers of the last hundred years? I must say, you disappoint me."

He pointed at Sierra. "Tell me, young lady, what's your name?"

"Sierra," she replied.

"Is your name Spanish?"

"Yes, it means mountain."

"A beautiful young lady with a Spanish name, but you've never heard of Miguel de Unamuno? Unamuno started out as a rector in the Roman Catholic church before his questioning mind led him to write. He's written numerous essays, novels and poetry. Unamuno became part of the famous '98 Generation in Spain. 1898 that is. He was willing to question his—and Spain's—blind acceptance of the Catholic faith. His masterpiece, *San Manuel Bueno, Martir* centers around Manuel the priest who leads others to trust in God, even when he has lost his own faith."

The professor put his thick glasses back on and strode down the aisle between the chairs. Stopping in front of me he stared down. His eyes, swollen and distorted behind the heavy lenses, reminded me of the eyeballs of a dead zebra.

"Mr. Andrews, is it?" he asked.

"Yes, sir," I answered.

"Do you have faith in God?"

"Yes, I believe in God," I shot back.

He rubbed his chin. Dandruff drifted down from his wispy beard. "Do you really? Is it your faith? Or is it a blind faith you received from your parents? Have you ever questioned whether God really existed? How do you know there's a heaven or even a hell?"

Without waiting for me to reply, the professor turned and spoke to the class. "That is the nature of Unamuno's quest. I believe Manuel the priest in *San Manuel Bueno, Martir*, mirrors the author's real-life spiritual journey. Saint Manuel is a priest who, after an agonizing period of questioning, no longer believes in an afterlife. Yet he goes on with his work as a priest. He leads others into faith and they join the church. Ironically, he gives them faith in something he no longer believes in."

He cleared his throat and scuffled to his desk. Shuffling some papers he lifted a stack of handouts. He motioned for someone in the front row to help him pass out the papers. "This handout gives a summary of Unamuno's novel *San Martin Bueno, Martir* and also outlines some of Unamuno's questions. I want you to read them and think. I want you to ask yourself the same questions Unamuno asked. I want you to take a critical look at your own faith. Why do you believe? Why are you at a Christian college? Are you here because your parents sent you? Or because you really have a personal faith in God? Is your faith blind? Before next Friday I want you to write a three-page essay answering one or more of Unamuno's questions."

My mind focused on the professor's last question. Was my faith blind? Did I really believe in God? The professor's questions knocked the center out of my comfortable but unquestioned faith. I didn't listen to anything else that class period. Instead, I trembled as I looked into my heart. I had never questioned before, but now I wondered if I really knew God personally. I'd heard about him all my life. But I'd kind of basked in my parents' faith. What would I discover if I truly questioned what I believed? Was there really a God? There had to be. But what if there wasn't? Had my parents wasted their lives? Was Christianity *bure* or worthless as we said in Kenya?

That evening during a tough practice Coach Davis pointed out where my poor positioning might lose us the game. "Cal State Fullerton has a striker who can pound the ball," Coach pointed out. "You can't give him that much space. They might not be able to shoot the ball well in Kenya, but in this league you have to smother the strikers or they'll score."

Tired and bruised in spirit as well as body, I lay on my bed that night and pulled out the handout on Unamuno and started reading. Manuel, the Catholic priest, lived in Spain, a society that was forced to believe the church doctrines without questioning. I pondered how I'd been brought up. My parents had a firm faith. I accepted it. I never questioned. Our teachers at Livingstone had pushed us into a routine of devotions, chapel talks, Bible classes and Sunday services. We knew the truth. Why test it? I loved the Bible stories, but I'd lived my life for myself. I didn't feel that intimate closeness to God my parents talked about. And I realized our life at Livingstone had been much like the Spanish society Unamuno wrote about. The Catholic church knew what was best for the Spaniards and the church expected its members to follow its instructions. Livingstone knew how to order our Christian lives. And for the most part it worked. Titch and some of the others seemed to have a rich spiritual life. But maybe I had only been acting out a faith that really wasn't mine.

I rubbed my aching eyes and read on. Manuel's biggest question was whether there was a heaven or a hell. All the rules, the deprivations to please God here on earth made sense if there was a heaven and a hell. But what if there wasn't? Manuel, a priest who'd studied at seminary, felt he couldn't prove an afterlife so maybe there was none. And if there was no paradise or place of eternal punishment, he was left with now—this life on earth. He decided to make the best of life now while he had it. Manuel's life became a constant striving to work and do things on earth because he decided nothing existed after this life. Manuel tried to make this earth his paradise, his eternity.

I stopped reading, intrigued, but afraid to probe too deeply into my own beliefs. The next day in class, the professor opened the discussion by asking, "So, is there an afterlife?" Several students argued that of course there was. The professor listened politely, then asked. "Can you prove it?"

"Well, the Bible says there will be an eternity—paradise for those who believe in Jesus and punishment in hell for those who don't believe," said a girl in the front row.

"Good, very good," said the professor. "But can you prove those words? Have you experienced this eternal state?"

"No," the girl admitted, "but that's where faith comes in."

"A blind faith?" the professor questioned.

"I wouldn't call it blind faith. Faith is our belief in something unseen. Believing in a promise not yet fulfilled. My faith is based on what I've read in the Bible. But it's also based on what I've seen God doing in my life."

"But you're basing your faith on the here and now. Perhaps you agree with Manuel that you can only really know what you can experience?"

"I don't think so," the girl said in a halting voice. She seemed to lose confidence.

"Keep thinking, keep questioning. Get personal with this essay. Wrestle with Unamuno's questions. It will have a profound effect on your lives. I want God to become real in your lives. Or if there is no God, then live authentically based on what you believe or don't believe. Don't base your lives on what others tell you."

He pulled out a transparency sheet and laid it on top of the overhead projector before switching it on. The lamp blinded the professor for a few seconds. He fumbled with the sprocket-shaped handle and focused the projector. "Here's another quote from Unamuno," he said. "Copy it down and don't be afraid to question. Dig until you find the truth."

I flipped open a blank page in my notebook and began writing down the quote.

"Those who believe they believe in God, but without passion in the heart, without anguish of mind, without uncertainty, without doubt, and even at times without despair, believe only in the idea of God, and not in God himself."—Miguel de Unamuno.

The girl in the front row twiddled her blue ballpoint pen between her second and third finger. "So Unamuno would say that without seriously working through our doubts about God, we'll only have a second rate belief in God?"

"Excellent thought," the professor said. "Now keep grappling with Unamuno's questions for your essay."

That evening I waded into my essay. "I have to be ready to doubt my faith before I can cross the bridge into a deeper experience of God," I wrote as my theme sentence. In my paper I discussed Manuel's struggle to prove the existence of heaven or hell. "I can't prove heaven exists either, but I'm not ready to throw out all my childhood beliefs yet," I concluded. "I need to keep searching for the truth. As I explore, I must use my time on earth to make the world a better place in case there isn't an afterlife."

The professor liked my paper. "Keep seeking," he wrote next to the A grade he gave me.

My questioning mode didn't develop a deeper faith. Instead I drifted into apathy. If I wasn't sure God and heaven were real, why bother with church? I began sleeping in on Sundays. I wrote to Leah, "I've changed denominations and now I'm a Bedside Baptist."

Leah wasn't impressed. "Don't forsake meeting together with other believers," she wrote back on pink stationery doused in flowery perfume.

I wrinkled up her letter and tossed it away. *What does Leah know?* I thought to myself. *I'll live for now and make a difference and help people, just like Manuel the priest.* The Christian rules I'd followed at Livingstone—being in church on Sundays, reading my Bible and praying—began to seem like legalistic duties. So I stopped doing them. Despite Leah's warning, my life didn't fall apart. I enjoyed the extra hours of sleep on Sundays.

One Sunday morning I went to breakfast at almost 10 a.m. I poured several glasses of orange juice and filled a bowl with Frosted Flakes, a cereal I'd fallen in love with. It sure beat gray oatmeal with toenails.

As I sat at a table myself, two shaggy haired students hurried into the dining hall. They stopped by a table next to mine and grabbed a tired looking senior. "Woody, you're late. We've got a game in Riverside this afternoon."

Woody shook his head. "Sorry guys. I partied late last night. No way I can play a rugby game today."

Rugby! Who played rugby around here? I thought. I turned and asked, "Do you guys really have a rugby game today?"

"We're supposed to, but we may not be able to raise a team," said one of the rugby players. "Guys like Woody here are copping out on us."

"I play rugby," I said. "I'd love to play."

The two guys looked at me. "You know how to play?"

I nodded. "I've been playing rugby since I was in fourth grade," I said.

They left Woody's table and sat down next to me. "I'm Dan Fuller," the one with black hair and a full beard said. "But everyone calls me Mad Dog. And this is my younger brother Dave. We've played rugby since we came here to college. We have a team called the Grunions."

"Grunions?" I asked.

"I know," Mad Dog said. "Everyone wonders what a Grunion is. It's a kind of fish that lives in the ocean around here. Anyway, if you're really up for a game, we're leaving in an hour from the parking lot."

"I'll be there," I promised.

39

I wolfed the rest of my breakfast and ran back to my dorm. I unzipped a blue sports bag that had orange mud-stains from the many times I'd stuffed filthy boots into it. Inside I found my black rugby shorts with pockets. They were frayed at the hems. A pair of red and white hooped rugby socks nestled next to my well-worn boots. I also found my old Livingstone rugby shirt and a half-empty tube of deep heat muscle rub. I unscrewed the cap and sniffed. My nose bristled at the harsh smell and I closed my eyes and saw myself back in my dorm room at Livingstone suiting up for a rugby game. I took a deep breath, hoisted my bag and headed for the parking lot.

I met Mad Dog and the others. "We're only one player short," Mad Dog said, a smile revealing a missing front tooth. "But we'll be fine. We'll play without a blindside flanker."

I piled into the backseat of Mad Dog's convertible Volkswagen beetle. He cranked up a Chicago cassette tape and we roared off. We headed down Highway 101 and soon we could see the Pacific Ocean on our right. Black dots in the ocean turned out to be surfers riding breakers near Ventura.

"Where are we going?" I asked.

"Riverside," answered Mad Dog.

"Where's Riverside?"

"It's part of greater L.A. We're playing against U.C. Riverside at a park. Last year we hammered them, but I hear they've really improved."

I nodded and watched in amazement as herds of cars sped past us like wildebeest in their annual migration from the Serengeti to the Mara. I thought of trips I'd made with my Dad in Kenya where we didn't see another car for a whole day.

At Riverside, we parked and changed into our rugby kit behind the cars. The car with the shirts hadn't arrived yet, so I pulled on my Livingstone rugby jersey. The white shirt with the red hoop across the chest looked more tan than white. As I warmed up, I saw a bald man in a yellow shirt with a whistle wrapped around his wrist coming towards me. He looked familiar.

He came right up and looked at the Livingstone badge on the left corner of my jersey. "I thought that looked like a shirt from Livingstone Academy," the man said.

"Did you go to school there?"

"I did," I answered. "I just graduated last year. How do you know about Livingstone Academy?" I stared at him, wondering.

"I used to teach there," the man said. "In fact, I started the rugby program at the school."

"Mr. Prinsloo!" I reached out and hugged him. "I thought you looked familiar! You were my first coach on titchie colts at Livingstone. You taught me how to play second row forward."

Mr. Prinsloo smiled. "You can call me Frank. Now which one of my many rugby titchies were you?"

"I'm Clay. Clay Andrews. I fell in love with rugby when Ox kind of adopted me and helped me through my second grade year at the school."

Frank nodded. "Ox captained my best team ever. So how'd you do against the other schools this year? Did you win the Safari Cup?"

I looked down at my boots. "Last minute loss against Lenana in the final this year. But we won the Safari Cup last year. First time since Ox's team. Mike Layton was my coach."

"Yeah, I'd heard Mike went back to teach at Livingstone." He paused. "This is quite amazing to run into you here, Clay."

"Yeah. What are you doing in America? I'd heard you went back to South Africa."

"We did," Frank answered. "My Dad was quite ill. But he died after one year. And I just couldn't stand to watch the injustice of the apartheid government. I tried getting involved in one of the political parties that was pushing for change. But then I got threatening letters from the police. I decided we couldn't really live there any longer. So we came to California."

"Do you still coach?" I asked.

"I'm a referee these days," Frank said. "Which reminds me, I'd better get this game started."

I ran over to where the other Grunions were pulling on the green and blue rugby shirts that had just arrived.

"Where do you normally play, Clay?" Mad Dog asked. "Not that we'll put you there. We fill gaps where needed." Everyone laughed.

"I'm normally eighth man or anywhere else in the backrow."

Mad Dog nodded. "Well, you'll play second row today instead."

"That's where I first played in fourth grade," I said, happy to be playing with an oval ball for a change.

Some of the others looked puzzled. "You've played rugby since fourth grade?" asked a tubby player whose shirt didn't reach his elastic gym shorts. If he played prop, I knew I'd have a hard time gripping his shorts and I sure couldn't reach his shirt. I made a mental note to choose to bind on the other side of the scrum.

"I grew up in Africa and we started rugby in fourth grade," I explained. We ran through a few stretches, then lined up to practice lineouts. The scrum-half said, "I'll give the signals. I'll say all kinds of crazy things, but they won't mean anything. Watch my hands. If my hands are on my knees, throw it to the first jumper. I think that will be you, Clay." I nodded. He went on. "When my hands are on my hips, that means the throw goes to the second jumper. And when my hands are dangling by my side, throw the ball long to the last man in the line-out."

Our hooker gathered the ball and walked to the sideline. We lined up starting on the five-yard line. The scrum-half had his hands on his knees. I crouched and as the hooker moved his arm back to throw, I leaped. The throw barely reached my chest.

"I can jump higher than that," I said.

The hooker nodded and threw a couple more until he got the range. We didn't even have time to organize the scrum before Frank Prinsloo shrilled his whistle and called for the captains. Mad Dog trotted out to the center of the field for the coin toss.

We received the opening kick off and the ball floated end over end right at me. I called for it and then found that American rugby differed greatly from the well-drilled game I'd played at Livingstone. I caught the ball and started churning forward to take on the opposition. I hit an opponent and then turned to present the ball to my teammates, expecting them to be bound tightly around me. No one was within five yards of me. "Bind on me," I shouted.

The tubby prop frowned and yelled, "Pass, pass."

I knew if I threw a loose pass in the horde of forwards we'd likely lose possession. The Riverside forwards overwhelmed me. I went to the ground and set the ball back with my hand for a ruck, but none of our forwards drove over the ball and the other team grabbed the ball.

"You've got to pass the ball faster, Clay," Tubby chided. "I thought you knew how to play rugby."

I started to protest, but realized arguing with my own team during a game wouldn't help. Instead I ran at an angle toward our corner flag. I managed to tackle their winger as broke through our backline. He knocked the ball on when he hit the ground. Mr. Prinsloo's whistle blew for a knock-on. He leaned over to me and whispered, "I see you didn't forget how to corner flag, Clay. That was a good tackle. But I don't think the rest of your forwards know much about the game."

His words seemed prophetic at the ensuing scrum. I insisted on playing second row on the left side since Tubby had lined up on the right. But the front row forwards, though big enough, didn't know how to bind properly. As a result our scrum splintered and collapsed. I felt a sharp pain as my neck twisted left. I heaved myself out of the pileup and ran in pursuit of the ball.

Even though the Grunions didn't know some of the basics of forward play, they tackled hard and U.C. Riverside couldn't score. When our players did get the ball, they passed with abandon. It didn't look pretty, but we had a speedster on the wing and he managed to get his hands on the ball a few times and outpaced his marker to score twice. Our kicker missed both conversions and we won 8-0.

After the game, my chest felt tight and my eyes streamed. "Something's wrong with my eyes," I commented.

"It's just the smog, Africa boy," said Mad Dog. "I can tell you're new to California."

Frank Prinsloo came over. "You're a classy player, Clay," he said. "I wish I'd stayed at Livingstone and had the chance to coach you. I seem to remember you had a good friend who played scrum-half. Tiny chap."

"Titch," I answered. "We played side by side all the way through Livingstone. He was a great scrum-half." I suddenly choked up. I couldn't remember when I'd played a rugby game without Titch.

Frank put his arm around me. "You miss your good friend, don't you?"

I nodded.

"Why don't you come home with me for the evening?" he offered. "I'll make sure you get back to college before your classes tomorrow. I live in Ventura."

I accepted his offer like a starving hyena grabbing a bone. As I walked into the Prinsloo's home I felt like I'd come back to Africa. They had a zebra skin on one wall. A mounted buffalo head glowered down at me from above the fireplace. Some large African drums served as end tables beside the couch. His wife greeted me with a hug. "This is Clay from Kenya," Frank said. "He went to school at Livingstone when we were there."

"I'm so glad you could come visit," she said.

"Thanks for having me, Mrs. Prinsloo. I love the decorations in your house even though they make me more homesick for Africa than ever."

"We tried to bring a little of Africa with us when we moved here," Frank explained. "But I'm homesick for Africa, too. Sometimes I think I'll shrivel up inside if I don't get back to Africa. I see a picture of a flat-topped acacia tree and my heart flips upside down." He turned to his wife. "Carol, I thought we'd have a good old Kenyan *nyama choma*. I bought some meat on the way home and I'll fire up the barbecue."

"I'll make some lemonade and some salad while you get the fire going," Carol said.

"So you don't coach rugby anymore?" I asked as I stood next to Frank and the smoking barbecue in the back yard.

He shook his head. "I ref a bit. But I've been too busy making a living to coach."

"The Grunions could use some good coaching," I said.

"You're right there, Clay. What a shambles in the scrum today."

"If I ask Mad Dog and he agrees, could you come coach the Grunions? Even if it's only once a week."

"I'd like that, Clay. Check into it and we'll see what works out. Tell me, how did Mike manage as a rugby coach?"

I began giving a blow-by-blow description of Mike's tenure coaching the Livingstone rugby team. Frank got a faraway look in his eyes. He sighed. "I really enjoyed those years at Livingstone. I wish we could have stayed on."

"Why didn't you come back after your Dad passed away?" I asked.

"We couldn't get a visa to stay in Kenya because of our South African citizenship," he answered. "Apartheid is a stain on our country. Not only are our black friends oppressed, but those of us who tried to help were harassed into leaving. We applied to return to Kenya but our visas were rejected. Black Africa wouldn't accept us because they saw all of us as white racists. Prejudice is a shotgun with barrels pointing both ways." He stopped talking and checked the coals.

"A few more minutes and we can put the meat on," he said. "I guess we could have gone to Rhodesia, but Rhodesia had its own racial tensions. So we came here. America's nice, but deep inside I long for Africa."

"I feel the same way," I said. "I remember being homesick at Livingstone when I was little. I missed my parents then. I miss my parents now, but I ... well, I know this sounds bad ... but I think I miss Africa more."

We put the meat on the grill and talked as we seared the meat and burned our tongues testing whether it was done just right. "I saw Ox back in Kenya after our last rugby game," I said.

Frank chuckled. "Ox was quite a player. And a real trailblazer. Did you know he was the first black to play on Kenya Combined Schools?"

We talked on and on, mostly about rugby and Africa. After supper, Frank drove me back to Santa Barbara. As I got out in front of my dorm, I felt a twinge in my neck. I reached up and massaged my neck as Frank said, "I hope this coaching thing works out. And when your longing for Africa gets overwhelming, give me a call and I'll bring you home for a weekend. We'll talk Africa."

"I'd enjoy that," I answered. "Thanks."

He drove off and I walked into the dorm, still rubbing my neck.

40

My neck still hurt on Monday, so before practice I went to the trainer who put me on a table and used some deep heat rub and probed my neck with his fingers. It hurt, but felt good as the muscles released. Coach Davis came by and frowned. "What's your problem?"

I grinned and said, "Rugby injury. I somehow twisted my neck in Sunday's game."

Coach's face turned red and he planted his hands on his hips. "You played a rugby game yesterday?"

I sat up on the table. "Uh, yeah. I love rugby and was amazed to find a team here in Santa Barbara. They were a few players short so I joined them."

Coach Davis shook his head. "Not on my team, Clay. No rugby during the soccer season. I can't risk having you injured. That's a game for guys with rocks in their heads."

"But Coach, I've had fewer injuries in rugby than in soccer."

"No more rugby, or you're off the squad. That's final."

Other players stopped and listened to the exchange. I wanted to scream out. "I live for rugby, Coach. Soccer's fun and I'm glad it's paying my tuition, but rugby's my passion. I need to play rugby." I wanted to walk out, but I knew that without the soccer scholarship, I'd have to leave school. I went to practice in a confused mood. In the first offense against defense drill, I got caught out of position. Coach yelled at me. Inside I got angry and determined to show him that I could play soccer. I focused on the drills, played my position well and attacked the ball with ferocity.

In one collision with our striker I kicked his shin along with the ball. He crumpled to the ground and I cleared the ball. "Careful Clay," Coach warned. "This isn't rugby."

I didn't know what he wanted, but I clenched my jaw and continued to play aggressive defense. At the end of practice Coach Davis called me over. "You're playing good defense. Just remember that we need our strikers in the next game, so please don't break anyone's ankle in a drill. Save the tough stuff for games." He slapped my back with his clipboard. "I know you love rugby. Just don't play it during the soccer season."

In the locker room Ron joked, "The guys are calling you Killer Too. Just remember we're all on the same team."

"I was ticked off at coach for saying I couldn't play rugby. Sorry if I took it out on everyone who came near me during the drills." I peeled off my socks and piled them on top of my soccer boots. "Why's Coach so against rugby, anyway?"

"From what I hear, coach lost a good player two years ago. Brian was a senior and the captain of the soccer team who also moonlighted playing rugby on Sundays, but he didn't let coach know. The weekend before Rockpoint's west coast divisional playoff game, Brian broke his collarbone playing rugby. When coach found out, he was livid. Rockpoint lost the soccer game and coach has had a vendetta against rugby ever since."

"Well, I guess I may have to miss a few rugby games," I said. "I can't see why I can't enjoy both rugby and soccer at the same time. But if Coach insists, I'll wait until soccer's over and then play for the Grunions some more. You should join, Ron. You'd make a great rugby player."

I told Mad Dog the next day I couldn't play rugby until soccer season was over. "I considered quitting soccer, but that's how I'm paying for school."

"Don't worry," Mad Dog said. "We only have one more friendly this fall. The main rugby season starts in January and ends with the huge Santa Barbara Rugby Tournament."

"That's great," I answered. "I love rugby. You know that guy who reffed our game on Sunday?"

Mad Dog nodded. "We've had him before. He's fair and knows the rules well."

"He's offered to help coach our team if you like. He used to be our school's coach in Kenya."

Mad Dog agreed that the Grunions could use some coaching.

Soccer season didn't end until Thanksgiving. We kept winning and qualified to play in the nationals in St. Louis.

The weather was foul. It rained the first day and I'd never felt so cold. Muddy rugby games in Nairobi had the advantage of being played in warm weather. In the first game I blocked a shot with my thigh and when the ball splatted against my leg it left red pentagon marks that stung long after we'd lost the game 2-0 to some midwest team that knew how to play in cold weather.

The next day got worse. It froze overnight and all the puddles from the day before turned to ice. "I bought gloves for those of you who aren't used to cold weather," Coach Davis announced, setting out a box of winter gloves. I swooped down and gathered a pair and pulled them on before going out to warm up.

What an oxymoron. How could anyone warm up for a soccer game in freezing weather? My fingers felt swollen like a bunch of African bananas. I kept making fists, but my hands were dead before the game began. My nose turned numb and the mustache of the beard I'd grown froze with small sprinkles of ice as my breath condensed. My pink African lungs burned from the cold. They felt too stiff to inhale enough air.

Our opponents, a Christian college from upstate New York, chugged through the frozen mud like they'd grown up playing soccer in the cold. I went to cut off a cross and slipped in the mud and cut my leg on the frozen rime of ice. The cross reached their striker who headed the ball into the top right corner. They led 1-0 at halftime.

Coach Davis led us into the locker room, his eyes squinted and his jaw clenched. "You're letting the weather beat you!" he began his assault. "You men can play better than this. This is a beatable team. If you lose now, there's no chance to win the national championship. We have to pull this one out." I shivered, but began to thaw out. Water dripped off my mustache. I blew my nose on my shirt sleeve.

Ron whispered. "My body's stiff. It doesn't get this cold in the Philippines."

Our play did improve in the second half even as the field became muddier. I stopped every few minutes to reach down and unclog my studs. My new gloves clotted up with frozen mud. We tightened up the defense and forgot trying to play nice control ball. We hammered the ball downfield anytime it came close. The strategy worked when one of my long balls rolled into the penalty area. Their keeper came out to collect the easy roller, but he slipped giving our left wing the chance to reach the ball first and flick it into the goal.

The game ended in a 1-1 draw. Coach Davis took us out for pizza to celebrate.

The next day's game wasn't quite as cold, but the field had been churned into a sloppy mess. We played a college from Florida who seemed as stunned by the cold as we were. We pulled off a 2-1 victory, leaving us in fifth place among the eight teams, not good enough to qualify for the semi-final.

Coach Davis congratulated us for pulling off a victory. "You played against the best," he enthused, "and showed you can win. Next year we'll go all the way." I didn't want to think about next year. I only wanted a hot shower. I stood under the stinging hot water longer than anyone else, hoping the warm water would seep into my frozen bones. I thought of the big concrete bathtub at the Kenya Harlequins rugby clubhouse in Nairobi and remembered how Titch and I had soaked in the tub with the other players after our annual friendly match with Quins. Thinking about Titch reminded me he'd given me his phone number the only time he'd called me on the phone. Maybe I'd have a chance to call him when we drove through Oklahoma.

The next day we set off for California, the paved road slick from sleet and icy rain. In Oklahoma at a truck stop, I found a payphone and popped in some coins and dialed Titch's number, which I'd copied onto a scrap of paper.

I heard the phone ring six times and was about to give up when I heard a tired voice on the other end. "Hello?"

"Titch?" I ventured. "Is this Titch?'

I heard a chuckle. "No one's called me Titch since I came to this country. Clay, is that you?"

"Yeah, we're just passing through after a soccer tournament in St. Louis. How are you?"

"Lonely," Titch replied. "Where are you? Can I come see you?"

"We're at a truck stop on the edge of Okalahoma City. We'll probably only be here another ten minutes."

"I've got wheels," Titch said. "Tell me what road you're on and I'm coming."

I called out to Ron and asked him to tell me what street we were on. I relayed the directions to Titch.

"I can be there in fifteen minutes," he stated.

"Our convoy may leave before that," I pointed out.

"Stall them. I've got to see you. You don't know how lonely it is without someone from Livingstone nearby."

"Actually, I do. See you soon."

I hung up the phone and went over to Coach Davis. "Coach, a friend of mine from Kenya is hurrying over to see me for a few minutes. Can we wait a few minutes?"

Coach frowned at his watch. I pleaded with my eyes. Coach released a puff of air from his cheeks. "It's a long way to California, Clay. But okay, we'll wait so you can see your friend. I'll go have another cup of coffee."

I went outside and stood in the brisk wind, scanning the road for Titch and his car. Several cars pulled in to fill up. I peered inside the cars in vain for a glimpse of my friend. A black Chevy pickup flew into the parking area. I could see Titch behind the wheel. I ran towards him. He flung open the car door. "Clay!" he shouted.

We met and clutched onto each other. Finally I released my grip and looked him in the face. "We're a long way from Africa," I said.

"That's for sure," Titch replied, leading the way into the smoke-filled café.

I introduced Titch to Ron and Coach Davis. Coach glanced at his watch again. "I'll give you another five minutes," he said. "Then we'll have to be on our way."

I nodded. Titch and I sat opposite each other in a booth with overstuffed red vinyl cushions. "How have you been?" Titch asked.

"California is nice and warm," I said. "But I sure miss Africa. I keep busy with classes and soccer. And you'll never guess who I met."

"Tell me," Titch prompted.

"Coach Prinsloo now lives in California. He's going to start coaching our rugby team in Santa Barbara." I paused. "So what have you been up to?"

"The place where I'm working as an apprentice is torture," Titch said. "But in another year-and-a-half I'll be a qualified water well driller. I've already got some contacts for work back in Africa. Sudan has opened up after years of civil war. There's a Christian company called Water for All and they're looking for people to drill wells and set up water projects in southern Sudan. I just wish I could go tomorrow. The thought of a winter alone in this place makes me want to shrivel up like those slugs we used to douse with salt."

I recoiled at his picture, but inwardly I admitted feeling much the same way. "We'll get back to Africa soon," I said. "This is only temporary."

"I can handle it, knowing I'll be back in Africa in less than two years. But if I had to live the rest of my life here, I think I'd die."

Coach Davis stood at the glass door and rang the little bell that hung there to alert the proprietor when someone walked in. "Time to be on the road," he called.

I stood up and shook Titch's hand. "Hey, it's been great to see you again."

"How's Leah?" Titch asked as we moved to the door.

I shrugged. "We wrote a lot at first. But I think she's got a boyfriend. She wrote about some hunk of a wrestler and then I haven't had a letter for a month."

I piled into the college van and waved at Titch. "Stay in touch," he called. I nodded and we drove away.

41

We arrived back in Santa Barbara late in the afternoon, exhausted by the long drive. A group of students met us near the dining hall with balloons and posters. "Congratulations. National soccer heroes," one of the posters read. Sierra and her friends stood behind a huge cartoon with caricatures of each player. Sierra's smiling face peered over the poster and she pointed frantically at a cartoon of a soccer player with long hair and a beard. "I drew this picture of you!" Sierra shouted.

I smiled as Sierra came around and gave me a hug. "We didn't win," I pointed out. I'd heard of rugger huggers, but it seemed we had soccer huggers, too. Coach gave a thank you speech before we unloaded our bags and went into the dining hall. I sat at a table, almost too tired to go get food. Sierra sat next to me and Ron.

"You guys look wiped out. Can I bring you anything?"

"Sure," I said. When Sierra arrived with two trays of food, I suddenly felt hungry.

"Thanks, Sierra," I said. Sierra asked all kinds of questions about the tournament, which Ron and I answered. When I finished, Sierra walked me to my dorm.

As I said good-bye, Sierra reached out and took my hand. "It's good to have you back, Clay. I missed you."

"We were only gone a week," I commented.

Sierra looked down. "I know, but I missed you."

I felt queasy. I'd danced with her once and talked with her between classes. I'd seen her watching all our games, but we'd never even had a formal date. Now it sure seemed to me that she liked me. I reached over and gave her a glancing kiss on the cheek. She responded with a hug and full kiss.

She pulled back and smiled. "I'm glad you're back. I'm sure we're going to see a lot more of each other." She turned and walked away. I wiped my lips with my fingers and saw the red of her lipstick.

I hoisted my bag onto my shoulder and walked into the dorm. In my room, my roommate, Troy from Hayward, looked up. "You're back! What's all over your lips?"

"A welcome home kiss from a friend," I said.

"Watch out," Troy said. "Don't let some girl carry you away with a kiss."

A few days later, the soccer team met after school in the locker room to turn in all our equipment. I carried my rugby ball with me. Coach, a clipboard in his hand, glared at the oval ball I gripped as I turned in my practice soccer ball. "I don't like balls shaped like that," he growled.

"Come on, Coach, soccer season's over. Rugby will keep me fit during the spring."

"Just don't break anything," Coach said. When we finished Coach announced, "We'll be having a soccer awards dinner at Pancho Villa's restaurant and each of you can bring a date."

"I think I'll ask Sierra," I whispered to Ron.

After chapel the next morning, the students erupted from the auditorium. I'd been staring at Sierra's shiny yellow hair instead of listening to the speaker. Now I elbowed my way through the crowd to catch up with her. I touched her shoulder and she turned around and smiled. The sun shimmered on her hair. I almost lost my courage.

"On your way to class?" she asked.

"Uh, yeah," I started. I walked a few strides next to her. "Actually, I wanted to ask you something."

Sierra stopped and looked up at me, her face puzzled.

"Well, there's this soccer awards dinner next Friday evening, and I wondered if maybe you'd like to go with me. As my date, I mean."

Sierra hesitated and my face heated up. I looked away. *What a fool I am*, I thought to myself. *Just because she acts nice and smiles at me, it doesn't mean she wants to go on a date with a wog like me.*

"I'd love to go with you," Sierra said.

I looked down at her. "Really! You mean it?"

"Sure. I'd love to go on a date with you. I just want to know why it's taken you so long to ask me on a date? If you hadn't asked me out soon, I'd have been forced to ask you out myself."

My heart leaped like a baby gazelle. "I'll let you know what time I'll pick you up," I said.

That evening I told Troy I had a date for the next Friday. "How are you going to drive to the restaurant?" Troy asked.

His question stopped me. "I'm not sure. I hadn't thought about it. Maybe I'll catch a ride with one of the other soccer players."

"Clay, you can't hitch a ride on a date. You've got to have your own wheels." Troy rubbed his chin. "Do you know how to drive a stick shift?"

"That's all we have in Kenya," I answered. "Why? You don't have a car, do you?"

"Not here. My Dad wouldn't let me keep my car on campus during my freshman year. But I parked my car at my Mom's place. After she divorced Dad three years ago, she moved to a beach cottage up near San Luis Obispo. We could skip classes on Friday morning and go up there and pick it up for the weekend. Dad will never know."

Friday morning found Troy and I driving up Highway 101 with Rich, another student who'd been happy to skip class and give us a lift. I stared down at the choppy Pacific Ocean on our left and longed to swim in the warm Indian Ocean. I remembered walking with Leah on Kenya's white beaches. I forced myself to focus on today.

We drove into the driveway of Troy's Mom's beach house. A light blue car cover had been stretched over a car on the edge of the driveway. "That's my car over there," Troy pointed out.

"What kind is it?" I asked. "It's not a big American car."

Troy pulled the cover off and lovingly stroked the dark green finish of the sports car. "It's a Triumph," Troy said proudly. "A TR-6. It has a rag top and if the weather's good on Friday, you can drive it with the top down."

The door to the house opened and a disheveled middle-aged man stepped out and squinted into the sunshine. "Jeez, what are you kids doing here?"

Troy looked embarrassed. "I'm here to see my Mom," he said.

The man hitched his belt tighter and his face flattened slightly as he squinted at us. He stuck his head in the door and shouted, "Lizzy, some kid out here says he's your son." He disappeared into the house.

Troy's Mom came out in a shiny short red kimono. "Troy, you should have called first." She made a vague attempt to straighten her hair.

Troy motioned for us to move away and he went to his Mom. "Who is that guy? And why's he calling you Lizzy?" I heard him hiss at her.

His Mom crossed her arms in front of her chest and answered fiercely, "It's my life and I'm entitled to have a few friends if I want." The two of them disappeared into the house.

A few minutes later, Troy came out, twirling his car keys on his forefinger. I could see cold anger on his flushed face. "Thanks for the ride, Rich," Troy said curtly. "I'll drive Clay back to Santa Barbara."

"I'll wait to see if your car starts," offered Rich.

Troy slipped into the driver's seat of his Triumph sports car and turned the key. The engine sputtered and coughed before catching with a leopard-like growl. Troy looked straight ahead. "Get in," he ordered.

Rich waved and drove off. Troy popped the clutch and the Triumph spun gravel as we tore out the driveway.

We flew down the freeway in silence. Finally I ventured, "I'm sorry."

Troy choked back a sob. "It's bad enough my parents divorced. But when I see Mom with some other man, it hurts so bad. I hate it." The knuckles on his fingers turned white as he gripped the steering wheel.

"Sorry," I said again, at a loss for any comforting words. I had missed my parents while I was away at boarding school. But I knew my parents loved each other and they loved me. I always knew I had a warm home to go back to during mid-term holidays and school vacations.

Back in Santa Barbara Troy gave me lessons in driving the Triumph. "The clutch is fussy," he pointed out. I stalled out a few times, but got the hang of it after a while.

On Friday evening I picked up Sierra. She had on a low-cut white dress, which made her tan legs and arms look even darker. "What a great car!" she enthused.

"I'd be more comfortable driving a Land Rover," I said, "but this will do."

I had the top down and as we drove down the road, Sierra's hair streamed backwards. "Sorry for ruining your hair," I said as we pulled up to the restaurant. She shook her hair and laughed. "It was worth it." She slipped into the ladies room to repair her hair. We sat next to Ron and his date. Sierra ordered a vegetarian burrito. "Beans only," she pointed out.

I had chicken enchiladas. At the end of the dinner Coach Davis stood up and gave a recap of the season ending with our trip to the nationals. Then he began passing out awards. Our captain received the most valuable player award. Our keeper had been selected best defensive player. Ron and I clapped and hooted.

"Our last award is for Rookie of the Year," Coach Davis droned on. "In order for our soccer program to continue to be successful, we need new talent every year. This award is for the best first year player on our club and it's my pleasure to give Rookie of the Year to Clay Andrews."

My feet wouldn't move at first. Sierra pushed my shoulder. "Get up there!" She clapped wildly. I pushed my chair back and almost tripped as I stood up.

I heard coach's words as I made my way to the podium. "Clay will be a great anchor for our defense in the years ahead—that is if he doesn't ruin his health playing rugby."

I reached out for Coach Davis's hand and gripped it tightly. "Congratulations," he said, handing me the trophy.

I waved the award and stumbled back to my seat.

Sierra took the award and admired it before passing it around the table. She reached over and snuggled her arm around my elbow like it was the most natural thing in the world.

After the dinner, we went to the Triumph. "Let's go cruising," Sierra suggested.

I aimed the TR-6 towards State Street, Santa Barbara's main commercial street. At the first stoplight, I stopped gently and turned to admire Sierra's face in the soft glow of the streetlights. The signal turned green. "Go! Go!" Sierra commanded. Startled, I pulled the clutch out too fast and the Triumph stalled. The car behind me honked.

Sweat beaded up on my forehead as I turned the key to start the car. Cars passed and jeered. I finally got the car going and lurched forward. I couldn't seem to get it right. Sierra ducked down and swore at me. "This is so embarrassing!"

I finally got the car moving smoothly. But within a minute I reached another red light. Sierra shrunk down below window level. "Do it right this time!" she demanded.

My sweat-slick palms felt greasy on the steering wheel. The light changed. I slipped the clutch out gently and the Triumph started moving. Then it began to jerk and lurch. I stepped on the gas and the car lurched some more until I dropped it into second gear.

"Let me out of here," Sierra gritted as I drifted to a stop at the next traffic signal. "Don't you know how to drive a car?"

I started to defend myself when the light turned green. I focused on the road, crammed my foot on the gas pedal and released the clutch. This time the car roared and leapt forward. "Just take me home," Sierra pleaded. I turned onto a side street. Once the Triumph got moving, it drove sweetly enough. The wind began to dry the sweat on my forehead. I drove silently up a back road to the college.

At Sierra's dorm, I stopped and turned off the engine. Looking straight ahead I mumbled, "I'm sorry."

I heard a muffled laugh. I turned to look at Sierra. She flashed a smile and said softly, "I was just thinking about how ridiculous we must have looked lurching up State Street."

"You're not angry?"

"I always react loudly when I'm embarrassed. Sorry for swearing at you and saying you didn't know how to drive. Now that it's over, I think it's kind of funny."

"Well, let's drive around a little longer," I suggested. "But this time, you drive."

I got out and Sierra slid across the stick shift into the driver's seat. "Ready to ride, Africa boy?"

"Let's see you start it without jerking," I challenged.

Sierra nodded and turned the key. The car started to move forward and then stalled. "Hmm, a bit harder than I thought," Sierra said. She tried again. The Triumph bucked across the parking lot like a wildebeest with flies hatching in its nasal passages. Sierra slammed on the brakes. "I'm not driving this thing any further." I put my arm around Sierra's shoulder and drew her towards me. We kissed.

"This is better than cruising with the top down," Sierra murmured. We kissed again.

42

I sat in the grass with Sierra outside the student center one Friday in late spring soaking in the California sunshine and studying. I toyed with a rugby ball on my lap as Sierra read from the Merchant of Venice by Shakespeare.

I spotted a black Chevy pick-up. "There he is! Titch is here!"

I jumped up and waved at Titch who slowed his car and stepped out. "Wow, I'm stiff," Titch said, putting a hand on his hip and stretching his back sideways.

I enveloped him in a hug. Sierra, standing behind me, said, "I thought he only hugged me like that." I released Titch and Sierra stepped forward. "I'm Sierra, Clay's girlfriend," she introduced herself, shaking Titch's hand.

Titch gently grasped his right forearm with his left hand as he shook Sierra's hand, an African gesture of respect.

"I wasn't sure you'd make it," I said.

"I couldn't miss playing rugby with you, Clay. It's been almost a year since we last played together." I'd invited Titch to join us for the Santa Barbara Rugby Tournament, which had attracted over 100 teams for the weekend.

I gathered up the rugby ball and flicked a pass to Titch. He caught the ball and turned it over in his hands lovingly. "I'd almost forgotten how good a rugby ball feels in my hands."

I frowned at Titch's chapped and cracked fingers. One of his thumbnails was missing and several other fingernails were black and blue. He saw my stare. "Working on water drilling rigs isn't easy on the hands." Grasping the rugby ball between his hands, he spun the ball sweetly to me. "But I can still pass a rugby ball."

"Come, we'll meet the rugby guys down at the field. We're having a last minute practice before the Santa Barbara Tournament tomorrow."

"Is Mr. Prinsloo there?"

"Frank can't make it today, but he'll be with us tomorrow. Our team has really improved under his coaching. Man, Titch, if we'd had Frank as our coach at Livingstone, we'd have never lost a game."

"This is my good friend, Titch," I called out to the other rugby players when we arrived at the field.

"Glad you could make it," Mad Dog greeted him. "Clay tells me you're a scrum-half." We ran through our moves unopposed while Titch watched. Coach Prinsloo had chosen me to play eighth-man.

After about ten minutes Mad Dog called Titch to step in as scrum-half. His passes flew straight as arrows without the wobble that our normal scrum-half put on the ball. At the first unopposed scrum, I played the ball back to my right foot. Titch crouched low over the ball with his back foot near the ball. He scooped the ball and passed all in one fluid motion. Suddenly our backs were flying.

After practice Mad Dog said to Titch, "You'll get some playing time tomorrow."

Titch grinned and turned to me. "I feel whole again for the first time since I left Africa. I'm doing something I really know how to do well. And I'm with my best friend."

The tournament started early. We'd been entered in the second division at the tournament.

Frank Prinsloo met us at the playing fields. Titch ran over to him. "Mr. Prinsloo! Coach! Remember me?"

Frank grasped Titch's hand firmly. "How could I forget the mightiest little scrum-half I ever coached? You had greatness imprinted on you at an early age. I still remember you tackling some of those bigger boys around the ankles. They toppled over like trees in front of a chain saw. I'm looking forward to seeing you play today."

Frank and Mad Dog went over to sign in at the tent where they'd set up tables to organize the tournament. "Look at those players," Titch whispered, nudging me. A group of hefty Pacific islanders strutted past.

"I heard a team from Samoa had entered this year. There's also a team from New Zealand and two club teams from England. But they'll all be in the first division of the tournament. We won't have to tackle them, but we can watch."

Coach Prinsloo came back with Mad Dog. "Here's our schedule," Coach said. "We have three group matches today. If we win those, we'll go into the knockout round tomorrow. We have to be alert and play hard from the start. Our first game is against Bakersfield at 10 a.m."

Since Titch had just joined the team, Mad Dog opted not to have him start against Bakersfield. We lost the toss and Bakersfield kicked off to us. One of our forwards knocked the ball forward off the kick. The ref blew for a scrum. The Bakersfield forwards, built like hippos, won the strike and pushed us backwards. I released my bind and hung behind our back-pedaling scrum. When their eighth man picked the ball up to run with it, I got under his hand off and hammered him to the ground. They won the ensuing ruck and passed the ball out to their backs. Without possession, we had to tackle like mad. By half time we were bruised and exhausted. But we'd held them out. The score stood at 0-0.

Coach Prinsloo knelt inside a circle of tired and discouraged players. "Your fighting spirit is good. But we need the ball to score. I'd like to put Titch in this half. Since we can't push them back, I want you, Tom, to hook the ball hard to your left. Let the ball come out in front of the left flanker. This is called channel one ball. It's not as protected as sending it back to the eighth man, but it will give us the ball. Titch, you have to get on the ball immediately and fling it to the backs. It's not quality ball, but it is possession and if we're running with it, we don't have to keep tackling."

Titch nodded. "I can do that."

"I know you can. As for lineouts, Clay, let's play our throw-ins with only two men in the lineout. That should give you the opportunity to get clean ball."

We kicked off to start the second half. A Bakersfield flanker caught the ball and charged straight at Titch, who ducked low and tackled him. The flanker went down so quick and hard I could hear the hollow thud as his head cracked the ground. He dropped the ball forward and groaned.

The ref called for the scrum. The Bakersfield player tried to sit up but fell over to one side. Their trainer came out and held two fingers in front of his eyes. "How many fingers do you see?" the trainer asked.

When the injured player couldn't even guess at an answer, the trainer took him off the field with a suspected concussion. We bound and crouched, ready for the scrum. Titch looked at me knowingly. "Channel one ball, remember?"

I nodded. As soon as he put the ball in, our hooker booted it sideways. I saw the ball spill out the left side of the scrum and broke off. Titch picked the ball up and swung his arms as if to pass. Two Bakersfield players went for his dummy pass. Titch cut inside and only had two men to beat. By now I'd caught up with him. Titch drew the first man then popped a pass to me. I charged straight at their fullback. Just as his shoulder hit my thighs, I turned with the ball. I saw Titch at my side and loaded the ball off to him and landed in a heap on top of the fullback. I looked up to see Titch putting the ball between the posts for a try.

He ran back to me. "Just like old times!" he enthused. Our fly-half converted Titch's try and we led 6-0. We held on to beat Bakersfield 6-3. Our next two games were easier and we qualified for the knockout stage on Sunday.

"I'll probably be late tomorrow," Coach Prinsloo told us after our last game. "I can't get here until after church."

We waved good-bye to Coach as he headed for home.

"Will you be going to church tomorrow?" Titch asked me. "Or will you skip it this time for rugby?"

"Actually, I haven't been to church for months," I confessed. Titch frowned at me but didn't comment.

Sierra hoisted a five-gallon jug of ice water onto a nearby table and we poured water to slake our thirst. Mad Dog and the others broke out a cooler of cold beers. "Celebrate boys," he commanded. "But don't get too wasted. We have to win some games tomorrow."

Titch looked at me with a question on his face. "No beer for me," I told him. "This ice water will be fine."

"I'm glad," Titch said. "I tried beer once. All the drillers are heavy drinkers and they're always offering me booze. But I didn't like the taste, so I figured, why bother."

Sierra joined us as we crowded into the main stadium to watch the Samoans and the Kiwis. "I'd love to play rugby at that level," I said after one of the Samoan players had powered his way through three players to score a try.

"Someday," Titch answered, a faraway look in his eyes, "maybe we could both play for Kenya when we go back to Africa."

I slapped his hand and grasped it in an African handshake. "Deal!"

"Are you planning to go back to Africa?" Sierra asked Titch.

"Absolutely. I've got African blood in my veins. I don't know anywhere else I could live and feel whole. I'm sure not comfortable here in America."

"What about you, Clay?" Sierra asked.

"When I'm done with college, I'm hoping to work in Kenya. I'm not sure where or what. I just know it will be in Africa somewhere."

Sierra started to speak, but then shut her mouth quickly.

The next morning Titch and I arrived early for our first game in the knock-out round. "Where are the others?" Titch asked.

"I'm not sure," I answered.

Our players began straggling in, eyes puffy and red. Mad Dog's grin revealed his one broken tooth. "Man, what a party!" he said almost with a sigh.

"We have a game to play," I pointed out.

"Whatever," Mad Dog answered.

I tried vainly to organize the team, but no one seemed to care. Five minutes before the kickoff for our first knock-out game, Coach Prinsloo arrived. He called us together. Rapping his knuckles on the leather Gilbert rugby ball, he pursed his lips tightly. "It may not mean much to some of you, but I believe playing rugby is a great privilege. And we should always play the game with the greatest possible vigor. When you get wasted the night before a game, I'm afraid there's not much I can do to help."

"We've played with hangovers before, Coach," Mad Dog explained. "For some of us, we play better after a binge. We're too fuzzy headed to worry about things like being tackled, so we play full tilt."

Mad Dog's little speech didn't mollify Coach Prinsloo. He gave Titch and I some hasty orders on controlling the game from the base of the scrum, then withdrew and folded his arms across his chest.

"He's a bit grumpy today," Mad Dog whispered to me.

I didn't answer, disappointed by the condition of the other players. We pulled on our rugby jerseys, wet and sour with yesterday's sweat. "Maybe wearing stinky shirts will give us an advantage," I said wryly to Titch. He wrinkled his nose.

The only thing that kept the game close was the fact that their team seemed to be suffering from a group hangover as well. Titch and I each scored an early try. But our backs didn't want to tackle and the other team from Santa Cruz had two wingers called Wheels and Jeep. Wheels whipped around the outside of our defense and scored three tries. Jeep motored straight ahead and carried three players, including me, over the in-goal line to score another try.

After the final whistle blew with us on the losing end of a lopsided score, I put my arm around Titch. "Not much of a display today. But it sure was good to play rugby with you again."

"I wouldn't have missed it for anything," Titch answered. "I'm glad I came."

"I need a beer," Mad Dog called, limping through the grass with one bare foot. A golf-ball-sized lump had purpled under his ankle. He grasped one sweaty boot in his hand, while the other boot flopped unlaced on his good foot.

Coach Prinsloo drew us aside. "If I had fifteen players like the two of you, we could win the first division cup in this tournament. Come, let's go watch some good rugby in the main stadium. Then I'll take you home for a good South African *braai*."

43

Titch headed back to Oklahoma the next morning. "I'll see you," I shouted in the vague farewell we missionary kids use to avoid saying good-bye. I had no idea when I'd see him again, but I knew it would be in Africa. I focused on finishing college and getting back to Africa as soon as possible.

I hardly heard a word from Titch until he finished his two-year training as a well driller and called me. "I've gotten a job back in Africa," he enthused on the phone. "I'll be drilling water wells and providing clean water all over Southern Sudan."

"That's great, Titch," I replied, secretly jealous that he would beat me back to Africa. "I'll be there as soon as I finish college two years from now."

"Right, I'll see you in Africa. I'll write and tell you how things are. I'll be in Nairobi for a couple of weeks of orientation before we drive up to Sudan with a new drilling rig."

I hung the phone up with an empty feeling in my gut. Titch was going home.

Rugby and soccer provided pockets of pleasure amidst the homesickness I felt for my birth continent. I tried to enjoy America, but I pined for Africa. During my junior year of college I grew especially close to Sierra. We studied together, ate together, did just about everything together. I'd never felt so relaxed with a girl. I began to consider the day I would ask her to marry me. One warm Sunday afternoon we hiked up Cold Springs Canyon.

I admired Sierra's legs as she walked ahead of me, her waffle-soled hiking boots making intricate patterns in the dust. At a pool of water near the head of the canyon, we took off our shoes and dangled them in the cool water. "This reminds me of a place I used to hike to in Kenya," I began.

"Tell me," Sierra said, flicking water at me with her toes.

I laughed and splashed her back. "We called the place Celebration Falls. In the old days at Livingstone lions and leopards were a threat and the missionary teachers and dorm parents killed them when they had a chance. When they shot a lion, the boys got to hike to the falls to celebrate. When a leopard was killed, the girls hiked to the falls."

"You killed lions and leopards?" Sierra asked, shocked.

"That was years ago. When I was at school, we just enjoyed hiking down to the falls and swimming in the pool at the bottom." I looked into Sierra's brilliant blue eyes. "I've been thinking," I went on, "how nice it would be for me to take you there."

"To Celebration Falls?" Sierra questioned.

"To Kenya. Sierra, would you marry me?"

A gentle smile tugged at Sierra's lips. "Clay, I'd love to be your wife. And I'd love to visit your old home in Kenya."

I pulled out a slave ring crafted in a zigzag pattern, which I'd bought years before from a silversmith in Mombasa's old town. "I know it's not a diamond," I said, "but I'd like you to consider this as a promise ring."

Sierra fondled the ring and then slipped it on her left ring finger. "Clay, this ring is exquisite. You know, you'll still have to ask my father if you can marry me."

I gulped and nodded. We walked down the canyon hand in hand planning our honeymoon to Kenya.

Back at school Sierra called her parents and told them we'd be going to their home in L.A. on the next weekend. "The sooner you ask him the better," Sierra pointed out. I couldn't argue, but my stomach twisted as I thought of facing Sierra's father.

I figured I'd better ask my parents as well. I stopped by the post office to buy an airmail stamp. As I passed my post box I could see a letter through the tiny window. I fiddled with the combination lock until it finally opened. The flimsy blue air form from my parents had a new Kenyan stamp with a chambered nautilus on it. I stuck a finger inside the flap and ripped it open poorly, tearing some of the lines written in my Mom's fluid script. She chatted in the letter about her work at the clinic. Near the bottom she wrote, "We've been asked to take on a new assignment with the mission. Your Dad's been called to the U.S. office as the candidate director recruiting and processing new missionaries. After much prayer, we've decided to take the job. We'll be back in the States this summer. I hope you can spend the summer with us at Grandma's. We'll start the new work in the mission headquarters in New York in late August. It will be good to be on the same continent with you again. We've really missed you."

I sat down on a nearby bench, my mind confused. My parents were coming back to the States? What would happen to our home in Kenya? If I went back to Kenya, then I'd be half a world away from my parents again. I decided I'd wait a few days before writing to Mom and Dad about my marriage plans.

Sierra drove us down to her parents' house in an exclusive suburb of Los Angeles. She told me her parents ran a pricey health food store. I wondered if they'd try to convert me to vegetarianism.

Her parents welcomed me with open arms. They had a pitcher of fresh carrot juice. I wasn't sure what to think of this new treat. My tongue told me I preferred milk shakes.

After supper, Sierra announced, "I'm going to help Mom with the dishes. Why don't you and Daddy talk." She motioned encouragingly with her head.

"Uh, sure," I said.

We sat down in his den, which had a big color TV. "I used to play football for USC and I'm a big fan. I go to all their home games here in Los Angeles and watch their away games on TV."

"We played USC in rugby a few weeks ago," I said. "Most of their team is made up of the football players."

"Rugby, huh. Now that's a wild and dangerous sport. No pads."

I decided not to argue with him. I cleared my throat. "One of the main reasons I've come this weekend is because, uh, well, Sierra and I …" I faltered.

Sierra's Dad raised his eyebrows. "Yes? What about you and Sierra?"

"Well, we're in love and I wanted to ask for your permission to marry her," I blurted.

Sierra's Dad leaned back in his brown leather recliner and put the palms of his hands together like a man in prayer, rubbing his chin with his forefingers. His eyes bored into me. "You want to marry Sierra? Tell me, what are your prospects?"

"Excuse me?" I asked.

"How do you plan to make a living? Sierra is my only child and I need to know how you plan to care for her."

"I'm planning to go back to Africa. I'm going to finish with a business administration major. So I thought I could work for some multinational business, or perhaps start a tour company, or manage a hotel, or …"

"Africa? Sierra did tell me she was dating a boy from Africa. Do you mean to tell me you plan to take my daughter to Africa to live?"

I nodded, worried that my appeal for Sierra wasn't going too well. We sat and stared at each other. His jaw clicked as he worked his chin sideways like a camel chewing its cud. Sierra came in carrying two coffee cups on a tray. Her face broke into a smile and she winked at me. "Coffee anyone?" she asked.

"Sierra, did you know he wants to take you to Africa to live?" her Dad answered.

"We talk about Africa a lot, Dad, but I doubt if Clay really wants to live there." She set the tray down on a glass table. "We may visit though. I'd love to see the animals. But no, we're not considering living in Africa. How would we make a living? Clay says he doesn't want to be a missionary going around and begging for funds from churches. Right Clay?"

"I did say I didn't want to be a missionary …" I began.

"See, Daddy, Clay doesn't really want to live in Africa. It's just a big part of his past. I'm sure he could help you in your business with his business degree. Then maybe he could do a master's in business administration."

Sierra's words stunned me. Ice filled my heart. Who hadn't been listening?

"Well, as long as Clay doesn't plan on taking you to Africa, I might consider letting the two of you get married. But I think you should wait until you finish college."

"I agree, Daddy. Thanks so much." She leaned down and kissed him.

My wind swirled. Sierra and I had talked at length about our future in Africa. Had she forgotten? Or did she want to deceive him so he would approve of our marriage and then she'd gently break the truth to him later on? That must be it, I decided. I took a cup of coffee and drank it with Sierra's Dad.

"I've always wanted a young man to take over my business," he said. "I'm sure we'll get on fine."

I wondered how he would respond when I took his precious daughter to my home in Africa. Custom in Africa dictates that when the wife is married she joins the husband's family in his home area.

As Sierra drove us back to college—she still didn't trust my driving on the freeways—I asked, "When will you break it to your father that we really do plan on living in Africa?"

Sierra didn't answer. Her eyes focused on the gray road as it blurred and disappeared under the Camaro's tires. Finally she sighed. "Clay, you can't really want to live in Africa. I mean, I know you talk about it all the time. But I figured we'd make a visit, a honeymoon in Kenya perhaps. But after that, I assumed you'd forget about Africa and stay here in the States. If you work with Daddy, you'll get a good salary, we can buy a house with a pool and have a good life. Right here. In America. I'm really a California girl, Clay. I'm a Chevy girl. My home is here."

"Well, I'm a Land Rover guy," I answered curtly, "and my home's in Africa." I stopped talking and stared out the window watching the guardrails curl and unravel as we whipped past.

Sierra reached over and stroked my arm with her perfect fingernails. I looked into her sea blue eyes. "I love you Clay," she mouthed, before turning her attention back to the road.

"I love you, too," I said, automatically. I really meant it, but a maelstrom seethed in my heart. Could my love for Sierra conquer my desire to return home to Africa?

"We don't have to decide our future right away," Sierra said. "Let's not talk about it right now. It's enough to have you beside me." She stole a glance at me and smiled.

My heart melted. I loved this girl. I wanted to spend my life with her. I'd take her on a honeymoon to Kenya and Africa would enchant her and we'd stay and live in Africa. I was sure that if she walked a few miles on my continent, her dust-covered feet would never want to leave.

Back at school, I walked Sierra to her dorm and kissed her goodnight. Our relationship continued, but Sierra seemed to tense up whenever I talked about living in Africa, so I learned to avoid the topic and we got along fine. I told myself she'd choose Africa when I took her there to visit. I desperately wanted to believe myself.

When school closed for the summer, I headed for my Grandma's house in Yakima. My parents arrived two weeks later. As they stepped into the airport lobby, Mom rushed me, dropping her hand luggage. I gave her a gorilla hug and looked over her to where Dad stood, smiling. He looked thinner than I remembered.

"A bad few months with hepatitis," Dad said as I gripped his hand and commented on his gaunt appearance.

I picked up Mom's carry-on bag and it almost jerked my arm out of the socket. "Still putting all the heavy things in your hand luggage?" I teased her.

"These airlines give you such a small weight allowance," she complained.

We collected their scarred and battered suitcases. The latch from one suitcase lolled to one side. "I hope nothing fell out of that suitcase," Mom said.

"You'd never know what was missing," Dad pointed out. "I don't know why we always carry so much back from Africa. Within a few days, we realize how hopelessly out of style and worn out all our clothes are and we throw them away. We'd do better giving them away in Kenya."

"We did give a lot away. Almost everything," she said.

"What about my trunk?" I asked. I'd left my school trunk filled with the mementos of my life in Kenya that had been too heavy to carry back to college:

Safari Rally programs, ticket stubs from various game parks, some letters, rugby schedules from each of my years on Livingstone's First Fifteen.

"Dad burned it," Mom said flatly.

"You burned my box?"

Dad looked away as we heaved the luggage into the back of the farm pickup. "We were leaving Africa for good and had no place to store it. I pulled out a few pictures, but everything else was just papers."

"You should have left it with some missionaries so I could go back and get it," I complained. "I can't believe you burned my treasure trunk!"

We didn't talk much as I drove the pickup back to Grandma's farm. "You don't seem happy, Clay," Mom said finally. "I didn't know that box meant so much to you. I threw out things I wished I could have kept as well. But we could only carry so much."

"Oh, it's not just the box," I answered. "Your leaving Africa seems wrong to me. Why'd you decide to come back?"

"Well, for one thing, we missed you," Mom said smiling.

"But I'm almost finished with college. I managed to get a bunch of language credits for already knowing Swahili and I'll graduate in December a whole semester early. And I'm planning on getting married and going out to Africa. But now you're here in the States."

"Did you say you're getting married?" Mom's eyes sparkled. "Tell me about this girl. Why haven't you told us before?"

"I was going to write, but then I got your letter saying you were coming home, so I decided to wait until you got here. Maybe when I go back to college at the end of the summer, we could drive down to California together. You could meet Sierra and her family."

"Sierra?" Dad jumped into the conversation. "What kind of name is that?"

"A different one, Dad. But you'll love Sierra."

Dad looked out the window. "As long as you love her, Clay. That's the most important thing in a relationship."

"I do love her, Dad," I stated.

He nodded.

Mom asked, "You say you're going to live in Africa. How did you persuade Sierra to move there? Does Sierra know what Africa's like? I remember my first years there; all I could think of was running home to my Mom. If we'd had any money, I would have left."

Dad's face broke into a sideways smile. "I almost lost you during those first years."

I'd never heard my parents talk about the struggle Mom had in adjusting to Africa. I stretched my shoulders upwards, thinking of Sierra's concerns. I pushed my chin forward and stated, "I've told Sierra all about Kenya."

"I'm so glad you've found the right girl," Mom went on. "We've prayed all your life that God would lead you to the right woman. Maybe we'll have to go back to Africa when you move out there."

Dad looked sad. "What's the matter, Dad?" I asked.

"I miss Africa already. And thinking of you and your new wife going out there makes me miss it even more."

"Well, why not go back like Mom said?" I asked. "You can do the desk job for a year, then go back to Kenya."

He shook his head. I noticed that Mom was biting her lower lip. Dad took a deep breath. "There's another reason we decided to come back to the States," he said. "After this latest bout with hepatitis, the mission doctors told me I couldn't stay in Africa. They say another tropical disease will kill me."

I glanced over at his hollow cheeks and gray-pouched eye sockets. He didn't look well. He went on. "I've had multiple cases of malaria, intestinal parasites, bilharzia, brucellosis from drinking unboiled milk with the Maasai, and now hepatitis. My health is shot."

We pulled into the ranch driveway. Grandma stood on the porch waving, her white apron framing her stocky figure.

44

Sierra invited us to stay with her parents for two days before school started. My parents agreed and planned to fly to New York after the visit between the two families.

"This is exciting!" Mom blurted as we drove into the Sierra's driveway. "I've never been a mother-in-law before."

"You're not one, yet," Dad said, smiling. "Just a mother-in-law-to-be."

My right hand trembled as I shifted the car into park. I hadn't seen Sierra for almost three months, though she had called several times a week. Sierra, wearing white shorts and a yellow tank top, burst out of the house. I barely had time to get out of the car before she leaped on me. We hugged while my parents unfolded themselves from the car. Dad rubbed his back and frowned at us. "That's probably enough hugging, Clay," he reprimanded.

Sierra pulled back and looked at me, puzzled. Holding her hand, I turned to my parents and said, "Mom, Dad, this is Sierra."

"I'm so glad to meet both of you," Sierra gushed. "Clay has told me so much about you."

Now it was my turn to be puzzled. One topic I'd rarely talked about was my parents. Having lived so much of my life away from them, I sometimes felt I hardly knew them.

We walked into the house and met Sierra's parents.

As we drank vegetable juice, Sierra's parents regaled us on the benefits of the vegetarian life. Dad's eyelids drooped. I whispered to him, "What would the Dorobo think about a vegetarian?"

Dad chuckled and pulled his eyelids up with an effort.

"I'm sure a vegetarian diet would help you recover from all your tropical diseases," Sierra's Dad said to my Dad.

"Oh, yes, yes," Dad agreed.

"So tell me," Mom said to Sierra, "are you looking forward to living in Africa with Clay? I have to warn you, these men make Africa sound so romantic. Clay's Dad swept me off my feet in college. But I hated Africa at first. I still remember trying to keep the floor clean. No matter how many times I mopped that gray concrete floor, it seemed to get browner with the mud from everyone's shoes."

Sierra looked over at me and frowned. A twinge gripped my heart. I tried to stop Mom, but she soldiered on.

"Oh, yes, those first days in Africa were the worst of my life. At night at the language school I'd crawl under the mosquito net, my mind fried from subjunctives and imperatives and a language that felt like spaghetti in my mouth. I cried and longed to be home with my parents here in America where everyone speaks the same language."

"Well, actually, Clay and I will probably only be in Africa for a few weeks on our honeymoon," Sierra put in firmly. "I'm sure there will be bugs and things, but I'll be able to put up with it for a few weeks. I'm looking forward to being at a tented camp in Tsavo and watching fiery sunsets through the baobab trees."

"Just a few weeks for your honeymoon?" Mom asked. "But I thought ..."

I touched her shoulder and whispered, "We'll talk about this later, Mom."

After a few awkward moments, Sierra's Dad invited us to swim in their pool. As we floated in the deep end, Sierra hissed at me, "Why does your Mom think we're planning to live in Africa?"

"Oh, I just hadn't told her all our plans," I blundered on. "I guess she assumed that since she followed Dad to Africa, you'd do the same thing."

Sierra glared at me. "And do you expect me to follow you to Africa?"

My heart melted to water. "I kind of hoped you would."

"I can't believe you think that! After what I've already told you!" Sierra shot back. I put my arm around her shoulder, my hand kneading her muscles gently. Sierra relaxed a bit. Neither of us talked. Holding onto her in the pool, I wanted her so much. But I began to doubt whether she really would ever want to live in Africa. And if she didn't? Then where would I be? Tied down to a job earning money to live the cushy American life?

Finally Sierra said, "Well, I'm not even so sure a honeymoon in Africa is such a good idea. I mean, it will cost a lot of money and we could use that money renting our first apartment here in L.A." She leaned back and stared into the sky. "I can't wait to be your wife."

The smog-choked sky of Los Angeles seemed to mirror the gray blanket I felt smothering my heart. We had to honeymoon in Kenya. How would Sierra fall in love with Africa if she wouldn't even visit?

"I'd still like to take you to Africa on our honeymoon," I told her. "You'll love snorkeling in the Indian Ocean. The water is warm as a bathtub and the white beaches gleam like teeth on a toothpaste commercial. And you have to experience sleeping—or trying to sleep—with hyenas howling nearby. Oh, Sierra, I just want to take you home."

She gave me a squeeze. "I know Clay. And you will. But maybe not for our honeymoon. Maybe a few years later when we've put some money away. Or after we have babies. Then you can show them where you grew up. Can you imagine visiting Africa with our kids?"

The thought frightened me. I wasn't ready to think about kids. I forced a smile at Sierra and then challenged her to a race across the pool. With her fluid strokes she beat me easily.

On our last night at Sierra's home her parents took us out to a Mexican restaurant. "We love this restaurant," Sierra's mother said. "They mark the vegetarian entrées with a little "no meat" symbol. They have some of the best vegetarian burritos in the city."

Years of working in Africa had stolen my parents' ability to enjoy a meal out. They looked at the prices on the menu. "One entrée costs as much as one of my Kenyan nurses earns in a month," Mom whispered to Dad, horror etched on her face.

I nudged them. "Just enjoy it. You're not paying."

"It just seems immoral," Mom said.

Sierra's parents, on the other side of the table, broke into our family huddle. "Were you discussing the prices? Please don't worry. We already told you this meal is our treat."

"Oh, I'm sorry, I didn't mean …" Mom began.

"Thank you," Dad said. "It always jolts us to realize how much we Americans are ready to spend on a meal out when so many others in the world don't have enough to eat. We do appreciate you taking us out, we really do."

Sierra's parents shrugged and buried their noses into the menus again. "Maybe I'll try something different tonight," Sierra's mother said.

I felt relieved the next day when I dropped my parents off at the airport. As we said good-bye for yet another time, I hugged Mom and shook Dad's hand.

Dad pulled me aside. "Clay, I want you to know I think Sierra's great, I really do. But I can also see you two haven't come to an agreement on Africa. If you love her, marry her. But you have to be ready to spend your lives together at a place you both agree on. Until you've settled that, I would suggest you be careful. Either she'll be miserable in Africa. Or you'll be miserable in America. Or you may split up. And you know how God hates divorce."

I shoved my hands into my pockets. "I know, Dad, I know. I'm sure Sierra will learn to love Africa like I do."

Dad's eyes penetrated my soul like the harsh stare of a tawny eagle. "Be careful, Clay. I'll be praying for you. And remember, it would be better to break it off before you marry rather than live with regret the rest of your life."

"Don't worry, Dad. I'll persuade Sierra to see things my way." My voice expressed a hope I no longer felt in my gut.

Back at school Sierra and I often talked about our wedding, planned for the following summer after she graduated. I'd agreed to work for the spring with her father to learn the health food business as his buyer.

One evening after looking at a catalog from a printer and trying to decide which wedding invitations we wanted, I commented, "You know Sierra, I don't mind what kind of invitations we send. I don't care what color the flowers are or what kind of tuxes the guys will wear. At the end of the day, we'll be married. And I want to take you to Kenya for our honeymoon."

"You spoil everything, Clay!" Sierra snapped. "Why do you keep harping on that subject? We'll visit Africa sometime. But not on our honeymoon. I can't imagine having to hide from bloodthirsty bugs under a mosquito net on our honeymoon. Now, my parents have a lovely cabin near Lake Arrowhead. That's my idea of a honeymoon."

I dropped the subject of an African honeymoon. Doubt draped over my heart. I did love Sierra. I thought I did. But could I survive a life away from Africa? Of course I could. I'd be with the woman I loved. Anywhere with Sierra would be heaven. But Africa seemed like an elusive mistress that might seduce me away from Sierra. I chased away my rampant doubts and focused on what Sierra was saying about the invitations.

45

Our soccer season ended early that year. We played a rival college from San Diego in the regional playoffs. At full time the score was deadlocked at 0-0. During sudden death overtime, their striker rifled a shot from just outside the penalty area. Our keeper made a leaping save and punched the ball away. I had instinctively run towards the goal to clear any sloppy saves. The punched ball rebounded straight at my head. Before I could duck the ball hammered into my forehead and into the net over the prostrate body of our goalie. I fell to my knees and covered my head. I'd lost the season. A few of the guys mumbled comfort, but I ached inside. In the locker room, coach took me aside and told me, "You were doing the right thing. I'm the one who taught you to run back to cover up any spilled shots. It was just one of those plays."

"Thanks, Coach," I murmured. Coach called all the players together. "It was a good season, boys. Just an unlucky break. But we've learned a lot, and I'm sure we'll go to the nationals next year."

I realized there wouldn't be a next year for me. Soccer had ended. *At least coach won't be upset if I go out and play in a rugby sevens tournament this weekend,* I thought to myself.

I turned out for the Grunions rugby practice the next day and poured out my frustration over my humiliating own-goal and my confusion about Sierra's refusal to consider Africa for our honeymoon. "Take it easy, Clay," Mad Dog warned after I'd hurled him to the ground in a rucking drill. "We're on your team."

"Sorry," I told him. "I'm just letting off steam. Wait until Saturday."

I invited Sierra to watch the rugby tournament. "Not this Saturday, Clay," she answered. "I'm going home for the weekend."

"Why didn't you tell me?" I asked. "Do you want me to go with you?"

"No, you've got the rugby tournament. I just need some time alone with my parents. I need to think about things."

"What kind of things?"

She leaned over and kissed me. "Don't you worry. I love you. The wedding plans and who to invite are such a political thing with my mother. I ask you and you say you don't care who comes, as long as we're married at the end of the day.

But I need to sit with my Mom and iron out who we're inviting and where everyone will stay."

"But the wedding isn't until next June, more than seven months away," I protested.

"I just want to get a head start," Sierra answered. "I'll miss you, but have a great rugby tournament."

That Friday after waving good-bye to Sierra, I collected my salary for working in the school post office. I'd been saving up every paycheck for the past two-and-a-half months. I cadged a ride with my roommate and we drove down to the mall. I edged my way in to a small jewelry store where Sierra had admired engagement and wedding ring sets a few weeks before. I'd noted her size and the designs that made her eyes brighten. I asked to see engagement rings. The jeweler smoothly drew out a tray of sparkling diamond rings. I pointed at the one Sierra had tried on during our previous visit.

"An excellent choice," he said.

I told him Sierra's ring size, then took a deep breath and asked the price. The figure he quoted stunned me. I fingered the notes wadded into my pocket. "Uh, do you have something with a smaller diamond?" I asked.

The jeweler frowned. "I think this is the right one for your fiancé. If you don't have enough cash, you can leave a down payment, then pay off the rest with easy monthly payments."

"I want to give it to her on Sunday."

"No problem, I'll write out a payment contract and you can take the ring."

I signed the contract and paid the down payment. I barely had enough money left to take Sierra out to a fancy restaurant when she came home on Sunday evening where I would surprise her with the ring. I realized how much I missed her. Even with the rugby tournament the next day, it would be a lonely weekend without Sierra.

When we arrived at the tournament, we found Frank Prinsloo waiting for us. "Hurry up, you guys. You're late. The other teams have already arrived and I need to teach you some sevens tactics."

We gathered in a circle and pulled on our socks and boots as Frank gave us pointers on how to play rugby with only seven on a side. "The key to winning at sevens is possession. If you have the ball, you can control the pace and wait for gaps to develop. With only seven people on a team, the field will look wide open and you'll be tempted to make a break through the line early. But here's how to win. Stretch your line. Get the ball all the way to the wing on every possession, then I want to winger to run straight sideways."

"Sideways?" I asked. "I've always been taught to run straight."

"That's fifteens. In sevens I want the winger to sprint sideways. But only the winger. As he races sideways, the rest of you must hustle to line up in a good deep offensive line. Once the winger gets within five meters of the sidelines, I want him to stop and whip the ball back. As you swing the ball down the line, you'll find gaping holes in their defense. Run through the gaps, support each other and you'll score easy tries and win the tournament."

"I wish we'd had time to practice this," grumbled Mad Dog.

"It would have helped. But just do it, and you'll be fine."

In our first game, we received the kickoff. On the first play, Mad Dog thought he saw a gap in the defense. He darted in, got tackled and lost possession. The other team passed the ball crisply. Their tank-like winger crashed into our defensive line. It took two players to drag him down. He passed to an unmarked player as he went to ground and they scored easily.

Coach Prinsloo frowned on the sidelines and waved at me. I ran over before the kickoff. "You have to pass it all the way out to the winger on first phase ball."

"Remember to stretch our line and use the whole width of the pitch the way coach told us," I told the others.

"Sorry," said Mad Dog. "It looked so open."

Our fly-half kicked off, a high end-over-end kick. I sprinted under it and leaped in front of one of their players and caught the ball. I hurtled past him and outran the defense to score a try.

The first half—only seven minutes long—ended with the scores level. I stood with my hands on my head, sides heaving as I sucked in air. Coach Prinsloo came in and reiterated how to spread the ball wide.

We won a lineout and our scrum-half passed the ball out. Two more quick passes and our winger had the ball. He ran directly sideways sucking their defense across the field. I hurried to get in position for when the ball came back. Our winger stopped near the sideline and threw the ball back. By the time we'd passed the ball halfway across the field, the other team's defense was so badly out of position Mad Dog had an easy run through to score.

"It works, guys," Mad Dog shouted. "Keep it up."

We sailed through that first game and got more skillful as the tournament went on. The final against a team from Old Mission Bay Athletic Club was tough. They ran hard and scored two tries early. But Coach Prinsloo calmly repeated his strategy at half time. "You're receiving the kickoff second half. Run it the way I've told you and you'll score. Nothing can stop you lads." We controlled possession in the second half, scoring four tries and winning 24 points to12. As Mad Dog stood up to receive the cup, we pushed Coach Prinsloo in front of the crowd and gave him a loud cheer. Someone threw a cooler of ice on Coach's head.

I instinctively looked around for Sierra. I shook my head. I knew I was in trouble if even winning a rugby tournament didn't drive that girl out of my mind. I smiled as we celebrated our win, happy at the thought of having won the tournament and also having such a beautiful girl in love with me. One dark cloud tried to choke my happiness. I wanted Sierra, rugby and Africa. But Sierra didn't seem to want Africa.

I shook off the thought and planned how I'd surprise Sierra with the engagement ring the next evening. Back at the dorm, I called Sierra. "Having a good weekend?" I asked.

"No," Sierra answered. "I miss you. My world seems to move in slow motion when you're not here. How'd you do in the rugby tournament?"

"Great, we won!"

"And I missed it. Oh, Clay, I'm sorry. Coming here was a bum choice."

"What time are you coming back tomorrow?" I asked.

"Mid-afternoon. I have to go to church with my folks."

"I want to take you out to supper. Maybe that little bistro on Olive Mill Road."

"Sounds romantic. I can't wait."

After hanging up I felt a twinge of conscience when I thought about Sierra going to church with her parents. I no longer thought church was worth the trouble. I'd gone with my parents during the summer. I didn't want to battle with them. But inwardly I shut myself off as I sat on the hard shiny pews. Sierra knew I didn't bother with church anymore. I wondered if I'd have to attend church with her when we got married.

I slept in on Sunday, waking up just in time for lunch. I did some studying after lunch while I waited for Sierra to arrive. I called and made reservations at the bistro for 7 p.m. I went outside and sprawled out on the grass next the parking lot. I jerked my head up every time a car drove into the dorm parking lot. Finally Sierra arrived. I leaped up and ran to open her door. She stepped out and I gathered her into my arms. After a quick kiss, she pulled back and asked, "What happened to your forehead?"

I rubbed the lump above my eye and grinned. "Rugby game."

She peered at the lump. "It's covered with a network of squared off red lines. You sure you don't have some sort of tropical rash?"

I laughed. "It's the impression from someone's sock."

"A sock?"

"Yeah, I dove on the ball as someone was trying to kick it. His shin blasted my forehead and the spot where his sock hit my head left a fabric imprint. Haven't you ever seen one before?"

Sierra shook her head. "Do you think you'll survive until our wedding?"

"Definitely. Hey, I missed you and I've made reservations for the bistro at 7 p.m."

Sierra shook her left arm so she could see the face of her silver watch, which dangled loosely on her wrist. "That will give me just enough time to get ready."

"Three hours to get ready?" I questioned.

"You want me to look good don't you? Now, grab my suitcase out of the trunk."

At the bistro we ordered a plate of calamari as a starter. I ordered filet mignon and Sierra asked for chicken cordon bleu. As we waited for the calamari to come, I couldn't take my eyes off Sierra. "You really look good tonight."

"So you don't begrudge me the three hours it took to get ready?"

"No, it was worth the wait. Thank you so much for agreeing to be my wife. I can only think of one thing that might match your beauty." I reached into my pocket and pulled out the black velvet jewelry box. I set it on the table in front of Sierra.

"What's this?" Sierra asked, her aqua eyes open in surprise.

"Just open it."

Sierra reached out and stroked the top of the box. She took it with her right hand and set it in her open left palm. She gave me a quizzical look.

I nodded and smiled. "Go ahead and open it."

She squeezed the top of the box between her right thumb and forefinger. As she pulled the box open she tilted her head to peek in. "Oh!" Sierra exhaled and the box snapped shut.

"You don't like it?" I asked.

"Oh, I do ... I just didn't expect ... I ... it's beautiful!"

I reached over and took the box, opening it with one swift motion. I took the engagement diamond ring and slipped it onto her finger.

"I know I'd given you a slave ring when I promised to marry you. But I wanted you to have a proper engagement ring."

Tears began to leak out of Sierra's eyes. "Oh, Clay, I've never seen anything so beautiful." I stopped her words by leaning over the table and kissing her. She grabbed my shoulders and we kissed again, her tears adding salt to the sweet taste of her lips. The waiter, who had just arrived with a plate of calamari, cleared his throat.

I pulled back. "I just gave her an engagement ring," I explained, trying to smooth down the table cloth where it had rucked up under my plate.

"Very good sir," the waiter said with a mock bow. He served the calamari and retreated.

Sierra's eyes were transfixed on the ring. "Oh, Clay, the ring sparkles. I can't believe it." She looked at me. "I can't wait to be your wife. Forever."

46

She stood up and came to my side of the table and bent over and kissed me again. I could feel my pulse beating against my temples. As she released me I whispered, "Do you want to leave now and continue with the kissing?"

Sierra laughed. "No, let's enjoy this meal together." She lowered her voice. "We can kiss later."

I raised my eyebrows and smiled as I picked up a piece of calamari with my fingers from the plate.

"Use a fork," Sierra hissed.

"Sorry, too many years eating *ugali* with my hands in Africa."

Sierra's eyes clouded over and she frowned briefly. "This isn't Africa."

"Sorry," I answered, chastened. I took a fork to spear my next piece of calamari.

Sierra's words—"this isn't Africa"—haunted me in the months that followed. I graduated from college in mid-December, a goal I'd pushed towards since leaving Livingstone three-and-a-half years before. I'd held myself in tight control during those college years, just waiting to finish so I could go back to Africa, but now I was engaged to Sierra. And this sure wasn't Africa.

I moved into a small apartment built over Sierra's parents' garage and started working for her Dad after Christmas. As I unloaded my African skins and other trophies into the small room, I looked out the window at the sprawling suburban landscape. Africa suddenly seemed to be very far away, like an image viewed through the wrong side of a pair of binoculars.

I took out my box of shells and rummaged through it, the sparkling cowries clinking as I dribbled them through my fingers. I found the dawn cowrie I'd been searching for. The size of my thumbnail, it was dark chocolate brown with white zigzag stripes on its back. I loved the dawn cowrie with its distinctly African-looking pattern. I rubbed the shiny shell between my fingers, and then pocketed it. I sat on the bed and sighed.

Sierra had driven back to school earlier that day. I thought about our future. Could I really survive living in America the rest of my life? Could I ever persuade Sierra to go to Africa with me? I wanted Sierra and Africa. Could I have them both?

I changed into an old t-shirt and rugby shorts and pulled on a pair of Nike waffle-soled running shoes. I went for a long run carrying a rugby ball under my arm. When I came back, sweat dribbling down my forehead, Sierra's Dad came out and told me Sierra had called to say she'd arrived back at college.

"That's great! I'll give her a call after I shower," I said.

He nodded before saying, "Are you ready for your first day of work tomorrow? We need to leave at 7 a.m."

"I can't wait," I lied.

I called Sierra and we talked briefly. She seemed distracted by all her preparations for her last semester at college. I hung up, strangely disturbed.

Sierra's Dad showed me the ropes the next day. I learned who supplied what health foods and how to bargain for the best prices. The work wasn't hard, but after a couple of weeks my soul felt as withered as a corn stalk in an Africa drought.

I called Sierra that evening. "I can't do this," I stated.

"What?" she asked.

"I can't spend the rest of my life ordering carob chips and honey. I need to get back to Africa and do something meaningful."

"Earning money so we can get married seems pretty meaningful to me," Sierra replied.

"I can earn money anywhere. I've got to do something that will make a difference. I know I'm not much for going to church anymore, but I still need to make this world a better place."

"And you don't think providing healthy food for people is meaningful enough?"

"No, I don't. People here are so spoiled they can spend tons of money buying a certain type of wheat bran to add a few days of colon-cancer-free life. But it seems so pointless. I'm restless. Africa's calling me. I need to go home. I'm going crazy here."

"Here we are having our first argument and we're doing it on the phone," Sierra reprimanded me. "I think you just miss me. Why don't we get together and talk?"

"Let's meet at that all night restaurant next to the freeway in Ventura," I suggested.

"Tonight?" Sierra asked. "I have an English paper due tomorrow."

"Tonight," I insisted. "I'm leaving right now. Will you be there?"

"Of course."

I hung up and hurried out to my car, a small Datsun I'd bought with graduation money.

I got to the restaurant before Sierra. I ordered a Coke and sipped on the straw as I waited. My stomach churned. Sierra walked in the door and I stood up and waved. She smiled and waved back.

Sitting next to me at the booth, she slipped off her black leather coat. "So you're not getting along well with my Dad?" she asked.

"Your Dad is great. I'm just dying inside. I told you, I need to get back to Africa."

Sierra grabbed the menu and ordered a chocolate sundae. "If you go to Africa now, how will you earn money for when we get married?"

"I don't have to go right now. I'm willing to stick it out with your Dad until we get married if we go to Kenya after the wedding."

"Are you trying to blackmail me into taking the Kenyan honeymoon?"

I sighed. "No. I want to share the rest of my life with you. I love you, Sierra. But I've realized I can't spend the rest of my life in America. I have to get home to Africa. Either we go together or I go alone."

"What do you mean you'll go alone, Clay? You'll marry me and then go off to Africa on your own?"

I surprised myself by stating, "I mean that if you don't want to go with me to Africa, the wedding's off."

Her sundae arrived. She stared at it with a vacant glaze in her eyes. "I thought you said you loved me?"

"I'm confused," I answered. "I do love you. I can't see any way to live without you. But at the same time, I can't see any way I can go on living in America. If you can't go with me to Africa, maybe it's best if we break it off now. Otherwise I'll be miserable …"

"You'll be miserable with me as your wife?"

I shook my head. "It's not you, it's Africa. How can I explain it to you?" I closed my eyes and thought. Finally I went on. "When I hike through the forest in Kenya, I have to watch out for the wickedly hooked thorns of the wait-a-bit bush. If I get a row of wait-a-bit thorns stuck in my arm or leg, I have to move backwards to release the barb or risk ripping the thorns through my flesh. That's the best picture I can paint of Africa's hold on my heart. As long as I'm here in America, the imbedded thorns are tearing at my heart. I have to go back."

"I won't make you happy?"

"I'm sure you'd make me happy. But I couldn't really be fulfilled living here all my life. I'd end up making your life miserable as I pined for Africa."

Sierra's sundae began melting, but she made no effort to pick up a spoon. She leaned her head forward and rubbed her temples with both hands. She finally looked up at me, her eyes bulging with tears. "Clay, I don't think I can live without you. But I can't do Africa. It scares me." She paused. "If you make a trip back to Kenya, do you think you can unhook the wait-a-bit thorns and come back to me?"

I gently shook my head. "I don't know, Sierra. Maybe when I've made my visit to Africa, I'll be able to pull out the thorns that hold me tight. But somehow I don't think it will happen. All I know is right now I need to go home."

Sierra's lips trembled and the tears began to flow. I pulled some paper napkins out of the black metal dispenser and gave them to her. She wiped her eyes.

Sierra shook her head. "It's no good," she finally said, her voice husky from crying. "It just won't work. I've dreamed all my life of meeting my perfect man and then settling into a nice house in suburban Los Angeles with a swimming pool, having two kids and being a great mother. I can't give up that dream. Africa sounds exotic, but it also sounds dark and ominous. Your stories of Kenya thrill me. But when you insist that I live in Africa … I just can't. If you're giving me an ultimatum then I have one answer." She slipped off the engagement ring. "I can't do Africa. Take your ring back."

I felt like two different people. Half of me cried inside at the thought of losing Sierra. I put my arm around her and said, "Oh, Sierra, I'm so sorry for hurting you." But the other half of me surged with elation. If I was no longer engaged, I could go back to Africa!

"So what will you do now?" Sierra asked hoarsely.

I shrugged. "Buy a plane ticket for Nairobi."

"But what will you do there?"

"I really don't know. Maybe find a job with a tour company. Maybe hook up with Titch in Sudan."

"How can you just head off with no real plans?"

"I have to go home."

Sierra stood up. "I'm leaving, Clay. I love you. I probably always will. But you already have a mistress. You're so in love with Africa that I really couldn't compete."

I escorted her to the parking lot. "That's not true, Sierra. I love you. Just come with me to Africa."

"And if I don't? Would you choose me over Africa?"

I had no answer. She slipped into her car. She took a long ragged breath. Her nose twitched as she sniffed and a fresh flow of tears came. "Go home Clay. Just go home."

I felt the lump of the dawn cowrie in my pocket. I pulled it out. "Take this, Sierra, to remember me."

She took the shell and stroked it. She looked up at me with a confused puppy-like expression. She shook her head slowly and slammed the door shut. I could see her hands tensely gripping the steering wheel of her Camaro as she pulled out of the parking lot.

I went and sat in my car and found myself crying. Had I made the right choice? "I need to get back to Africa," I told myself, sitting up and starting the car.

I broke the news to Sierra's parents. Her Dad didn't seem too upset and promised to keep a box full of my African skins and other treasures. With my wages in my pocket I set off to drive to New York where I'd leave my car with my parents and catch a plane for Nairobi.

I turned my back on California and headed down the freeway. I was going home!

Book Five
Sudan

January 1983

47

I arrived in the Nairobi airport in the early evening. The warm cloak of the African night welcomed me home. I caught a taxi to a nearby mission guesthouse where my parents had often stayed. They had space and I booked in for a week.

"Long enough to figure out what I'll be doing," I told the white-haired missionary lady who sat behind the reception desk. She smiled stiffly and handed me a room key attached to a huge plastic disk with the name of the guesthouse. She had a questioning look on her face as she eyed my shoulder-length straw-colored hair.

"Don't ever take the key off the compound," the receptionist warned me.

I fell into bed, exhausted by the trip. Soon a mosquito woke me up by dive-bombing my ears. I'd forgotten how annoying they could be. Maybe it was a good thing I hadn't brought Sierra to Africa. Thinking of Sierra caused my heart to drop. Had I done the right thing? I wadded up the pillow and pulled the sheet over my head to keep the mosquito away. Though tired, I couldn't sleep. My body seemed to think it was time for lunch. When I woke up in the morning I felt terrible. My twisted sheet and blanket had fallen to the floor.

I pulled the curtain back and welcomed the Kenyan sunshine. I rubbed my eyes and grabbed a towel and walked down the hallway to take a shower. At the breakfast table I met some missionaries who knew my parents.

"So your folks gave up on Africa, did they?" the man with drooping jowls asked.

"Actually they took a job recruiting new missionaries back in the States. They felt it might be a more strategic ministry."

The man looked sour and repeated, "I think they just gave up on Africa. To tell you the truth, young man, I don't know what will really help this continent. Our mission has been starting churches for almost eighty years and it doesn't seem like the Africans have learned anything. If it weren't for us missionaries, the whole church enterprise would fall apart." His fleshy cheeks jiggled and a small shaving nick on his neck began to weep a trickle of blood.

"Now, Harold," his wife reprimanded. "Don't get all worked up. You know what the doctors said about your blood pressure."

Harold humphed and then asked me, "So what have you come out to do? Are you going to your parents' mission outpost near Narok?"

"Actually, I didn't come out to do mission work. I'm looking for a job. Maybe in the safari business."

Harold opened his mouth but no words came out. He looked at his wife, questions filling his eyes.

"Good to meet you both," I said politely and stood up and went back to my room. I gathered my passport and a few travelers' checks and stuffed them deep in my pockets. I walked out of the guesthouse and hopped on the yellow city bus with a green stripe under the windows, much like a one-hooped rugby shirt. Passengers filled the bus like popcorn in a pot without a top. At every stop people tumbled off while others squeezed on. Downtown, I shouldered my way off the bus, one hand in my pocket to protect my money and passport.

I produced my passport and signed a few travelers' checks in the presence of the foreign exchange teller in the big Standard Bank on Kenyatta Avenue.

With shillings in my pocket, I stopped by a safari company to offer my services. The manager just shook his head. "I'm sorry, but we're nationalizing most of our positions."

"But I was born here in Kenya," I pointed out.

He showed me to the door. "I'm sorry, but our policy is to hire real Kenyans, not Kenya cowboys."

After a morning of closed doors, I slumped into a chair at the Blukat Restaurant on Muindi Mbingu Street opposite the city market. "Do you still make the best *samosas* in Nairobi?" I asked the waiter.

"*Ndiyo Bwana*, Yes sir," he responded with a smile.

"Then bring me four with a cold Coke. I'll eat them while I wait for you to bring me a plate of chicken curry and rice." The waiter came back with a small clear plate with four triangular pastries oozing grease onto a white torn-in-half napkin. Four lemon wedges festooned the edges of the plate. I squeezed a lemon wedge onto the first *samosa*, then took a bite. The spicy meat filling bit my tongue. "Mmmh! I've missed *samosas*," I said to no one in particular.

I wondered if Sierra would like to try a *samosa*. Most restaurants offered both meat and vegetarian *samosas*. "Forget her," I ordered myself.

After lunch I visited a missionary mechanic who'd been asked to sell my Dad's old Land Rover. My heart surged as I walked into the missionary compound. There stood our Land Rover, sagging a bit to the left and covered in desiccated purple jacaranda flowers. I went over and stroked my old friend.

"Not one person has expressed any interest in your Dad's Land Rover," the mechanic said, wiping his greasy hands on a greasier old towel. "His price is good, but I told him it's just too old."

"It's almost old enough to be a classic," I joked.

The mechanic laughed. "It's a classic, all right." He opened the hood. "Easy to fix. You only need a screwdriver and a pair of pliers. And occasionally a hammer."

"Dad said if you hadn't sold it yet, I could use it as long as I needed it." I handed him a letter from my Dad.

The mechanic squinted at the letter, leaving a greasy thumbprint on the top corner. "It's all yours. The battery's probably dead, but otherwise, I had it in running order when your Dad left. Of course that was seven or eight months ago."

We jumpstarted the Land Rover and the engine roared and belched smoke. Coughing, I tried to move away from the toxic cloud. The mechanic handed me an envelope. "All the paper work is in there. You'll have to renew the road license and get third-party insurance."

I thanked him and lurched and jolted out of his compound. A uniformed guard opened the spiked metal gate. The stone wall surrounding the compound had shards of broken glass set in the concrete on the top.

That afternoon I drove to Udongo Rugby Club, my rugby kit in an Adidas shoulder bag. I walked into the Udongo clubhouse and greeted the Kenyan players who were arriving for practice. One frowned at me. "*Kwa nini huyu mzungu amekuja kwa kilabu yetu ya wana wa udongo?*" he asked a friend. "Why has this white guy come to our club for sons of the soil?"

I smiled and answered, "*Nimekuja kwa sababu mimi ni mwana wa udongo pia.*" My answer, "I've come because I'm also a son of the soil," didn't please him.

He pointed at the door. "Why don't you go and join a club with others of your kind. We don't need you here at Udongo Rugby Club. We have enough good players."

I hadn't expected such open rejection. I edged towards the door, when a massive hand gripped my shoulder. I turned and looked into Ox's face. "Ox! How are you? I thought I had an open invitation to join your club."

The stern look on Ox's face told me he wasn't pleased. I wasn't sure whether his ire was directed at me or the Kenyan player who'd been so rude. "Come with me, Clay." He walked me out to the rugby field and we sat on the stone steps that served as a grandstand.

"How have you been, little buddy," Ox asked.

"Dying in America. I thought I'd never finish college. You'll never guess who coached our rugby team in Santa Barbara. Coach Prinsloo! He said you were the best player he ever coached."

Ox had a pained look on his face and he looked over his shoulder. "Please don't mention Coach's name around here," he warned.

"Why not?"

"He's South African, and right now anyone with South African connections is being ostracized."

"But he taught you everything you know about rugby, Ox."

"I know that and I owe Coach a lot. It's just not a convenient time or place to announce it. You saw how those guys responded when you came into the clubhouse?"

"Yeah, what's up? When I saw you a few years ago after my last game for Livingstone, you said I'd be welcome here."

"That was our original intent. Sons of the soil, no matter what color. But we've gotten some more radical players in and they are so determined to prove Kenyans can play rugby that they don't want any whites on their team, regardless of their birthplace."

"So you're kicking me out?"

Ox shifted his weight onto his left foot. "Hip injury," he complained. "It happened last year. These Nairobi fields are hard as concrete. I don't get to play anymore, Clay. I'm just a coach these days."

"I guess I understand. Well, I just wanted a run around. I arrived in Nairobi yesterday and couldn't wait to play some rugby. I'm also looking for a job. Any suggestions?"

"There's not much available right now. The economy isn't doing well since last year's attempted coup. Besides, the government is reducing the number of work permits given to expatriate workers."

He turned to the players who had filed out of the clubhouse, their rugby cleats clicking on the stone steps. "Stretch out and run two brisk laps, then I'll join you," Ox instructed.

"I'm from Kenya," I told Ox. "I'm not an expatriate."

"What passport do you travel on?" Ox asked.

"A U.S. passport," I admitted. "But I have a Kenyan birth certificate."

"The government will regard you as an expatriate. Tell you what. I've got to run this practice. If you want a game, drive half a mile up the road to Kiboko Rugby Club. They're a relaxed club with a good mix of black and white players and no racial agenda. If I hadn't been one of the founding members of Udongo,

I'd be tempted to join them. Kiboko used to be based out at Naivasha during colonial days, but the numbers of available players shrank and they moved the club to Nairobi. I hate to send a good player like you to join our rivals, but if you're anything like me, you live to play rugby. And since Udongo isn't welcoming white players at the moment, join Kiboko. We actually play them in the season opener this Saturday."

"Thanks Ox. You're all right. I'll see you around."

I wandered back to my Land Rover and tossed my bag on the passenger seat. Considering how much I loved Africa, the continent hadn't exactly welcomed me home with open arms. Thinking of arms reminded me of Sierra.

I shook my head in an attempt to forget her and then chugged the Land Rover over to Kiboko Rugby Club. A large painted signboard with a grinning hippo in a hooped rugby shirt holding a mug of beer pointed the way to the clubhouse. A small wooden plaque above the bar read: The Drunken Hippo. I wondered if this was just a social club. I met a couple players and introduced myself. One said, "I remember you, Clay. You used to captain Livingstone. You broke my collarbone when I played for Nairobi School."

I cringed. Would my history at Livingstone set up impenetrable barriers for entering this club as well? Instead the young player thrust out his hand and pumped mine up and down. "Welcome to Kiboko Rugby Club. I'm Owino and if you're here to play for us, we'll take the Barclays Cup this year. We used to fear the way you guys from Livingstone tackled. Didn't you have a short little scrumhalf?"

I smiled. "My best friend, Titch. He's up in Sudan working. When he comes out for a break, I'm sure we can persuade him to play for us."

Owino called some of the other players over. "This is Clay, and he wants to join Kiboko." I was pleased to see mostly black Kenyan players with a smattering of whites.

"Welcome to Kiboko," said a tall balding Kenyan with a booming voice. "I'm Sam Kariuki and I'm the captain this year. What position do you play?"

"Eighth man, back row, second row. Actually, I'd even play in the front row if it would help me get a game."

Kariuki laughed. "I'm the eighth man and I'm not giving you my spot, but I'm sure we'll find a place for you in the forwards. The changing room is back there." He pointed to a white enamel-painted door beside the bar. Black-and-white team photos looked down at me from the walls as I headed to the changing room.

I donned my rugby clothes and ran out to join the others. The forwards were gasping and groaning as they shoved a scrum machine back and forth in the grass behind the in-goal area. "Second row, Clay," Kariuki commanded. I bound tightly to the other second row forward and we pushed and shoved until my ears were raw. I had forgotten to smear my ears with Vaseline.

After practice we showered and I sat on a long-legged stool in front of the bar. "Let me buy you a drink, Clay," Owino offered.

"Thanks, I'll just take a Coke."

Owino grinned. "Still following the straight and narrow even now that you're out from under those strict missionary rules at Livingstone?" he teased.

He poured a Tusker beer, which frothed over the edge of the glass beer mug.

I shrugged. "I never acquired a taste for beer."

Kariuki and some others huddled together around a table at the far end of the bar. Finally Kariuki stood up and carried a sheet of paper to the bulletin board. "Here's the roster for Saturday's season-opening fixture against Udongo. We'll have a second fifteen game the same day. Both games are here at Kiboko Field."

The players all crowded around, but I hung back. I'd worked hard in practice, but I really couldn't expect to be named to the first fifteen right away. As the tide of players around the team lists ebbed away, I edged over. I read the second fifteen list first and was disappointed not to find my name. I looked up and there was my name as second row for the first fifteen. Kariuki leaned over my shoulder. "Be here at 3 p.m. We'll go over strategy and work on lineouts. We're glad you joined us, Clay."

"Thanks, Kariuki. It's good to be back playing rugby in Kenya."

48

As I drove back to the mission guesthouse I came to a police check. Two sets of metal spikes had been set across the road leaving just enough room for one car to get past by maneuvering with a sharp S turn. A policeman wearing a dark blue overcoat waved at me with his flashlight. I pulled over. He peered at the road license on the windshield, which I'd renewed that afternoon. He slowly circled the car, then came to my window and stated in a solemn voice. "You have a problem with your right rear brake light. It is not working."

"Thanks for telling me. I'll make sure I get it fixed tomorrow," I promised.

The policeman shook his head. "This is a problem. What do you think we could do about fixing it now?"

A wave of irritation flashed through me. "I have a screw driver. Maybe I could fix it now, but it's pretty dark outside and I'm not sure I have a spare bulb."

The policeman laughed. "You don't understand. I don't want you to repair the light now. I want you to fix the problem with me. If not, I will have to charge you."

The light dawned. He wanted me to give him a bribe so I wouldn't get a ticket. I followed my Dad's example. "I'm sorry, I don't have any money with me to fix the problem right now. So if you have to charge me for driving with a broken brake light, then go ahead and write me a ticket and I'll go pay my fine in court."

The policeman cleared his throat. "Oh, just go. I'll release you this time. But be sure you fix the light tomorrow."

"Yes sir, thank you sir," I replied, and twisted the steering wheel to fit between the two rows of metal spikes that looked like tyrannosaurus teeth.

The next day I decided to drive out to Baridi to see Livingstone. I was pretty sure Titch's parents still lived there and I could spend a night or two with them and find out any news about Titch.

I pulled into the school parking lot. A shudder swept from my shoulders down my back. All the painful leavings tumbled over each other in my mind. Green tree stood sturdy and climbable. I had to fight back the urge to climb the tree like I used to as a little kid. As I stood next to the Land Rover I gazed at the old yellow-brick administration building. I turned and the green grass of the rugby field stretched out before me. I shivered. I was home. A bell rang and students poured out of the classrooms. I was shocked to see students without uniforms. Where were the boys in khaki? Where were the girls in gray skirts, white blouses and red sweaters? What had happened to Livingstone?

I expected to see Leah and Titch and all the others from my class. But as I peered at the teeming mass of faces, I couldn't recognize anyone. Some of these kids must have been at Livingstone when I left, but they'd grown. The school buildings looked the same, but the people had changed.

"Can I help you?" I short brown-haired man with a moustache asked me.

"Uh, yeah. I'm Clay Andrews. I graduated from Livingstone a few years ago and I just wanted to see my old school again."

"I'm John Dobson and I've been teaching physics here for two years. The students are heading to chapel. Come with me and I can introduce you to the teachers at staff tea. What did you say your name was again?"

It seemed funny to have to introduce myself as a newcomer to this teacher. "I'm Clay. Clay Andrews." Inside I screamed. *You've only been here two years. I lived here for ten years. This is my home. Don't you know who I am?*

My eyes wandered around the assembly hall during the chapel. I recognized a few of the kids and saw some teachers I remembered. I couldn't see Coach Layton.

I walked to staff tea with the physics teacher feeling like I was in some sort of time warp. The trees, the buildings, everything looked so familiar. But Livingstone had moved on without me.

At staff tea the physics teacher stood up during announcements. "I found one of Livingstone's former students in the parking lot. I'd like you all to welcome … ah … Clint. Clint Anderson."

I stood up, embarrassed. "Actually I'm Clay Andrews, class of 1979. It's good to be back at Livingstone."

During the prayer time, my senior English teacher, Miss Fleet, prayed specifically that God would continue to guide me in my Christian faith. Her words burned my soul and I squirmed. What would she think if she knew my faith had dwindled away? When the prayer time ended, Miss Fleet came over to talk to me. "Where's Coach Layton?" I asked.

"He and his wife left last year," answered Miss Fleet. "We've had a huge turnover in teachers. Say, can you visit my class next period? I'm sure this year's senior class would love to ask questions about college life."

"I'm not sure I have much to share," I said, trying to put her off.

"Sure you do," she insisted, herding me away to senior English.

I slouched against the black board as Miss Fleet introduced me to her class. "We'll give Clay a few minutes to tell us how God has been leading him since he left Livingstone."

I left God's leading out of my story. I'd made my own way since Livingstone. "I studied business administration at college," I finished, "hoping to get a job overseas."

"So what job did you find?" asked a boy with red hair and freckles.

I glanced sideways. "Actually, I'm still searching."

"How did you pay for college?" one of the girls asked.

"I had a soccer scholarship."

The girl looked puzzled. "How did you get a soccer scholarship from here? Did you play sports at Livingstone?"

"Well, yes I did ..." I began but Miss Fleet cut me off.

"Thank you so much for sharing with us, Clay. Now, we're going to have to get on with reading Shakespeare this morning." She escorted me to the door. "Thank you again for coming."

I slipped out the door. I hadn't even been away from Livingstone for four years and already people had forgotten who I was. When I'd graduated I had thought I'd built myself a permanent place in the Livingstone rugby firmament. And now some dame had asked if I used to play sports when I was at school!

Disappointed at my less-than-heroic welcome, I wandered to the Land Rover and drove down to see Titch's parents. "Clay!" Titch's Mom called, stepping onto the porch to hug me. "How lovely to see you! I didn't know you were back in Kenya. Come in and have some *chai*."

I sat down at the kitchen table while Titch's Mom boiled some water. She set a plate of peanut butter cookies in front of me. "How's Titch doing?" I asked.

"It's hard work up there in the Sudan," she answered, pouring hot water into two mugs. "But Titch loves it. He says there's nothing more satisfying than drilling a good borehole and leaving the community with clean drinking water. Titch also installs hand pumps so people can get clean water right near their homes and the people save hours walking back and forth to the nearest river."

"Do you know when Titch is coming out again? I really want to see him. I'm actually kind of looking for work and hoped that maybe his water company might be looking for someone to handle the business side of their operations."

"Titch said he'd be out next week. They're flying out and then driving back up with a big truck filled with pipes and other equipment."

"I'd love to travel back up with him."

"Well, why don't you stay with us until Titch comes out. You can stay in his room. I think his plane flies in next Tuesday. You could go in and pick him up. He has a week of vacation before they head back to Sudan."

I thanked her and went out to the Land Rover and carried my backpack and sports bag up to Titch's bedroom. Nothing had changed. Even the covers from the East African Safari Rally programs that were stuck to the wall with yellowing sticky tape had been there since our days at Livingstone. We'd had slumber parties in this room on special weekends back in grade school. I sat on the bed to think. I was glad to be back home in Africa. But it seemed like some drama director had filled the familiar stage with new characters.

49

Saturday I drove to Nairobi to play rugby with Kiboko. The smell of liniment hammered me in the face as I walked into the changing room. Our captain, Kariuki, had a bottle of horse liniment and was applying it liberally to his thighs.

"*Sasa*? How are you Clay?" Kariuki asked, offering his gigantic hand in greeting.

"Fit," I said using the new sheng greeting before slouching down on the wood-slatted bench and dropping my bag at my feet. Leaning my back against the brick wall, I rubbed my neck with my thumbs. "All that practice on the scrum machine really did a number on my neck," I complained. "I'm still stiff."

Kariuki offered his liniment. "No thanks," I said smiling. "That stuff's too strong for me."

Owino came in with a bag full of jerseys and dumped it on the floor. Players began grabbing for their numbers. "Here's number five," Kariuki said. "It's yours, Clay." He wadded the shirt up and threw it to me.

I tossed the rugby jersey on my bag and started to change. My only white shorts dated back to my years at Livingstone and several rugby seasons slipping and sliding on Kenya's red mud had left the shorts more orange-brown than white. I pulled them on and slipped my gum guard into the front pocket. Next I pulled up my knee-length black stockings. I pulled my jersey on. I shoved my feet into my worn and comfortable rugby boots before taking a gob of Vaseline and rubbing it thickly around my ears to reduce earburn in the scrums.

Outside, Kariuki called us into a circle where we did a short, methodical stretch. Angawa knelt, desperately trying to wind some tape around the front of his boot in an attempt to keep his foot from sliding out of the hole that had ripped open between the instep leather and the studs.

"Five minutes to kick off, lads," the ref said trotting out to the center line. He blew his whistle and called for the captains. Kariuki went out for the coin toss.

"We kick off," Kariuki said when he came back, "and we're on this side."

Osimbo, our fly-half, gathered the ball from the referee who turned and counted to be sure each team had fifteen players. He shrilled his whistle. Osimbo looked at the forwards, raising his hand as a signal. As he dropped his arm and stepped into the kick, Angawa and I started sprinting, timing our run to reach the line just as Osimbo kicked the ball.

Osimbo lofted a beautiful floater. A tall Udongo second-row forward called for the catch. The black-shirted Udongo forwards wrapped tough arms tautly around him and formed a perfect wedge. I felt like I had run into one of the red anthills that littered Kenya's drylands.

Dropping low into a horizontal position, I wrapped myself around the man with the ball and began pushing. Our other forwards crashed into the slow-moving human caterpillar and halted Udongo's forward progress. Udongo slipped the ball out to their scrum-half who dipped his shoulder and gave a long underhand spiral pass back to their fly-half. The fly-half took one quick step and kicked the ball deep behind our winger. The ball bounced once in the field and then into touch. We jogged back for the lineout.

I won the lineout and passed the ball to our scrum-half. With two searing passes, the ball reached our first center, Githugu, a quick-footed runner. He faked a pass to his right, selling a dummy as we call it in rugby, and cut left, just inside his man who had bitten at the fake. Surging ahead with a curious, slippery sidestep, Githugu slanted his run to the right to join the second center. Udongo's eighth man, the surly player who had told me to leave their clubhouse, hustled across the field in hot pursuit. Seeing the tackler coming, Githugu shoveled a quick pass to his right without looking.

An Udongo defender picked off Githugu's pass and sprinted past our back line, now badly split apart because of the attacking move. I turned and tried to chase down the runner, but he had too much of a head start. He set the ball down between the posts for four points. The Udongo kicker slotted the two-point conversion and we were behind 6-0.

Kariuki, a flame glinting in his eyes, scolded us. "We can take these guys, but we have to work at it. Now, no more mistakes."

We battled on with no change in score. Late in the half their fly-half kicked the ball deep behind our backline. Nzomo, our winger, caught the ball and sprinted forward in a quick counter-attack, carrying the ball in front of him with two hands. I hustled over to support him. I found Angawa matching me stride for stride.

Nzomo looked in at us and moved both arms as if to swing the ball to us. The Udongo winger took a half step toward us and Nzomo squirted around him, eyes on the try line. Their fullback had drifted across and took Nzomo across the thighs with a diving tackle. Nzomo half-turned as he was hit and popped a short, soft pass, which I gathered in at full tilt. Angawa still surged alongside of me, arms pumping in his full body running motion. I ran straight at one last defender. Lowering my left shoulder I hit him as I tossed the ball to a grateful Angawa. I tumbled to the ground on top of the tackler and looked up to see Angawa romping across the try line and making a belly flop dive as he grounded the ball for a try. Osimbo fluffed the easy conversion. We trailed, but we'd cut the margin to 6-4.

A few minutes later the ref called one of our backs offside on a loose scrum. The Udongo fly-half kicked a field goal cleanly between the posts for three more points. When the whistle blew for half time Udongo led 9-4.

During the five minute break, we stood on the field downing water while Kariuki exhorted us. "If we take the ball cleanly on the kick off, I want to run a play we call the Kiboko." He looked at me. "That's where we fake the pass to the backs and pop the ball to Owino on the blindside."

We lined up ten yards behind the center line to receive the kick off. Their fly-half put his boot to the ball. It floated like a wounded pigeon hit with a pellet gun. Muniafu, a strong young player, called for the ball. As he caught it, I drove into him, stripping the ball down with my shoulder. Our other forwards converged around us. Holding the ball down and away from sight of the Udongo players, I checked to see if Owino was ready. He had retreated about ten yards, pretending to limp as if he'd been knocked in the leg on the play. As our scrum-half faked a pass to the left, I popped the ball to Owino as he sprinted by the right side of the maul. He caught the ball and squeezed it tightly to his taut, balloon-sized gut. Owino burst past the loose scrum and into the open field. Veering to his left, Owino headed for their fly-half who drifted across to cover. The reedy fly-half managed to grab Owino's shirt sleeve and hang on as Owino dragged him down the field.

Our backs had streaked up in a tight line. Owino dished the ball off neatly to Osimbo who passed the ball back to Githugu. Githugu ran straight at the remaining defender, drawing the tackle and passing off at the last second to Nzomo. Nzomo carried the ball triumphantly into the in-goal area and set it down with a flourish between the posts.

Osimbo made the kick, putting us in the lead 10-9.

We clung to our slim lead. The Udongo forwards became more ponderous, but they still managed to control most of the possession and, behind the magic leg of their talented fly-half, they kept driving us back towards our goal line. Eventually Udongo scored a pushover try from a five-yard scrum. Their fly-half neatly chipped the kick over and Udongo led 15-10.

Kariuki's shoulders hunched forward. Owino had a pained look on his sweat-beaded face. We only had a few minutes left. "Come on, Kiboko!" I said. "We don't want to lose now." I gathered in Osimbo's kick-off and charged at an Udongo forward. Just before contact, I put my left arm out, fully extended, and hit the player on the forehead with my palm in a classic rugby hand-off. My maneuver successfully held off the tackle and I was past him. Another black-shirted player came in for a tackle as I reached the twenty-two meter line. I crashed into him and we both went to the ground. I played the ball back as I hit the hard earth, but the other Kiboko players lagged behind. A player from Udongo picked the ball up and passed it to their fullback who kicked it into touch. In his haste, the ball squibbed off his foot and went almost straight side-ways. Kariuki reached down and gave me a hand up. "All right guys," he said, the fire back in his eyes. *"Twende kama yeye.* Let's go like he did. Two-man lineout."

Angawa and I stayed in the lineout. The other forwards dropped back ten yards.

"Simba," Kariuki called out, giving the code for a play we'd practiced once before the game. Ken, our hooker, licked his fingers before gripping the ball. I took three quick steps forward, while Angawa drew his man to the back of the line. Ken lobbed the ball in the gap between us. Job, our small but slippery scrum-half, darted into the lineout, caught the ball and then squirted around his opposite number and ran for the line. The Udongo forwards converged on him. He faked past one, but had no room to slip around anyone else.

As a big forward swallowed Job, I reached him and drove in hard, ripping the ball down. I felt a comforting thump as Angawa bound in on the side protecting the ball and driving forward. The other Kiboko forwards piled on as well. Job managed to extricate himself and, thinking he saw an opening, he called for the ball. I noticed Owino standing about ten yards back from the play, nodding vig-orously. I pointed with my chin back at Owino. Job understood instantly and stepped a bit to the right to camouflage the ball. Owino was running now, get-ting up a head of steam. I tossed the ball to him. Owino brushed off two players, but they slowed him down enough for a player to stand him up on the goal line. Angawa and Kariuki had peeled off the last maul and joined Owino immediately, securing the ball and binding tightly around it. As the Udongo players frantically tried to steal the ball and push us off the line, we gave the ball to Job who swung it out to where our backs waited eagerly.

With deft passes the ball flew out to Nzomo at the right wing. The Udongo line had tightened, fearing an inside break. Nzomo caught the ball about ten yards away from the goal line but he had fifteen yards of lateral space. Spreading his legs wide, Nzomo swung right around his opposite number and made a diving leap into the corner for the try. We pounded Nzomo on the back and retreated behind the halfway line to await the kick. Nzomo's try left us trailing 15-14 and Osimbo had to make a difficult conversion. Taking the ball in a straight line back from the spot where the try had been scored, Osimbo jammed his heel into the grass to make a divot and gently propped the ball up. He moved back almost to the forty yard line to increase the angle.

Osimbo took four long steps back from the ball followed by two strides sideways to the left. He reached down and adjusted his boot. We waited. Osimbo took two short jerky steps, got into stride, and swept his right foot soccer-style into the oval ball. He caught this one right. It flew toward the uprights, end over end. It was high, but it looked like it would miss wide right. At the last second it curved a bit to the left and dropped over the cross bar. The kick counted! We led 16-15! Before Udongo could bring the ball up for a kick off, the ref blew three long blasts on his whistle. The game was over! Kiboko had won!

We ran to the fifty-yard line and formed a congratulatory tunnel for the Udongo players, clapping for them and shaking their hands as they walked through. Most only mumbled congratulations and then sat down bad-naturedly on the stone bleachers. Ox stood at the end of the line and shook my hand firmly. "You've grown up to be quite a rugby player," he rumbled. A laugh wrinkled the skin around his eyes. "I think some of my Udongo players are rethinking their decision to tell you to join Kiboko."

I sat down next to some of the Udongo players. "Great game, you guys," I began.

"We'll beat you next time," one of them smiled.

When I reached out to shake their eighth man's hand, he ignored me and turned and limped into the bar.

"Don't worry about him," Ox said. "I always knew you'd be a tough rugby player, Clay."

The win felt so good I didn't notice the lumps on my shins, the ache in my shoulder, the abrasion on my forehead or the cuts on my knees. I'd feel them later in the shower. A strong hand clamped itself on my shoulder. I looked at the dirty cracked fingernails and thought my Dad must have showed up.

I leaned back and looked up. "Titch! What are you doing here?" I stood up and hugged him.

"One of our team members came down with a bad case of malaria so we had to airlift him out. They needed someone to nursemaid him on the plane so they sent me since I was due for a break in a few days anyway."

"Is he okay?" I asked.

"He should be. He's in hospital getting pumped full of quinine right now. Seems the malaria is chloroquine resistant. But he'll survive. Great game!"

"Did you watch all of it?"

Titch shook his head. "Just the last few minutes. I read about the game in the paper and came over to see some rugby. I didn't know I'd see you here."

I turned and called, "Ox, Titch is here."

Ox lumbered over from where he'd been talking with the Udongo players. He gripped Titch's hand. "If all you Livingstone players join Kiboko, we'll never win the Kenya Cup," he said, a smile on his face.

"I'm just down from Sudan," Titch said. "I doubt I'll have a chance to play any rugby."

Titch faced me. "So when did you come to Kenya? Last I knew you were working in the States and scheduled to marry some California babe."

"I missed Africa. I called the wedding off and came out. I was just with your parents this morning. Need a ride home? I've got my Dad's old Land Rover."

50

"Come back to Sudan with me," Titch insisted as we bounced down the winding road to Baridi. "Our project has been looking for someone to do logistics. Ordering supplies, paying wages, keeping track of money, everything. We've got three engineers and we know how to drill wells, but everything in our little office is a mess."

"Well, I haven't had much luck finding work in Nairobi. They're into nationalization these days. You're sure they'd hire me?"

"We'll go into our Nairobi office on Monday. If we're not careful, they may poach you to work in that office. But you've got to see Sudan. It's old Africa. The place has been hammered by war since the late 1950s. Right now there's peace, but no one's certain how long it will last. There's some unrest boiling right now with some soldiers in the South. But there's so much need, it's a great place to serve God. Every little thing we do makes such a difference."

Some uncomfortable guilt feelings pricked my mind. I'd tried to leave God out of my life, but Titch still seemed to have faith.

On Monday we visited the Water for All office in Nairobi. "We could certainly use you in Sudan," said Dwight, Titch's boss. "We've just gotten a grant to drill twenty new boreholes. A good logistician could help us get the drilling team in the field more efficiently. You say you have a business degree?"

I nodded, surprised at the whirlwind pace at which the interview was being conducted.

"Well, if you want to drive back up with Titch, I can have your contract ready in a few days." He turned to Titch. "Bill will recover from this bout with malaria, but the doctors have told us to invalid him back to the States. So you can't have your ten days off. We'll have the truck filled with supplies by Wednesday. Can you and Clay drive it up?"

Titch's eyes caught mine. He smiled. "No problem. Sudan, here we come. What route will we use?"

"Uganda's still unstable. You'll have to drive through northern Kenya on the road through Lokichoggio."

Two days later with Titch balanced in the driver's seat, we inched the old Mercedes truck through the Nairobi traffic. My backpack with everything I owned in the world had been tossed in the back. The stench of billowing black diesel fumes from other trucks filled my nostrils as the truck labored up the narrow blacktop road, strewn with potholes. After the first day, the tarmac ended and the truck bucked over the spring-breaking dirt and rock roads of northern Kenya.

Titch looked over at me. "This is Africa. Wait until you see Sudan."

I scanned the horizon and couldn't see any signs of habitation. I smiled. "It's good to be back in the bush," I answered.

We had no major breakdowns and after almost a week on the road we arrived at the Water for All compound in Tindilo smothered in dust. Two old Sudanese men hurried to the truck, smiles wrinkling their smooth faces. "Titch! You have come back to us." They took turns pumping Titch's hand.

Titch introduced them to me. "This is Pastor Paul. He's the pastor of the church here."

Pastor Paul grasped my hand. "Welcome to Sudan! We're glad you've come to serve the Lord with us."

"And this is Joshua," Titch went on. "He runs our kitchen."

Joshua solemnly bowed his head as he shook my hand. "Food is ready," he said, leading us to a long table under a thatched roof.

I met Luke, the project director, and Titch introduced me to the rest of the team who had just served themselves and were sitting at the table.

"I see we have a guest tonight," Titch said as he reached a girl with short dark hair. "Meet Amani Hunter. She works at a clinic here in town." He turned to Amani. "Tired of eating by yourself?"

Amani laughed. "Anything wrong with wanting some company?" she asked.

"Come get your food," Joshua said, taking me by the arm.

Titch and I, our plates overflowing with food, sat on either side of Amani. "You're new to Sudan," she began.

"Yeah, but I'm not a tourist," I defended myself. "I grew up in Kenya."

"I feel like I should have grown up in Kenya," Amani said.

"How'd you get a Swahili name?" I asked. "Did you know your name means peace?"

"Yes, actually. My Mom gave me the name."

"How'd your Mom know Swahili?" asked Titch.

"Haven't I told you about my Mother?"

Titch stuffed a potato into his mouth and shook his head.

"Well, Mom grew up in Kenya like you guys. She even went to school at Livingstone."

"You never told me this before," Titch said.

"You never asked," Amani replied. "She always expected to come back to Africa to live and work. But after she went to college in the States, she got married, I came along and life went by. Whenever Mom talked about Kenya, she got a faraway look in her eyes. I was raised on her stories about hiking in the forest, eating *ugali* at Kenyan homes, the homesickness and camaraderie of roommates in the boarding school. Her stories tasted and smelled like Africa. I sometimes felt I was right there with her. So it's kind of like I was raised in Kenya. The Kenya of my Mom's memories."

"Is that why you came to Africa?" I asked.

"Yeah, I think so. I've had wanderlust since I was a kid. I always wanted to visit my ancestral home. I wanted to walk barefoot in the African mud."

"You sure got a chance last month when you stuck your Land Rover in the river," Titch pointed out.

Amani laughed again and gazed into Titch's face. "I sure did. Up to my knees. Thanks for rescuing me."

Titch gave a blow-by-blow account of winching Amani out of the river.

Mosquitoes began to nip at my ankles under the table. Others were taking their plates out to the kitchen. I stood up and helped clear the table.

"I'd better be on my way," Amani said, going over to a motorcycle. She mounted it, kicked the starter and it thundered in the still, dark night. She flicked on the headlight, which listed to the left. "I'll see you guys later. Thanks for supper." The motorcycle stirred up the dust and she roared out of the compound.

"Quite a girl," I said to Titch. "Is she your girlfriend?"

Titch laughed. "She's a good friend, Clay, but no, she's not my girlfriend. I'm too swamped with work here to think about having a girlfriend."

"Didn't you see how she looked at you?" I teased.

"We're just friends. And she needs the company sometimes. She's the only expatriate at her clinic and we're her closest neighbors. Come, I'll show you where you'll be sleeping."

Titch led me to a small one-bedroom *tukl* or oval house with a thatched roof. A bat swooped out of the open ceiling. "You're lucky," Titch said. "You've got a house with a bat. That should keep the mosquito population down."

An orange cat strolled by and stopped to rub my leg. "Looks like I have a cat, too. Does he keep the rats out?"

"Pretty much. We have three compound cats. No one's bothered to name them, but they are good mousers. Not too good with snakes, though. We used to have four cats, but a cobra bit one a few weeks ago. So be careful where you step."

I dropped my backpack on the small table next to the bed and unfurled the mosquito net. "Thanks for bringing me here. It's good to be back in Africa. And it's even better to be together with you again."

"Sleep well. You'll need the rest. Tomorrow we'll start early and you've got a lot to take care of in the office."

I gathered the mosquito net under the mattress and lay back on the crumpled pillow, my fingers laced behind my head, elbows pointing out. I drew a deep breath of warm African air. Through the window I could see the first crescent of the moon and more stars than I could ever hope to count, pricks of brilliant light against the night sky. I prayed my first prayer for years. "Thanks Lord, for bringing me back home. Home to Africa." I could feel my lips curling in a smile. How could I pray to a God I wasn't even sure existed? But someone powerful had to have hung those stars. I had forgotten how bright stars could be on an African night.

A hoarse rooster crowing in a nearby courtyard woke me up the next morning. I grabbed a towel and stumbled to the shower, a canvas bag hanging above a cement slab surrounded by walls of grass thatch. An old Sudanese man stirred up the fire under a metal drum filled with water. He stood up when he saw me, a big smile on his face. He shook my hand vigorously. "I am Simon," he said, poking a finger into his sunken chest. He turned and dipped a bucket into the hot water and hobbled ahead of me to the shower. Climbing a pyramid-like three-legged African ladder, he poured the hot water into the shower bag. "Your water is ready," Simon said. I washed off the grime from our days in truck.

I joined Titch and the others for breakfast. I washed down pancakes with a sweet cup of *chai* made with dried milk powder. Clots of undissolved milk floated on the top. I sucked one of the milk clots into my mouth and chewed on it before looking at Titch. "Monkey turds. Just like our *chai* back at Livingstone."

"Yep," Titch answered. "Some things never change."

A hand rested on my shoulder. I looked up into Luke's freckle-flecked face. "Radio call's in five minutes. Come and I'll show you the ropes. It'll be your first job every morning."

I gulped the rest of my *chai* and followed Luke. Titch and the others moved to the truck we'd driven up and began unloading their drilling supplies.

Luke pulled a straight-backed wooden chair up to a green-painted table with a radio on top. He flicked on some switches and the radio hummed and whirred.

"Pull up a chair," Luke instructed, taking a hand-held microphone. "Whiskey Alpha Sierra calling Whiskey Alpha November," he said into the microphone.

The word Sierra tore into my heart. I'd abandoned my Sierra back in America. Had I broken her heart? "Who's Sierra?" I asked.

"Radio alphabet code for our project. Whiskey's for Water. Alpha is for All and Sierra refers to our location, Sudan. Code for our headquarters in Nairobi is Whiskey Alpha November." He released the button on the microphone and listened.

A faint voice came through the crackling static. Luke listened carefully before replying, "Titch and Clay arrived safely with the truck last night. Over."

I couldn't make out the answer, but Luke rattled off some instructions about equipment, food and supplies that needed to be purchased in Nairobi before signing off.

He showed me how to leave the radio on a common frequency for emergencies. "Emergencies?" I asked.

Luke explained. "Most projects like ours have their own radio frequency and time for radio call. But we all leave our radios on the common frequency. If some kind of emergency comes up at some other project, they can call for help and hopefully someone will be listening and pick it up."

"What kind of emergency?" I asked.

Luke shrugged. "Who knows? This country is a shambles. Sudan has always been divided between the North and the South. The North and the city of Khartoum are Arab-controlled and strongly Islamic. The South under British colonial rule was open to missions who started churches. The North uses Arabic, while the South prefers English. After independence in 1955 Sudan drifted into civil war between the North and the South. Missions were kicked out and several million Sudanese died, not only from battles but from the after-effects of war—starvation as the Northern soldiers destroyed crops, roads and bridges."

"What stopped the war?"

"People got tired of fighting. The war ended in a giant stalemate. So in 1972 both sides met for peace talks in Ethiopia where they signed the Addis Ababa Agreement. It called for an end of hostilities. According to the agreement, the country's president would always be an Arab located in Khartoum in the North. The country's vice-president would always be a Southerner and would operate out of Juba, here in the South. Effectively, Sudan is operating now as two countries. Because the South has a large degree of autonomy, Christian-based organizations like ours have gotten permission to come back into southern Sudan."

"Sounds like a good arrangement. What's the problem?"

"All money from taxes goes to the North and precious little if any money trickles back into the South. Many of the soldiers here in the South are frustrated and they blame the North for breaking the Addis Agreement. Then Chevron Oil did some exploration around Bentiu and announced in 1980 that they'd found extensive oil fields. That's here in the South. But when the oil fields are developed, will any money stay in the South? Rumor has it the Southern soldiers will start fighting against the North again. The army garrison at Bor, north of us, seems to be quite volatile right now. Anytime you have disgruntled soldiers running around with guns, the situation can get dangerous."

"So we leave the radio on to pick up any emergency calls," I said.

Luke nodded and pulled out some drawers from a sagging desk in the corner. "Our record keeping has slipped up in the last month or two. I want you to sort it out and develop a plan to get us organized. Titch and the others are great well-drillers and we've gotten ten new boreholes established this year. But unless we can send out some coherent reports, we may lose our funding." He pulled out two yellow manila envelopes. "These are requests from overseas donors asking how we're spending the money. So get to work. Read these requests. As soon as you have enough information to fill them out, do it. I have to go visit with some local officials so we can get permission to drill a new well near a town where another aid organization wants to start a hospital."

I nodded and began wading through papers and trying to make sense of expenses and expenditures. It was like doing a giant jigsaw puzzle without the picture on the box. *At least it's more challenging than ordering health food in California*, I thought to myself.

I heard Luke's motorcycle sputter as he pulled out of the compound. Titch stuck his head into the disheveled office. "We've unloaded. We're taking off now to repair a pump on one of our boreholes next to a school. We'll be back by supper time. Joshua will make sure you get some lunch."

I sucked on a pencil eraser and squinted at a wrinkled piece of paper with a row of numbers and names that looked like wage records. Elaborate squiggles representing signatures at the end of each line confirmed my conclusion.

I waded through the mess all morning with only a brief break for lunch. After lunch, the staggering heat clogged the office. I needed some light and fresh air. I took the manila envelopes and decided to study them outside. I saw a hammock slung underneath a mango tree. I kicked off my flip flops, peeled my sweat-soaked shirt off my back and eased my backside into the hammock. I laid back and started to read what the report required. My eyelids drooped and I covered my face with the envelope and fell asleep.

51

Water dribbled onto my face. I battled away the cobwebs of sleep and wiped the water off my face. A giggle drifted into my sleep-sodden brain and I jerked to a sitting position. The hammock swung and whipped me back-first into the gray Sudanese dust. I looked up into the Amani's laughing face. She held a glass of water.

"Sleeping in the middle of the day?" she asked. "You sure know how to get work done."

I scrambled to my feet and grinned. "Just a short siesta." I rubbed my eyes and shook my head. "Man, it's hot."

Amani agreed. "110 degrees in the shade to be exact." She paused. "I went to a nearby village to do a well-baby clinic this morning. Weighing babies, giving inoculations, that kind of thing. I finished up earlier than I expected." She shook her head. "Probably because there aren't that many healthy babies around. When our clinic is open we have sick patients all day long. That'll start up again tomorrow. I just stopped by to see how you're doing."

"Starting to make sense of the jumble," I answered. "Once I have a clear picture I can start writing some financial reports to our donors." I reached down and picked up the envelope that had fallen to the ground. "I just didn't expect it to be so hot!"

"Don't worry, you'll get used to it," Amani said. "And to tell the truth, most of us start work early in the morning and take a two to three hour nap after lunch. Come, I know a place down by the river that's cooler."

I followed Amani on a path that led out of our compound. A fighter plane streaked across the clear Sudanese sky and I ducked. "Get used to it," Amani told me, a grin on her face. "Sudan has endured years of civil war. Right now we're in a brief window of peace, but we might be on the brink of war again."

We passed some ladies collecting water from the river in large clay pots. Amani waved and greeted the ladies. They smiled at us. My sweat-soaked shirt clung to my back. Under the shade of the trees the temperature cooled slightly. We walked along the river's edge to a place where a huge strangler fig tree flanked the water, roots clinging to rocks.

"You can barely see the original mahogany tree," Amani pointed out. "The strangler colonized it, sucked the life out of it as it grew and choked the mahogany tree to death." She paused. "Kind of like what's happened here in Southern Sudan."

"I guess I didn't pay much attention to what was going on in Sudan when I was growing up in Kenya," I said.

Amani sat on a flat water-worn rock and looked up at me. "I wish I could have grown up in Kenya." Her dark chocolate eyes matched her rich brown hair. She patted the rock and I sat next to her looking down at the muddy river. "Tell me, what was dorm life like at Livingstone Academy? Did you miss your parents? My Mom's told me so much about Kenya. She loved Africa, but all her memories about boarding school are colored with homesickness."

"I had my share of homesickness," I began as I reflected on my early days in the dorm. "My first memories of boarding school in Africa are blurred on the edges of my mind. Blurred and salt-stained by tears that flowed down my cheeks as my parents drove away in our beat-up Land Rover after dropping me off at school for the first time. I remember clinging to my Dad's leg with a grip more tenacious than a pinching ant. Tears ran down his cheeks, too, dampening his bushy brown beard. My Mom cried like a busted faucet. Even now my chest tightens when I think back on that day." I told Amani the story of my first lonely days at Livingstone.

"I'm sorry, Clay," Amani said, eyes glistening as she touched my arm. "Mom didn't give me too many details of the hard side of boarding school. She just said she was homesick. I had no idea."

"I learned to cope," I said.

"Did you ever blame your parents for leaving you at school?"

"I don't think so. But all my years away created a distance between us," I answered. "I knew they loved me, but our time apart made me wonder about God's love. Obeying God's call led my parents to be missionaries. I reasoned that if I had to be at boarding school so my parents could tell people about Jesus, then it must be God's fault I had to spend so much of my childhood away from my parents. I loved Africa. I still do. But I missed being home with my parents."

"I feel homesick for my parents in America right now. I can't imagine what you felt as a second grader in the dorm," Amani said.

"At Livingstone we used the word homesickness to describe the heartsick feeling we had at being away from home. It meant the fear we felt being on our own. It meant missing our parents. Funny, during my first term at boarding school I felt the most homesick for my dog Rocky. He went frantic when I drove away that morning to go to school. He followed the billowing dust for almost a mile. I ached for a chance to hug Rocky around the neck and have him give me a slobbery lick on my face." My voice choked as I told Amani how Rocky had died of tick fever while I was away at school.

"When I finally came home from my first term away, home had changed. My friend Lempapa had gone away to become a man. Rocky wasn't there any more. And my time in school had changed me."

"Did you have a chance to visit your old home when you first arrived in Kenya a few weeks ago?" Amani asked.

I shook my head and flung a rock into the river. "You know, Amani, I'm not sure where my home is anymore. For a time Livingstone Academy became my home. But when I stopped by there last week, I found things had changed. I hardly knew anyone. Life at Livingstone has gone on without me. Livingstone isn't home anymore."

We sat silently, watching the sluggish river flow past. My back ached from sitting on the hard rock and I stood up. "I probably should get back to work," I said.

"Me too," Amani agreed.

As we headed back to the Water for All compound, I asked, "So you still wish you'd grown up in Kenya and gone to Livingstone?"

Tears bulged out of Amani's eyes. "Oh, Clay. So much of your story was sad and lonely. And it sounds like you're still trying to figure out where you belong. I guess I should be glad I grew up in America and got to stay home with my parents. But thanks for telling me about the hard times. It's helped me understand my mother better."

"Boarding school wasn't all hard times. Titch reached out to me there in second grade and became my best friend for life. And I fell in love with rugby at Livingstone. You should hear some of our rugby stories. And the pranks we pulled in high school."

"I'd like to," Amani said, her soft smile etching an image in my mind.

Back at the compound we found the drilling truck, covered in dust, parked next to a frangipani tree. "There you are," Titch called out from the back of the truck. "Come help us put things away. You're not just an office boy. Catch!"

Titch hurled a tightly wrapped blue tarp at me. I caught it easily. "Good pass! This is good rugby practice."

Titch stood up and looked over at Amani. "Visiting again? You must be really lonely, Amani. Or are you chasing Clay?"

Amani's soft white face reddened, but she tried to ignore Titch's comment. "I just came over to invite you and Clay for supper," she said, moving towards her motorcycle. "But if you're going to be rude …"

"Hey, I'm just kidding, Amani," Titch apologized. "We're all lonely up here. We'll come for supper."

"All right, I'll see you guys in a couple of hours. I'll go make sure my cook has the curry and rice ready." Amani mounted her motorbike and rode out the gate.

52

I finished helping Titch and the others. With all the gear locked into the brick storeroom, Titch said, "I'm going to take a cold shower to wash off this dust."

I had two shirts on my bed when Titch came by after his shower. He frowned at the shirts. "I'm trying to decide which shirt to wear tonight," I explained.

"Trying to impress Amani? I thought you'd just called off a wedding. Isn't it a bit soon to start chasing someone else?"

"I'm amazed how she loves Africa. She wants to be here. Even in Sudan where things are tough. Anyway, I'm not trying to impress her."

Titch laughed. "Yeah, tell me about it. You're smitten. Wear the Santa Barbara Rugby Tournament T-shirt. When she asks you about it, we can tell her about playing in the tournament. When she knows you're a rugby jock, you'll melt her heart for sure." His eyes sparkled.

I pulled on the rugby T-shirt and Titch and I climbed into the project Land Cruiser and drove over to Amani's house.

The rich smell of curry wafted out of the bullet-ridden house, which Amani called home. "Come in," Amani called, ushering us to a table set on the screened-in veranda. I traced one of the bullet holes with my finger. "Souvenirs from the civil war," Amani explained lightly. Then her face grew serious. "The war has really left its mark on the people of Southern Sudan. But amazingly, their faith has grown through the troubles."

We sat at the table and Amani's cook brought out a steaming plate of rice and a battered white-enamel bowl of curry with chicken parts on the bone floating in the dark yellow sauce. Amani asked me to pray for the meal. I felt like a hypocrite. I hadn't thanked God for a meal in years. But I summoned the words of a prayer from my memory.

"What do you mean, their faith has grown?" I asked after Amani had served the food. "Faith in what?"

Amani and Titch looked at each other, puzzled. "Faith in God, Clay," Titch answered around a mouthful of chicken.

"How can faith in God grow when things are going so horribly wrong? Seems to me all we can really be sure of is the here and now. So I don't understand how getting hammered by a war would strengthen anyone's faith. If anything, seems like it would turn people away from God."

"Don't you remember anything we learned at Livingstone?" Titch asked. "Consider it pure joy when you face trials of many kinds because you know the testing of your faith develops perseverance so you may be mature and complete. That's my paraphrase of some verses in the book of James."

"I guess I haven't been thinking about the Bible much since I left Livingstone," I explained. "A philosophy class I took in college made me doubt God's existence and the concept of eternity. The professor encouraged us to question our beliefs and not to have blind, unthinking faith. He quoted a Spanish philosopher named Unamuno who said unless you've gone through a time of doubting your faith, your belief in God isn't real. I began doubting God's existence."

"One philosophy class and you lost your faith?" Amani asked. "Maybe your faith wasn't too real to begin with."

Her comment needled me. "I think I experienced a second-hand Christianity. I accepted the form of Christianity modeled by my parents and poured into us at Livingstone. No offense, Titch, but they did shove Christianity down our throats. We had nightly devotions in the dorm, Bible classes in school, Sunday school classes and church every Sunday. Christianity surrounded me like a comfortable blanket. I didn't rebel or question the teachings handed down to me. Going to church, worship, all that God-stuff became ritual. A bit worn and tiresome, but comfortable. When I was encouraged to question my beliefs in college, I was afraid of what I might find. Maybe I only believed in an idea of God and not God himself. Maybe God didn't even exist. So I kind of drifted."

"Are you still drifting?" Amani asked.

I stared at a moth fluttering around a candle that lit the table. Finally I answered. "I guess I am still adrift. One thing that struck me from what Unamuno wrote. What really matters is the present. The best I can do is try to create a little bit of heaven on earth."

"Is that what you hope to do here in Sudan?"

"Yeah," I answered.

"Then you'll be disappointed," Amani pointed out. "Sudan doesn't make any sense without an eternal perspective."

We ate the rest of the meal in silence. As we drank tea, Amani stood up and disappeared into the kitchen. She came back with her cook, a thin dark man with deep smile lines marked into his forehead along with small triangular scar patterns. She pulled a chair up for the cook and he sat down.

"Clay, this is Joseph. I'd like him to tell you his story."

Joseph nodded, telling his story in halting English. "I love Jesus," he began. "He saved me when I was a young boy. I was baptized in the Yei River. I married and had a small farm with two children. Then the British left and the war began." He paused.

"Did you join the Anyanya rebels?" I asked.

"No," Joseph answered. "I didn't want to fight. But the war came to us. A group of the rebels came through our area. The government soldiers moved in and started shooting. They shot me." He lifted his leg up and I saw a puckered scar in his calf. "I fell in a pool of my own blood and looked up and saw the bullets rip through my wife and children and two of my brothers. They were all killed. I pretended I was dead. A soldier's boot kicked me and I heard the soldier grunt. Then they left."

I sat stunned. "They killed your whole family?"

"Yes," Joseph said quietly, sadness clouding over his eyes.

"I guess you were pretty angry with the Northern soldiers. Did you join the war to get revenge?"

Joseph looked puzzled. "No, I forgave the soldiers. They didn't know what they were doing."

"You forgave them for killing your wife and family?" I asked.

"Jesus told us to forgive those who do wrong to us. It's the only way. In our church we've learned the only way to overcome the bitterness is to forgive. Not everyone in the South knows this. But we as Christians have to show the rest of our people the way of forgiveness."

Amani looked at me. "Joseph's faith amazes me. He clings to Jesus. And he's not alone. His story can be retold many times. By people whose daughters were taken and sold as slaves. By women who've been raped. By families who've had their houses burned. This country's been devastated. But the body of believers has flourished. New churches have sprung up. They know there is only hope in Christ. And at the final accounting in heaven, God will right all the wrongs."

"God is good," Joseph said. He stood up and limped back to the kitchen. Before he disappeared around the wall, he turned and added, "This world is not my home." He smiled and pointed upwards.

"I've never heard anything so amazing," I said to Amani and Titch. "He lost his whole family and yet he smiles and forgives the Northern soldiers."

"It's the way Jesus taught, Clay," Titch answered. "Watching the faith of these battered Christians has humbled and challenged me."

"Their lives only make sense in light of an eternal end with God," Amani put in.

"Yes, but …" I stopped. I had some thinking to do.

Titch stood up. "We've got a long trip tomorrow to check on another bore-hole pump gone bad. So I think we'd better be going."

"Thanks for the meal, Amani," I said as I walked out to the Land Cruiser. "And thanks for letting me hear Joseph's story."

Amani just smiled and nodded. She waved and shut her door.

"I'm puzzled," I said to Titch as the Land Cruiser rattled my teeth on the washboard road.

"What about?" Titch asked.

"How can Joseph be so filled with peace having lost his whole family? Everything. He's lived through hell on earth. Yet he smiles, talks about loving God and forgiving others. How can anyone forgive the atrocities he's suffered?"

"Weren't you listening when old Pastor Cord preached to us at Livingstone? Weren't you listening while he crammed the Bible down our throats?" I could sense an edge to Titch's tone. "Pastor Cord had a three month series on Christian forgiveness."

I laughed trying to ease the tension. "I didn't listen too closely. I spent most Sunday services day dreaming about rugby. I think in some ways rugby had become my god in junior high and high school. How do you remember what Pastor Cord preached about anyway?"

"It reached deep into my heart. I had a lot of anger and bitterness. You know how difficult it was for me to learn at Livingstone? Still is. But back then, many of my teachers just wrote me off as dumb and stupid. Miss Marker back in eighth grade was the worst. The things she wrote on my papers hurt. A lot. 'When will you learn to spell?' 'What's wrong with you?' 'Are you dumb?' 'Can't you spell the same word twice the same way?' Things like that."

"I could tell you were sad, but I never saw you show anger."

"No," Titch answered. "I swallowed it. I tried to joke it off. I couldn't really tell you how much it hurt because school was so easy for you. Sometimes I resented your straight "A"s without cracking a book. I appreciated your help with my homework, but life didn't seem fair. The bitterness ate away at my heart. I couldn't look at Miss Marker without feeling an inner rage and contempt. I wondered if she was even a Christian. She sure never showed any compassion on me and my spelling problems. That's when Pastor Cord preached about forgiveness. I think we were in tenth grade. My inner anger felt like it would erupt. I often used rugby as an outlet for my frustrations. I'd hammer people and think I was getting back at the ones who called me dumb."

"I thought you were just psyched to play rugby."

Titch smiled. "I fooled you. Anyway, God touched me as Pastor Cord preached. After one sermon I went to his office and cried as I poured out my anger and frustrations to him. He helped me forgive, first in prayer before God. Then he helped me to meet with each teacher I still had bad feelings about and I forgave each of them. It was tough to forgive Miss Marker. I think it shocked her that her words had hurt me so deeply. It was a real healing time in my life. And people here in Sudan like Joseph have learned that forgiveness is the only real answer to offer against the hurt and pain of war."

I sat silently. Finally I said, "Forgive me, Titch. I was your best friend and I never knew this was going on. I guess I only thought about myself."

"No need to apologize. You weren't down on me. You helped me, remember? It was your taking time to read to me and help me with my homework that encouraged me to keep ... Whoa!"

53

He slammed on the brakes and skidded to a stop. I flew forward and bounced my forehead off the windshield.

Titch rolled down his window and dust from our fast stop swirled into the cab. I rubbed my forehead. A lump was already forming. A soldier carrying an automatic rifle pushed his head in the window. "Didn't you see our road block?" he demanded.

I looked out and saw a dim kerosene lantern next to a log that had been dragged diagonally across the road. Several other soldiers lounged nearby.

"This road belongs to Southern Sudan. We control this road now," the soldier informed us. "No more money is going to the North. You need to pay us a road tax to proceed."

"But ..." Titch started to protest. Then he closed his mouth and reached into his pocket and handed the soldier some Sudanese pounds.

The soldier laughed and barked an order. Another soldier rolled the log off the road.

"Who were those guys?" I asked, still rubbing my head.

The glow of the dashboard illuminated Titch's face a pale green. A grim look masked Titch's face. "Insubordinate soldiers. Looks like they have control of the roads around here. We'll have to be careful. We may have another war erupting."

Back at our compound, Titch reported to Luke about the soldiers and their freelance roadblock. "I'll look into it tomorrow," Luke said. "I have to visit the commander of the garrison anyway. He'll want to know what his men are up to. In the meantime, no driving around at night."

"Got any aspirin for a headache?" I asked Titch as we headed for bed.

Titch examined the lump on my head. "No worse than some rugby injuries I've seen," he said, giving me some aspirin.

I swallowed the pills without water and grimaced at the bitter taste.

"Those soldiers didn't seem too happy," I commented.

"No, not everyone in the South has the capacity to forgive the North for the years of war. The South has been plundered since before Gordon tried to impose some British governance in this region almost one hundred years ago. Seems the

Arabs have always regarded the South as a source of wealth. Ivory, slaves, whatever. There's a long history of exploitation and resentment."

"So it's not a normal Sudanese thing to forgive?" I asked.

Titch shook his head. "It's not normal for anyone to forgive. Only God can change a bitter heart so it produces love and forgiveness." He looked me directly in the eyes and I thought he wanted to say more, but he didn't.

In bed I pondered God. The hot night air hovered over me like a prickly wool blanket. Sweat soaked my pillow. I turned it upside down, hoping the other side would be cooler. It wasn't. The scalp on the back of my head itched.

I scratched and cried out to God. "You must be there God. I've seen a powerful example today of forgiveness. Without you, I know Joseph could never have forgiven the ones who killed his family. I haven't talked with you for a while, God. I've been too busy enjoying myself. But I have to ask you now to forgive me. Forgive me for doubting you. And help me to have faith again." I sighed and finally drifted off to sleep. When I woke up, a verse about faith that I'd memorized years before at Livingstone popped into my mind.

I got up and shook the sleep out of my head. I went outside and saw Titch stumbling out of the grass-thatched shower. "God just spoke to me," I said.

Standing in worn-out cut off jeans, Titch rubbed his afro dry with a towel and asked, "I thought you didn't believe in God anymore. What'd he have to say?"

"He just reminded me of a verse I learned as a titchie." I hesitated. Here I was, someone who had thrown God out of my life in college, quoting from the Bible. "Faith is being sure of what we hope for and certain of what we do not see."

"Hebrews 11, the faith chapter," Titch responded with a smile. "So does this mean you believe in God?"

"I think God's there even if I can't see him. I'm still working on exactly what I believe. I've been wandering, Titch. It's good to be back home. Not only in Africa, but in touch with God again. Do you have a spare Bible?"

"I'll get one for you after breakfast."

Luke joined me for the radio call. "Whiskey Alpha Sierra calling Whiskey Alpha November," Luke intoned into the microphone. The name Sierra jolted me more deeply this morning. Had I ruined her life because of my selfish need to be back in Africa?

When Nairobi replied, Luke reported, "Groups of soldiers encountered last night on the road asking for money to get past road blocks. Any news of similar events in Sudan?"

The radio hissed and sputtered while Luke cocked his ear and frowned. I decided I'd better have a lesson in radio listening before I took over this job.

"Did you hear that?" Luke asked.

I shook my head. "I heard something garbled."

Luke translated. "The army garrison at Bor, made up mostly of Dinka soldiers, has mutinied. It looks like other army units in the South are deserting as well. Full scale war might not be too far away."

"So what do we do?" I asked.

"We'll stay put for now, but I'll cancel today's trip. Nairobi said they're monitoring reports from the United Nations. They haven't recommended evacuation yet. But they say to be cautious."

A few days later I watched a shirtless soldier shoot some branches off a palm tree near our compound with his automatic rifle. He smiled, revealing a gap between his front teeth. He waved and swaggered on down the road. "Khartoum hasn't responded to the desertions yet," Titch commented. "Looks like the soldiers are getting bored waiting for war to start."

Luke was in twice-daily radio contact with Nairobi, but nothing much seemed to be happening in our area. After a week, Luke gave Titch and the drilling crew the go-ahead to work. They left early the next morning to repair a pump and survey an area for a new borehole. I got back to work sorting and sifting records and writing reports. I finally got everything organized after a month on the job. Southern Sudan remained tense but quiet.

"All the project paper work and accounting is up to date," I reported to Luke. "Do you think I can join the drilling crew on their next job?"

"Go ahead," Luke agreed. "It'll do you good to get out of the office."

We loaded the truck early the next morning and bumped over the dirt track for four hours. We met several groups of soldiers, but they all waved us on. The truck growled to a halt next to the clinic.

We'd brought Joshua along to cook for us. I helped him set up his kitchen and pitched the tents while Titch and the others set up their drilling rig. By early afternoon we'd eaten and the drilling rig thudded steadily as it pounded a hole in the earth.

That evening Titch and I sat under the stars drinking steaming cups of *chai* after the others had gone to bed. "This country is so beautiful," Titch said. "I wish the war would just go away."

"It hasn't hit yet," I answered. "Maybe it will stay peaceful."

"We can hope," Titch replied. "So how are you doing with your search for faith?"

"I've done a lot of thinking," I said. "I've been uncertain about so many things the past few years. I wasn't sure I could trust God even if he was real. I know my parents believed. They even made a huge sacrifice to send me to boarding school so they could get on with doing the Lord's work. I know it was hard for them. But some days I thought I'd been sacrificed on the altar of their faith. I really felt lonely, even abandoned when I first went to school."

We sat staring at the stars.

"This world is full of hurting people," Titch began. "Tons of missionary kids hurt when they have to give up normal family life for the sake of the Gospel. Seems like a picture of what God did when he dropped off his only Son to be born as a baby and then live thirty-three years at the boarding school called earth with Joseph and Mary for dorm parents. God abandoned his own son to die so we could be forgiven."

I mulled over Titch's words as I sipped some *chai* from the enamel mug. "That sure makes me think of my MK experience in a new way. At least I didn't die at Livingstone. I missed my parents and wondered how God could really love us if he broke our family up."

"I thought you loved your time at Livingstone," Titch said. "You were so full of life, always positive and enjoying everything. Especially rugby."

"I did love the school, rugby, my friends. You were my best friend. I don't know if I've ever thanked you, Titch, for pulling me through those first difficult days. Funny, talking with Amani last month about my life at Livingstone dredged up all kinds of emotions I thought I'd buried. I managed at school, but I missed having a normal family life. And underneath I now realize I blamed God and gradually stopped believing in him. I filled my life with rugby instead. I made rugby my idol. I've had to ask God to forgive me for loving rugby more than I loved him."

"Does this mean you won't play rugby again?" Titch teased.

"No way. I just won't make it the most important thing in my life. Maybe we can play a game of touch rugby when we get back to base."

"Why wait?" Titch asked. "I brought a ball here. We can play tomorrow."

54

We pulled into the Water For All compound a week later around 4 p.m. Luke met us. "How'd the drilling go?" he asked.

Titch signaled with thumbs up. "They've got clean water," he shouted as he hopped out of the truck. I stretched my aching back and noticed a familiar motorcycle leaning against the mango tree. Had Amani come to visit Luke while I'd been away? A hot surge of jealousy flowed through me.

We started to unload. I glimpsed Amani coming out of the radio room and I dropped a box of food. Joshua the cook scrambled after the cans. I heard Titch laugh. "I think someone's in love," he whispered loud enough for me to hear.

"Let's finish unloading and play another game of touch rugby," I suggested.

"Absolutely," Titch answered. We'd played a one-hour game of touch every afternoon at the drilling site.

"We can add two players," I said.

Titch raised an eyebrow.

"Amani and Luke. One on each team," I pointed out.

"Amani's on our team," Titch said.

"I agree."

We unloaded in record time and Titch started tossing the rugby ball around with the others as I marked off a field in the dirt using a long stick.

"I don't know how to play," Amani protested when we put her on our side. "I think I'd rather watch."

"Nothing to it," I said. "Pass the ball backwards and run forwards. What could be simpler?"

Titch kicked off. "Stay in a flat line on defense," I called to the others. "Man for man." Amani lagged behind and Luke, playing opposite her, slipped through our defense to score.

"I told you I didn't know how to play," Amani pleaded. "I want to sit out."

"Don't give up now," I said. "Then we'll be one player down. We need you."

On the next play Titch dummied his man and ran in a try.

"See," I said to Amani who stood next to me. "We've just scored. I'm glad you're on my team."

"But I didn't have anything to do with Titch scoring," she pointed out.

"I didn't say you did. I'm just glad you're on my team." I smiled at her and she blushed.

After the game Amani agreed to stay for supper. I still worried that she'd come to see Luke, but she nestled next to me as we ate. A strong breeze whisked away the normal after-supper mosquitoes, so Amani, Titch and I stayed at the table and chatted.

"Thanks for letting me play rugby with you guys today," Amani began. "I can see why you love the game so much."

"Touch rugby is just a shadow of the real game," Titch said. "You should have seen Clay and I play back at Livingstone."

"Yeah, Titch and I made the second fifteen rugby team in eighth grade," I boasted to Amani. "Then we both played one game for the first team when we were ninth graders. And from tenth grade on we played varsity. We even won the Safari Cup our junior year. We were the best school team in Kenya."

"What about your senior year?" Amani asked. Titch and I looked at each other. His sad face resembled a basset hound and I burst out laughing.

"I never thought you'd recover from losing that last game." Titch sounded miffed. "Now you're laughing about it?"

"It still hurts," I admitted, "but I had to laugh at the look on your face. It made me realize how silly it is to be moping four years after losing that game."

"Rugby molded our identity at the school," Titch said. "Girls wanted to sit by us because we were rugby players."

"I'm sure they wanted to sit by you because of your afro and Clay's long blond hair, red sideburns and freckles," Amani teased.

I smiled. "It was against the rules at Livingstone to have long hair or sideburns. I did grow my sideburns out one vacation, but I had to shave them off the first day of school or risk a demerit. Inside, I was scared to death of girls. I didn't know what to say to them."

"You seem to have learned. Was high school everything you expected?"

I scratched my neck. "You know, you have these dreams of how great everything will be, especially your senior year. But things don't always turn out the way you hoped. I enjoyed high school, but it had its ups and downs. Especially that last second loss to Lenana in the Safari Cup final."

"With all those girls chasing you rugby players, did either of you ever have a steady girlfriend?" Amani asked.

Titch shook his head and said, "I didn't, but Clay did."

Amani looked at me with a question mark in her eyes.

"Yeah, I dated a girl named Leah our senior year. But we went our separate ways at graduation. You know, I always thought graduation would be the pinnacle of our time at Livingstone, but now I remember it as the saddest day of all."

Titch nodded. "So much ended that day."

"What do you mean?" Amani asked.

We told her about the trauma of splitting up from friends we'd lived with for so many years.

"Going to college was a major shakeup for me," I said.

"When I first went back to America, nothing seemed to work," Titch concurred. "I'd been driving on back roads in Kenya for years so I figured I could easily pass my driving test. I went in and failed the written test. Four times!"

"I got my first paycheck for cleaning the gym showers and had no idea how to cash a check or even open a bank account," I said. "It took me a week before a nice girl named Sierra offered to drive me to town and help me open a checking account. She even had to show me how to write a check!"

I noticed Amani tighten up when I mentioned Sierra.

"So who was Sierra?" Amani asked.

"A girl in my philosophy class."

"Did you fall in love with a California girl? Is that how you adjusted to America?"

"I don't think I ever really adjusted to America. I learned to cope, but it never became home. How could it? My roots are here in Africa." I paused. "But I did fall in love with a California girl. My friendship with Sierra grew after she helped me open my checking accounting. I invited her on a date to our soccer awards dinner."

I narrated my disastrous first date with Sierra and the difficult-to-drive Triumph. Amani and Titch laughed at my story until tears ran down their cheeks.

"Somehow the shared embarrassment of lurching down State Street in the Triumph drew us together and we later got engaged."

Amani crossed her arms and leaned back in her camp chair. "So when are you getting married to this Sierra?"

I felt my jaw tighten and click from the time I'd been upended in a lineout and landed on my chin. I didn't answer Amani's question directly, but went on to tell both her and Titch the details of how and why I'd broken off the wedding with Sierra.

"You really left Sierra like that?" Amani asked. "How could you? She must have been devastated."

I rubbed my eyes. "Don't remind me. I feel like a jerk. But America was suffocating me." I drew a deep breath. "Amani, do you remember the strangler fig tree you pointed out to me down at the river?"

She nodded.

"You said it reminded you of how Northern Sudan is squeezing the life out of the South. I see it as a picture of how America started strangling the life out of me. As I got more comfortable with fast food and swimming pools, I felt like that mahogany tree in the middle. Something foreign was taking over my life and if I didn't get out of there I'd die."

"So you feel like you escaped from America?"

"I'm home in Africa. Bad as I feel about jilting Sierra, I know she'll find someone to fulfill her suburban American dream. I needed to come home."

"I think my Mom would empathize with the way you felt when you thought you might never get back to Africa again," Amani said softly.

"What do you mean?" I asked.

"She always thought she'd come back to Africa. But after she finished college, she married and I was born followed by my three brothers. I could see the sadness in her eyes when she talked about Africa. I know she loves Daddy and all of us. But I think a little part of her died when she had to stay in America."

"I would certainly have died if I had to live in America," Titch cut into the conversation. "I belong here in Africa."

"So do I," I agreed. "You don't know how freeing it has been to my spirit to come back home to Africa."

"I feel like I belong here, too, Clay," Amani stated. "There's a saying here in Sudan. Once you've drunk from the Nile you're infected for life."

Luke walked over to the table. "It's getting late. I don't want to break up the party, but with the soldiers on the roads, it might be dangerous for you to ride home alone on your motorcycle. Maybe I can give you a lift?"

"We can do it," Titch offered.

Luke forced a smile. "OK, but I want both of you to go so no one comes home alone."

"Yes, boss," Titch intoned in an African accent.

Luke laughed and tossed the Land Cruiser keys to Titch. We hoisted Amani's motorcycle into the bed of the pickup.

The soldiers on the road stopped our car. After Titch explained who we were they finally waved us past their barricade, but they didn't look pleased. We arrived at Amani's house and she jumped out. "Thanks for the rugby game and supper," she said. She held onto the door as I started to close it. "Hey, why don't you come for lunch on Sunday after church?" She addressed her question to me and even in the dim light I could see her beautiful eyes and I gazed into them. Amani finally dropped her eyes and added quickly, "Both of you are invited of course."

As we drove out of her driveway, Titch commented, "She loves you, Clay."

"I hope so. Is it immoral to fall in love so soon after breaking off an engagement?"

Sunday dawned hot and heavy. Gray clouds boiled over the horizon. "When it's this hot, it means a big rainstorm is on the way," Titch said. "Come, let's go to church."

I grabbed the Bible Titch had given to me and we hiked to the clay brick church. My thongs flipped quietly as we slipped into the church and sat down on the cement benches.

After several vigorous songs, Pastor Paul stood up to preach. "We have to love our enemies, like Jesus said," he began. "We need to do good to those who persecute us."

"No!" a voice erupted off to my left. "The time has come to fight our enemies!"

I saw a young man stand up. A small group stood up with him and they marched out of the church.

Pastor Paul watched sadly as others stood and walked out. Finally he went on speaking to the now-decimated congregation. "Not everyone is ready to listen to God's Word. But without love and forgiveness, our land is doomed to many more years of war. We as Christians must be the first to offer love and forgiveness. It's not easy. I, too, have lost many family members to this war. But I know I'll see them again. In heaven. For those of us who are left, we must work for peace, not war."

After the service Titch and I talked with Pastor Paul. "It's hard for me to believe you can forgive when you've lost so many members of your family," I said.

Tears welled up in Pastor Paul's graying eyes. "You can't understand the pain of losing your only son to bullets, but Jesus taught that revenge is not the answer."

"Not everyone thinks the way you do," Titch pointed out.

"No, I have great fears for our country." Thunder boomed in the distance and a spray of lightning forked golden yellow on a nearby hill. "War is coming as surely as the rain."

Amani sidled through the throng and joined us. "Don't forget you're coming over to my place for lunch."

"We'll be there," Titch answered for both of us. "Clay wouldn't miss it for the world."

Amani smiled at me before mounting her motorbike. Titch put an arm on my shoulder. "I think she's perfect for you Clay."

"She's nice, but I'm not really looking for someone," I lied. "I've decided the scars from breaking up with Sierra are still too tender."

Titch's eyes bored into mine. "Baloney! You like Amani. You said so the other night. She loves Africa and I think she likes you. Let's go get the Land Cruiser. We'll definitely need four-wheel drive to make it home through the mud if it rains as hard as I think it will."

After the meal at Amani's we sat on her screened in veranda and sipped tea. Amani pulled out a battered Scrabble game and challenged us. Titch declined. "I can't spell well enough to play that game."

"We could help you," Amani offered.

"I'll be happy to watch," Titch answered.

I admired Amani's delicate fingers as she placed her tiles on the board. She won the game by over fifty points.

"Congratulations, you really know how to play Scrabble," I said.

"Thanks for being a good sport. The last person I played against was Luke and he sulked the rest of the afternoon after I beat him."

Luke? I thought.

"Let's play again," Amani begged. We whiled away the afternoon playing Scrabble.

Titch dozed on the nearby sofa. After Amani beat me again, I leaned over to help her shuffle the tiles into the bag. She had leaned forward too and our noses touched. I bent my head slightly and kissed her on the lips. As I pulled away her smile glowed. "Trying to distract me, are you?"

My hand was on her shoulder and I let it gently slip off. "Sorry, you overwhelmed me."

Titch snorted himself awake and sat up on the couch. "Must have fallen asleep. Combination of good food and the heat, I guess." He stood up and stretched. He suddenly stepped to the edge of the veranda and pressed his nose against the fine screenwire.

"What's up?" I asked.

"I thought I saw some movement over in those bushes." Titch continued to peer. Finally he said, "I guess it's nothing."

"Well, we'd better head home," I said. "We don't want to have to argue our way through any more night time road blocks." I turned to Amani. "Watch yourself, now."

"Yeah," Titch agreed. "You notice anything unusual, call on the radio. Clay sits beside it all day as he organizes our office."

"I'll be okay, guys. All the people here know me and are happy for the help we give at the clinic. I'm not worried by any rumors of war."

Titch swung open the screen door and we walked to the Land Cruiser. As we reached the car, an armed soldier rolled out from underneath and pointed his AK-47 at us. I caught glimpses of other soldiers racing at us from the bushes.

A sharp cry behind me caused me to jerk around. A soldier had an arm around Amani's neck.

55

"Let her go!" I shouted, moving towards her. Something cracked into the back of my head and I fell to my knees. Bright spots of light spun in front of my eyes. Someone shoved me roughly onto my stomach. I wanted to jump up and tackle my tormentor, but I felt the cold metal barrel of a rifle pushed behind my ear and I lay still.

I heard a slap and a groan beside me. A soldier dragged me to my feet. I saw Titch, nose bleeding, glasses broken. A soldier pushed him and he staggered toward the Land Cruiser. They picked him up and hurled him into the bed of the pickup. They threw me in next. I sat up as they shoved Amani in beside me. Another soldier came from the cookhouse leading Joseph, Amani's cook. His eyes were wide as he took in the scene. "You can cook for us," the soldier commanded.

A tall soldier, who had been standing off to the side watching, came to the car. "We're at war with the North," he informed us. "We need your car. And you can pray someone loves you enough to pay for your release. Because if they don't, we have no reason to keep you alive. Give us the car keys."

Titch pulled the keys out of his pocket and handed them over. Other soldiers leaped into the back with us while the tall soldier wedged his giraffe-legs under the steering wheel. Two other soldiers slipped into the cab with him. The car started and bounced out of Amani's compound. At first, dust poured in over us. But soon the heavy clouds opened and the rain gushed down like a waterfall, soaking us in the back. Rain dripped off the end of one soldier's nose. The car slithered in the slippery mud and slammed into a ditch. I cracked my already-throbbing head against the wheel well. I could see a pained look in Amani's face as well.

The wheels spun uselessly. "Guess I'd better show them how to put it into four wheel drive," Titch muttered, sitting up. "If I don't, we'll spend the rest of the day sitting here in the rain."

A soldier waved his gun as a threat to Titch. "We're stuck in the mud," Titch explained. "I want to show the driver how to get out."

The soldier looked doubtful, but hammered with his fist on the roof of the cab. The tall driver rolled down his window.

"I'll lock the hubs and show you how to get out of the ditch," Titch said.

The driver nodded. "But no trying to escape."

Titch hopped off the pick-up and knelt down to lock the front wheel hubs. He went to the window and showed the driver how to shift into low ratio four-wheel-drive.

I leaned over to Amani. "Are you okay?" I whispered.

She nodded bravely, her rain-soaked hair plastered to her forehead. A smudge of mud colored her left cheek.

The car jerked and jolted out of the ditch. Titch hopped back into the pick-up. The Land Cruiser ploughed steadily through the mud for another half hour before pulling off the road. We coasted to a stop in front of a dilapidated brick house with rusted iron sheets on the roof. The soldiers jumped off the back and used their rifles to motion us into the building. Inside they locked us into a small room with wads of cobwebs in every corner and drooping down from the ceiling. The door slammed shut.

"Where are we?" I asked. "It reminds of the boogey man's room at Livingstone."

Titch laughed. "What an adventure that was. This is an old Presbyterian mission house. It's been abandoned since missionaries were expelled from Sudan in 1963."

"What are they going to do to us?" Amani asked, her voice quavering.

"Nothing," Titch said, confidently. "They said they're holding us as hostages so our friends will buy us free. So they'll protect us."

"What happens when Water for All refuses to pay?" I asked. "I've been reviewing some of the papers in the office and one is a no-ransom policy. They say it will encourage other abductions."

"For now we'll pray and hope that Amani's boss in Nairobi, or her parents or somebody will pay and the soldiers will count the payment towards all three of us," Titch said.

A bolt on the other side of the door clunked and the door swung open with a creak. The tall gap-toothed driver filled the doorway. The rain still pelted down behind him. He smiled. "I am Captain Kelei. Do not fear. I have sent messages to your people. We told them to pay $10,000 for your release. We need US dollars for our war effort. We are very happy with your work for Sudan and mean you no harm. But this war is very important to us. We must be released from our bondage to the Arabs in the North."

He turned and ordered, "Feed them!"

"Yes, Captain!" a gangly soldier with toothpick legs answered as he drew himself up and saluted.

"Enjoy your stay. This used to be a house for white missionaries. I'm sure you will find it comfortable."

Joseph arrived after about an hour with rice and beans. "They had no meat or fruit," he apologized.

Amani cried. "It's okay, Joseph. Thank you so much. Are they treating you well?"

Joseph smiled. "They only kicked me once and told me to hurry up and make their tea before bringing you this food."

He slapped the food onto some yellow enamel metal plates. "Before I go, I must pray with you," Joseph insisted. He looked up to heaven and lifted his hands. "Oh God, protect your people. Be the hiding rock for my friends. As the wall surrounds Jerusalem, surround these servants of yours. We have known too many years of war. But we know that you are a faithful God. You are able to deliver us from evil. And even if your answer for us is death, we know that is only our doorway to heaven." He paused. I opened my eyes and saw tears trickling down the old man's cheeks. He sighed and then finished, "I make this prayer in the name of my Savior Jesus Christ. Amen."

"Amen!" Amani agreed loudly. "Thanks Joseph."

He nodded and backed out the door. I heard a soldier shout. "Hurry up, you stupid! We need more tea." A dull thump followed.

"His faith still amazes me," I said, shaking my head.

"It's all he has to hold onto in this country," Amani said. "It's called having an eternal perspective."

"I was so quick to dismiss God and the concept of heaven a few years ago," I said.

The sharp crack of a gunshot made me jump. Amani shivered. I put my arm around her. Titch cocked his ear towards the door. We heard shouting, but the hubbub eventually subsided.

"Heaven becomes much more real when you're standing at the edge of death," Titch pointed out. "I wonder what happened out there?"

We had no answers. Titch prayed for all of us. We tried to sleep, but the adrenaline flowed. Amani, exhausted from the abduction, eventually fell asleep with her head leaning against my shoulder. My arm turned to pins and needles and I tried to shift my position. Amani's head slipped off and landed on my lap. "Sorry," she muttered before drifting back to sleep. Titch curled up on his side and soon snored louder than a diesel generator. I stroked Amani's hair, and tried to sleep.

Titch's snoring annoyed me. *How can he sleep so soundly while we're locked up in this dilapidated old house?* I thought. I railed at God. "Why can't you answer Joseph's prayers? Deliver us like you delivered the Israelites again and again. Prove yourself." My mind swirled with half-formed prayers and foggy nightmares.

I jerked awake in the early morning when a cock in the yard began to crow. All I could think of was how Peter had denied Christ three times before the cock began to crow. My doubts and accusations against God filled me with guilt. "I'm sorry, God," I prayed silently. "I do want to trust you. I really do. I'm just so worried. Things seem so out of control."

I tried to stretch and my neck stabbed me with pain. Amani moaned and rolled off my lap. Titch shook his head and stood up. "Wow, where does a man go to relieve himself?"

He began hammering on the door. A red-eyed soldier finally opened the door. "I need to use the bathroom," Titch explained. The soldier shouted. Eventually a cracked blue plastic bucket was handed into our prison. Titch set it in the corner. "Well, turn the other way you guys."

"Hurry up, Titch," Amani urged. "When a girl has to go, she has to go."

We waited for breakfast, which never came. About mid-day, the door swung open and Captain Kelei stood there, a stern look on his face. "Your cook was too slow last night. He's no longer with us."

Amani grasped my arm. "Oh no, not Joseph!" She began to sob.

"You shot Joseph?" I asked.

Captain Kelei frowned. "We have to keep discipline. He was an old man. Too slow. And your people are too slow. There has been no payment."

"Keep the car as payment," Titch bargained. "It's worth $10,000. Then let us go."

Captain Kelei laughed. "We already have the car. We also need the money. We will try to be patient. But if your people take too long, we'll have to move. And we can't carry you with us."

Amani's quiet sobs shook her slim torso. I pulled her tight against me as if I was binding onto another rugby second row forward.

Captain Kelei dropped some bananas on the floor then slammed and locked the door.

I released my grip on Amani and she crumpled to the floor and wailed. "They shot Joseph. Gentle old Joseph." She pulled her knees to her chest, locked her arms around her legs and began rocking back and forth.

Titch rubbed his hand over his forehead and then flattened the afro on top of his head. He looked up at the rain-stained ceiling. "Anyway to escape out of here?"

"Here, stand on my shoulders," I said. I faced Titch and cupped my hands just above my crouched knee. Titch stepped into my hands and I boosted him up. He clambered onto my shoulders and pulled his red Swiss army knife out of his pocket. "Still can't believe they didn't search us for weapons," he said through clenched teeth as he sliced an angled cut through the old ceiling board. He changed directions three times until he had cut out a square. He pushed it upwards. Dust and bat droppings showered onto my head. He dug his toes into my shoulders as he tip-toed to see into the attic.

"What do you see?" I asked, squelching the impulse to scream as his toes drilled into my shoulders.

Amani stood up and shook the bat dung out of her hair. "Can we escape?" she whispered.

"There may be a space on the other side of the building where we can slip out. But we'll have to wait until dark." He settled back onto my shoulders and fit the ceiling board back into the space he'd cut. He leaped lightly onto the floor and knelt to sweep the bat dung and dust into the corner using his hands.

He stood up and faced Amani. "I'm sorry about Joseph. At least we have the hope that he's now in a better place."

Amani began crying again. "Yes," she sobbed. "He's in Jesus' hands with the rest of his family. But it still hurts. It's so senseless. Why kill an old man? He wasn't the enemy."

We sat quietly waiting for evening to try our escape. "Where will we go if we do escape?" I asked.

"I'm not sure," Titch said. "But it's better than waiting here for them to come in and pull the trigger."

Amani shivered. I looked up at the ceiling. "I can shove you and Amani up into the attic," I said. "But how will I get up?"

Titch tapped his belt. "I'll rig up a harness and Amani and I will haul you up."

I raised one eyebrow. "Are you sure?"

"I'm a water drilling engineer. It's my job to lift heavy deadweight objects up and down. Don't worry."

Conversation dropped off. Flies had penetrated the dingy storeroom and buzzed around our bucket latrine. I wrinkled my nose.

No one brought us any supper. Finally Titch stood up. "It's almost eight o'clock," he said, tapping his glow-in-the-dark watch. "Let's go."

I heaved Titch to my shoulders and pushed him up through the hole in the ceiling. I lifted Amani up next. As she disappeared through the hole, I felt all alone.

"Hurry up with the harness, Titch!" I hissed.

Suddenly the crackle of gunfire exploded right outside the door. Wood splintered and a bullet whizzed thumped into the wall. I dropped to the ground and folded my arms around my head. I heard shouts, screams, and groans. Bullets whistled. I vaguely heard a car engine starting. Then the firing stopped. Someone kicked open the door. An Arab soldier swept in waving his AK-47. Others followed carrying powerful torches. "We have come to rescue you from the rebels," he said.

I stood up shakily. I looked up and called, "Titch, Amani, we're rescued."

Titch didn't answer. I peered up in the gloom. A hand hung limply over the edge of the hole. Blood trickled off the fingers and dripped onto my forehead.

"Titch! Titch!" I called.

The soldiers focused their torches at the ceiling. I heard a rustle and then Amani's head appeared over the hole. "Oh Clay," she wailed. "Titch has been shot!"

56

"Titch! Hang on! You'll be okay!" I cried out. A soldier rolled in an empty 50 gallon metal petrol drum. I climbed on it and grasped Titch's hand. Someone handed up a torch.

Titch's eyes rolled briefly and he groaned, "I'm on my way to heaven."

"No, Titch, no!"

Amani, on her knees beside Titch, shook her head sadly. "He took the bullets across his chest. The blood is frothing out. He doesn't stand a chance."

"We've got to get him down," I insisted, fighting back tears. Grabbing his arms, I pulled him across the filthy ceiling and onto my shoulders. I gently eased him down into the waiting arms of a giant soldier. He cradled Titch in his arms and carried him outside. I pulled Amani down, smearing her with Titch's blood.

Almost in a stupor, we walked outside. Titch lay on a blanket. Amani knelt beside him and felt for his pulse.

Tears streaming, she choked out the words I couldn't comprehend. "Titch has gone, Clay. He's dead."

I stood beside Titch's body. Amani leaned against me. I held her tight and I cried.

The soldiers transported us to the Water for All compound where Luke and the others hugged us and cried with us. Luke called Nairobi and organized a plane to come the next morning. The trip to carry Titch's body to Kenya seemed like a never-ending nightmare. Finally we had arrived at Wilson airport and I stood at the immigration desk. I glanced back at the airplane where some white-coated men bustled around the door. I forced myself to look away. The immigration official flipped through the passport, frowning. My brain couldn't absorb anymore.

A muffled thump startled me. The Kenyan official had just stamped my passport. He snapped the passport shut and said, "Welcome to Kenya." I stuffed the passport into my pocket. I turned and looked back at the plane and thought of Titch. The friendship I forged with Titch during those first tough days in boarding school had endured for a lifetime. His lifetime, anyway. Fighting back a sob, I groaned in my heart, "Ah, Titch. I'm so sorry."

I'd been unaware of Amani next to me. She clenched my hand in hers and led me to the door of the immigration shed.

Amani summoned a nearby taxi. "*Karibuni* Kenya," the driver said. "Welcome to Kenya." I nodded a greeting but couldn't find any words to say. I tossed my tattered backpack into the broken down Toyota saloon.

The taxi jerked forward and the driver hurled the car into Nairobi's frantic traffic. A *matatu* mini-bus with passengers oozing out the door cut in front of us, prompting our driver to slam on his brakes. An African proverb had been painted on the back of the *matatu*. "You can't wash the dust of Africa off your feet." I remembered the white powdery volcanic dust that seeped into my shoes when Titch and I hiked Longonot, a dormant volcanic crater on the floor of the Rift Valley in front of Baridi. The dust of Africa had penetrated my skin pores and entered into my soul.

"It's true," I said to the driver.

"What's true?" the driver asked, as he eased our taxi around the *matatu*.

"You can't wash the dust of Africa off your feet," I murmured.

We met Titch's parents at the mission guest house. His Mom's eyes were red and swollen like the wattles around the eyes of a ground hornbill. I gave her a hug and said, "I'm so sorry."

She couldn't talk, but nodded up and down and clung to me as if I were her own son.

Titch's Dad's voice was husky. "They've taken Titch's body to the mortuary. We're planning the funeral for Saturday at Baridi so as many of his friends as possible can come. I was hoping you could say a few words."

I almost choked as I said, "Of course."

I noticed the denim jacket on my shoulder. I handed it to Titch's Mom. "Here. This was Titch's." She took one look at the blood-stained jacket and burst into a fresh waterfall of tears.

On Saturday at the funeral held at the old missionary cemetery at Baridi I stood up and gave a tribute to my friend. "Titch and I have been best friends since we met here at Livingstone Academy in second grade." I cleared my throat. "He reached out to me when I was a scared and lonely little boy. We learned to play rugby together. We both had dreams of playing for Kenya. That's one dream Titch never got to fulfill. But he loved God. And that love spilled out to others. Titch struggled in school, and as a result always had compassion on those who'd been given a hard deal in life. Maybe that's what prompted him to go to Sudan."

I paused and looked down at Titch's parents. "Titch's life wasn't wasted. He showed God's love to people who had survived years of war. His warmth and friendliness charmed the people he worked with. He went to bring water to Sudan. And he brought true living water by being an example of Christ in serving others." Titch's Mom pulled out some more Kleenex. A fine misty rain swept across the field. Black umbrellas opened.

I lifted my chin and took a deep breath. "I can imagine Titch right now in heaven. I'll bet he's already playing scrum-half for heaven's first fifteen. I'll miss you, Titch. And I look forward to meeting you once more on the playing fields of heaven."

I was surprised to find myself talking so confidently about heaven and God but realized that after my period of doubting I really did believe in God again. God had finally brought me home. Not only to Africa but also to himself.

I knelt down and gave Titch's Mom a hug and shook his Dad's hand.

I heard sniffles all around the crowd of mourners. The Kenyan pastor who officiated the funeral prayed and then called for the pallbearers to lower Titch's casket into the grave. A mound of red earth from digging the hole had been piled to one side. Taking a handful of soil, the pastor intoned, "From dust we were created, to dust we shall return," and sprinkled it over the grave.

I stepped forward and took a handful of red dirt clods from the mound. Reaching out over the hole I dropped the clods, which rattled sharply on the coffin. I grabbed a shovel and helped pour dirt into the grave. The brief drizzle had stopped and the sun blasted through the gray clouds. An eager Kenyan took the shovel from my hands. I stood and wept, my tears spilling into the dust of Africa.

Epilogue

Dubai 2002

I sat back in the stands and watched the young New Zealand rugby player power his way over an Australian to score a try in the corner. I clapped. "Did you see that?" I enthused.

My wife Amani gave me a tolerant smile as she looked up from her book. "Wonderful play," she murmured.

A crowd of young players from South Africa had colonized a section of the stands beside me. "Did you see that running?" I asked leaning toward one of the boys.

"The All-Blacks are magic," he answered in a clipped South African accent.

"Are you boys playing in the tournament?" I asked.

"Yes," the boy answered. "Our school flew up from Port Elizabeth. But we just lost in the semi-finals of the Schools Division."

"I'm sorry," I said.

"It was a great experience. And here we are watching the best rugby players in the world. We can't wait for the Springboks to play Samoa in the other semi-final."

I nodded. "It will be a good match. I'm from Africa myself, and I'd like to see the Springboks win."

"Where do you live in Africa?" the boy asked.

"My wife and I do development work in East Africa. We've moved back and forth between Kenya and Sudan for the past nineteen years," I began. But the boy lost interest as the Springboks sprinted onto the field in their green shirts with gold trim.

The South African schoolboys cheered themselves hoarse, but the Samoans snatched the game away from the Springboks, winning 19-12.

"Sorry lads," I commiserated.

"I can't believe it," one of the South African boys said. "No African team in the finals."

"Don't give up on Africa yet," I said, standing up and hoisting my sports bag over my aching left shoulder. My knees creaked and I'd split my lip.

275

"What do you mean? Where are you going?" the young South African asked.

"To play in the final," I answered.

"Go on!" he said. "You're too old!"

I raised my eyebrows. "Veterans Division," I told him. "My team from Nairobi is in the final."

The boy told his mates and they all started clapping. "We didn't know we were sitting next to a finalist," one of them said. "There will be an African team in a final."

I smiled and started to limp down the steps. "Are you sure you're not too old to play rugby?" another schoolboy asked.

Amani giggled and put her book down. I gave her a wink.

"I'm old and bald and gray. But rugby's like the dust of Africa. It works its way into the deepest crevices of your body and you can never wash it off. There's always one more rugby game to play." I stepped back to squeeze Amani's hand before hobbling away to play one last rugby game.

End